CW01276948

THEOPHANO

EMPRESS OF THE WEST

JAN HERBERT

THREE ABBEYS

Published by Three Abbeys in 2007

ISBN: 978-0-9555244-0-0

Copyright © Jan Herbert, 2007

Printed and bound by CPIAntony Rowe, Eastbourne

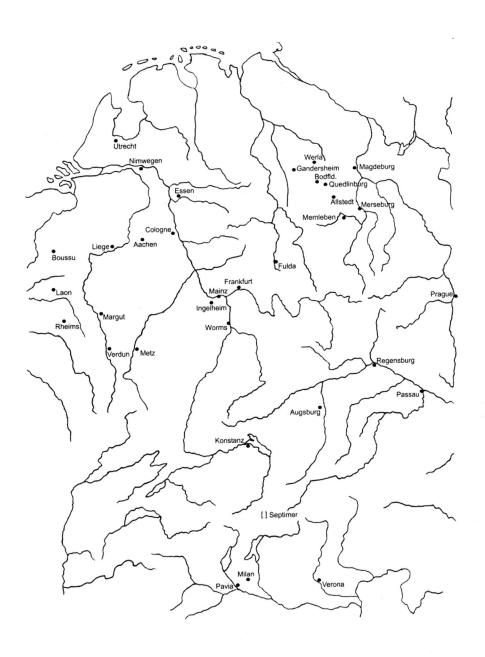

10th Century Germany and Surrounding Areas

i

DRAMATIS PERSONAE
Historical characters in capital letters

In Constantinople

THEOPHANO SCLERINA: Princess of Byzantium and
Holy Roman Empress

THEOPHANO: Empress of Byzantium; Widow of
Romanus II; Wife of Nicephorus II Phocas;
Mistress of John Tzimisces; Godmother of
Theophano Sclerina.

Children of Romanus II and Theophano
BASIL II: Co-emperor of Byzantium
CONSTANTINE VII: Co-emperor of Byzantium
ANNA: Princess of Byzantium

Philip: tutor to the imperial children and Theophano
Sclerina

BASIL THE EUNUCH: chief minister; distant relation
of the imperial family

NICEPHORUS II PHOCAS: usurping emperor and
great-uncle to Theophano Sclerina; husband of
Empress Theophano

LEO PHOCAS: his brother; grandfather of Theophano
Sclerina; Lord High Chamberlain

BARDAS PHOCAS: his son

SOPHIA PHOCAS: his daughter; Theophano
Sclerina's mother

CONSTANTINE SCLERUS: soldier; husband of
   Sophia Phocas; father of Theophano Sclerina

BARDAS SCLERUS: his brother

MARIA SCLERINA: his sister, wife to
JOHN TZIMISCES: usurping emperor; lover of
   Empress Theophano; uncle-by-marriage of
   Theophano Sclerina

Maria and Helena: Bulgar princesses held as
hostages

LIUDPRAND: A Lombard, Bishop of Cremona and
   envoy of Otto the Great, Holy Roman Emperor

GERO: Archbishop of Cologne and envoy of Otto the
Great

Emilia: lady-in-waiting to Theophano Sclerina
Anastaso: lady-in-waiting to Theophano Sclerina

In the Ottonian Empire

The LIUDOLFINGS or OTTONIANS

OTTO I 'the Great': Emperor of the Germans and
   Italians (Holy Roman Emperor)
ADELHEID: his second wife; Empress; Princess of
   Burgundy; widow of King Hugh of Italy

Their children:
   OTTO II: Emperor; husband to Theophanu,
      formerly Theophano Sclerina
   MATILDA: Abbess of Quedlinburg

Grandchildren of Otto I by his first wife
   OTTO: Duke of Swabia
   OTTO: Duke of Carinthia

Children of Otto II and Theophanu, also
grandchildren of Otto the Great
   SOPHIA, educated at Gandersheim
   ADELHEID, educated at Quedlinburg
   MATILDA, educated at Essen
   OTTO III: Emperor

Nephews and nieces of Otto I
   HENRY 'the Wrangler': Duke of Bavaria, claimant
      to the throne
   GERBERGA: Abbess of Gandersheim
   HEDWIG: former Duchess of Swabia

BEATRICE: Duchess and regent of Upper
   Lotharingia; mother of
THIERRY or DIETRICH: Duke of Upper Lotharingia

LOTHAR IV: King of France; father of
LOUIS V: King of France

CHARLES: brother of Lothar IV; Duke of Lower
Lotharingia

HUGH CAPET: Duke of France
ADELAIDE: his wife

EMMA: Queen to Lothar of France; daughter of
   Empress Adelheid and Hugh of Italy
CONRAD: King of Burgundy; brother to Empress
   Adelheid

Churchmen:

WILLIGIS: Archbishop of Mainz; Archchancellor of the Empire; friend and supporter of Theophanu

DIETRICH: Bishop of Metz; cousin of Otto I and enemy of Theophanu

GERBERT: Abbot of Bobbio; later Archbishop of Rheims then Pope Silvester II; supporter of Theophanu

ADALBERO: Archbishop of Rheims, supporter of Theophanu; kingmaker of France

JOHN PHILAGATHOS: Chancellor of Italy; Archbishop of Piacenza; reputed lover of Theophanu

ASCELIN: Bishop of Laon; reputed lover of Queen Emma

BERNWARD: Bishop of Hildesheim; tutor to Otto III

Others:

IMIZA: lady-in-waiting and friend to Theophanu

ECKBERT ONE-EYE: rebel and kidnapper

CONRAD: Duke of Swabia

AB'UL KASIM: Emir of Sicily; invader of Calabria

CALONYMUS of MAINZ: Jewish merchant and soldier; rescuer of Otto II

HENRY ZOLUNTA: Slavic knight and rescuer of Otto II

FAMILY TREES - Eastern Empire

SCLERUS FAMILY

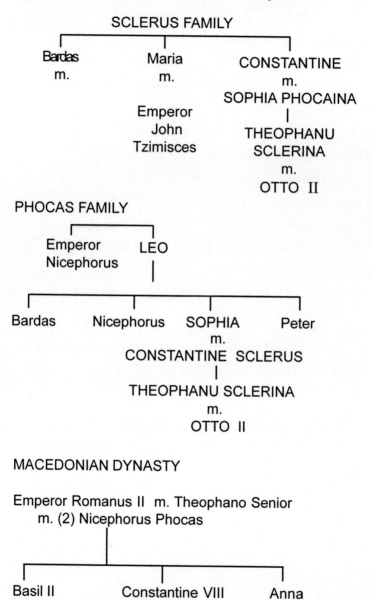

Bardas
m.

Maria
m.

Emperor
John
Tzimisces

CONSTANTINE
m.
SOPHIA PHOCAINA
|
THEOPHANU
SCLERINA
m.
OTTO II

PHOCAS FAMILY

Emperor
Nicephorus

LEO

Bardas   Nicephorus   SOPHIA   Peter
m.
CONSTANTINE SCLERUS
|
THEOPHANU SCLERINA
m.
OTTO II

MACEDONIAN DYNASTY

Emperor Romanus II m. Theophano Senior
m. (2) Nicephorus Phocas

Basil II   Constantine VIII   Anna
m.   m.
Helena   Vladimir of Kiev

OTTONIAN DYNASTY

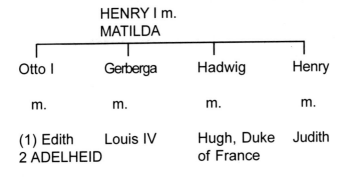

HENRY I m.
MATILDA

Otto I	Gerberga	Hadwig	Henry
m.	m.	m.	m.
(1) Edith 2 ADELHEID	Louis IV	Hugh, Duke of France	Judith

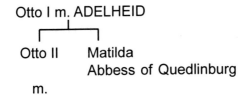

Otto I m. ADELHEID

Otto II   Matilda
           Abbess of Quedlinburg
m.

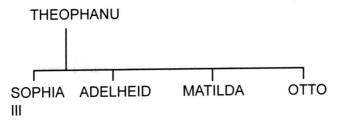

THEOPHANU

SOPHIA III	ADELHEID	MATILDA	OTTO

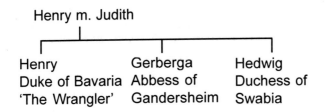

Henry m. Judith

Henry Duke of Bavaria 'The Wrangler'	Gerberga Abbess of Gandersheim	Hedwig Duchess of Swabia

CAROLINGIAN DYNASTY

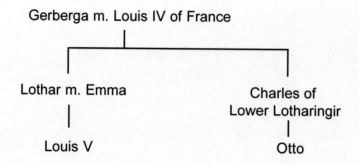

Gerberga m. Louis IV of France

Lothar m. Emma

Louis V

Charles of
Lower Lotharingir

Otto

CAPETIAN DYNASTY

Hadwig m. Duke Hugh of France

Hugh Capet m. Adelaide

Robert II

PROLOGUE

For the last time, Imiza removed the emerald and ruby rings from the Empress Theophanu's pitifully thin fingers. Then she signalled to Anastaso, the other lady-in-waiting, to bring forward the rough-textured nun's habit which the dying empress had requested. Carefully they eased it over her shoulders and smoothed it into place, then laid her back against the pillows and pulled the sheet straight. A slow, contented smile spread across the Empress' wasted features, the first relief the sick woman had known for days. Imiza's eyes opened wide in surprise.

'Did you realise that she always wanted to be a nun?' she whispered to Anastaso, who had known their mistress longest.

'No, I had no idea. I know her faith is important to her and she always seemed to enjoy staying in convents, but I would have said she was a woman concerned with this world.'

Hearing them the Empress smiled again but could not summon up the energy to speak. They had not understood. Now that the last of the imperial robes, which she had loved so much, had been taken away, she was no longer Domina Theophanu, Empress-Regent of the Germans and the Italians, of lands stretching from the Baltic to the Mediterranean and from the North Sea to the Adriatic, but simply Theophano Sclerina, who had once been an unregarded little girl, merely great-niece to an usurping emperor, amongst the many children of the Great Palace in Constantinople. She felt the burden of empire slip from her shoulders like the robes. Whether the Danish fleet attacked England or Germany was not her worry any more. It no longer even mattered whether her illness had really been caused by that odd-tasting flask of wine from her mother-in-law or by poison from the King of France. She was as free in her dying as she had been in the schoolroom of the Great Palace, when she had only her lessons to worry about. How had that carefree child Theophano Sclerina turned into the woman she had become? Perhaps the process had started on the day when she had first seen Bishop Liudprand.

1

CHAPTER ONE

The Princess Theophano Sclerina gazed wistfully out of the palace window as Constantine stumbled through his reading. It was so slow and painful to listen to him that she could hardly follow the story. He was only seven, of course; you couldn't expect him to read as well as an eight-year-old like herself, but even so.... it would be at least half an hour before the three children were released. From the schoolroom window over the tops of the trees Theophano could just see a galley swinging out from the Golden Horn into the choppy, blue waters of the Bosphorus. She imagined it sailing through the Sea of Marmara round the Gallipolli Peninsula, all the way to Thrace and home.

Suddenly the door flew open and the Empress burst into the room.

'The girls are to come with me. Quickly – and quietly,' she snapped to their tutor, Phillip.

Even as they all leapt to their feet, Constantine was protesting.

'And me! And why Theophano? She's not even really royal.'

He stopped short as his mother looked at him through half-closed lids.

'I'm sorry,' he muttered.

'Yes. When I desire your company, Constantine, I shall send for you. Now hurry,' she added to Anna and Theophano.

Obediently the little girls followed the Empress along the corridor. No guards fell into place behind them. This was unusual, but they were given no explanation as they left the Daphne Palace, home to the women and children of the Great Palace of Constantinople, and made their way across the gardens to the Magnaura. This was where important state events took place. When they reached a spot where nobody could approach or overhear them unobserved, the Empress stopped.

'Listen to me carefully, Anna,' she said to her five-year-old daughter. 'You are here to learn a lesson, about the importance you have as a princess of the Macedonian dynasty. You must stand quite still where I show you, and watch and listen, but you must make no sound. That goes for you as well, Theophano. Your great-uncle the Emperor wants you too to learn how affairs of state are conducted. Now, follow me.'

Once inside the Magnaura Palace they turned into a side-corridor. A servant opened a door and the girls found themselves in a long, narrow space with a wooden lattice running along the wall at waist-height. Theophano did not need the Empress' warning finger on her lips to stay silent. Through the lattice she could see her grandfather, Leo Phocas, who ran the affairs of the palace for his brother, the Emperor Nicephorus. He was seated on a chair in a small audience chamber. She distrusted the Empress but she simply feared her grandfather and would take great care not to anger him.

A slave threw open the door of the audience chamber and announced,

'Liudprand, Bishop of Cremona, envoy of the King of the Franks, seeks audience of the Curopalates, Leo Phocas.'

With these words an elderly, splendidly-robed Italian entered the room and bowed low to Theophano's grandfather. Men carrying gifts, which they laid in front of Leo before retreating, followed him.

Leo neither rose to his own feet to welcome his guest nor waved him to one of the other chairs. The Italian was left standing awkwardly in the middle of the room and Theophano could tell that he was annoyed by the insult. Although he tried to keep a smile on his lips, his black eyes were furious.

'Your business?' Leo's voice was cold and curt.

My master, the Emperor Otto, seeks the hand of the Princess Anna in marriage for his son and Co-Emperor, also named Otto.'

Theophano glanced at Anna, ready to warn her to make no sound, but the five-year-old had obviously not understood. She merely looked puzzled at the mention of her name and Theophano turned her attention back to the interview. The Bishop was extolling the virtues of his master's son, who, although only thirteen, a suitable age for Anna, was already skilled in the arts of peace and war, a handsome youth on whom Fortune had showered her gifts, etcetera. Leo cut him short.

3

'I cannot believe your master's insolence in asking for this marriage. He has invaded our territories in Italy for no reason and put our subjects to the sword. This has angered Emperor Nicephorus very greatly. Now Otto adds insult to injury by calling himself an emperor. The Empire of the Romans has only one emperor and that is Nicephorus II, and his two Co-Emperors, Basil II and Constantine VIII, who are still boys. Your master is not an emperor but merely the King of the Saxons. There can be no marriage between an emperor's daughter and a king's son.'

The Bishop's face flushed still redder with annoyance.

'*Basileus* in Greek and *rex* in Latin mean the same thing,' he retorted. 'My master is the successor of Charlemagne and of the Roman emperors of the West, just as your master is successor to the Roman emperors of the East.'

Leo shot to his feet.

'The Emperor Nicephorus II Phocas is the heir of Constantine the Great,' he shouted at Liudprand. 'You have simply come to stir up trouble, not to make peace as you claim.'

'At least receive my master's letter and read his own words,' entreated Liudprand, holding a piece of parchment towards Leo, who shook his head angrily and motioned to a servant to take the letter. Then, without another word, Leo strode from the room, leaving Bishop Liudprand standing with his mouth open.

As soon as Leo Phocas had gone, the Empress signalled to the children to follow her out. She was smiling but there was no humour in her smile, just a look of satisfaction.

'Did you understand what happened?' she asked Anna when they were back in the Daphne Palace.

'No, Mama,' answered Anna honestly. 'Just that Theophano's grandfather was very angry.'

'And you?' said the Empress to Theophano. 'Did you think that was what happened?'

'Not exactly, Most Pious Augusta,' replied the girl carefully. 'I know Grandfather when he is really angry and I think he was pretending today.'

The Empress laughed. 'Let us hope that Liudprand is less perceptive than the child,' she said. Then aloud, 'Yes, you are partly right. He was indeed angry at the impertinence of this Otto the Saxon, but a marriage might not be completely impossible if the Saxon is willing to pay a big enough price for Anna. Why do you think I brought you both to watch today?'

Anna was silent, wondering how she could have a price like a piece of cloth. Theophano ventured

'Because it could affect Anna's future.'

'Yes, although it almost certainly won't, but both of you need to understand that your marriages will affect many people beyond yourselves. Anna especially can alter the fate of nations by whom she is allowed to marry and even you, Theophano, have a place as a bargaining counter. So when the time comes, I want you both to accept your destinies without complaint. It is best you understand this from a young age.'

'But I don't want to leave Constantinople and go to live somewhere else miles away,' wailed Anna, suddenly understanding what was meant.

'I have said you are not likely to marry this German. But when your emperor, whether it will be your stepfather or your brothers, tells you to marry, it will be your duty to him, to God, and to the Empire to do as he says.'

Anna bowed her head but silent tears trickled down her face. Theophano put her arm round the younger girl and said

'Of course, Lady.'

The Empress nodded, satisfied, and smiled at her goddaughter and namesake. The child was worryingly intelligent but at least appeared biddable. Since Theophano was such a favourite with her uncle, John Tzimisces, who happened to be the Empress's lover, it was fortunate that she found the girl an acceptable companion for Anna. As young

Theophano was also Emperor Nicephorus's great-niece, the friendship pleased her husband, the Emperor Nicephorus too, although the Empress had long ceased to care much for his wishes.

Her smile encouraged Theophano to venture a question.

'Will we be told the result of the embassy, Lady?'

'You are outspoken for your years,' observed the Empress.

Theophano lowered her eyes modestly. Had she gone too far? No, the Empress was still speaking.

'Yes, you will be told the progress of the embassy but I think you may be sure that nothing will come of it. Now come, you must return to your tutor.'

As soon as they were re-occupied by their wax tablets and styluses, the Empress signalled to Philip the tutor to follow her out of the room. Once they had gone, Theophano was free to resume gazing out of the window, this time with much more to think about.

She would feel pity for Anna if the little girl had to leave her family and the Great Palace where she had been born and which she had hardly ever left. But for Theophano it was different. She was not palace born and bred and was not entirely happy there. Her early childhood had been spent on an estate in Thrace, over in Europe, which belonged to her father's family, the Scleri. Although her mother, Sophia, niece of Emperor Nicephorus Phocas, had died when she was born, her father's sister, Maria, married to John Tzimisces, had looked after her. Theophano had flourished in the less formal atmosphere of the country. She had been allowed to play with the estate children, which would be unthinkable at the imperial court, and at four she had been given her own pony, a grey called Shadow whom she loved passionately. When Uncle John, or even occasionally her own father, Constantine Sclerus, came home on leave, they would take her riding in the wild hills around her home, days of absolute delight for her. They would tell her exciting stories about the army or their days out hunting and sometimes, forgetting her age, they would talk about the politics of the Empire in front of her.

When Theophano was six, Aunt Maria died of a sudden fever. The child missed her desperately but at least she had her beloved hills and tumbling streams, her pony and familiar servants and playmates. Imperial politics soon changed all that, however. In distant Constantinople Theophano's mother's uncle, Nicephorus Phocas, had usurped the throne and become Senior Emperor three years earlier in 963. With the help of the Scleri he had achieved this by marrying the widowed Empress, mother of Anna and her brothers. The children's father, Emperor Romanus II, had died suddenly two days after Anna's birth.

Even in Thrace Theophano had heard plenty of rumours about that time. Rumours that the Empress had poisoned Romanus. Rumours that she and Romanus together had murdered his father, the previous emperor. Rumours – which were actually true – that the Empress had forced her five sisters-in-law to go into convents against their will and had allowed her mother-in-law to die of neglect in a secluded part of the Great Palace. The Empress, despite her beauty, was not liked by her people and Theophano herself did not trust her, despite her apparent kindness.

One of Emperor Nicephorus' first appointments was to make Theophano's grandfather, his brother Leo, *Curopalates*, Chief of Staff of the Great Palace, which was really a small city in itself, lying at the heart of government. Within its walls were several palaces, churches, factories and workshops and even a university. As soon as Grandfather Leo learnt of Maria Tzimisces' death, he persuaded the imperial couple to summon Theophano to the Palace, to be a companion to little Anna and to be educated with the imperial children. And so Theophano lost her freedom and her pony but she gained high status and an excellent tutor. Anna, who did not remember her own father and so did not resent Nicephorus, became a friend, but the two boys regarded her as an upstart intruder and let her know it. On the whole she thought that if she had been Anna, she would have been rather excited by the thought of travelling across the world to be empress of a different country. Still, that would not be her fate and meanwhile she had her lessons, which she enjoyed, not least because she was better at them than Constantine.

At this point in her musings Philip returned, looking troubled.

'The Empress wishes me to explain to you the background to what you have just seen,' he said to the girls. 'You listen too, Lord Constantine. You know that in the old days the Roman Empire included all the lands around the Middle Sea and went as far north as the south bank of the great River Rhine and the island of Britain?'

'Yes, but it split in two,' answered Constantine.

'Nearly six hundred years ago,' agreed Philip. 'The Empire of the East continues to this day, although the followers of Mohammed have taken North Africa and Syria from us, but in the west it has been a different story. The last *real* Emperor of the West was killed in 476, nearly five hundred years ago. Barbarians, especially a tribe called Franks, occupied all our land in Gallia and Germania and for a long time there was chaos. But eventually the teachings of our Lord Jesus Christ reached even these people and they became more civilised. Then in the year 800 the Bishop of Rome even crowned their king, Charlemagne, Emperor of the West and we acknowledged his title.'

'Why did we do that?' broke in Constantine indignantly. 'He wasn't an emperor.'

'It suited us at the time,' Philip retorted curtly. 'Anyway Charlemagne's sons couldn't hold his empire together and it split into three parts, East and West Francia and the Middle Kingdom. The father of this Otto the Saxon became King of East Francia and Otto himself added the Middle Kingdom to his domains. Now *he* calls himself Emperor of the West but we do not recognise his title.'

'Why not, when we did Charlemagne?' asked Theophano.

'It does *not* suit us at the present time, Lady Theophano. There is only one Empire of the Romans and it is ruled from Constantinople.'

'Yes but,' began Theophano but Philip interrupted her.

'Leave it, child', he said smiling. 'It's politics, not logic. Now back to our reading.'

CHAPTER TWO

The following day at Mass in the great church of Holy Wisdom, Haghia Sophia, from the women's gallery the two girls caught a glimpse of Bishop Liudprand in the throng of men in the body of the huge basilica but they heard no more of the western embassy. On Monday Philip told them that the Emperor himself had given an audience to the Italian but no progress had been made. They had to wait another week before they heard anything definite, and at first the news seemed disturbing. Anna would be given in marriage if Otto handed Rome, Ravenna, all eastern Italy, Istria and parts of Dalmatia back to the Eastern Empire.

Anna's jaw dropped in horror.

'I've got to go,' she wailed.

'No, no, Lady Anna,' Philip soothed her. 'The Saxons will never agree. If they did, they would only have Germany and Lombardy left – not much of an empire. Bishop Liudprand said that he could not consider it.'

'So why did the Emperor make the offer, if he knew it would not be accepted?' asked Theophano.

'Because to refuse outright might well provoke open war. This way it is the Germans who have refused. Do not worry, Lady Anna.'

'So I'm not going?'

Theophano hugged the little girl to comfort her, while Philip decided that assurances were needed rather than explanations.

'No. You will definitely not marry young Otto,' he said firmly. It might prove not to be true but there was no reason for Anna to start worrying yet.

Later that week there was an unusual break from routine for Anna and Theophanu. Accompanied by Philip, they visited one of the silk manufactories within the Great Palace. These factories provided useful occupation and income for the ladies of the court, because the Palace kept the monopoly of silk manufacture in Europe and production and prices were strictly controlled. The girls loved to examine the beautiful fabrics with their rich embroidery and to watch them being made, perhaps even be able to choose a length of fabric for themselves.

They were engrossed in this delightful task when a shadow interrupted the light and, looking up, they recognised the foreign bishop, Liudprand of Cremona, standing next to them. On meeting their eyes he bowed formally and asked leave of their tutor to introduce himself. Politeness forced Philip to agree, although inwardly he was dismayed at this turn of events.

Once the introductions had been completed, Liudprand talked to them easily about the fabrics. He was buying silk, he said, to take home to his master, the Emperor Otto, and his son, young Otto, because it was very rare in the West, although they had skilful embroiderers. Did the young ladies like the pretty materials, he asked.

Anna's face lit up.

'Yes,' she answered eagerly, 'I love wearing silken clothes. They feel so soft on my skin.'

'What if you are outside?' asked Liudprand. 'It is not so easy to ride in silken garments, is it?'

'Oh, but I never do ride,' replied Anna, 'Theophano used to, before she lived in the Palace. She had a pony called Shadow.'

Liudprand politely turned his attention to the other girl and felt a sense of shock. Anna seemed like any little palace-reared princess, sweet, pretty, and rather soft, but the other child was stunning. A beautiful bone-structure rather than childish chubbiness made her attractive. Dark hair surmounted wide-set black eyes and a chin that tapered to a determined point. The eyes, large and intelligent, were her most striking feature. Even at her young age they watched the world with an appraising detachment. There was a wiry toughness about her, which, he thought, would equip her to be a western empress much better than Anna's soft gentleness. Because the western imperial court was constantly on the move, never stopping anywhere for more than six weeks or so, an empress needed to be strong, both physically and mentally.

'Are you fond of riding, Lady?' he asked, trying to work out who this child was.

'It used to be my great pleasure when I lived in Thrace, before my great-uncle sent for me,' the girl answered formally.

'Do you miss it?'

'Oh yes, to be outside and.....' Theophano broke off, remembering, then said swiftly 'but please do not think me ungrateful. I know how fortunate I am to be here.'

Dignified and diplomatic, thought Liudprand, what a pity this was not the *porphyrogenita*. This child might even be worth Italy, although his master would never think so. While the girls' attention veered back to the silks, Liudprand engaged their tutor in conversation. It occurred to him that the other girl might be more affordable, if she was suitable in other respects. A useful second string.

'Your other charge is also a princess?' he said to the tutor, whose frown indicated how worried he was by the whole encounter.

'Yes,' Philip answered swiftly. 'She is the Emperor's great-niece, Theophano Sclerina.'

It was public knowledge, after all.

'Sclerina? She is not a Phocas, then?'

'Her mother was Sophia Phocaina, daughter of the *Curopalates*.'

Liudprand grimaced involuntarily. The *Curopalates* was a man who would cut your hand if you tried to lean on him, if ever he had seen one. He began to feel sincerely sorry for Theophano. Still, he had the information he needed, although it was not as satisfying as he had hoped. Theophano was of noble, very noble, birth and was being given a royal education but was not herself royal. All the same, she was worth bearing in mind. He started to talk to the tutor about the children's curriculum and gradually steered the conversation round to Theophano's prowess. Her tutor was concerned, he learned, because Theophano was definitely clever and was being held back by Constantine's indolence, for naturally the boy-emperor's needs took precedence.   Liudprand saw his opportunity.

'Why do you not teach her something extra?' he enquired. 'Another language, perhaps.'

Philip stared at him suspiciously. 'Why should it benefit her to learn another language? She will never need it.'

A typical Byzantine attitude, thought Liudprand. 'You can't be certain. Anyway if she were to study Latin, for example, there are many great books she could read. You 'Romans' spoke Latin once, don't forget,' he added waspishly.

Philip ignored the gibe and considered the idea. He nodded. 'It would certainly be more interesting for her. I will have to consult the Empress, of course.'

'Indeed.' Liudprand smiled to himself. One never knew what might happen but he was increasingly sure that the marriage between Anna and young Otto was never going to materialise. There were other young noblemen in the West, however, and a semi-royal Byzantine princess, who knew some Latin, might be of serious interest.

So it came about that Philip kept Theophano back after the others three times a week and gave her a Latin lesson. The Empress agreed readily to the suggestion, thinking that pique at being excluded from the lessons might drive her idle son into exerting himself more, but she was displeased about the encounter with Liudprand. After that the Italian was confined to his quarters, until he was finally sent home, his mission a failure, in late September. By that time the girls had news of other new arrivals to occupy their minds.

The newcomers were two small Bulgarian princesses, Maria and Helena, sent as possible brides for Basil and Constantine. They were nieces of Tsar Peter of Bulgaria, who hoped that such a marriage alliance would secure Byzantine support against Bulgaria's greatest enemies, the pagan Rus from Kiev. What Tsar Peter did *not* know was that it was actually Nicephorus Phocas who was bribing the Rus to attack the

13

Bulgars. In reality the little princesses were hostages, not prospective brides, but none of the children knew that, any more than Tsar Peter. Theophano and Anna were both shocked and spellbound when Nicephorus told them that the Tsar of the Bulgars was a barbarian, who dressed only in the skins of animals.

To their disappointment Maria and Helena arrived wearing long, straight tunics and stoles to cover their heads like anybody else, and seemed shy and homesick rather than barbaric. Basil and Constantine paid them little attention, acting, it seemed, on their mother's orders, but Theophano remembered her own loneliness when she first came to the Palace and Anna was delighted to have a companion as near her own age as Helena.

In November, during one of their Latin lessons, Philip told Theophano that he had bad news for her. Her favourite uncle, John Tzimisces, had been exiled by her great-uncle. As a result he could not come to Constantinople at all but was to stay on the other side of the Bosphorus.

'What about my birthday-feast?' asked Theophano, not quite understanding.

'He will not be able to come.'

Tears filled Theophano's eyes but she fought to control them. Not merely did she like Uncle John for his own sake but he was her only real link with Thrace and her happy life there. As for her imperial great-uncle, he was very ugly, rather short with a head too big for his body. The head seemed to grow straight from his shoulders with scarcely any neck. He was quite dark-skinned with thick, bristly black hair. He was always stern and unbending and very, very pious.

Still, he was the Holy Emperor and his great-niece wished she could feel more affection towards him. It was so much easier to love Uncle John Tzimisces, with his curly red hair and beard and his bright, blue eyes, always ready to share a joke with her on the rare occasions when he was in the city and came to see her. Curiously the Empress usually seemed to decide to visit the schoolroom on the days when John was there. Otherwise she was an infrequent visitor.

'Why was Uncle John sent away?' she asked.

'He is a very good general and sometimes it is not wise to appear to be a better commander than the commander-in-chief,' replied Philip.

Theophano considered this.

'The Empress will be sorry. They are good friends,' she observed.

'Perhaps too good,' Philip said softly.

'What do you mean?'

Philip sighed. 'It is also not wise for a general to become too friendly with the Empress.'

'Do you mean an empress can never have a friend?' asked Theophano indignantly.

Philip hesitated. 'That is almost true. Her best, and perhaps only, friend must be the emperor. Certainly you must not mention your uncle's banishment to the Empress.'

The birthday-party went ahead in December but, despite the Empress honouring it with her presence, Theophano thought it a rather lacklustre celebration. Indeed the whole court seemed to be becoming increasingly gloomy. Even the Christmas festivities did less than usual to lighten the spirits. The little Bulgars, still suffering from homesickness, were cast into fresh floods of tears by the news of the death of their uncle, Tsar Peter, in January. The court went into formal and, in the circumstances, hypocritical mourning.

No sooner had that period of official grieving expired, than they were in mourning for Princess Olga of Kiev. A Viking Rus princess, she had converted to Christianity whilst staying at the Byzantine court. The children managed to overhear some gruesome but thrilling stories about her pagan past. They heard that to avenge the murder of her husband, she had pretended to forgive all his murderers and summoned them all to her. As a mark of honour she suggested that they should be carried into her court in their longship. Unknown to the murderers, Olga had a huge pit dug in her courtyard and covered it with a light screen. Her followers carried in the unsuspecting enemy in their boat, which they dropped into the pit. The earth was hastily shovelled back on top of the assassins and they smothered to death in a parody of a Viking ship-burial. The boys and the Bulgars were inclined to admire Olga's ingenuity but the soft-hearted Anna was appalled. Theophano listened to the story without comment then asked

'How many murderers were there?'

'About forty,' answered Philip, to whom they had rushed with the tale.

'So that made forty more blood-feuds,' said Theophano. 'That was not so clever.'

'Nonsense,' snapped Basil, who had come to see his brother. 'She hit them so hard she suppressed their faction for good,'

Theophano shrugged but said nothing. You didn't argue with even a boy-emperor. Philip said to Basil

'The Lady Olga must have repented of her sins. You were present at her baptism, Lord, when you were a babe in arms. She took the name Helena after her godmother, your grandmother.'

'Her son was not converted though,' said Maria, the elder of the Bulgars, with a shudder.

'Sviatoslav? No, I'm afraid he still remains a great threat to your new Tsar, Boris,' agreed Philip.

The atmosphere in the city grew more and more tense. Nicephorus had become deeply unpopular, because of high taxation, endless and unnecessary warfare and bad harvests. Serious riots in 967 had persuaded the Emperor to fortify the Great Palace, and even to build himself a small citadel down by the seashore near the Bucoleon harbour. People said that he no longer slept in his bed at night for fear of assassins, but wrapped himself in a panther-skin on a dark corner of the floor.

Maria's fears of Sviatoslav were confirmed in August when the hordes of the Kievan Rus, commanded by him, stormed into Bulgaria and captured its capital, Preslav. They took the whole of the Bulgar royal family, Maria and Helena's family, prisoner. There would never be any question of imperial marriages now for the two girls, but otherwise they were still kindly treated. Indeed as the autumn wore on, the Empress came herself most nights to say goodnight to them and to check that they were well, before going back down the hill to the Bucoleon. The Bulgars made brave efforts to suppress their tears but Theophano was puzzled by the Empress's concern. She had never bothered before to say goodnight to her own children or to Theophano. Why such attention to two girls whose political importance had disappeared? It was out of character for the Empress. Perhaps she too was suffering from the mounting tension. It was widely known that in August an anonymous monk had confronted Nicephorus during a procession through the city and pressed on him a note saying, 'O Emperor, it has been revealed to me, although I am only a worm upon the earth, that in the third month after the coming September you will die.'

The news from Bulgaria grew worse and worse throughout the autumn. Theophano grew worried about her home in Thrace, because by the beginning of December the Rus were massed along the Thracian border of the Empire. They had started as Nicephorus' allies but by now they were a two-edged sword, utterly out of control. Something had to be done and the hated and compromised Nicephorus was not the man to do it. The Empress decided it was high time she intervened herself, even if it meant getting rid of her husband the Emperor.

CHAPTER THREE

At first the Empress' intervention seemed innocent enough. She decided to give a party on the 10th December to lighten the gloom. A party in Advent was unusual but the girls thought it an excellent idea, until Constantine informed them that they were not invited.

'It's only for grown-up ladies,' he said smugly.

'So you're a grown-up lady?' challenged Theophano.

'I'm an emperor. People tell *me* things.'

This was disappointing but not wholly unexpected. Nevertheless by judicious loitering around the corridors, they would see what the ladies were wearing and possibly speak to those they knew. They did not for a moment believe that Constantine was really invited.

The loitering scheme too was doomed to failure. The day of the party turned out to be bitterly cold and when the guests arrived at the Daphne Palace in the afternoon, they were wrapped from head to foot against the weather, so that even their eyes could only be glimpsed. The girls could not recognise anyone except the Empress herself. The other guests all looked grotesquely tall and bulky in their travelling cloaks and Theophano wondered if it was a fancy-dress party, because when one cloak fell open a little way for a second, she was sure she had caught the gleam of a sword-blade. There was no chance to investigate, because the girls were constantly returned to the children's quarters whenever they were noticed. They were all thoroughly frustrated and bored by the time darkness fell.

Just after nightfall the snow started, slowly at first but as the wind rose, it turned into a blizzard. The Empress left just after the snow began, presumably to join Emperor Nicephorus in his citadel. Surprisingly the other guests stayed and the girls could hear them being shown to various empty rooms all over the palace. Boredom eventually drove the children to bed, even before the Empress came back to say goodnight to the little Bulgars. She must really be worried about Maria and Helena, if she

18

struggles up through the blizzard to see them, thought Theophano, feeling guilty about her lack of affection for her godmother.

The Empress checked all four girls were in bed and told the nursery maids to make sure they stayed there.

'It is not a night for wandering,' she said sombrely, before going off to see the boys.

Anna quickly dropped to sleep but Theophano was restless. The wind moaned constantly and she thought what a strange day it had been. Some of the servants seemed to have been exchanging odd looks all day and even the dopey Constantine was full of suppressed excitement. It was as if everyone knew a secret from which the girls were excluded.

Late in the evening she heard the Empress go, but many other footsteps followed hers. Why were the party-guests going when the blizzard was still blowing? The snow muffled all noise outside and she could not be sure which way they went, but it sounded like downhill rather than towards the Chalke, the great bronze gate which was the only exit from the whole palace- complex.

Still the wind blew and still Theophano lay awake. At one point the storm eased for a few minutes and in the quiet Theophano clearly heard a low whistle, coming from the area of the Bosphorus shore. Then the wind started up again and she was nearly drifting off to sleep when suddenly there was noise everywhere. Running feet and people shouting, inside and outside the building. Someone rushed past her room towards the boys' chambers, then the whole group pounded back down the passageway. The confused shouting settled into a rhythmic chant, 'John, Emperor of the Romans,' repeated over and over again. What did it mean? Who was John and where was Nicephorus?

The chant was soon drowned out by the hubbub as the little girls woke terrified and each screamed louder than the other. The nursemaids, frightened themselves, had their hands full trying to calm them and nobody noticed as Theophano grabbed her cloak and slippers and crept out of the room. She reached the main door of the now-deserted Daphne Palace unseen, then sank back into the shadows as the Emperor's bodyguard, the red-clad Varangian, thudded past *uphill*, their battle-axes over their shoulders. Emperor Nicephorus was not with them.

Theophano slipped out to follow them but she could already hear shouting from the Magnaura Palace and knew that was where they were going. Unobserved she got to the Room of the Golden Thrones – and there she stopped short.

This was the room used for the really big audiences of state. In the centre were the thrones. The Emperor's had a mechanism which would suddenly lift it several feet into the air as if by magic. In front of the throne was a tree of gilded bronze, its boughs filled with brazen birds who seemed to sing, and on either side were gilded lions, who threshed their tails and roared at the Emperor's signal. None of these mechanical marvels had ever astonished Theophano as much as the sight that now met her eyes.

The Emperor was enthroned as normal, with Basil and Constantine at his side, surrounded by a cheering crowd. The Emperor, however, was not Great-uncle Nicephorus but Uncle John Tzimisces, wearing the purple tunic and red boots of empire.

Suddenly terrified, Theophano turned and ran, blindly into the snow, straight down the hill towards the shore. The snow was falling more gently now and as she neared the Bucoleon citadel, she skidded to a halt. Something dark lay on the white snow, just underneath her great-uncle's window. She realised instantly that it was a body but something was wrong with the shape. Trembling she approached it and saw what was missing – there was no head. All the same she knew it was Nicephorus' body; she recognised the barrel chest and short legs. Cautiously she touched the dark area around him and her fingers were covered in sticky, congealing blood. Holding her other hand over her mouth she darted into an archway and was violently sick.

Gradually the horror subsided a little and she forced herself to think rationally. She grieved for her great-uncle, who had been as good to her as his stiff nature would permit, but she had to work out what personal danger she was in. She was a Phocas on her mother's side. What if the pretend party-guests who were, she now realised, the assassins, had orders to kill all the Phocas? Should she see if she could find an untended boat and get out of the Palace by sea?

On the other hand she was equally a Sclerus and they were close friends of John Tzimisces. Anyway her Uncle John would not harm her – but then she would never have thought that he would murder Nicephorus. It seemed the dead emperor had been right about not trusting anyone; not that his suspicion had kept him safe in the end.

It dawned on her that, whatever happened, she had to find physical shelter. She was shaking from head to foot, as much from cold as from shock. She forced her frozen limbs to take her up the hill, back to the warmth and safety of the Daphne Palace – she hoped.

Halfway there she ran into a pair of nursery maids who had been sent to look for her. She was rushed back to her bedroom, rubbed dry with warm towels and given fresh clothes and a drink of a strange-tasting hot wine, before being put back to bed.

'What was in the drink?' she managed to ask.

'Something to help you sleep without nightmares,' was the reply.

Yes, Theophano thought. Even if it was poison, so long as there were no nightmares, she was too exhausted to care. Obediently she closed her eyes, for the last time hoping for the simplicities of childhood, where you just did as you were told and other people looked after you. She slept, the rest of the night and all the next morning.

She woke to find the world shrouded in fog and eerily silent from the snow. Anna knelt by her bedside, tears rolling down her face. As memory came back, Theophano shot up in bed then stopped, puzzled. Why was Anna so upset? She had had no great liking for her stern stepfather and she should not be in any danger. Her mother would protect her, after all.

She got the rest of the story in bits from the weeping child. John Tzimisces was indeed the new emperor and Basil and Constantine were still his co-emperors, but Anna's mother was not to be the empress any more. It seemed that she had conspired with John and many others to rid the Empire of her disastrous husband, which made her a murderess. Patriarch Polyeuctus, the chief bishop of the Empire, would not crown John, if he married the elder Theophano. John cared more for his crown than for his lover, and so Anna's mother had been deposed and was already imprisoned on the island of Proti. Anna would never see her again and Basil and Constantine did not even care.

Theophano wrapped her arms round the little girl and rocked her gently while she considered the new situation. It was to be several days before she fully understood what had happened. The Empress' kindness to the Bulgars had been a sham, a pretext to persuade Nicephorus to leave the door to his citadel unlocked on the fateful day, so that the 'party-guests' could reach his bedroom. John Tzimisces, whose arrival by boat was signalled by the whistle Theophano had heard, joined them. They battered Nicephorus to death before cutting off his head and throwing his torso out of the window.

A few days later the new emperor summoned his niece. She went with her heart in her mouth, unable to reconcile her picture of Uncle John with the barbarous details of the murder, which were now circulating round the court. John looked at her consideringly as she entered and made her obeisance.

'No more kisses, Theophano?' he asked gently.

'It would not be fitting, Most Pious Augustus.'

John sighed. 'In private I am still Uncle John,' he said. 'Tell me, do you blame me for what I have done?'

Theophano swallowed. This was a dangerous question, despite the gentle tone.

'I do not understand why you did what you did,' she answered carefully.

'You know Nicephorus was not a good emperor?' he began and waited.

'He was a good man,' Theophano objected.

'True but that is not necessarily the same thing as a good emperor. Think, little Theophano. You know that the Rus are massed all along our Thracian border. It was Nicephorus who brought them there and he was doing nothing to stop them. Come the spring, they would push right into the Empire and thousands of men, women and children would die, while he did nothing. Meanwhile our people are starving from the bad harvests, but he has done nothing for them, no food stores, no doles, nothing.'

Theophano nodded doubtfully. Philip had been saying as much during her lessons over the last few days. In any case, what was done, was done. Her opinion could make no difference but John was continuing to talk.

'Don't think that I am happy that I had to gain the throne through trickery and violence,' he was saying. 'I am not and I will do penance for my sin for the rest of my life. But I had to think of the Empire and I want you to do the same. I have a great destiny in mind for you but I have to be sure of your loyalty.'

Theophano shot him a troubled glance. This sounded like what she had dreaded since the question of Anna's marriage had been raised – being made to marry Basil or Constantine and being trapped in the Great Palace for ever. She regarded the two young emperors as brothers of whom she was not particularly fond. Constantine was annoying and she was a little frightened of Basil. She certainly did not want to marry either of them.

John waited for her response but when she was silent, he continued,

'You are the daughter of my very dear friend and brother-in-law, Theophano, but you are also a Phocas on your mother's side and I must be sure that you will not intrigue against me with them.'

Theophano shook her head forcefully.

'Of course I would not,' she said. 'I am not close to my mother's family – but I would not wish them to be harmed.'

'If they accept the situation as it is, they will not be,' replied the Emperor, a hint of menace in his tone. 'They have been sent into exile, your grandfather on Lesbos and your uncle Bardas Phocas in Pontus. A bit cold there but it will serve to cool his temper.'

Against her will Theophano smiled. She knew Uncle Bardas Phocas' temper. She nodded.

'Then I promise you loyalty,' she said simply.

'Good then,' replied John smiling. 'Now let me tell you what I have in mind for you.'

Theophano stiffened but his next comment took her completely by surprise.

'You are studying Latin with your tutor. He tells me that you are quick to learn. Do you remember that, when you were small, an embassy from Otto the Saxon came to the court?'

'Bishop Liudprand, yes. They wanted Anna to marry the German Emperor's son.'

'So Philip told me.'

Theophano stared at him in surprise and he laughed.

'Philip was appointed by the former empress at my suggestion and he has kept me closely informed about you. I could not let my – and my wife's – favourite niece grow up unprotected in a place as dangerous as the imperial court.'

Nothing was ever as it seemed, Theophano thought. Sometimes it was better, sometimes worse, but never simple.

'How old are you now, child?'

'I will be ten after Christmas.'

'Nearly old enough for marriage. Have you ever thought about it?'

Theophano's reply was an indistinguishable mutter. No great enthusiasm but not a complete refusal, John thought to himself. That would do.

'The Franks cannot be allowed to have Anna. As a *porphyrogenita* she is too valuable and the Empire may need her more later on. But how would you feel about marrying this young Otto? By all accounts he's a handsome lad and people speak well of him. It would be a very different life from here.'

Theophano did not know how to answer. Part of her – a small part at the moment – was thrilled at the idea of getting away from the Palace and seeing new places, but most of her shrank from the thought of leaving everything familiar.

'I do not know, Uncle,' she said finally. 'I think I am too young to think about marriage yet. I will not be twelve for two years.'

John laughed again. 'And no doubt that seems a long time to you but at my age it will pass in a flash. Still, you are right that you should not be married until you are twelve and there is no need for you to worry about it yet. Just work hard at your Latin. Philip will teach you more about the Franks and their empire and you must listen carefully.'

'How do you know that this Otto will want to marry me anyway?' objected Theophano.

'He will not be allowed to make a personal choice, my dear, any more than you will' answered John. 'He is an emperor; you are a princess. You both have your duty but I would not wish to force you if you really hated the idea. If you could not bear leaving Constantinople, for instance.'

'No, I didn't mean that,' said Theophano quickly. 'I meant the Franks altogether. Do they still want an alliance? I thought we were at war.'

'That is exactly why we need an alliance. I cannot fight three wars at the same time, two of them provoked by your great-uncle's folly. I must ensure the defeat of the Rus and make peace with the West, then I shall go back to Syria and the Saracens.'

'Yes, but do the Franks want peace?'

'So my spies tell me. Otto the Saxon has been in Italy fighting this pointless war for several years now. If he doesn't keep more of an eye on Germany, he could be in for some nasty surprises.'

John looked at his niece with fresh interest. She was not just a pretty and intelligent child, he thought, but someone who had the makings of a stateswoman.   She could see the pertinent questions to ask about a situation. The Germans would be lucky to have her, although he doubted whether they would see it that way.

The door opened and a eunuch came in with yet another file of papers about the coronation, which was to be on Christmas Day. With a kiss John sent the girl back to the Daphne Palace and put the Western Alliance to the back of his mind for the time being.

CHAPTER FOUR

Back in the schoolroom, life changed slowly but gradually. Constantine left to join his brother with another tutor. The boys also had to spend more time with the Chief Minister, a distant cousin of theirs known as Basil the Eunuch, who had acted as kingmaker to both Nicephorus Phocas and John Tzimisces. His eunuch status meant he could never be emperor himself, but he was determined to exercise power through his influence on the boy-emperors. Once John Tzimisces went back to his troops, as he intended, Basil the Eunuch would be the real power in the land.

The two girls also increasingly had to watch the process of government, so that they would be able to play their parts in the rituals of court and church life. Unlike the boys, they were not allowed to be present publicly but had to observe from behind a lattice or from the women's gallery in Haghia Sophia. One of the first such audiences Theophano witnessed took place a few months after John's coronation and she was very glad that Anna was not there to see it.

Theophano had been told that the deposed empress, Anna's mother, had escaped from her prison and sought sanctuary in Haghia Sophia. Basil the Eunuch's guards had dragged her from her refuge but she was to be allowed one last interview with the Emperor, before going into exile in Armenia. Young Theophano could hear shouting as she entered the latticed corridor, which was unheard of in the Emperor's presence. When she could see into the chamber, Empress Theophano, flanked by guards, was berating John and Basil the Eunuch, who faced her.

'You never loved me. You just used me to get the throne and when it suits you both, you'll murder my poor little sons as well.'

She paused for breath and Basil shouted to the guards

'Stop her mouth.'

The Empress was too quick for them. Still screaming abuse, she darted across the room, arms and fingers outstretched, and raked her long

27

nails down Basil the Eunuch's cheeks before she was overpowered. Even that could not make her hold her tongue. She had been an innkeeper's daughter before becoming empress and she applied several words to John which young Theophano did not understand. The Empress was dragged from the room as the girl herself was hustled away and the incident was never mentioned to Theophano again. She could not help feeling some sympathy for her godmother over her attitude to the two men. Her wickedness was not obviously greater than theirs but she had lost the power-game. In this world perhaps that was all that counted.

In time she came to realise that her uncle was genuinely remorseful about his treachery to Nicephorus and intended to atone for it. He gave away almost all his own money to the poor over that spring and summer and to Theophano's delight sent much of it to the peasants of Thrace, who were suffering from both the bad harvests and the Rus attacks. He also endowed orphanages and a hospital for lepers across the Bosphorus at Chrysopolis. He went there every week to help, sometimes even bathing the patients' sores with his own hands, and he often took Theophano with him, although she was never allowed to touch a patient. On such days, on the way back, Theophano would lean against the side of the imperial barge, the wind ruffling her hair, and look up at the city on its hills on the European bank. The dome of Haghia Sophia dominated the graceful skyline and she would be gripped by a feeling of pride. This city, the centre of the world and surely its most beautiful town, was *her* city and she would not wish to live elsewhere.

Her content and her security increased in the autumn when her father and his brother Bardas Sclerus won a great victory over the Rus host in Thrace, using the tactic of a feigned retreat, which they had learned from fighting the Saracens. Tales of the brothers' personal heroism reached the city – Constantine Sclerus had saved his brother's life by decapitating a warhorse with one blow and Bardas had sliced a Rus warrior in half lengthways. Theophano wrote to her father to congratulate him and was surprised and delighted to receive a reply. Her father assured her that he heard good reports of her and regretted that his duties kept them apart. She was, however, to regard her uncle John as her father and to obey him in all things. Such a letter could not compensate for ten years of neglect, but it was better than nothing.

In the spring of 971 disturbing news reached the capital. Theophano's Phocas relations did not accept their defeat by John after all. Her grandfather started a rebellion in Thrace and her Uncle Bardas Phocas proclaimed himself emperor. Theophano found her loyalty under suspicion again and the courtiers started to avoid her, especially when John crushed Leo Phocas' revolt with his usual decisiveness and sentenced him to death. Her heart in her mouth, Leo's granddaughter requested an audience with the Emperor. This was quickly granted.

Theophano was relieved that, when she was admitted to John's study, he was obviously going to be the uncle rather than the emperor.

'Well, child, what can I do for you?' were his opening words, as she rose from her obeisance.

'I have heard that my grandfather is sentenced to death,' began Theophano, a tremble in her voice.

John looked at her in some surprise.

'I didn't know that you were so fond of him.'

'I'm not, really, but he *was* good to me. He had me brought to the Palace when Aunt Maria died. I owe him gratitude, Uncle.'

'Hm, but his son, your other uncle Bardas, is challenging my throne.'

'I know,' Theophano admitted miserably, 'but Grandfather is old now. Too old to do any real harm'

John gave her a long, considering look.

'Do you remember you made a promise to me?' he asked.

'Oh yes, Sir. Indeed I do. I am not asking for mercy for Uncle Bardas Phocas, because he *is* dangerous, but I truly don't think Grandfather is now.'

John grunted.

'Well, you will be glad to know that I have already commuted his sentence to blinding and perpetual exile.'

Theophano expressed her thanks, adding 'A blind man can't be any threat, I suppose.'

For the first time in her life she found herself feeling sorry for her grandfather. He, who was so used to command, would probably prefer death to the dependency brought by blindness.

John hesitated.

'Actually,' he admitted, almost shame-facedly, 'I have sent secret orders for the hot irons to be withdrawn at the last moment, so he will keep his sight – this time. I have no wish to commit more sins against your mother's family, Theophano. Let this help to pay for Nicephorus. But you must say nothing of this to anyone.'

Impulsively Theophano abandoned formality, throwing her arms round her uncle and kissing him. She could find no words to express her relief but the gesture spoke louder than words. Eventually she said tentatively

'Uncle Bardas is a different matter, of course?'

'Theophano, do you remember what you once said to Philip about the Princess Olga of Kiev's revenge simply creating more bloodfeuds? You were right and you were thinking like an empress. A private man can perhaps afford the luxury of such a feud but an emperor must not; he must think of the good of the country. I admit that I would personally sleep sounder in my bed if Bardas Phocas were out of this world, but all the same, if I *can* persuade him to give in, I will. We have infidel enemies enough without fighting within the Empire. The peace of Christendom should be our ultimate aim. Always remember that.'

True to his word, John put the Sclerus brothers in charge of the loyalist troops with orders to disperse the rebels by bribery if possible. As a result the rebel army simply melted away and in the end Bardas Phocas, his sons and his wife crept under cover of darkness to a small fortress nearby, where they were besieged. In August 971 he surrendered. John forced him to accept a monk's tonsure and sent him with his family to the island of Chios, where they began a pleasant life in exile.

Theophano fervently hoped that he would stay there and cause no more trouble. Seeing the Emperor's obvious favour towards her, the court had become friendlier again but the boy-emperors, Basil and Constantine, lost no opportunity to taunt her with her relatives' treachery. Anna burst out one day in the schoolroom

'I hate my brothers for being so horrible to you. Basil is just a cruel bully. It would be worth getting married to get away from them.'

'Our husbands might be just as bad,' pointed out Theophano with grim humour. 'I think Basil is frustrated actually. Look at him – he'll be fourteen and a man soon but my uncle and Basil the Eunuch don't give him any power or responsibility at all. He hits back at John through me.'

Anna disagreed. 'He's always been a bully,' she said obstinately.

Theophano was silent. It was true that there was a cruel streak in Basil, which any opposition to his will brought out. All the girls had suffered from it at times. Like Anna, she found herself in the autumn very ready to be distracted by the news of two forthcoming weddings.

CHAPTER FIVE

The first wedding was that of the Emperor himself. John Tzimisces decided to legitimate his claim to the throne by marrying into the Macedonian dynasty. There was plenty of choice available. Romanus II had had five sisters who had all been forced into convents by their ruthless sister-in-law Empress Theophano, but twelve years' hard labour – Byzantine convents observed no distinctions of rank – had left them neither youthful nor pretty. Nevertheless Theodora, John's choice, was kindly and her young nieces were delighted and revelled in the wedding preparations. Then a thunderbolt struck. Bishop Liudprand was coming back, because Otto the Saxon still wanted a Byzantine bride for his son. Suddenly Anna decided that she could tolerate her brothers after all.

As soon as John Tzimisces had definite confirmation that the envoys were under way, he sent for both Theophano and Anna. One glance at the younger girl's pale face and trembling lip was enough to make her feelings clear. Anna was still only seven and lacked the curiosity that might make Theophano receptive to new experience. This was convenient in view of his intentions and he hastened to reassure Anna that she was not going to Germany.

'The Empire will never give a princess born in the purple to a foreigner. Your grandfather laid down that that must never happen.'

'Why does being porphyrogennate matter so much?' Theophano was frowning as she considered this. Why should being born in a particular room be so important?

'Because only the children of reigning emperors may be born in the purple chamber,' answered John. The girls both knew the room he meant in the Magnaura, a room lined with the rare and precious reddish porphyry marble. Anna and her brothers had been born there.

'To be born to a reigning emperor is more sacred than being the child of one who becomes emperor later,' added John. 'Even the Saxons know this. Some of their people say that it is not Otto who should be king, but his younger brother Henry, who was born *after* their father became king. That is why it is important to Otto to marry his son to a *porphyrogenita*. It would increase his own legitimacy.'

Anna merely looked puzzled but Theophano nodded. She could see what John meant. To the Byzantines the Emperor was the Thirteenth Apostle, more sacred than anyone else on earth, but he only became so when the Patriarch put the imperial diadem on his head. Obviously a child born to him after that would be more numinous than one born before his crowning.

John was not sure that Anna fully believed his reassurances but he did manage to coax a hesitant smile from her, which pleased him. Childless himself, yet fond of children, he wanted to be on good terms with the imperial princelings. He would certainly miss his own niece when she went.

Next he turned his attention to Theophano. He knew there was no need to repeat to her his reasons for needing peace in Italy; Philip would have made sure she understood that. It was her own attitude he wanted to assess now. In response to his query she shook her head.

'I don't know what I feel, Uncle. If it will serve the Empire then it is my duty to marry this Otto, and I will do it, but I know nothing about him and little about his people. I don't know what they will expect of an empress. I don't understand exactly what you want me to achieve. In the books I've read, Germany seems like a land of nothing but huge forests inhabited by savage barbarians. It will be like going back in time.'

'Not entirely,' John said gently. 'Tacitus is nearly a thousand years out of date, you know. For a start their so-called empire includes parts of Italy as well as the land north of the Alps. Even under the old Romans, the lands west of the Rhine were civilised and there were some great cities which still exist – Cologne, for instance.'

'Yes, but the Saxons live a long way north-east of the Rhine.'

'The Saxons were converted to Christianity by Charlemagne nearly two hundred years ago. That is a long time, Theophano. They are not the primitive savages their ancestors were.'

'Do they speak Latin?' asked Theophano doubtfully. This was her main worry. The idea of not being able to talk to anyone was appalling.

John glanced at his notes. 'Let me see. I asked that too. Yes, your future husband is fluent in Latin, as are his mother and sister. His father has some Latin, although he only learned it late in life.'

'Young Otto's mother is still alive?'

'Very much so,' answered John. 'It is through his wife that Otto the Saxon rules in Italy. She is Burgundian by birth but married the former king of the Italian Kingdom.'

Theophano frowned. 'Italian Kingdom? But I thought Southern Italy was ours.'

'It is. Listen carefully, child. The Italian Kingdom is not the same thing as Italy. It means the parts of Italy which were conquered by the Lombards, roughly from the Alps to just north of Rome. These are the areas Otto controls, or thinks he does. Then there are the Papal States in the centre, which he effectively rules, because of the weakness of the Pope. In the south, as you say, are Apulia and Calabria, which we rule. There they speak Greek, not Latin or Italian. And lastly, south of Rome is the problem, Capua and Benevento. Independent Lombard principalities. Otto wants to control them as a buffer against us. We want the opposite and that's where you come in.'

'Me?' Theophano asked baffled. 'How?'

'If a marriage is arranged, I shall release the Lombard Prince of Benevento, Pandulf Ironhead, from prison. He is Otto's ally and in return for his release Otto must agree to stop attacking Apulia and Calabria. If he does that, then we will recognise his title as an emperor, which matters a lot to him. We had to do the same with Charlemagne eventually and there is no point in fighting about titles. Then, if all this is agreed, I will be free to push Sviatoslav back to Kiev and the Saracens back beyond Jerusalem, for the first time for three hundred years. A lot is depending on you, Theophano, because you will be the guarantor of all this.'

Theophano gulped. I'm only eleven, her mind screamed but she pulled herself together. There were many more questions she needed to ask while somebody was willing to answer them.

'Two – no, three things, Most Pious Augustus,' she said.

He nodded.

'What sort of people are they – the family, I mean?'

John frowned. How much to tell her?

'The boy, Otto II, is a good age for you, sixteen or seventeen. His nickname is Otto the Red, from his red hair.' Unconsciously he touched his own auburn curls. 'He is said to be handsome, brave, well-educated, perhaps a trifle spoilt, as boy-emperors tend to be.'

Theophano thought of Basil and grimaced. John saw it and guessed why.

'No, this boy is said to be good-natured, of an open disposition. In terms of character, it seems that you could do far worse, Theophano.'

Theophano sensed that there was something she was not being told. 'His mother?' she asked.

'It is a second marriage for both of them and there is a complicated history on both sides, too complicated to explain now. Adelheid is brave and resourceful, as well as very pious, and she is used to command. You will need to respect that, Theophano. I'm sure you will.'

The girl nodded obediently but she was not so sure. The one advantage of growing up at court both motherless and without an empress was that, on the domestic side, she and Anna got their own way quite a lot. It sounded as if it might be different in the West.

John watched her face and smiled to himself. Some people considered Theophano insufficiently submissive for a woman. It would do her no harm to learn to defer to a mother-in-law for a time. From what he had heard, Adelheid was formidable and no doubt sparks would fly.

Theophano moved on to her second point.

'Have they said that they are willing to have me instead of Anna?'

This was certainly the weakness of John's scheme, but he judged that Otto I was as pragmatic as he was himself.

'It's their choice,' he replied. 'I will not let them have Anna. They can take you and make peace, or carry on fighting a pointless war, which keeps Otto trapped in Italy with a risk of losing Germany. It's very simple.'

Not simple at all for me, thought Theophano, but anyway. There was still her third point, a sensitive one. She looked straight at her uncle.

'Uncle, when I am married, my duty will be to my husband and his empire but now my duty is to you and to this empire. What happens if the agreement is broken after I am married?'

'It will be hard for you,' John answered. 'It always is for royal brides. The law of nations and the law of God say that you must support your husband, not your own country. That is for your protection, because otherwise you would always be a potential traitor and thus in reality a hostage. By the same token, I will not prejudice the interests of the Empire to keep you safe.'

'Queen Esther worked for her own people after she married Xerxes,' objected Theophano.

'But Dalilah was universally reviled when she betrayed her husband Samson to her own people,' retorted John.

'I'm on my own then,' said Theophano slowly. As you always have been, a voice in her mind added.

'I'm afraid so,' agreed her uncle. 'We shall not break the treaty,' he added. 'It is for you to influence your future family to keep it too.'

Then, rather hastily, he dismissed the girls. The trouble with Theophano was that she saw rather too clearly. It was not a comfortable trait in a woman; she would need to learn to cloak it.

The actual arrival of the western envoys in early November was overshadowed by the preparations for John's own wedding to Theodora. Theophano learned that it was a large delegation, which included Bishop Liudprand but whose leader was a German, Archbishop Gero of Cologne.

A bodyguard of mailclad knights escorted them. Otto I was not having his envoys mishandled again. In fact they were received with great honour but John would not discuss their mission until after his wedding.

Theophano had quite a major role in this ceremony, her first real public engagement in front of a mixed audience. Inside the New Church, now a hundred years old and blazing with gold and jewels in the light of the many candles, she was to take the bride's flowers when she needed her hands free and return them as required.

Theodora was nervous, especially when her husband had to go alone through the *iconostasis*, the screen which separated off the sanctuary. It was at this point that the Patriarch could forbid the marriage because of John's past. Theophano moved unobtrusively to support Theodora as John went forward, then an audible sigh of relief swept the church as the Patriarch beckoned him through. Theodora sagged at the knees with relief but Theophano's arm held her up until her husband returned through the screen and they could process out together as man and wife.

Theophano was not surprised to find that, at a banquet to celebrate the marriage, she was placed next to Bishop Liudprand and within earshot of Archbishop Gero. This evening was another first for her, her first grown-up dinner engagement, and she wished she had been free to enjoy it without having to watch what she said so carefully. Liudprand soon had her chattering away, however. His lively, black eyes, darting everywhere with a hint of amusement in their depths, were irresistible and he set Theophano at her ease by reminding her of their earlier encounter in the silk manufactory. He had never forgotten her, he told her, and was delighted to see that she had indeed grown into a beautiful and accomplished young lady, as he had expected. Theophano deflected the flattery skilfully and used the opportunity to pump him for information about the Western imperial family.

It gave her plenty to think about. She learned that the Ottonian dynasty was quite recently formed. When Otto I was born, his father Henry the Fowler had been only Duke of Saxony, not King of Germany.

'Why Henry the Fowler?' interrupted Theophano, laughing. 'Surely he didn't catch birds for a living?'

Liudprand laughed too. 'No, but legend says that one day he was out trapping birds and fell asleep beneath a great oak-tree on the hill below his castle at Quedlinburg. Suddenly the princes of the East Franks, the Germans, appeared, bearing the royal insignia. They greeted Henry as King of Germany. King Conrad, the last of the East Frankish descendants of Charlemagne in the male line, had just died and the princes had elected Henry king. So the nickname stuck to him.'

'It's like something from a story,' observed Theophano, thinking that such a thing could never happen in the East. How could you 'elect' an emperor, she wondered. Only God could do that.

'And about as likely to be true,' agreed Liudprand cheerfully. 'Really he was elected by the assembly of the nobles at Fritzlar in the normal way.'

'You *choose* your emperor?' Theophano found this incredible.

'We choose our king. The Lord Pope bestowed the emperorship on King Otto much later in Rome.'

'So it *was* God who appointed him?'

'It is always God,' answered Liudprand, 'but the Western Empire is not quite like the East. In the East you can have an emperor like young Basil's grandfather. He had a long, successful reign, although he was a scholar and an administrator, not a soldier. In the north the ruler still has to be a warrior and the nobles have always chosen the best war-leader out of the royal kin.'

'So is Emperor Otto's son a warrior?' asked Theophano.

Liudprand smiled, apparently pleased by the question.

'Now that is a very interesting point. Young Otto has been trained as a knight, of course, but he has been reared in Italy since he was quite small, not Germany. He was given the same kind of book-learning that he would have had here and he has never taken part in a proper battle, although he is nearly seventeen. His father has had him crowned co-emperor, but I think he will still need to convince the German princes of his worthiness to succeed.' He watched her carefully. 'He will need a wise wife to help him.'

Theophano's face gave nothing away.

'Why? It doesn't sound as if women count for much in the world you describe.'

'That's what one would think, but actually it's not true. When men ride off to fight, their wives must rule their estates for them and for their sons. Our women are less secluded than the women of the Eastern Empire. The Empress Adelheid, for example, brought many of his lands to my master and her youth was full of adventure and danger. Beyond all this, though, my young master, like most men of his age, can be hotheaded. A wife whom he loved could exercise a moderating influence.'

'Princess Anna is very young for such a responsibility,' observed Theophano neutrally.

Liudprand almost laughed aloud. His informants had left him in no doubt that Anna would stay in Constantinople and that Theophano was aware of the proposed substitution. Her discretion would be a good counterpart to Otto II's impulsiveness.

'This is not the first time my master has sought a marriage-alliance with Byzantium, you know,' he said, to change the subject. 'Nearly twenty years ago he wanted to wed his niece Hedwig to Romanus II.'

Theophano looked up, startled for the first time.

'Anna's father? The Empress Theophano's first husband?'

'He was a boy and Hedwig was only a child. She was – and is – wilful. She pulled hideous faces to stop her portrait being painted for him, because she did not want to leave Germany. The engagement dragged on for some years, but when he reached his majority, he fell for his innkeeper's daughter and that was that.'

'Hush,' said Theophano automatically then remembered that it was now safe to mention the deposed empress's low ancestry again. 'So Hedwig never came here?'

'No, but she and her sister Gerberga learned Greek for many years. That whole branch of the Family, the Bavarian line, were angry about the slight to Hedwig and she and her brother Henry, Duke of Bavaria, still have no love for anything Byzantine. Gerberga does not bear such a grudge, I would say.'

Liudprand loved imparting gossip for its own sake but in this case he had a purpose. If Theophano came west, from the start she would need to understand the likely hostility she would receive from the Bavarian line.

As Theophano turned to talk to her neighbour on the other side, Liudprand caught the eye of the Archbishop of Cologne. Since they had been speaking Latin, he had been able to overhear most of the conversation. Gero nodded slightly. After his first embassy, Liudprand had suggested privately to Otto I that Anna would probably remain unobtainable but that another young princess, Theophano, night have the personal qualities to make an acceptable substitute. Only Gero and Liudprand knew that they had private authorisation from Otto to make such a change, but they certainly did not want the Byzantines to guess it until there was no chance of getting the *porphyrogenita*. Emperor John had granted them an audience the following day and Liudprand prayed that the situation would be resolved then. At least Gero's response to the girl was favourable; that was a big step forward.

CHAPTER SIX

Late the following afternoon Theophano received a summons from her uncle. She arrived to find an intimidating line-up waiting for her – her uncle, his Chief Minister, Basil the Eunuch, Archbishop Gero and Bishop Liudprand.

'This is it then,' she thought. 'They've decided.'

It was indeed so. Theophano listened carefully as the Emperor launched into a résumé of the agreements they had reached. She was to marry Otto II and the Eastern Empire would recognise his title as co-emperor with his father. John did not specify what the father and son were emperors of. She was to be married and crowned Empress by the Pope in the Church of St. Peter, Rome. The Ottonians would give up their claim to Apulia and Calabria and stay away from these territories. In return, as well as recognising the title, John would release Prince Pandulf Ironhead, Otto's vassal, from prison and he would keep the peace in Capua and Benevento – 'Which will be the August Lady's dowry,' broke in Archbishop Gero, with a bow to Theophano.

There was a sharp intake of breath from Basil the Eunuch and he and John exchanged glances. 'Pandulf Ironhead will keep the peace in Capua and Benevento,' repeated John as if Gero had not spoken.

It was now Gero's turn to glance at Liudprand, whose face for once was expressionless. From where she stood Theophano could see Liudprand's hand making a quick, suppressing gesture. The Archbishop said nothing more. John was still talking.

'I will give you an entourage fitting your rank as my niece and gifts to match it, worthy of your imperial husband and his illustrious family. Are you content this should be so?'

All four men looked at her while she fought down rising panic. It was one thing to think about it in theory, but now the decision was becoming reality. She would have to leave Anna, Philip, her governess Lady Emilia, her maids, the other young women of the court, her books, everything that was familiar. Really she knew nothing about her bridegroom; she could not speak German; although she and Otto were both Catholic Christians, she knew that Roman religion differed in some ways. No, she did not want to go, yet what choice did she really have? She thought she could detect sympathy in the eyes of all but Basil the Eunuch, who merely looked bored, but the sympathy would no doubt vanish if she dared to upset their plans. Bracing her shoulders, she said in a clear voice

'Yes, I am content.'

A wave of relieved congratulation broke over her. She had hesitated just long enough to make them doubtful. Almost immediately the conversation turned to practicalities. It became humiliatingly obvious that her uncle wanted her to go quickly, so that he could resume his campaign against the Rus. Liudprand demurred. That would mean the Princess would have to travel through the worst of the winter and take unnecessary risks. He did not add that he himself was no longer young, but he thought it.

'It will be better for the Princess,' John said. 'She is leaving everything she knows. If you must do that, it is best done quickly.'

Gero agreed. 'My master wishes the marriage to take place as soon after Easter as possible. The question is which way to travel, by sea or by land.'

'By sea,' John replied promptly. 'Our navy will protect her.'

'Precisely,' thought Liudprand. 'And it only needs a feigned attack by pirates and *you* have Apulia and Calabria and *we* have no bride.'

He also had no wish to repeat his last sea-voyage from Constantinople, which had involved theft, mutiny, starvation, three earthquakes and a shipwreck.

'The sea-route is too dangerous,' he said hastily. 'The weather around Greece is too stormy in January and those Sons of Ishmael, the Saracens, would be watching for the opportunity to snatch such a valuable hostage.'

'The same is true of the Rus and the Bulgars if you go the land route,' objected Basil the Eunuch.

'The Rus have withdrawn well to the north of the Via Egnatia, as you know,' said Gero.

'The Bulgars haven't.'

'The Bulgars are not officially your enemies and anyway you have the two little hostage-princesses. An attack on Lady Theophano would seal their fate.'

There was a brief silence while everyone considered whether that would make any difference to the Bulgars. It might; if Sviatoslav chose to massacre the imprisoned Tsar and his family, Maria and Helena were all the royalty the Bulgars had left. Theophano felt a stab of pity for them and for herself. They were all just pawns in a game of chess. If she ever had daughters....

Archbishop Gero was pressing home his argument.

'The old Roman road is still passable most of the way. It will be the quickest, surest, and, I think, the safest way. Such treasures as you have promised would be an irresistible magnet to pirates.'

'And to bandits,' John pointed out. 'But you have well-armed guards and I will send more with you as far as Benevento. You will still have to sail from Albania to Italy,' he added rather waspishly.

In the end the Germans won the argument. Gero genuinely thought it the safer mode of travel but he also wanted to see how well the bride stood up to it, which a boat-ride would not tell him. He was concerned by Theophano's slight figure. He hoped it indicated a healthy toughness but if not, it was better to find out soon, rather than to shackle his master's son to a woman who could not cope with the semi-nomadic life of the Western court. He also hoped those slim hips would be adequate for childbearing. She was young yet, of course, but he had been assured that she was ready for marriage, which time would tell. Otto I's anger if the girl turned out to be unsuitable was not pleasant to contemplate. Gero had only got his archbishopric after a vision of an angel with an unsheathed sword had persuaded the Emperor to appoint him despite Gero's brother's opposition to Otto. He certainly did not want to make any mistakes on this important mission.

Life for Theophano now turned into a whirl of riding-lessons, gown-fittings and dowry inspections. She needed silk brocades to illustrate the glamour and magnificence of the Eastern Empire as well as fine linens for more ordinary occasions. There also had to be finespun woollen garments and fur cloaks for both the mountain journey and for later on, when she went north. Her riding-habits had to be full skirted with the underskirts slashed, so that she could ride astride through the mountains. Fur-lined boots and jerkins completed her travelling outfit, while her bedroll was made of sheepskin with woollen blankets to go on top.

She also had to see and approve items for her dowry. She examined carpets and wall-hangings from Persia and Anatolia, woven with patterns of flowers and little, stylised animal-figures. There were porcelain dinner-plates and drinking-vessels made of rock crystal and agate. Bolts of rich silk were embroidered with designs of real and legendary animals. Precious stones abounded, sapphires, rubies, pearls, often set in gold filigree chains. Cameos, dating from classical times, of the Emperor Augustus and the imperial eagle signified recognition of Emperor Otto's title – or reminded him where the true successor to Augustus ruled, depending on how one interpreted the gift. Richly ornamented covers adorned illuminated manuscripts and golden reliquaries enclosed the most valued gifts of all, relics of the saints. It was much more than Theophano had expected, as she said to Philip one day. He nodded soberly.

'You know you told me that Archbishop Gero seemed to think that Capua and Benevento were your dowry? I think your uncle has given you such a rich bride-gift so that there can be no mistaking that they are not, without the need to say so.'

'It could still cause trouble then,' commented Theophano, 'if they think they've agreed to one thing and we think we've agreed to another.'

'Yes. While Otto's vassal Pandulf Ironhead lives, it should make no practical difference, but if anything were to happen to him, look out for squalls.'

Theophano decided that there was no point in worrying about it for the moment. She was more concerned about the immediate question of her entourage. Philip had refused to come. It had been a joy to teach her, he said, but now she was grown, it was time for him to return to the Magnaura University fulltime. Privately he doubted whether she would be allowed to keep any adult male Greeks near her, with the possible exception of a chaplain. Theophano was relieved to hear that her governess Emilia had volunteered to accompany her as lady-in-waiting. A childless widow and a distant Sclerus relation, Emilia had little other than a convent to look forward to in the East once her charge was gone, and the prospect of travel appealed to her. Theophano was fond of her, although she rarely heeded her, and was grateful for her decision.

She still had to choose which of her maids to take. In the end she called them together and described in detail the hardships of the journey which awaited them, drawing on her own memories of Thrace. She watched their faces carefully, noticing whose eyes lit up with curiosity and who looked appalled. Only two girls passed the test and one of these was noted for stirring up quarrels. She would be no asset at all but the other girl, Anastaso, was one of her favourites and she got the job.

Theophano kept managing to avoid the finality of her departure. First of all Christmas was still to come, so she could pretend that leaving was a long way off. Then there was her birthday, her twelfth, the day a girl became an adult. Her uncle's birthday gift filled her with more delight than all the dowry put together. It was a beautiful black Arab mare called Windswift, who had the speed and stamina of her race, as Theophano discovered when she tried her out.

Inexorably, however, the short days drew on and on the evening of the Feast of the Epiphany, called Theophany in the East and so her nameday, it was time to bid a private farewell to Anna. The little girl clung to her friend, protesting

'I'll still see you in the morning.'

'Yes, but everyone else will be there and we have to be on our way early. This is our real goodbye, Anna.'

Anna shuddered. 'I can't bear it, being left alone with those horrible boys and Uncle Basil'.

'Anna, listen to me,' said Theophano in a grave tone. 'Those boys are the Sacred Emperors. You must be more careful in what you say about them. If you are, my Uncle John will look after you. At least you are going to stay here for a long time. I shall never forget you and I will write to you. Will you send me letters?'

Anna nodded but clung to Theophano even more desperately. Eventually the older girl persuaded her to go to bed, while she attended to last-minute details. At least the need to comfort the child kept her own tears at bay.

A magnificent cavalcade headed towards the Golden Gate the next morning just after the dawn of a cold, clear day. First was a guard of Byzantine cavalry, then half the heavily-armed German knights. Then came Theophano, her ladies and the bishops, flanked by outriders, followed by the rest of the knights. Byzantine soldiers escorted a large mule-train and a group of craftsmen, and yet more of them brought up the rear. Banners fluttered in the breeze; the Patriarch blessed the procession; the Emperors gave Theophano the formal kiss of farewell and then they were off. Tears misted her eyes as she twisted back in the saddle for a final look at the beloved city, but the wind and the sunshine dried her tears and the Via Egnatia stretched invitingly away. Theophano turned her face to the future.

CHAPTER SEVEN

At first they were lucky with the weather and the going along the flattish coastline of the Sea of Marmara was easy. It was possible to talk as well as ride. To pass the time, Theophano reminded Bishop Liudprand that he had told her that her future mother-in-law, Empress Adelheid, had encountered adventure and danger in her youth but he had not said what these adventures were. The storyteller in Liudprand could not resist this overture and he embarked on his tale.

'My mistress was the daughter of King Rudolf of Burgundy and his Queen, Bertha,' he began. 'When she was six, her father died, leaving her unprotected, and she was forcibly married to Lothar, son of King Hugh of Italy. The marriage proved successful and Adelheid bore Lothar a daughter Emma, now Queen of France. In 951 Lothar died suddenly and the throne of the Italian Kingdom was seized by Berengar of Ivrea, a cruel and greedy man. He captured the young widow, who was only nineteen, and he and his wife Willa, a woman noted for her avarice, imprisoned her in a castle on Lake Garda in the north of Italy. There they cruelly mistreated her; she was beaten and kicked –' he paused for Theophano's horrified gasp – 'and they stole her jewellery. Nobody was allowed to see her except her serving-maid and sometimes her chaplain, a priest called Warin.

'The castle was on a rocky headland overlooking the lake. Warin got word to her supporters of where she was and a plan was made to free her. One dark night Adelheid and her maid climbed out of their chamber window while the guard was at the other end of his beat. Both young women were dressed as servants in dark clothes.

'A dangerous, winding path led down the cliff to the shore. At first the girls had to run in the dark, dreading that they would miss their footing, so that they would be round a curve in the path before the guard returned. When they heard his footsteps, they froze, then very, very carefully and quietly they climbed down the rest of the path.'

Liudprand stopped, enjoying Theophano's wide eyes.

'Oh, do go on,' she said involuntarily. 'Did they escape?'

Gero chuckled to himself to see the sophisticated young noblewoman returned to childhood by the power of a story. He was enjoying Liudprand's embellishments himself.

'There was a boat waiting at the foot of the cliff,' Liudprand went on, 'a flat-bottomed fishing boat with a top like a covered cart on it. Queen Adelheid and her maid hid in it and the boatman took them to the south of the lake, where he put them ashore. Then they had a weary walk to the rendezvous, a hut deep in the marshes near Mantua. They were exhausted by the time they got there, and extremely hungry, because they hadn't been able to bring any food with them. You can imagine how they felt when they reached the hut as day was dawning, but there was no Warin

'They waited several days but he did not come. Finally they were so hungry that they risked going out on the marsh by daylight, to see if they could catch anything to eat. Suddenly they saw a fisherman. For a time they hid and watched him, but when he caught a fat fish, they could bear it no longer. Adelheid called to him. He asked who they were and what they were doing. Adelheid answered

'Can't you see that we are wanderers without any human support, alone and hungry? If you can, give us something to eat.'

'The fisherman took pity on them. He lit a fire and they grilled the fish and ate it together, queen, maid, and fisherman. Their smoke guided Warin, who had become lost in the marshes, and he arrived with a company of knights just as they finished the meal. They escorted Adelheid over the wetlands to the Castle of Canossa, where she was safe.'

'What an amazing story! Is it all really true?' asked Theophano.

'Most of it,' said Archbishop Gero. 'The Empress really is a brave and resourceful lady.'

'In a way she's a bit like the Empress Theophano,' observed young Theophano thoughtfully. Both men regarded her with astonishment turning to disapproval.

'The Lady Adelheid is no murderess, nor an adulteress,' said Gero sternly.

'No, no, of course not. I mean she takes action on her own rather than waiting for things to happen to her,' Theophano tried to explain.

'Hm. At all events, Emperor Otto sent his brother Duke Henry of Bavaria to rescue her. When she married the Emperor, Otto became King of Italy as well as Germany. Then they had two children, your betrothed and a daughter, Matilda.'

The thought of her sister-in-law pleased Theophano. She was already missing Anna.

'Is she in Italy too?' she asked.

'She is a nun, abbess of Quedlinburg in Saxony,' Gero answered.

'Abbess already? How old is she?' Theophano was startled.

'A little older than you. She was young when she was elected abbess. She is a virtuous lady who will make you welcome.' He was relieved to be able to say that with certainty, knowing Abbess Matilda's nature. He did not know whether Adelheid was aware of the substitution of Theophano for Anna or not, nor how she might react. She was not one to underplay the importance of rank.

Their good fortune with the weather held all the way to Thessalonica, even through the Thracian mountains. They made full use of the baths and palaces of the city but all too soon, it was time to be on the road again, and now winter set in in earnest as they headed for the mountains of Epirus and Macedonia. Wolves, wild boar, lynx and brown bears roamed these forests. The snow, which now fell thickly, kept the bears in hibernation but the wolves and the wild cats were hungry and the travellers had to be wary and keep close together. At night the howls of the wolves echoed eerily over the white landscape and the women huddled in their sheepskins and shuddered, wondering why they had ever left the comfort of Constantinople.

Bishop Liudprand, now well into his sixties, was also suffering. His normally ruddy face was pale and his lips had taken on a bluish tinge. He talked far less and often rode with his left arm clamped to his chest, an expression of pain on his face. As January gave way to February, however, they crossed the watershed and started the descent to the Adriatic Sea. Near the coast there was no snow and the first flowers were in bloom. It had taken them a month to reach the sea, a thousand kilometres along the road the old Romans had made.

'Imperial couriers used to do it in three weeks', grumbled Liudprand as they waited for their ship at Dyrrachium.

'Imperial couriers were neither girls nor old men,' snapped Gero in irritation. The weariness of the journey was affecting them all and the two envoys grew more apprehensive about the substitution the nearer they came to Rome. The sea-voyage would give them all a necessary respite.

Soon their galley and its escorts, ships of the Byzantine navy, arrived and they all embarked. Theophano spent some pleasant hours in cool February sunshine, sitting talking to Archbishop Gero under an awning on the rear deck. He explained more of her new family's history to her, how all Otto I's children by his first marriage to an English princess had rebelled against him, but how the rebels' sons, two little boys also called Otto, had been brought up with her husband and were his closest friends.

'Tell me more about him,' she said to Gero. 'You all talk about the family but I want to know about him.'

Gero smiled. 'How would I know what a young lady wants to know about a man?' he asked teasingly and she laughed too. 'Well, I'll try. He has short, reddish hair and brown eyes. I think he is good-looking, but of course you will be the better judge of that. He is certainly well-made and excels at all knightly exercises, but he likes to read as well'

'How does he get on with his parents?' Considering the readiness of Otto I's family to rebel against him, this seemed a pertinent question.

'He is loyal,' Gero replied immediately, answering Theophano's thought rather than her words. She was relieved to hear it but his next comment revived her anxieties. 'Nevertheless he is of full age and has not yet been given any land of his own. He may find that irksome.'

Theophano thought of Basil and was sure that it did annoy young Otto.

'Why do you think he has not been given any land?'

'His dead elder brother's example has made the Emperor cautious, I think. And then he would perhaps like to see the young Emperor think more before he acts.'

At that moment a sudden squall hit the ship and their leisure to talk was ended. The bad weather continued all through the voyage and made Bishop Liudprand seasick. By the time they landed, he was seriously ill. He admitted that he had been having acute pains in his chest and left arm, as they had guessed, and it was decided that he should leave them and go straight home to Cremona. Theophano was sorry. When Liudprand was in a good humour, he was good company and she sensed that he liked her personally, despite his dislike of all things Greek after his treatment by Nicephorus.

As soon as they landed, Gero sent fast couriers to Rome with the news of Anna's replacement by Theophano. As they journeyed through Apulia, messages came back. He shared some of the contents of these with the girl but kept others to himself. She would find out soon enough that when Otto I made the news public, the main reaction at court was horror, and demands that the intruder should be sent home straight away. So far Otto was ignoring the criticism and young Otto was reputedly pleased at the prospect of a bride nearer his own age than Anna would have been. Gero was confident that the Emperors were quite strong enough to bear down the opposition but he was disturbed to read that the welcoming delegation at Benevento would be led by Bishop Dietrich of Metz. Here for the first time Theophano would enter western imperial territory and here, beneath the Arch of Trajan on the border between the two empires, the delegation would await her.

Bishop Dietrich was the Emperor's cousin, an aristocrat of the old school, very conscious of his birth, wedded to his own will rather than his vocation. He was formidable and Theophano would need all the confidence she could muster to confront him. Archbishop Gero could see his charge's spirits sinking as they rode towards the town and so he decided to administer a stimulant.

'I'm afraid, my lady,' he said, 'that you will have to change your name now you are in the west. In Germany names that end in 'o' are boys' names – like Otto and Gero. You are Theophania in Latin, of course, but in German you will be Theophanu.'

For a moment Theophano was speechless from utter fury. She had given up her homeland and her language and now even her name was to be taken from her. It was too much. Then she remembered that if Basil or Constantine married a western princess, her name would be changed completely into a Greek one. Perhaps she should count herself lucky that only a syllable was to be altered. But they would have to learn that 'Theophanu' could not be pushed around, she silently resolved.

Full of this determination she looked along the Via Appia to where the walls of Benevento could be seen in the distance. They would learn, she repeated to herself, and, spurred on by the force of her anger, she set her horse to canter forward to meet the new challenge.

CHAPTER EIGHT

Accustomed to the kindly bishops Liudprand and Gero, Theophanu found her first sight of Dietrich of Metz rather a shock. At the head of his delegation, he looked much more like a warrior than a bishop. In reality, like all bishops of the Western Empire, he was both and a politician as well. When Gero learned that it was Dietrich who was to welcome them, his heart had sunk. The Bishop of Metz had no time for women, did not like foreigners, and was probably the last person Gero would have chosen for the task.

The two parties dismounted and Archbishop Gero performed the introductions. Theophanu knelt to kiss the Bishop's ring and they formally embraced, then turned aside to talk. She could not look more beautiful, thought Gero. Not merely had Emilia and Anastaso dressed her in a grass-green tunic and overdress kept especially for this occasion but the spots of anger still glowing in her cheeks emphasised the animation of her dark eyes. He noticed, though, that Dietrich's eyes travelled again and again to her slim hips and Gero could guess what he was thinking – how likely was this one to produce an heir?

The conversation was going reasonably well. Theophanu was startled into blinking when Bishop Dietrich welcomed her to the Empire. She was used to a different empire, but she pulled her wits together and replied politely. Remembering what Gero had said about Dietrich's fondness for gold, she talked about the gifts she had brought with her in her dowry, particularly describing a golden reliquary which would, she thought, cater for both his enthusiasms, money and relics. Gero had told her a comic but supposedly true tale in which Dietrich had browbeaten even the Lord Pope himself into giving him a length of St. Peter's chains. The Bishop's eyes lit up at the mention of the reliquary but he replied stiffly. Had Theophanu but known it, she was displaying a quality he particularly disliked in women. She was being talkative, as Greek women were reputed to be.

Eventually the stilted encounter came to its end and then there was a painful duty for Theophanu, bidding farewell to the Byzantine guards who had accompanied her from Constantinople. They would not ride into western territory but would turn back to Bari. Her women would stay with her and a number of courtiers would attend her wedding and coronation, but then they would go home, whereas she never would. She was acutely conscious of the finality of that breach as she stood with Emilia and Anastaso under the Arch of Trajan, watching the company in its familiar uniform jogging back east. The Germans had considerably moved aside and the three women were alone for a moment. Then Emilia gave herself a little shake and cleared her throat.

'Well, Lady,' she said in a brisk tone, 'you've got a smear right down the side of that gown. Anastaso will need to wash it before we leave Benevento, if you're to wear it to meet the imperial family, as we planned.'

It was the necessary distraction.

'Surely there will be time on the journey,' said Theophanu. 'Rome is many days away yet.'

'Yes, beyond the mountains,' answered Emilia. 'There are no big stopping-places.'

'More mountains!' groaned Anastaso. Some of the way from Bari had been through flat country where spring was obviously beginning.

'Not so high as some we've done already,' Theophanu encouraged her, 'and it's later in the year and the Via Appia is a very old road. Just think, St. Peter and St. Paul must have come along it.'

Judging from Anastaso's expression, she was unimpressed by this thought, but when they set out again, her spirits improved, whereas Theophanu became more and more apprehensive. Bishop Dietrich did unbend slightly as the journey continued, although she still sensed that he did not really like her. Such information as he provided seemed designed to intimidate. He spoke no Greek, and, rather then complimenting her Latin, he seemed to delight in pointing out that she would need to learn the

Italian vernacular as well, not to mention the language of Southern Germany. Then there was Saxon.

'Don't most Germans speak Latin?' Theophanu asked.

'Only the clergy. If you want to speak to most other people, you'll have to learn the northern languages.'

'Even the nobles?'

'Yes.'

'Aren't Latin and Italian the same?'

'No.'

'Is German very different from Saxon?' Theophanu wondered with increasing despair in her tone. Overhearing, Archbishop Gero intervened.

'They are different but many words are the same. You must not worry, Lady. You have been quick to learn Latin and you will find the other languages falling into place.'

Theophanu flashed him a grateful smile but she was not entirely comforted. They had all been saddened that morning by the arrival of a courier announcing that Bishop Liudprand had died of a heart attack on his way home. It was not unexpected but she was grieved that his friendly face would never be at the imperial court.

At last the day dawned when they would ride the last stage of the Via Appia to where her new family would be waiting outside the city walls. Her attendants dressed her with special care. The green brocade tunic, which Anastaso had managed to clean, was brought out again and they took great pains in displaying their mistress's rippling, dark hair to best advantage. It would be one of the last times she would appear in public with her hair loose.

As they approached the walls, the procession drew to a halt. Facing them was a finely dressed and mounted host with three figures at their head. In the centre was the Emperor Otto the Great, a broad-shouldered man with close-cropped grizzled hair and beard. His keen grey eyes fixed on Theophanu and held her gaze. For a few instants, she sustained his challenging stare then she was unable to resist looking at the man on his right – and could hardly hold back a gasp. He really *was* handsome. A clean-shaven young man with short-cut auburn hair and a pleasant, open expression was looking at her appreciatively. There was a slight quirk to his mouth; she could not tell whether it showed amusement or friendliness. Suddenly Theophanu began to feel that perhaps she *was* a lucky girl, after all.

Reluctantly the girl tore her gaze away and looked at the figure on the left. The two men both wore Saxon dress, short tunics in rich shades of blue or green over woollen leggings. Velvet cloaks covered their right shoulders, fastened on the left by large jewelled brooches. Empress Adelheid was more soberly dressed in a dark gown and veil, but the dark shades emphasised the strength of her face. With a shock Theophanu recognised that, whereas the Emperor was in late middle-age, the Empress was a generation younger. Her expression as she met Theophanu's eyes was ambivalent, not openly welcoming like her husband's and son's faces, but not forbidding either, more a guarded assessment. Theophanu too reserved judgement.

Formal introductions followed, conducted by the bishops. Theophanu had arranged with Emilia and Anastaso that they were to watch as well as listen, watch for the look in people's eyes and listen to the tone in their voices rather than their actual words, which they would have difficulty understanding. She knew that she would be fully occupied with saying and doing the right things, and so it proved, although it was less difficult than she had feared. Groomed as she had been, like all Byzantine princesses, to conform to the expectations of the court on all public occasions, she automatically moved gracefully and spoke graciously. Part of her mind was filled with the hope that she was making a good impression, whilst another part was just filled with the glorious image of Otto. She would have been hard put to say whether she meant the father or the son. Young Otto touched her heart by greeting her in a few words of Greek, which he had obviously prepared for the occasion, and the great Emperor himself smiled at her as if she had been his favourite granddaughter.   Since her own grandfather, Leo Phocas, had never looked at her with anything other than disapproval, the effect of this smile was overwhelming.

At last she seemed to have met everyone who had to be met, an utterly confusing jumble of unfamiliar names and faces, and she and her women finally found themselves alone in her bedchamber in the Vatican Palace. Otto had apologised that they were not staying with Pope John XIII at the Lateran, as she had perhaps expected, but as the ceremony was to be at St. Peter's, it seemed more convenient for them all to be nearby. He did not add that the Vatican Hill, near the Saxon quarter of the city, was surrounded by strong walls and much more easily defended if necessary. He also did not say that, as a recent pope had made the Lateran Palace notorious for his orgiastic parties before dying in his mistress's arms at the age of twenty-three, it was not the most suitable residence for a virgin bride.   Otto I had given the Romans more appropriate popes since, but the citizens were not markedly grateful and so his relationship with the Romans was often stormy, hence his caution.

'Well, how did I do?' Theophanu asked eagerly.

'Brilliantly, Lady!' exclaimed Anastaso. 'You were magnificent.   And oh, isn't he gorgeous? That hair and those eyes!'

'Yes, but it's his smile more than....'

'Ladies, ladies,' interrupted Emilia. 'Please keep your voices low and fitting.'

She glanced significantly round the room, looking for the lattices which in Constantinople would have indicated the presence of a listener. There did not seem to be any but you never knew. The girls understood her point and lowered their voices. Emilia tried to get their minds off Otto II's shapely legs, strong but delicate hands, voice that sent shivers down your spine, and all his other perfections, onto more serious matters.

'You did very well, Madam,' she said to Theophanu,' but not everyone was won over. You certainly charmed both the emperors and most of the laymen, but some of the bishops and abbots were not so impressed.'

'What did I do wrong?' asked Theophanu, slightly surprised.

'I don't think it was what you did. It is more who you are and how you look.'

'But I'm dressed correctly for a court reception,' protested Theophanu.

'Of course, Lady, in silk with gold thread. Did you not notice that your mother-in-law was much more simply dressed?'

'Yes, but....'

'The Lady Adelheid, as we know, is devout. It seems that she supports what they call here 'Church Reform', inspired by the monks of a huge abbey in Burgundy called Cluny. Empress Adelheid was a Burgundian princess before she became Queen of Italy. These monks believe that asceticism and simple living is for everybody, not just monks as our ascetics think, and they look reprovingly on those who are given to the vanities of this world.'

'But I'm not that vain. It's just that emperors and empresses have to dress magnificently,' said Theophanu, still rather puzzled. 'It's their job, to represent on earth the magnificence of the King of Heaven'

'I don't think my lady's bridegroom was averse to the gown,' said Anastaso slyly.

Her eyes met Theophanu's and the two girls collapsed in giggles, which were soon choked back when a slave entered the chamber announcing the Empress Adelheid. At home they would have been in trouble for such unseemly laughter, which, it had to be admitted, Anastaso's mischievousness was provoking in Theophanu more and more often. She was delighting in a companion near her own age, who took life less seriously than the princesses had. With grave expressions, though, they all sank into curtsies and as they rose from them Theophanu was relieved to see that Adelheid was smiling.

'It is a pleasure to see you are happy, my child,' she said benevolently. 'You are a long way from home and I am glad that you look forward, not back. To help you, I have had a little gift made for you.'

She held out a leather-bound book to Theophanu.

'I am so grateful, Most Pious ...' she began but Adelheid stopped her with an upraised hand.

'We do not use such titles in the West,' she said. 'On very formal occasions 'Your Grace', but in private 'Lady' will do, or even 'Mother.''

There was a brief pause then Theophanu bowed her head in acknowledgement.

'Of course, Lady,' she answered. 'I wished only to say that I will study hard to learn enough Latin to read it.'

'Look inside,' said Adelheid.

Theophanu opened the cover and saw that the book was truly beautiful, clearly written in gold letters on purple parchment – a gift for an empress indeed. Then she looked more closely. The work was a Latin psalter, but unlike in many Latin books, the words were not abbreviated, which made it much easier to read. Even better, between each two lines of Latin was the Greek translation of the lines. A more thoughtful gift could not be imagined. For a moment Theophanu was speechless, then she beamed at the Empress.

'Thank you, Thank you, Mother. You are truly kind.'

The two women embraced.

'Well, well,' said Adelheid. 'just do your duty as a wife and daughter and I'm sure we shall do very well together. Now you should go to bed. You must be exhausted and the rehearsal tomorrow will be gruelling. You need a good night's sleep. Goodnight, my dear.'

At that moment, overwhelmed by Adelheid's kindness, Theophanu was fully prepared to believe that all would be well between them, and in truth she was exhausted and longing for sleep.

Fortunately for her peace of mind she was unaware of the stormy meeting which was taking place between the emperors and their advisers. Bishop Dietrich of Metz was the main proponent of the view that Theophanu should be sent back to Constantinople. He was supported by Duke Henry of Bavaria, Otto I's nephew.

'She's not worth the treaty,' Dietrich insisted. 'She's the wrong girl, she carries no political clout, and she's a silly girl, always laughing and talking. She lacks *gravitas*.'

'She's twelve years old,' protested Archbishop Gero. 'She sometimes laughs and chatters but she knows well when to be grave and dignified, as she was today.'

'And she's beautiful and she looks like an empress,' struck in the young emperor, to vociferous agreement from his two nephews, the other 'Young Ottos', who were both slightly older than he was.

'The claim to the south of Italy is too much to give up for a girl's looks, when she's not a *porphyrogenita*,' sneered Duke Henry, whose father *had* been born to a reigning king. That settled it for Otto the Great, who was not *porphyrogenitus*.

'But *I* wish for peace in the south, so that I can go back to Germany,' he said, giving his nephew a menacing look. 'To me the princess seems suitable in all respects. We cannot expect a girl to have the wisdom of a man, my Lord Bishop,' he added to Dietrich. 'My son wishes to marry her. The Empress is pleased with her. They will be married and she will be crowned as planned on the fourteenth of April. The Council is ended.'

CHAPTER NINE

The morning before the wedding Theophanu met Willigis, the Chancellor of Germany, for the first time. She knew that his role was similar to that of Basil the Eunuch at home. He was the Emperor's first minister and right-hand man in the business of government.

To Theophanu's surprise, Willigis was a young priest, making him different in two respects from Basil the Eunuch, and she took to him instantly. Willigis was calm and watchful, but there was a suggestion of strength and intelligence about him which impressed Theophanu. They talked easily and when she asked him about his family, his reply was unexpected.

'No, I'm not related to any great house at all. My father was a smallholder in East Saxony and I was exceedingly fortunate as a boy to be noticed by Bishop Folkold of Meissen, who at that time was one of the Emperor's chaplains. He found me a place in the Court Chapel and so here I am.'

'The Court Chapel? What is that?'

'The body of clergy who surround the Emperor, to keep records for him and administer his decrees, as well as praying for him, of course. It's the nearest thing we have to an imperial administration like the old Romans had – which the East still has, of course.'

'So you are a bit of an outsider as well,' said Theophanu artlessly, making the thirty-year-old Willigis smile.

'Not one of the charmed circle of warrior aristocrats, you mean, Lady? That is true, but you will not be an outsider. You will be at the very centre of the kingdom. Let me explain to you how the coronation service makes this clear.'

He then went through the following day's rite with Theophanu. She would be both married and crowned in one service. Essentially her role would be defined by comparisons to queens of the Old Testament. The prayers would ask that she should be fruitful like the blessed and respected mothers Sarah, Rebecca, Leah and Rachel. More surprisingly she was to be like Judith, who freed the Jewish people by cutting off the head of the tyrant Holofernes. This meant, explained Willigis, that the Empress was not just to produce heirs but to be an active benefactress of her people, showing glory and strength as Judith had.

A little later she would be compared to Queen Esther, wife of Ahasuerus, whom the Greeks called Xerxes, King of Persia. Esther had saved her people from persecution by being a partner in the rule of her husband, as the prayer would put it. The Empress was not to be just a figurehead; she would actively share her husband's power.

Sunday morning, April 14th in the Year of Our Lord 972, saw Theophanu standing on the threshold of the great church of St. Peter at the Vatican, built over the burial site of St. Peter himself. Behind her lay the garden, the *paradisum*, and the courtyard thronged with the people of Rome. Ahead of her the church was packed to bursting point with the nobles of church and state, all waiting to see her, Theophano Sclerina, married to the heir to the Western Empire. She suddenly shivered, as if someone had walked over her grave, then reminded herself that she had seen equally splendid ceremonies in Haghia Sophia. As the music from the choir swelled up, she squared her shoulders and moved forward up the central aisle to the body of the church, where her husband and Pope John waited for her. Otto was now wearing the long robes of the emperor he already was, which made him look older and more distant, but as she reached him he gave her a sideways, reassuring smile.

Together with Otto, she followed the Pope up to the High Altar. Up to now she had been wearing a white shift and over-tunic, plain although made of the finest silk. After they made their marriage-vows and Otto placed a ring on her finger, the overdress was removed. The imperial vestments, like her husband's, long with bands of rich embroidery, were draped round her head and shoulders. The new clothes symbolised a new *persona*, cleansed from her sins by absolution and fit to take on her new responsibilities. Then she was anointed on the head and chest with holy oil, as a sign of the dedication of her life to the service of her husband and her people. Finally she received the crown, the gem-studded imperial diadem. Its outward lustre, the Pope told her, was to reflect her inward wisdom and virtue. Then the triumphant notes of the royal *laudes* burst from the choir and the huge congregation repeated the refrain:

'Christus vincit, Christus regnat, Christus imperat.'

Theophanu was now Empress of all the lands between Benevento and the Baltic Sea, between the North Sea coast and the River Oder. She was crushed by the weight of the crown and yet borne up by a sense of exaltation. She felt convinced that, as God had called her to this duty, so He would give her strength to carry the responsibility. She stole a glance at Otto and saw that his face mirrored her own emotions. Tentatively they smiled at each other before the next part of the proceedings, the High Mass, started.

After the service came ritual acclamations, as the new empress was presented both to the great inside the church and to the people outside. Byzantine forms were deliberately chosen for this to honour the bride. Then followed the state banquet. Theophanu was by now too emotionally drained to enjoy it much, despite the variety of delicious food. All evening faces of dukes and their ladies swam out of the crowd to be introduced to her, but remembering their names became increasingly impossible.

One or two faces did make an impact. One belonged to a rather short, burly man, hair already thinning round his red face, who radiated suppressed energy and discontent. This was Duke Henry of Bavaria, she learned, her husband's cousin, who was rumoured to want the crown himself. Emilia had used her genius for picking up gossip to learn that Henry's nickname was 'the Wrangler' or 'the Quarrelsome'. Looking at his expression, Theophanu could easily believe it.

As she and Otto were finally leaving the hall, he stopped to speak to a man at one of the lower tables and introduced him to his wife. This was Gerbert of Aurillac, a young West Frank already famed for his learning and his inventions. Otto himself had studied at his feet. Theophanu looked for resemblances to her beloved Philip but this was a different kind of man. Intelligence certainly shone from his piercing black eyes, but he looked to her more ambitious and cynical than Philip.

At long last they were alone together. The nobles and ecclesiastics had all withdrawn; even Emilia and Anastaso had finally gone, directing encouraging looks at their mistress and, to the young emperor, meaningful glances towards a flagon of wine. In truth Theophanu was so exhausted and so bemused by wine that she was completely relaxed and did not find her initiation into womanhood nearly as painful as she had been led to believe. Otto was a thoughtful and, she guessed, experienced lover and he seemed satisfied by what happened, so she presumed that she had done everything that was expected of her. When they made love again in the early morning, she found she could actually enjoy it and, as this time Otto stayed awake afterwards, they had time to talk, the first chance they had had to do so.

'You really are beautiful,' her husband told her. 'I'm so glad you're you, not the Princess Anna.'

Theophanu gazed at him with a slight doubt.

'You really are?'

'Of course. You're a woman, not a child. You heard it all yesterday. We can be partners in the kingdom, like my parents are. Isn't it like that in Constantinople?'

'Not exactly.' And so Theophanu began to tell him about Byzantium and her family. Soon they were exchanging anecdotes of childhood and her shyness vanished. She learned that Otto was apprehensive about the impending move to Germany. He had been away in Italy since he was a small boy and his memories of deep snow and endless forests did not make him eager to return. It was a relief to Theophanu to think that they would both be facing new experiences. It seemed to create a bond between them against the older generation and put her at less of a disadvantage.

Over the next few days Theophanu grew to feel more at ease. Otto introduced her to his two nephews and best friends, the other two 'young Ottos', and the three young men were happy to show off to her and include her in their jesting, although an occasional restraining glance from her mother-in-law reminded her that she still had to be decorous. Even so, this court lacked the stifling solemnity of the Palace in Constantinople, which pleased her.

Three days after the wedding came the ceremony of ratification in the Church of the Holy Apostles. Here Theophanu's morning-gift was confirmed and conveyed. She had been astounded to learn that this was an enormous grant of lands, which became her own property. If her husband died, it would become her *wittum*, her widow's portion. It consisted of two whole counties in Italy and Istria and many other estates, including the rich convent of Nivelles in Lotharingia, which alone owned fourteen thousand hides of land. There were also manors in the Rhineland and in Saxony. She was overwhelmed by the generosity of the gift but even more touched by the wording of the charter:

'I, Otto II, Emperor and Augustus, according to the advice of my great, holy and illustrious father and of God's holy Church, and of the loyal subjects of the Empire, and with the blessing of Pope John XIII, take Theophania, niece of Emperor John Tzimisces of Constantinople, to be my lawful wedded wife and sharer in the Empire, by the grace of Christ.'

When she saw the document, she was even more staggered. It was a beautiful object, written like her psalter in gold letters on purple-dyed parchment. Ornamented borders decorated the top and sides, while beneath the gold lettering was a double row of large red medallions bearing pictures of animals, lion and bull, griffin and hind in outward-facing pairs. These medallions were set against a dark blue background with a pattern of red tendrils. The workmanship was magnificent, as rich as anything Byzantium had to offer, and she guessed that that was part of the point, a way of proving that she was not coming to a land of barbarians. She decided that, wherever she went, the charter would be rolled up and taken with her. Her obvious pleasure in it repaid her new family for the trouble they had taken.

It seemed to Theophanu that she had only just got settled after her long journey when they were off again. It was now late April and the Emperor wanted to be across the Alpine passes by high summer, so they needed to set out. Emilia and Anastaso grumbled mightily at packing up again but, like their mistress, they felt a sense of relief as they rode out along the Via Flaminia, leaving the dark-red walls of the city behind them. In fact the journey over the Apennines in late spring was pure joy for the young couple, a carefree time which they would never be able to re-capture. They could ride along together, everyone else keeping a tactful distance, and they could talk and laugh freely. The young Ottos were much amused by Theophanu's horse, Windswift.

'She's a real lady's horse,' teased Otto. 'Very dainty but no power in her at all.'

'Rubbish!' retorted Theophanu. 'Look at her haunches. That's where she keeps her power. She could outrun your great carthorses any day.'

'Cousin, your wife can't even tell the difference between a carthorse and a destrier,' said Otto of the Wormsgau sympathetically.

'I can *show* you the difference between my horse and yours,' said Theophanu.

'Well, we can see that ourselves,' pointed out her husband.

'No, I mean in a race. Windswift could outrun yours anytime.'

'We need to test this out immediately,' cried the remaining young Otto. 'This valley is the last long, flat stretch before we start to climb the mountains.'

On being approached, the Emperor agreed to halt the cavalcade for an hour for the race to take place. He stipulated that, if Theophanu were to ride, there should be only two horses, hers and her husband's. He would have preferred that she did not ride the course herself and certainly did not want her crushed between two much bigger horses. He accepted Theophanu's argument that a strange rider would handicap Windswift and contented himself with a quiet word urging his son to use a little common sense. Young Otto grinned.

'I'm afraid she'll be left so far behind it won't really be a race,' he said cheerfully.

'I think you underestimate her,' said his father drily.

'Theophanu or the mare?'

'Both. Take care. They are both priceless.'

The course was set up and marshalls put in position. At first it seemed that young Otto was right. Although his riding-horse was smaller than a full warhorse, its great legs thundered ahead for the first stretch of the race. Windswift, however, was much quicker and neater on the turn and Theophanu inched ahead as they started the return. For a moment or two it seemed as if the big horse's superior strength would overtake its rival but as the winning-post came in sight, Theophanu's mount gathered her haunches and suddenly sprang forward like a streak of lightning, to the gasps and cheers of the spectators. Otto was beaten by a whole length.

He took it well.

'I'm so much lighter than you, my lord,' Theophanu hastened to point out.

'No, you won fairly,' Otto answered, looking at her with a new respect. 'To show I've no hard feelings, I shall kiss the winner.'

There, in front of all the court, he pressed a kiss on his beautiful wife, thinking that even on her wedding day she had never looked as lovely as she did now, her eyes laughing with triumph and her cheeks flushed.

'A prize for the winner,' proclaimed the Emperor. Otto the Great presented Theophanu with a small jewel-hilted knife he was wearing and a kiss on her cheek.. 'Just remember,' he added to his son. 'Never underestimate women or Arabs.'

Amidst the laughter Theophanu felt again the frisson that had disturbed her at the entrance to St. Peter's, a kind of shudder. 'Silly,' she said to herself and dismissed it. Anastaso, watching from the sidelines, noted it and wondered what the cause was. She had been observing faces all through the race. The indulgence and approval of the Emperor and the enthusiasm of most of the younger members of the court was obvious, but the Empress Adelheid's face was impassive and Bishop Dietrich looked disgusted. Anastaso sighed. It was fun and it was private but Theophanu had broken all the conventions of behaviour and of the right relations between men and women. Someone – Emilia probably – needed to speak some tactful words of warning to her. In fact Empress Adelheid got in before Emilia and dispensed with tact.

'I think you forgot yourself this afternoon, daughter,' she said acidly, having drawn Theophanu aside from the throng when they stopped for the evening.

Theophanu looked at her questioningly, although she could guess what was meant.

'Not merely did you race like a hoyden in public, but you dishonoured my son by outstripping him.'

Theophanu flushed red. Unfair as it was, she knew there was truth in what Adelheid said. Some of Otto's men might think less of him for being excelled by a woman. She was not going to admit it though.

'I intended no offence to my husband,' she protested truthfully. 'The mare is bred for speed, whereas his horse is bred for strength. The contest was between the horses, not the riders. But I am truly sorry if I did cause offence,' she added in a more conciliatory tone.

Adelheid decided to accept the olive branch.

'Very well, child. See it does not happen again.' She hesitated, genuinely wanting to advise the young bride for her own good. 'Young men are proud and sensitive. You think in terms of a schoolroom contest but it is not that to him. At present he is completely besotted with you, and I am glad of it, but when the enchantment wears off, as it will, you will need to be tender of his pride.'

Theophanu bowed her head in polite acceptance, but she knew her mother-in -law was talking nonsense. The enchantment – stupid word –

the love between Otto and herself would never wear off. It was much too special for that.

CHAPTER TEN

The first major stopping-place on the journey was Ravenna, which Theophanu was eager to see. This Adriatic town had a history that made it intriguing to her. After the Fall of Rome to the Goths in 410AD Ravenna had become the capital of the West. Chancellor Willigis told her more of its story as they rode up the coastline from Fano. An empress had once ruled in Ravenna, Galla Placidia, who had suffered many tribulations before she came to the throne. She ruled well and started the tradition of fine buildings for which the city was famous.

'What sort of tribulations did she have?' Theophanu wanted to know.

'She refused to leave Rome, when her brother Honorius and the court abandoned it to its attackers, and so she was taken captive by the Goths and held hostage for four years. Eventually they forced her to marry one of their leaders.'

'Was she unhappy?'

'I don't know. He died quite soon afterwards and she was sent back to her brother. She was unhappy then, because his court was dissolute and she hated it. Then he made her marry an elderly senator. I think that marriage was reasonably happy; at any rate she had two children before she was widowed again.'

The poor lady! What happened then?'

Willigis looked rather embarrassed.

'She returned to the court with her children, but she could not stay there, because her brother was...too interested in her.'

Theophanu stared at him in shock, wondering if he meant what she thought he must. He nodded and continued hastily

'Fortunately she managed to escape to her nephew in Constantinople, Theodosius II, and he sheltered her until Honorius died. Then he gave her an army and she managed to claim the Western Empire for her little son, Valentinian. She ruled well for him until he grew up.'

'She was the daughter of Theodosius the Great then,' said Theophanu, who had been working it out.

'That's right. I believe he built the great walls which have defended your city so long. His daughter built churches rather than walls, very special churches.'

'What's so unusual about them?'

Willigis smiled. 'I'm not going to tell you. It would spoil the surprise. Just wait until you see them.'

The day after they reached Ravenna and settled in, Willigis asked Otto for permission to take his wife to the church of Sant' Apollinare Nuove. Otto immediately understood him and chuckled delightedly.

'Of course, but I'm coming too. I wouldn't miss seeing her face for worlds.'

What on earth could they be on about, Theophanu wondered but as soon as she entered the church, she gasped in astonishment. It was full of the most beautiful mosaics, more than she had ever seen in Constantinople. As they walked up the aisle, her eyes out on stalks, she checked and pointed to the triforium. There were mosaics of the Emperor Justinian and his Empress Theodora. Because the style of imperial vestments had not changed down the centuries, just for a moment she thought she was looking at depictions of Romanus II and Theophano Senior. She realised her mistake instantly but was suddenly swept by an unexpected pang of longing for her old world and all its unquestioned assumptions. Her eyes misted but Otto, watching attentively, took her hand and squeezed it.

'That's Belisarius standing next to Justinian,' he said to cover her emotion.

'Yes, of course. It's wonderful to see them, and all the rest.'

She shook her head in wonder and carried on doing so all afternoon, as they went into church after church. She particularly liked the mausoleum of Galla Placidia, whose story as told by Willigis had impressed her. How much more Galla Placidia had had to overcome than just leaving her home, and yet she had not moped but had been a great ruler and builder. Theophanu thought that she should take her as a model and an inspiration.

After a few days rest the court set off again. At first it was a long, slow, flat journey across the plains of the River Po but soon they could see huge mountains looming up out of the north.

'We're not going there, are we?' asked Anastaso.

'I'm afraid so. Basically right over the top. Well, through a pass.'

Theophanu sounded much more confident and knowledgeable about it than she felt.

'If the old Romans could build a road through, I suppose we can manage to ride it,' said Anastaso, trying to be positive.

Empress Adelheid, riding near them, laughed.

'I'm afraid there's no road the way we're going, not even a cart-track. Just a bridle-path.'

'Are there no roads through the Alps then, Lady?' asked Theophanu.

'There are good roads through the western passes but they are too dangerous. Only this winter Saracen raiders kidnapped the good Abbot Maiolus of Cluny as he travelled the Great Saint Bernard Pass. He had to be ransomed. We are better off taking the Septimer, despite the nuisance of loading everything onto mules and packhorses.'

The girls were silent. They had learned already of the power and importance of the Abbey of Cluny. Such an outrage was truly shocking. Anastaso was struck by a sudden memory.

'Is the Septimer the one they call the Via Mala, the evil road?' she asked anxiously.

No, no. We always avoid that if possible. This way is difficult rather than dangerous.'

They soon found the truth of that. A steep path climbed up the side of the mountain. At first it wound back and forth, following a stream, but then it abandoned all caution and headed straight for the top. The mules and the big German horses took it in their stride but Windswift found it hard

72

going and eventually Theophanu dismounted and led her. They were both heartily glad to reach the hospice at the top of the pass.

They stayed the night there. The next morning proved that going down was even more difficult than getting up. For an hour they all had to guide the animals down a steep, rocky defile, then came marshy meadows where the humans had to trust to the animals' instinct for where to tread. They were exhausted by the time they came down to a village where another path joined theirs, making a proper road.

'Congratulations!' Otto said to the girls. 'You've done it.'

'What do you mean?'

'You've crossed the watershed. From here all the waters run north, eventually to the seas at the north and west of Europe. From the other side of the pass they all ran to the Mediterranean.'

'We're really in another world now,' said Theophanu thoughtfully, staring northwards. There lay Germany and the rest of her life.

'Where do we live when we're in Germany?' she suddenly asked Otto.

'Everywhere. Lots of places.'

'Yes but...where's the palace?'

'Ah!' he grimaced. 'They didn't tell you?'

'Tell me what?'

'Tell you that there isn't a palace or seat of government like Constantinople. We can't stay anywhere for more than about six weeks,' said the Co-emperor.

The girls gazed at him blankly.

'Why on earth not?' asked Theophanu in an icy tone. Anastaso decided that it was time to remove herself from the scene.

'You've seen the size of the court. It's never fewer than a hundred people. It can be a thousand. There's nowhere in Germany that can cater for that number of people for more than a few weeks. That's one reason. The other is that the King has to be seen by his people. He is the fount of justice and they need access to him, so he has to travel around.'

'Like these journeys all the time?'

Theophanu's voice made clear the horror she felt.

'No, no, no. It's not the same. We only move every few days, or perhaps after a week. And we have lots of palaces, perhaps not as grand as Constantinople but they're pretty luxurious – underfloor heating and glazed windows in some of them. You will be comfortable.'

He looked at her with some anxiety. Someone really should have warned her about this. He could understand how she felt and it was bound to be harder for a woman not to have a home. He had to admit that one of the things he had liked about Italy was that the need to keep on the move was less urgent there, but like his father he was restless by nature. Theophanu would just have to put up with it.

She could see that too.

'Well, at least it won't be boring,' she said. Then another thought struck her. 'Who organises all the moving?' she asked.

'I think you'd better talk to my mother,' said Otto miserably.

Theophanu had her answer. When the king moved, the queen organised it. Luckily the idea of any of the empresses of Byzantium condescending to do anything so menial was so comic that she burst out laughing. Otto heaved a sigh of relief.

'You don't have to do it yourselves, of course,' he pointed out quickly. 'The imperial ladies just tell the slaves what to do.'

'That's all right then.'

He glanced at her, uncertain whether there was sarcasm in her tone, but she was grinning.

'As you say, you won't get bored,' he promised her.

Despite the shattering realisation that she would never have a permanent home, the sight of the Abbey of St. Gall, where they would halt for several days, lifted Theophanu's spirits. Already hundreds of years old, the abbey had a mature, settled beauty which she realised she had been missing. It was a large, stately establishment with a residence for the imperial family away from their retainers, so there was a measure of privacy. The buildings were surrounded by gardens. Rows of shady fruit trees sheltered rose and flower- beds as well as the herb and vegetable patches. Throughout their stay the sun shone down on them. The days had an idyllic, out-of-time feeling.

The peace mellowed even Theophanu's restless and energetic father-in-law. On arrival he established his authority during the first service they all attended in the abbey church, by dropping his service-book deliberately. This was a favourite technique; if any of the monks looked round or lost their place in the chant, in Otto's view they were not concentrating enough on their devotions and would be disciplined. Fortunately – and possibly forewarned – nobody moved and the Emperor's good humour was undisturbed. This mood continued all the time they were there and Theophanu found him wonderful company. She felt that he was far more of a father to her than her own father had ever been.

She was, however, coming to realise that her husband's attitude to his father was complicated. He certainly respected and admired the Emperor but he also chafed under his authority. He sometimes complained to the other young Ottos, when he thought they were alone, which worried Theophanu. One afternoon the four young people were in the rose-garden when he burst out to Otto of the Wormsgau:

'He hangs on to all the kingdoms he's won like a lion, but he won't give the least little part of any of them to me.'

Theophanu was sure she caught the swish of a monk's habit vanishing behind a bush and knew she had to intervene.

'Have you still got that book you borrowed from the library yesterday?' she asked. 'It would be a good time for another lesson.'

To her surprise the previous day Otto had borrowed from the library a Latin-Greek psalter, this one designed to teach Latin-speakers Greek, the opposite of hers.

'Then I'll be able to understand when you're jabbering to Anastaso,' he had joked. 'You'll have to watch what you say.'

Otto swung round and looked at his wife. He was always quick on the uptake.

'A good time for watching what's said?' he asked softly.

'Exactly,' she replied and he nodded.

'Well, time will tell,' said Otto Liudolfson, apparently apropos of nothing, and the incident passed over, although it may have contributed to Otto II's irritation as they left the abbey the next morning. The Abbot asked for the return of the books the Young Emperor had borrowed. The library was St. Gall's greatest glory. When it had first been catalogued, one hundred and fifty years before, it already had hundreds of books, impressive even by Byzantine standards, and the Abbot did not want to lose any of his treasures. Otto ignored his protests and insisted on taking four books with him, including the bi-lingual psalter. He promised he would return them but the Abbot patently disbelieved him. As Otto wanted the book to learn Greek, Theophanu felt that the black looks of the Community were directed particularly at her, as if it was her fault, when she could quite see the Abbot's point of view. It did cross her mind that Otto was behaving in a spoilt, high-handed way, but she determinedly banished the thought. First love was still too powerful to admit analysis of the beloved.

CHAPTER ELEVEN

The first year of Theophanu's married life sped by. Although the constant travelling was disconcerting, she enjoyed the stimulus of new places, with a welcome rest in the depth of winter when the snow lay too thick for them to move on. Otto the Great's presence calmed any latent unrest and the year of his return was to culminate in a triumphal Easter-court at Quedlinburg, where the founders of the Liudolfing dynasty, Henry the Fowler and Queen Matilda, were buried.

Quedlinburg lived up to Theophanu's expectations. It was perched on top of a huge outcrop of rock a few miles from the northern edge of the Harz mountains, whose forests bounded the horizon to the south. Around the crag lay acres of marshy land with little rivers and streams winding through groves of willow and alder. The whole of the flat top of the hill was surrounded by massive walls of squared stones, with a gateway facing south to the mountains. Within the walls was a basilica where Henry and Matilda were buried and their memory was honoured by the canonesses of the convent on the site. The nuns also ran a school for girls and the imperial family stayed at the convent during the court. Abbess Matilda was the daughter of Otto and Adelheid and so, once the Holy Week ceremonies were over, there was a joyful family reunion. Theophano grew to like her sister-in-law very well; despite Matilda's rank as abbess, which gave her an automatic seat on the imperial council, she was only twenty years old and the two young women found much to talk about.

The assembly at the court was indeed glittering. The reigning dukes of Poland and Bohemia, Miesco and Boleslav, were there in person, as were ambassadors from the Eastern Emperors, the Rus, the Bulgars, and the Hungarians. From within the Empire came messengers from Rome and Benevento, and envoys from England and from the Fatimid Arabs in Sicily were reported to be on their way. All were seeking either alliances or missionaries from Otto the Great. As he said to Theophanu one night, it was the fulfilment of his dream for a peaceful, Christian Europe. She was thrilled for him, especially as he had seemed melancholy since visiting the graves of his three eldest children during the winter.

A particular joy for Theophanu was the chance to hear the news the Byzantine ambassadors brought, although it led to her first quarrel with her husband. While she had been crossing the Alps the previous summer, her uncle, John Tzimisces, had finally defeated the Rus in battle. He had used his favourite manoeuvre, a feigned retreat, and the unsophisticated Rus army had pursued his troops into an ambush. They were completely crushed and Sviatoslav withdrew towards Kiev with the remnant. Other enemies killed him on the way and turned his skull into a drinking-cup. Theophanu rejoiced at the removal of such a threat from Christendom but Otto was less enthusiastic.

'It seems rather dishonourable to me, pretending to retreat when you're not' he said to Theophanu. 'Men of honour don't fight like that. They attack and prevail by force of arms and the justice of their cause.'

'But the Rus are not men of honour and they will fight by any means they can,' argued Theophanu. ' So will the Saracens, who are always pretending to retreat,' she added.

'Two wrongs don't make a right,' said Otto rather stiffly.

'You can't afford to be pompous if you're a general,' snapped Theophanu. A moment of appalled silence followed.

'What do you know about it?'

The scorn and hurt in Otto's voice was palpable as he swung on his heel and left the room in search of more congenial company.

'Maybe not much, but I have got some common sense,' muttered Theophanu. Nevertheless she wondered why she had spoken so sharply over something that mattered so little. She had again felt that frisson of fear running down her back as Otto spoke; perhaps that had been why. She wished she could understand what provoked these shudders.

She and Otto made up their quarrel in the usual way of young lovers and they were both pleased to hear at the Easter-court that John Tzimisces had celebrated his victory with a triumphal parade through

Constantinople. Theophano was distressed to learn that the Bulgar royal family, including Maria and Helena, the hostage princesses, had had to walk behind John's chariot as captives.

'Why?' Theophanu asked the envoy, after reading Anna's letter,

'The Most Pious Augustus has taken Bulgaria back into the Empire as a subject province.'

'But he promised to protect Maria and Helena.'

Otto gave her a look which clearly said 'I told you he couldn't be trusted.' It was a most sobering consideration. How much did Theophanu's own position depend on John Tzimisces' good faith? Perhaps Otto was right in his assessment of John. If only she could conceive a child, she would be so much more secure, but every month her hopes were dashed.

'What is my uncle doing now?' she asked.

'He has gone back to Syria and the infidel are retreating before him.'

That was a relief. At least he was not intervening in Southern Italy, Theophanu thought. She continued to feel a vague sense of unease, however, until a sudden disaster on the Thursday of Easter week put it from her mind. Herman Billung, Duke of Saxony and Otto the Great's oldest friend and ally, suddenly fell to the ground dead outside St. Wigbert's Church down in the valley.

His death was a severe blow to the Emperor. All the recently conquered land on the east bank of the Elbe was only partly Christianised and assimilated into the Empire and it had needed a heavy hand to keep the lid on the pot. Herman had provided that hand and Otto knew that his son, Bernhard Billung, would have to be the man to succeed him, no matter how much it might disappoint the hopes of Otto's own son, or other members of the Billung family, who had resented Herman's appointment originally. The truth of this was demonstrated when the disaffected kinsfolk intercepted Herman's funeral cortege and refused to allow him burial.

Theophanu could tell that her father-in-law was deeply grieved by all this and when she found herself riding alongside him as the court left Quedlinburg, she tried to comfort him. He thanked her and went on:

'Think about it, Theo.' He alone used this nickname for her. 'In Mainz I prayed at the graves of three of my children. In Magdeburg at the tomb of my first wife, Edith of Wessex. In Quedlinburg at the grave of my parents. Now my great and longstanding friend Herman is dead. Yet still blood-feuds matter more to the Saxons than the safety of the Empire. I sometimes wonder if I have achieved anything at all.'

'But the land is at peace,' argued Theophanu, 'and you have a living wife and other children.'

Otto smiled sadly. 'And a lovely daughter-in-law,' he agreed. 'Yes, I must not be discouraged, but there are times when I would gladly lay the burden of kingship down.'

'Perhaps your son could take some of the burden from you,' suggested Theophanu tentatively.

'Yes,' said Otto meditatively. 'I've noticed him growing restless this last year. If only he would think more and listen to advice before he acted, I would feel happier.'

'It is difficult for him to do that until he has some real responsibility,' observed Theophanu. She knew how angered Otto II had been by his father's appointment of Bernhard Billung as Duke of Saxony and in her heart she thought that it would have been a good move to appoint her husband.

Otto the Great smiled again. 'You are a very good advocate, my dear. No doubt you are right. After I have seen the ambassadors from England and from the Saracens, I will consider the matter. Did you know that Edgar of England, my brother-in-law, has just been crowned King of All England, the first time the English have had one king really acknowledged by all of them?'

Theophanu accepted the change of subject gracefully, hoping she had carried her point. She could hardly wait to tell her husband in the privacy of their marriage-bed. The young couple continued to hope. Perhaps on Ascension Day at Merseburg? Again disappointment, but when they arrived at Memleben for Pentecost, Theophanu felt that the elder Otto was bound to make an announcement. Memleben was a significant place for Otto the Great, because his father had died here, and it would be an opportunity to replace the sad associations of the place with a happy event.

They reached Memleben on Tuesday, 6th May. The Emperor seemed rather low in spirits when they arrived but he was up with the dawn as usual and attended the first two services of the monastic day. He talked briefly to Otto and Theophanu after that before retiring to his room for a rest. This was so unusual that it worried Theophanu. He rejoined the company for Mass, however, and looked better. As he always did wherever he stopped, he distributed alms to the poor of the area, and then the court all breakfasted together. By the end of the meal Otto looked exhausted again and retired once more.

'Is he unwell, Lady?' Theophanu asked Adelheid, when she encountered the older woman sitting in the cloister, for once with no needlework or book to occupy herself.

He's very tired,' Adelheid answered shortly. 'If he had more help from the younger generation, instead of endless complaints and follies, it would ease his mind.'

Theophanu bit her lip, genuinely upset by the reproach. 'I am truly sorry, Madam, if we have added to his troubles. I would never wish to do that.'

Adelheid's grim expression softened slightly. 'No, I know you love and respect him,' she admitted. 'I wish I could be more sure of young Otto's feelings. Well, the Emperor is sixty-one years old. He has a right to feel tired if he wishes.'

She forced a smile, but her words left Theophanu deeply uneasy and she looked anxiously at Otto the Great's face as they sat down for the midday meal. He was much more cheerful than earlier and ate a full plate of cold meats and cheese, while chatting to his son about the prospects for the next day's hunting. Theophanu was reassured and took her place for Vespers just behind the Emperor with an easier mind.

The service progressed as normal through the psalms and the lesson but during the singing of the Magnificat Otto the Great suddenly swayed to one side. Empress Adelheid caught him before he could fall and a chair was fetched. His face was flushed bright red and by the time they had manoeuvred him into the chair, he was unconscious. Young Otto forced his head down between his knees to try to revive him and after a moment he did come round. He murmured 'The Blessed Sacrament' and Otto gestured frantically for a priest to bring the wafer. His father managed to swallow it but he was already slipping into unconsciousness again. The laboured breathing continued for a minute or two then stopped. Death the Leveller had come for the greatest Emperor of the West since Charlemagne.

CHAPTER TWELVE

For the living, time moves on and requires action. By mid-evening the dead emperor's viscera had been removed and buried but his body lay in state in the church, waiting to be taken to Magdeburg for burial next to his first wife, Edith of England. Otto and Theophanu withdrew briefly to their chamber, where Emilia and Anastaso had spiced wine waiting to hearten them. Despite the season the evening air struck cold and damp and they were still trying to adjust to the shocking change in their state.

Suddenly the door was flung open and the Dowager-Empress entered. One look at her face led Theophanu to wave the waiting-women out of the room. They obeyed promptly, carefully shutting the door behind them. As soon as they had gone, Adelheid launched her tirade. Otto was an undutiful and ungrateful son who had brought his father to an early grave, was the gist of it.

Otto listened to the storm for a time but he too was shocked and grieved and his temper rose to meet hers with counter-accusations.

'You can't talk, Mother,' he accused her. 'You always made him think that you would rather have married Duke Henry of Bavaria and you certainly prefer his son to me. My father never knew whether you really supported his claim to the throne.'

Theophanu gasped. This was common gossip round the court and it was true that Adelheid seemed to favour the company of the Bavarians, but for such a criticism to come from her own son at such a time was too hard.

'Henry the Wrangler is married to my niece Gisela, who is very dear to me,' Adelheid shot at her son. 'My own kin are just as important to me as the Liudolfings. If your wife had any family worth mentioning, she would understand.'

'Just leave Theophanu out...' began Otto heatedly but Theophanu interrupted him.

'Mother, we're all grieved and upset and we shall say things we'll wish unsaid tomorrow. Wouldn't it be better to sleep now and talk when we are all calmer?'

Adelheid glared at her. '*I* shall go to the church and keep watch with my husband,' she said pointedly. Without another word she left the room.

Otto turned a face full of misery to Theophanu.

'I loved him too,' he said wretchedly, 'even if he wouldn't see I was a grown man.'

'I know,' his wife answered,' but don't forget, this has all happened to your mother before and last time she was widowed, she ended up being captured and beaten by Berengar and Willa. She's hitting out because she's frightened.'

There was a short silence.

'What do you think I should do then?' asked Otto.

'Give her a bit of time to calm down, then we'll go and join the vigil. Nobody can say anything to anybody there but she might feel supported.'

Otto sighed. 'Doesn't she make you furious as well?' he asked curiously.

'She tries my patience. Well, yes, she can be a bitch but I do feel sorry for her too. She's very alone now.'

By the next day the imperial family had its emotions well under control and the apparent amity held through the funeral at Magdeburg, in the great cathedral which the dead emperor had had built, and through Otto's proclamation as sole emperor at Werla in Saxony. These occasions gave Theophanu a chance to meet properly the members of the Liudolfing dynasty who were not yet well-known to her and to form her opinions of them, especially Henry the Wrangler's two sisters, Abbess Gerberga of Gandersheim and Duchess Hedwig of Swabia. She liked Gerberga as much and as immediately as she had her husband's sister, Abbess Matilda of Quedlinburg. It was a particular joy that Gerberga could speak some Greek and was happy to practise her skills.

Unfortunately the same was not true of Hedwig, who, as Bishop Liudprand had warned Theophanu on the journey, had hated all things Byzantine ever since the failure of her projected marriage to Romanus II many years before. Her blatant cheating in a game of chess with Theophanu warned the Empress not to trust her. The wisdom of this was borne out within a year, when Hedwig and her husband outwitted the imperial couple over the important appointment of a new Bishop of Augsburg, who would control crucial areas of South Germany. By the support of both Henry the Wrangler and Adelheid as intercessors at court, Otto was tricked into appointing the Bavarian candidate against the wishes of the clergy of Augsburg. By the time the deception was discovered, it was too late to change it.

'What makes me so angry is that my mother knew all the time. It makes me wonder again, whose side is she on?' he raged to Theophanu, Willigis and the young Ottos later that night.

'The trouble is that, when the story gets out, it will make us look stupid,' observed Otto Conradson. 'Denmark, Poland, Bohemia, even France – they're all looking for signs of weakness now your father is dead.'

'My Lord, His Grace knows that is true. There is no great need to say so at the moment,' sighed Willigis.

'No, Lord Chancellor,' Otto said. 'I need good friends and my beloved wife to tell me what I don't want to hear. But the foreign problems can wait. It's what to do about my mother that is urgent.'

Since there was no real solution to that problem, the meeting broke up without reaching a decision, but fate swung the other way a few months later when the Duke of Swabia died suddenly and unexpectedly. Otto had a stormy interview with the widow, his cousin Hedwig, about the succession. She asserted – correctly – that she was perfectly capable of ruling the Duchy by herself, with the support of her brother Henry the Wrangler. As this was precisely what Otto feared, the meeting grew heated. Willigis tried to interpose the voice of reason.

'You must see, Lady, that His Grace cannot afford to have the whole of Southern Germany forming a potentially separate kingdom, with lands stretching as far as the Adriatic. He needs a man he can trust in Swabia and you have no son.'

'Plain speaking indeed!' Henry the Wrangler, who was present to support his sister, said meditatively.

'I will choose a husband and he shall be your new duke,' said Hedwig.

'The new duke is to be my nephew, Otto Conradson. He is already married,' the Emperor pointed out.

The Emperor's will prevailed and Hedwig withdrew to her castle to sulk. Much more ominously, the Wrangler returned to Bavaria to think about rebellion.

Luckily for him, Otto's attention was distracted from him for the whole first half of 974. Early in the year the Emperor besieged the castle of two robber-barons, the Reginar brothers, who had been terrorising their neighbourhood in the Low Countries. Their trademark speciality was hanging their victims in church belfrys.

'Apart from the sacrilege,' Otto explained to Theophanu, 'the point is that everyone knows exactly how long it takes the condemned man to die. When he stops struggling, the bell stops ringing.'

The siege was successful but the barons escaped to France with their grievances. Immediately Otto and Theophanu had to go north to counter a Danish invasion. It took most of the early summer to muster an army in the Lower Elbe valley and Theophanu accompanied her husband wherever he went. She was glad of the activity; she had been married for two years now but there was still no sign of a child. The covert glances at her belly and the half-heard murmurs of 'barren' we getting on her nerves. To counter the muttering, in the spring Otto gave her yet more estates in Saxony and Thuringia 'for her own free possession'. He could not have made his favour more clear and his wife loved him for it. Perhaps as a result, by the time the Danish campaign was underway in September,

Theophanu suspected that their prayers were going to be answered the following May.

King Harald Bluetooth of Denmark and his son Sweyn Forkbeard were soundly defeated and retreated behind the Danewerk which marked the border. Otto was able to enforce a peace-treaty, which lasted several years, and the whole campaign gave him a military credibility which he had lacked in the north before. He was also delighted by the news of his child and so his morale was high when he had to deal with the Wrangler's revolt in the autumn. Typically, Henry had set on foot an ambitious rebellion, to be backed up by invasions from the Christian Slav princes of Poland and Bohemia. Equally typically, he had declared his hand too soon, when his allies were still hundreds of miles away. He received less support than he expected, both in Bavaria and Saxony, and by mid-autumn he had to surrender and throw himself on his cousin's mercy. Otto, who had just learnt of the expected heir, was in a mood to be magnanimous, and Henry was confined in comfort at the royal palace in Ingelheim on the Rhine.

While all this was going on, Otto had also had to deal with a long-distance revolt. John XIII, the pope who had married Otto and Theophanu, died that same year and his replacement was one of Otto the Great's last appointees. Roman aristocratic factions considered control of the papacy to be their prerogative and after Otto I's death it did not take long for them to rise in support of their own nominee. Boniface VII deposed his predecessor and imprisoned him in Castel Sant' Angelo, where he was found strangled in his cell a few days later. This led to a counter-revolt by imperial factions and Boniface was expelled from the city. He fled to Constantinople, taking much of the papal treasury with him. Otto II's emissary was then able to secure the choice of a more suitable pope, Benedict VII.

'On the face of it, the Emperor has won on all three fronts,' Willigis told Theophanu when he came in late November to offer his congratulations on her pregnancy, 'but in reality the only secure victory is in the north. Boleslav and Miesco won't necessarily go home just because the Duke of

Bavaria is in custody, and Boniface is stirring up endless trouble in Constantinople.'

'Why, what's happened there?' asked Theophanu in surprise. 'I thought everything was going really well. I hear great news about my uncle's victories in Mesopotamia.'

'His success has indeed been astonishing,' Willigis answered. 'The greatest advances against the infidel for centuries. He was on the point of taking Baghdad itself, the seat of the caliphate.'

'Was?'

'Yes, was, because of Boniface. The administration in Constantinople wants to break off diplomatic relations with *us* because of the deposition of Boniface, but the Church, especially the Patriarch, supports Benedict. Your uncle has had to put his troops into winter quarters and go back to Constantinople himself to sort out the mess.'

'Boniface was deposed according to law by a Church council because he murdered his predecessor,' said Theophanu slowly. 'I don't see how anyone could support him.'

'Probably not so many would, if he did not have so much of the treasury with him,' said Willigis dryly. 'Even so, your great-uncle Nicephorus loathed the West. That faction is eager for the breach.'

Theophanu realised that that would be so.

'I doubt whether my Uncle John would agree, though.'

'With his record he can't be too censorious about murdering predecessors,' said Willigis.

Theophanu was silent for a moment.

'If this does happen, then the point of my marriage will be over,' she said at last.

'The political value of the marriage will be diminished,' Willigis emended. 'But since your husband adores you – and vice versa, I think – and you are about to bear the heir to the Empire, it should not make any personal difference to you. Many of us are very glad that you are here, Lady,' he added warmly.

Nevertheless Theophanu waited anxiously for news from the East. When it came, it was not good; against her hopes John Tzimisces had sided completely with the anti-western party, even though it meant he had had to depose the Patriarch and appoint another more amenable. The Eastern Empire refused any recognition to Pope Benedict VII and all official diplomatic contact ceased. John was then free to return to his troops. A stalemate ensued between the two empires, not too much of a problem while Otto stayed in Germany and John in the Levant.

Theophanu's attention became focussed on her pregnancy, so that she took little notice when Boleslav of Bohemia invaded Bavaria in the spring. She had stayed well and fit throughout, a bonus of her youth, but she was now too big to travel comfortably on horseback and a wagon was cumbersome and bumpy. She was relieved when the court reached the convent near Fulda where her confinement was to take place. It was pleasant, too, to move back for a time into a female world. She had enjoyed the challenge and stimulus of mixing so much with men, but Emilia and Anastaso joined her new friend Imiza, a relation of the Archbishop of Rheims, in looking after her and she relaxed happily into their care and the smiles of the nuns.

One of her hopes had been that the prospect of the baby would improve her relationship with her mother-in-law, but this was not the case. Her husband and his chancellor were engaged in an argument with the Dowager-Empress about her *wittum*, her widow's portion. This had originally been her morning-gift and, like Theophanu's, the lands comprising it were extensive. They would provide handsomely for her upkeep for the rest of her life, but in northern eyes they remained essentially state property, on loan, as it were. The widow was supposed to found a convent to pray for her husband's soul, where she would live in comfortable retirement from public life.

Adelheid was perfectly willing to provide for her husband's *memoria* but she had no intention of retiring from politics and allowing a couple of young hotheads like Otto and Theophanu to run the Empire. Moreover she wanted to use her *wittum* to make enormous donations to her favourite Cluniac foundations in perpetuity. In Otto and Willigis's eyes the economy of the Empire would be endangered if she made such huge perpetual gifts. The arguments were bitter, so much so that on a visit to Theophanu shortly before the baby was due, Otto made a startling announcement.

'If the baby is a boy, as we hope, he will of course be named Otto for his grandfather. But if it's a girl, she's not going to be called Adelheid. We'll name her after your mother.'

Theophanu gasped. 'That's a terribly public insult, Ottone.' She often used the Italian form of his name when they were alone. 'She will be hurt and humiliated – and furious. Is it worth it?'

'Don't you like the name 'Sophia'?'

'Yes, of course. It's a lovely name with a beautiful meaning, 'wisdom', but that's not really the point.'

'The point is that my mother has to learn who's the master now. Subtlety and gentleness are getting us nowhere.'

Theophanu said no more. With luck the baby would be a boy and anyway she was too tired and heavy to argue. She re-immersed herself with relief in the peaceful harmony of the convent – although she had no doubt that beneath the surface there were as many tensions as there had been in the Women's Palace in Constantinople.

CHAPTER THIRTEEN

The baby arrived in beautiful weather in mid-May. A trained midwife had been brought from the famous medical school in Salerno but in the event there was no real need for her skills. Theophanu's ladies encouraged her to walk about during the early stages of labour and bathed and massaged her when the pains grew severe. Then after only half an hour in the birthing-stool, a healthy baby with a frizz of her father's red hair dropped into the midwife's hands bawling lustily. The Princess Sophia had entered the world. There was, of course, both delight and disappointment.

Theophanu's disappointment melted away the moment the washed and swaddled bundle was put into her arms. In her eyes the baby was perfect and she was overwhelmed by the fierce, tender protectiveness which gripped her. This precious child was hers and nobody would ever be allowed to harm her, she vowed.

A commotion at the door distracted her.

'The Emperor, Madam,' the midwife called, sinking into a curtsey.

Theophanu lifted eyes filled with anxiety and defiance to her husband, but he was gazing at his family with an expression of reverence. Mutely she held the baby out to him.

'My little wisdom, my Sophia,' he said wonderingly, taking the child and holding her aloft as a sign of his acknowledgement of her as his own. The watching ladies applauded and the Empress signalled to the sister waiting by the door. She came forward with a pitcher of the best clear-gold Rhenish wine and pewter beakers for everyone.

'To Sophia,' toasted Otto, 'and to all her little brothers.'

'Not just yet,' murmured the Empress as the others echoed the toast.

There was no chance of conceiving a boy during the eighty days' seclusion which custom enjoined on the mother of a daughter. Initially Theophanu was glad of the rest and delighted by the chance to spend time with her child in a way which she knew would be impossible once she resumed public life. Towards the end of the six weeks the little one beamed in recognition whenever she saw her mother. That was sometimes a relief from the howls of fury which convulsed Princess Sophia when something did not suit her, but on the whole she was such an alert, sociable infant that she was forgiven her squalls. She did at least behave herself like a model baby when her grandmother visited her, even favouring the Dowager-Empress with a smile. After that Theophanu felt less bad about the child's name and less guilty about how much she preferred the name 'Sophia' herself.

By the time Theophanu came out of seclusion, Otto was preparing for war again. In retaliation for Duke Boleslav's invasion of Bavaria, he made a punitive raid into Bohemia and in his absence the Empress had to take over some of his duties, receiving petitioners and diplomatic envoys as well as ordering the household. Chancellor Willigis had been elected Archbishop of Mainz in addition to his other responsibilities in the spring, and so he could give her less support than usual.

A succession of thrilling letters from Anna in Constantinople reached Theophanu in the autumn. John Tzimisces, now back with his armies, was re-taking land which had been lost to the Eastern Empire since the original Muslim conquests in the seventh century. Homs, Baalbek, Damascus, Tiberias, Nazareth, Caesarea, Sidon, Beirut, one by one they fell into Christian hands in 975. The Byzantine armies were reported to be poised to take Jerusalem itself. Late one autumn evening Theophanu was thinking happily about this news as she rode home after an afternoon's hawking. Stars were already appearing in the sky and she was congratulating herself for choosing a dress of fine warm green wool in the German style for the hunt, rather than the more elegant but less convenient Byzantine robes, when shouts from the escort distracted her. Following their pointing arms, she saw that a strange star had appeared in the sky. Brighter than any of the others, it was shaped like a cypress tree on its side or like hair streaming back from a face. She knew she must be looking at the star called 'comet' because of its resemblance to hair. She also knew that its appearance was reckoned to foretell disaster, especially to princes. Had not the comet shone in the sky the night Julius Caesar was murdered? Otto's safe return from his raid reassured her, but reports of the comet came in from as far apart as England and Constantinople. Some prince could still be threatened.

The winter that year was hard in the north. Snow carpeted the ground before Christmas and did not melt, even in the valleys, until well into March. That meant that the sowing was delayed and there could well be famine later. People continued to mutter about the comet in a way Theophanu found irritating. Philip had taught her that there might be as natural an explanation for the comet as there was for eclipses, and the doom-laden atmosphere reminded her of the worst Christmas of her life, when Nicephorus Phocas was murdered in 969. She did not want Sophia's first Christmas spoilt by such gloomy thoughts.

Bad news started to reach them, however, even before the twelve days were up. Henry the Wrangler had escaped from his captivity in Ingelheim and headed for Bavaria to find his Bohemian allies. The court had perforce to set out in pursuit through the heavy snow. Then in February even worse tidings reached them. Willigis brought the news.

The previous autumn, instead of attacking Jerusalem, John Tzimisces had again left his armies to return to the capital.

'It seems that he learned of the level of corruption in Basil the Eunuch's government, or rather it was forced on his attention, because he could hardly have suspected nothing,' said Willigis. 'Unwisely he talked about the reason for his return and somebody told the Eunuch.

'Then a friend of Basil's in Bithynia invited the Emperor to a dinner-party on his way home. The next morning Tzimisces was barely able to move. His eyes streamed blood and his neck and shoulders were covered with sores.'

'He's dead then?' asked Otto.

'Not immediately. They managed to get him to Constantinople. He wanted to place Our Lord's sandals and John the Baptist's hair, which he had re-taken, on the altar of Santa Sophia. Then he died, on the 10th January.'

Rather to Theophanu's surprise, she was deeply distressed by this news. She still believed that John had shown her real kindness as a child, no matter how much he had later made use of and then abandoned her. Her last real link with home was severed.

'Is Basil the Eunuch accused of poisoning him?' asked Otto.

'Not officially, no,' replied Willigis. 'He is still in power, although everyone suspects him.'

Otto looked surprised. 'Surely young Basil II will take the real power now,' he said. 'He must be old enough.'

'He's eighteen,' put in Theophanu.

'Yes', said Willigis carefully. He was treading on delicate ground. 'He has never been allowed any real power and he has no military experience. He and Constantine may need to keep the Eunuch in post to maintain their thrones against those who would challenge them.'

A horrible certainty hit Theophanu.

'Who would challenge the legitimate emperors now they are grown?' she asked, but she knew the answer already.

Willigis looked at her apologetically.

'I'm afraid your uncle already has,' he said gently.

'Which one?'

'Bardas Sclerus. He had himself proclaimed emperor by his troops in the old Roman way last month.'

'Raised on their shields?'

'Yes.'

'Ever a stickler for the proprieties,' said Theophanu ironically. 'And of course my father is supporting him as always?'

'Yes.'

Otto forced a laugh.

'Well, we shall just have to keep a close eye on the Empress, Lord Chancellor. Rebellion runs in her family, on both sides'

Theophanu recoiled as if she had been struck. Otto appeared to be joking but she wondered that he could be so cruel, even in jest.

Willigis nodded soberly.

'Unfortunately that is what some people will say, foolish though it is. It's a bad business but meanwhile we have to deal with our own little Liudolfing rebel.'

He looked squarely at his master. Treachery and rebellion seemed to him to be innate in royal dynasties. Theophanu's family was no worse than the rest, but there was no denying that her diplomatic value was now less than nothing.

'Did you yourself get on well with young Basil, Lady?' he asked.

'I'm afraid not. I feared and disliked him.'

'What about his brother? Constantine?'

'He hardly counts, unless he's changed.'

'No, my sources would say the same. Basil II is the enigma. You are not timid, Madam, and yet you feared him. That such a man is content to allow a distant uncle to rule for him is strange.'

'It's not likely to make much difference in the West,' said Otto. 'Our dealings have had to be with the Eunuch for years while Tzimisces was on campaign.'

Willigis frowned. 'I'm not so sure, your Grace. Tzimisces was much feared in the Saracen world. You remember the Fatimid ambassadors from Sicily, who came to your father just before his death?'

Otto and Theophanu nodded. Nobody would forget the tall, grave men in their flowing robes.

'They wanted to drive the Greeks out of Eastern Sicily, but they needed our help, because they feared John Tzimisces. We refused, of course, but now John is gone, they may attempt it on their own. The Fatamids are a very different matter from the Abbassids.'

'But Sicily lies well beyond our territory, on the far side of land belonging to the Eastern Empire,' objected Theophanu.

'Even so, it could threaten all Christendom,' replied Willigis heavily.'
Then he smiled. 'Perhaps it won't happen, Lady. It is my function to
consider the worst possible outcome. That does not make it inevitable.'

Theophanu smiled back but she was troubled by the whole
conversation. Obviously she could not expect Otto to feel grief for a man
he had never met, but she would have thought that he would sympathise
with her sorrow rather than taunting her. For the first time she understood
a little of how his mother must often feel about him. Perhaps when he re-
captured Henry the Wrangler and dealt with him properly, he would be less
tense and jumpy.

In fact it took Otto two full years to defeat Henry. The Wrangler was
deposed from his dukedom *in absentia* while he raised allies in Bohemia.
The Emperor then split Bavaria in two, the western half going to Otto of
Swabia to add to his adjoining duchy, and the east, Carinthia running up to
the south bank of the Danube, being given to another Henry known as 'the
Younger.' The Wrangler promptly re-invaded, with the help of Boleslav
and the Bohemians. Henry of Carinthia and Bishop Henry of Augsburg
joined the rebels and the rising became known as the 'Revolt of the Three
Henrys'.

Theophanu found these years difficult. Otto's confidence was put
under severe strain by the disloyalty of so many of his nobles. To many of
his subjects, the Emperor's enjoyment of divine favour, whether that of the
God of the Christians or of Thor, was guaranteed and illustrated by his
success in battle, and if he did not have such success, there were doubts
about his fitness to rule. Otto did win victories but they were not enough to
dispose of the threat posed by Henry. Theophanu suspected that Otto
himself felt some of this uncertainty and it made him unapproachable,
unwilling to discuss his problems.

There was a brief, happy time around Christmas 976, which the court
spent in Cologne. This was fast becoming Theophanu's favourite town
north of the Alps. The city's Roman past and the trade flowing up and
down the great river made her feel more at home there than in the forests

of Saxony. Here too she was able to give Otto the good news that she was pregnant again and hopes ran high for the son and heir who would work wonders for morale.

Disappointingly the baby turned out to be another girl. Theophanu insisted that this child must be called Adelheid. Agreement had been reached about the Dowager-Empress's *wittum* after Sophia's birth and Otto accepted the name, although he still had suspicions about his mother's loyalty. She, however, seemed fully occupied at this time with the troubles of her daughter by her first marriage, Emma of France. Queen Emma had been accused by her brother-in-law, Charles, of adultery with Ascelin, Bishop of Laon. This accusation had naturally set the French court in turmoil and Emma had turned to her mother for emotional and practical support.

Little Adelheid, a placid, gentle baby, unlike her sister, was only a few days old when her father had to ride off to battle again. The rebel Henrys had captured several important cities on the Danube, including Passau. Otto's troops besieged the town but it was October before they could enter the city in triumph. The prize was worth waiting for; the Wrangler and Henry of Carinthia were both still in the city.

This took the heart out of the rebellion. Boleslav of Bohemia decided to change sides, which left Bishop Henry of Augsburg no alternative but surrender. In spring 978 Otto staged a grand reconciliation with Boleslav. The rest were all tried for treason.

The punishments were still not harsh. The Wrangler, along with his piratical henchman Ekbert One-Eye, was handed over to Bishop Folkmar of Utrecht, known as Poppo, to be kept in less comfortable custody there. His wife, Gisela, was sent to Merseburg in Eastern Saxony at the opposite end of the Empire. Henry of Carinthia was deposed and imprisoned and his duchy given to the remaining 'Young Otto', Otto Liudolfson. For a time it seemed that the imperial family could relax. The young couple played with the two little princesses, celebrated Theophanu's eighteenth birthday, and waited for the birth of her third child in the summer. This time it would surely be a boy.

CHAPTER FOURTEEN

By June they had left Saxony for the western rim of the Empire, the town of Aachen near the frontier with France. This had been the centre of Charlemagne's empire and Theophanu, now heavily pregnant, was looking forward to their stay there. She particularly loved the great Palace Chapel, an octagonal building built by Charlemagne in imitation of San Vitale in Ravenna. It was one of the largest and most splendidly decorated churches in northern Europe and another place where she felt at home. Many of the courtiers had returned to their homes now that the rebellion of the three Henrys was over and the atmosphere was relaxed.

The Empress was therefore happily supervising the final touches to the table settings for the main meal of the day in the great banqueting hall when her husband and his close retainers returned from the day's hunting. They had found plenty of game and there was much laughter and chatter around the huge room when the door suddenly flew open. A serving-man dashed in and fell on his knees before the Emperor.

'Your Grace, a messenger has just ridden in. He says that an army under the command of King Lothar of France and the Reginar brothers is heading this way. They are about five miles away, riding fast. The scouts say they mean to capture you and the Empress.'

There was a moment's stunned silence then Otto burst out laughing.

'What nonsense!' he exclaimed. 'How could a French army be coming to attack us when there's been no declaration of war? Lothar is a descendant of Charlemagne. He'd never behave so dishonourably. Come, we have a magnificent feast awaiting us.'

There was an audible hiss of indrawn breath around the hall. Willigis, now Archchancellor of the whole Empire, and Theophanu exchanged glances. Who could disagree most tactfully? Willigis tried first, in response to Theophanu's nod.

'Your Grace, should we not at least seek to establish the truth of the report? Why should someone invent such a story?'

'For a joke, I suppose,' replied the Emperor. 'Wasn't you, was it, Otto?' When Otto of Swabia shook his head, he continued, 'Stupid joke anyway. I'm hungry, as are we all. We'll look into the matter after the meal.'

'My Lord,' Theophanu said carefully.' Please for my sake and for your unborn child, could we not investigate further? I expect I'm being fanciful, but in my condition ladies do have such fancies.'

The Archchancellor's thunderous scowl was already making Otto doubt his own wisdom and Theophanu's plea gave him the chance to change his mind without losing face.

'Very well,' he said grudgingly. 'I shall go and see myself. Perhaps that will satisfy you, Madam, and then I shall be allowed to eat.'

'Thank you,' Theophanu murmured soothingly. The minute Otto had left the hall, she sent her ladies to collect up the most necessary things if they had to leave in a hurry. Once he left the palace, she sent orders to the stables to have horses saddled and paniers mounted for the children. She cursed that her own girth prevented her from joining in the preparations. She had a strong feeling that the warning was accurate, although it seemed incredible that an enemy army could come so close without being spotted. The forests around Aachen were particularly thick, however, and the woods grew right up to the city walls.

It was an anxious wait for those left in the hall until they heard hoofbeats thudding back into the courtyard and shouts shattered the quiet. The warning was entirely accurate; the French force was now about two miles away and advancing fast.

Pandemonium could have ensued at this point but Theophanu had made her preparations well. The saddled beasts were already loaded with the most necessary things and it was the work of a moment for the women and remaining fighting-men to mount. There was an instant's panic because of Princess Sophia's ill-timed decision that this was a good time for a game of hide-and-seek, but she was quickly found, grabbed and unceremoniously loaded despite her protests. The local servants were told to make no resistance but to scatter into the woods on the other side of the town.

As soon as the Emperor returned to the courtyard, the cavalcade set off at full speed, making for the Cologne gate. Otto himself took Theophanu up in front of him. Her pregnancy was too far advanced for it to be safe for her to ride and his destrier was strong enough to carry three.

As they rode out through the eastern gate, the French poured in through the south. King Lothar laughed heartily when he saw the banquet all spread and waiting, but nevertheless he was disappointed at losing his prey. He had succeeded to his throne when he was only a boy and for much of his life he had had to rely on his mother's brother, Otto the Great, to protect him from powerful nobles who were eager to take the throne from him, particularly his cousin Hugh Capet, Duke of France. Accepting Otto I's tutelage was one thing, but he was not willing to defer to his other young cousin, Otto II. If he had captured Otto and Theophanu, the price of their freedom would have been the handing over of the Duchy of Lotharingia to France. This prize had seemed to him worth the honour he had forfeited by an undeclared assault on a fellow-sovereign.

Lothar vented some of his frustration by allowing his men to plunder and burn the town as they wished. He also sent soldiers up onto the roof of the palace, which was surmounted by a great bronze eagle with outspread wings, the symbol of the Empire. It faced Francia in defiance of any threat from that quarter. Lothar's men turned it round to face Germany, to resounding cheers from his troops.

Lothar had a personal grievance against Otto as well as the general political situation. One of the great problems of Lothar's life was his younger brother, Charles. Two years ago Charles, in league with the robber Reginar brothers, had started a futile rebellion against Otto in Lotharingia. After his defeat, Charles slunk back to his brother's court at Laon. It was then that he made his outrageous allegation against his sister-in-law, Queen Emma, of adultery with Bishop Ascelin. Lothar was convinced of his wife's innocence and banished his brother from France. Charles took refuge in the Empire and appealed to Otto for help.

This presented the imperial government with a dilemma. Empress Adelheid, reasonably enough, held that the man was a slandering scoundrel who had plagued her innocent daughter Emma. He should receive no support. Otto and Willigis, however, realised that if they gave Charles the Duchy of Lower Lotharingia, as he was requesting, he would *ipso facto* become Otto's vassal for it. It would suit them well to have the brother of the King of France as an imperial vassal and as a direct descendant of Charlemagne Charles had a good claim to the duchy. When Adelheid heard this, she was white and speechless with fury and frustration.

As so often, Theophanu found herself torn. If the Queen of France was innocent, then Theophanu's own husband's behaviour was less than 'honourable' to use the favourite word of most of the men she knew. She had, however, heard so much from Adelheid over the years about the improbable perfection of Queen Emma as compared to herself, that she could not be entirely displeased by Emma's misfortune. It was easier to try to keep out of the quarrel by occupying herself with the children, which Adelheid naturally regarded as yet another betrayal. She convinced herself that it was the Greek woman who was influencing Otto against his half-sister. In truth, tired by her third pregnancy in three years, Theophanu just wished they would all go away and leave her alone.

The decision was finally made to give Charles Lower Lotharingia and he swore homage to Otto for it. When Adelheid learned that Otto and Theophanu were going to Aachen with only a small force, she wrote to tell her daughter. That was enough for Lothar to act to avenge the insult as well as to gain Lotharingia. When he failed to capture his prey, he sent urgent messages to Adelheid, warning her that she might be suspected of complicity in the raid. She knew that nothing could be proved beyond giving her daughter a bit of family news, but nevertheless she judged it wise to pay an extended visit to her estates in Burgundy and Italy. It was all Theophanu's fault, of course.

The imperial party escaped safely to the Rhineland and Lothar went back to France. Theophanu, meanwhile, was occupied with her own problems. It was no surprise to anyone that the baby came early after such a frantic ride but this birth was not as easy as the other two had been. Worst of all, the child was yet another girl. Her father acknowledged her and named her Matilda after his grandmother and sister but otherwise he showed little interest in either the baby or her mother. A third girl was useless to him, but in any case his mind was wholly set on obtaining revenge on Lothar, and Theophanu, for the first time in their marriage, was opposing him. So were most other people, as Theophanu discovered at a meeting of Otto's advisers, which she attended just before Matilda's birth.

'My honour is besmirched by Lothar's treachery,' the exasperated Otto pointed out to his assembled generals. 'I cannot suffer this without signalling that any man may insult me with impunity.'

'There is no dispute about that, Your Grace,' Willigis said. 'The argument is over *when* we should retaliate. We are already in July. There is no time to muster an army and take it to France in this campaigning season.'

'We should strike while the iron is hot,' insisted Otto. 'I don't want to give Lothar the winter to fortify every castle against us.'

'Sir, the north of France is notoriously wet in winter,' said Otto of Swabia. 'Our troops are heavily armed. We cannot move through mud and the river valleys will be swamps.'

'It'll all be over by Christmas,' snapped the Emperor.

'How will the Duke of France react?' asked Theophanu. 'His forces are at least as large as King Lothar's. He could hold the balance of power.'

'Hugh Capet will no doubt do as he always does,' answered her husband. 'See what happens and watch where his advantage lies.'

'But what exactly does Your Grace intend to achieve by this campaign?' asked Willigis. 'An apology or a change of government?'

'What's wrong with a change of government, Lord Archbishop?'

'The setting up of a dangerous precedent, as Your Grace well knows,' answered Willigis, not a whit abashed. 'Lothar is the legitimate King of France, elected and anointed. To unhorse him is to weaken the position of all lawful monarchs.'

After a tense silence Otto assented. 'Very well. An apology will satisfy my honour, but it must be now, not next year. Are we all agreed.'

He looked round the ring of faces, to see nothing but frowns. In the end Duke Bernhard of Saxony spoke for them all.

'You know we are not, Your Grace, but you are the Emperor. If this campaign is your wish, we shall follow you to the end.'

'And you, Lady?'

This time Theophanu found she could not give the automatic assent which custom required. She had worked out the timing and realised that it was indeed too late for this year.'

'I wish you would wait for the spring, my Lord,' she said in a low voice.

Otto decided that the best way to deal with a pregnant woman was to patronise her.

'Ladies are naturally fearful in your condition, my dear, as you showed at Aachen. No, I am resolved. Give the order to mobilise, Lord Archchancellor.'

Willigis bowed in acknowledgement, even as he wondered how many good men would lie dead by Christmas because of the Emperor's impatience.

The memory of the two occasions on which his wife had defied him publicly rankled with Otto, especially when she produced yet another girl, not an heir. His mother's possible support of Lothar further convinced him that women were a snare and a hindrance, not to be trusted. He set off on his campaign in September with a sense of relief.

At first all went well. The weather held and Otto's troops swept through Rheims, Soissons and Compiegne to the very outskirts of Paris. Otto satisfied his thirst for revenge by burning Lothar's palaces at Attigny and Compiegne as Lothar had burned Aachen. The land, including the harvest, was laid waste, which meant that as usual the real losers in the war were the peasants, especially with the winter coming on.

Despite his words to Willigis, Otto had not abandoned his hope of setting Charles of Lower Lotharingia up as a puppet-king in place of his brother. From Rheims the Emperor sent off a strong detachment commanded by Charles and by Theophanu's old opponent, Bishop Dietrich of Metz, to capture Lâon, capital of Francia. The fortified city was perched on top of a hill above the great plain of Northern France with a good water supply. It would have been impregnable if anyone had cared to defend it. As it was, Lothar and his family had left as soon as they heard of the imperial invasion and shortly afterwards Bishop Ascelin too, the man accused of being Queen Emma's lover, decided to leave his people to look to their own defence. Sensibly they surrendered immediately. Otto's troops held the capital but had failed in their main objective, to capture the king.

Theophanu and Willigis, waiting on the Rhine, heard this news with exasperation. Otto and Charles had obviously taken no notice of Willigis' warning. Then news came in from the main army and it was not encouraging; Hugh Capet, always the unknown factor in French affairs, had shut the gates of Paris against imperial troops. The city had strong stone walls and Otto had been obliged to make camp outside. The Indian summer, which had helped the Empire so much, came to an end. Rain poured down and winds blew. It was clear, even to Otto, that there was no time to besiege such a well-defended city with the winter approaching.

'I don't know why the Emperor ever supposed Hugh Capet might support him,' Willigis commented to Theophanu. 'Why should an imperial puppet-king suit him any better than a rather feeble Carolingian?'

'He said himself that Hugh Capet only consults his own advantage,' agreed Theophanu. 'It might be more to the point to offer him the throne. He'd make a better king than that toad Charles.'

'But not necessarily one any more wedded to the interests of the Empire', warned Willigis.

'Hugh is a nephew of Otto the Great through his mother, isn't he?' Theophanu pointed out.

'They all are – Hugh, Lothar and Charles. Charles is the only one who is an imperial vassal.'

'Not to mention a slanderous, treacherous trouble-maker,' grunted Theophanu.

'Oh yes, that too,' agreed Willigis.

The next despatch highlighted the almost farcical elements of this war. Otto had no alternative but to retreat; publicly, however, he could not afford to admit a defeat. He therefore ordered his soldiers and clergy to mount a triumphal parade on the hill of Montmartre, outside but overlooking the city. The clergy then sang a series of alleluias to celebrate the 'victory'. Almost immediately afterwards the withdrawal started.

Once the rain had begun, it did not let up. The retreating army struggled along increasingly muddy roads, ever more harassed by French troops, who had now had time to organise resistance. When Otto tried to re-cross the flooded River Aisne in Champagne, matters came to a head. Theophanu listened appalled to the messenger's account.

'The vanguard and the main body got across safely, Lady, but the French bank was churned up by their passing into a thick soup, and when the rear tried to move the baggage wagons through, they couldn't do it. There were all the boys and women getting in the way too, of course. Then a horn blew and the French attacked from both sides at once and our men couldn't move for the mud. It was a massacre. The Emperor and everyone else just had to watch from the other bank. They could do nothing to help.'

Theophanu shuddered.

'How great was the loss of life?'

'Oh, not too bad. Nobody of importance was killed. The army is on its way home now.'

'Nobody of importance? How many widows and orphans will there be?'

The messenger stared at her blankly. 'I'm sorry, Madam. I don't understand. The Emperor is safe,' he repeated encouragingly.

Theophanu sighed. 'Of course. Thank you for bringing me word. Here's for your trouble.'

She handed him a coin but when he had gone, she turned to Emilia, who had been giving her a progress report on the little princesses.

'I cannot make myself think like these men. 'Honour' is everything and the lives of ordinary men, women and children count for nothing in comparison. But some woman went through agony to bear each man or boy whose life has been spent, just as much as I did with my babies. I can't see them as so different from me that their lives don't matter.'

Emilia nodded slowly. 'It is much that the Archchancellor thinks as you do, Madam. He has no love of war for itself.'

'No, because he springs from those whose crops are ruined by the trampling hooves of passing armies. Of course force must be used to uphold the law and preserve order, but this war between cousins still seems unnecessary.'

Willigis was in agreement when they discussed the news later.

'It will change nothing in most ways,' he said. 'Lothar is already putting out feelers about making peace by negotiation and all will go back as it was on the surface. And yet underneath I feel it is more significant and more sad. It marks a breach between the two halves of Charlemagne's empire, between the East and West Franks. Already they call themselves French, rather than West Franks. And we too are growing into a separate people, of whom the East Franks are only a part. It does not bode well for the safety of Europe.'

CHAPTER FIFTEEN

As Willigis anticipated, relations between France and the Empire eventually returned to what they were, although it took over a year to arrange a peace conference. Meanwhile, once Otto returned from France, 979 was a bit of a breathing-space for the young imperial couple to re-establish their relationship free of the strain of Adelheid's constant presence. The illusions of first love were past. Otto now had a slightly wary respect for his wife, symbolised by his referring to her in a decree as *co-imperatrix*, the first time any woman in the West had held the title. He did not, however, accompany it with the endearments he had used in the early years.

Theophanu's love too had changed. She no longer saw Otto as the seat of all perfections, but was aware of his failings, whilst still loving his many virtues. His daughter Sophia's resemblance to him accentuated this process and occasionally Theophanu felt that she had four children rather than a husband and three. Certainly the longer he ruled, the more headstrong he seemed to become. In the summer he even managed to exasperate his faithful friend Otto of Swabia over his handling of a judicial duel.

Nevertheless the imperial family was happy at this time. Otto and Theophanu together planned the details of a great memorial church which they would build at Memleben, deathplace of both Otto the Great and Henry the Fowler. They also had important decisions to make about the children's future. Sophia was four and it was time for her to go to school.

While the princesses were tiny, it was possible for them to be transported with the court, but Sophia was now too tall to fit into a pannier and any pony she could ride would not be able to keep up.
It would be too exhausting for her anyway. Both her parents had dedicated this much-loved child to God even before her birth, when they had waited so long for her conception. It did occur to Theophanu that little Adelheid might have been more fitted by nature for this vocation, but

Sophia's nature required to rule and as an abbess she would have scope to do exactly that, probably more than she ever would as a wife. It was a great pity she was not a boy. Anyway the only appropriate match for the eldest daughter of the Emperor would be a son of Basil or Constantine and so far they had none. From Anna's letters, Theophanu rather doubted that they ever would have a legitimate one.

The Empress wanted her daughter to go to Gandersheim, whereas Otto preferred Quedlinburg.

'It really is more fitting, Theophanu,' he argued. 'It's the main family shrine, my sister is abbess there and eventually, as abbess, Sophia will have a seat on the Imperial Council. And we go there every Easter, so we would see her regularly.'

'Taking those points in reverse order,' Theophanu replied, 'Gandersheim is on more of the trade routes; we shall drop in more often. Your sister is a delight but you have to admit that Sophia can twist her round her little finger already. She needs a tougher governess. Gandersheim is the oldest shrine of your family.'

'What about the seat in parliament?'

'Well, I grant you that, but look at the positive points for Gandersheim. The education there is superb; they offer the full *trivium* and *quadrivium* and teachers like Rotswitha and Rikkardis are renowned, not to mention Abbess Gerberga herself. Gerberga is versed in the Greek and Latin authors, not just the Church Fathers, and I *would* like Sophia to keep up her Greek.'

'Gerberga herself is perhaps the main problem, though. I know we both like and trust her, but when all's said and done, she's still sister to Henry the Wrangler and Hedwig.'

'Yes, she has their strength of will. She's strong enough to stand up to her brother – and even to young Sophia.'

Otto laughed. 'That will need a miracle,' he said ruefully. Very well then. You're right that Sophia will need a sound education if she is to follow the religious life. I'll tell you who will be devastated when she goes and that's our Lord Archchancellor.'

Theophanu nodded thoughtfully. 'I never know whether she adores him more than he does her,' she agreed. 'She's certainly the daughter he never had.'

They decided that they would go to Bothfeld in the Harz Mountains for the usual autumn hunting and then Sophia would be handed over to her new mentor. They agreed that the placid, sweet-natured Adelheid would eventually go to the care of Otto's sister at Quedlinburg. Unlike Gandersheim, Quedlinburg numbered boy choristers among the pupils, which was another reason why Theophanu did not want the tomboy Sophia to go there. Already her best friends were stable-boys and pages. Adelheid was much more law-abiding. That left Matilda, still a baby, in whom both her parents found it difficult to take much interest. Theophanu, particularly, felt guilty about this. It was not the child's fault that she was female, nor could she help being slower than her sisters. When Otto of Swabia suggested that she should eventually be put into the care of his sister, another Abbess Matilda, who was both the baby's godmother and herself a granddaughter of Otto the Great, both Otto and Theophanu felt it an ideal solution. Matilda would stay with them for a year or two anyway.

Otto wrote to Gerberga announcing their intention and stressing that it was the child's mother's desire that she should come to Gandersheim. In the autumn they delivered Sophia to school with promises that her mother would come to see her soon. They stayed overnight in the imperial guest-rooms and when they left, Sophia assured them that school was the bestest thing she had ever done. As they rode firmly away without looking back, following Gerberga's instructions, they could not tell whether the enthusiasm was maintained as they vanished, but Gerberga had promised to keep her little charge too busy to fret.

By this time Theophanu was feeling distinctly queasy. She was pregnant again and finding this pregnancy more troubling than the others, even Matilda's. She could not account for the permanent exhaustion that she was feeling and she was actually quite relieved when Otto rode off on a military expedition into Poland.

The Empress was also worried by the way events were shaping in the Eastern Empire. The Sclerus revolt had finally been put down. Her other Uncle Bardas, Bardas Phocas, had been recalled from exile to lead the loyalist armies and a tit-for-tat civil war had lasted for two years. Finally he and Bardas Sclerus met in single combat in early 979. Both gigantic men, they urged their destriers at each other across a flat plain in front of both armies. Each swung a massive blow at the other. Phocas managed to deflect the thrust onto his horse but Sclerus took the full force and fell to the ground senseless. Victory had to be conceded and the Sclerus brothers sought refuge, and the prospect of revenge, with the Saracen caliphate in Baghdad. Theophanu thus became not merely the daughter of a rebel, but of a supporter of the enemies of Christendom. It did not make her position any easier. The only saving grace, she supposed, was that her father had not fled to her.

Now that the east was free of the Sclerus threat, the two Basils were free to look westwards. They had never recognised Pope Benedict VII and decided that the time was now ripe to have him deposed and replaced by Boniface VII, whom they were still harbouring in Constantinople. Boniface would be a useful Byzantine puppet. By midwinter 979 news reached Otto's court that Pope Benedict, a man who was more concerned with church mission and reform than with international politics, had been driven out of Rome and had appealed to the Emperor for help. Otto would have to go back to Italy.

In the short term he could not. Theophanu's pregnancy would mean that she could not cross the Alps before the next autumn and the peace conference with France was already fixed for May at Margut-sur-Chiers in Lotharingia. That went ahead as planned. Lothar brought his thirteen-year-old son Louis along as his heir and peace was duly restored. The Empire recognised Lothar, not Charles, as the rightful King of France. In return Lothar gave up any claim to Lotharingia.

Theophanu was present at the negotiations but contributed little to the conference. She was feeling absolutely drained of energy. Her belly seemed larger than it had been in other pregnancies and in her worst moments she had a secret fear that she was going to give birth to a monster with twice the normal number of arms and legs.

In early July they were making their way through a forest called by the locals the Ketilwoud, en route to Nijmegen where the baby was to be born. Theophanu had been having the odd cramp for some days now and her ladies kept glancing anxiously at her pale face, where her lips were tightly compressed. They urged the wagon-driver to take more care to avoid the ruts in the track, but at last Theophanu could bear it no longer. She gave a huge groan and simultaneously her waters broke, although the child was not due for several days yet.

The cavalcade drew to a halt and her ladies formed a protective screen round the Empress. Scouts were sent off to look for the nearest shelter. Otto glanced anxiously round the thick, deciduous forest, which could easily harbour wild animals, but sooner than he could have hoped a scout returned to say that there was a hunting-lodge only two hundred yards ahead. By this time a stretcher had been made and Theophanu was carried as quickly as possible to the building, where the lodge-keeper's wife had already kindled a fire and heated water. The men made camp in a large circle outside and the real work started.

The first birth was not too difficult. Theophanu had managed to restrain the urge to push until she reached the house and a small but healthy boy-child headbutted his way into the world without injuring any of his limbs. Shouts of joy and triumph conveyed the glad news to the men waiting outside and riotous jubilation broke out. At long last God had favoured the Emperor with an heir.

Inside the lodge delight was rapidly turning to consternation. The baby was fine, although the noise outside completely drowned his angry yells. The mother was not so well. The afterbirth had followed normally but Theophanu's pains did not seem to be lessening at all, rather the reverse after a short lull. Then the explanation struck both Theophanu and Emilia at the same time. Just as Theophanu gasped out 'Another!', Emilia cried

'They're twins! Anastaso, leave the prince to the others. Come back here.'

The second birth was far more difficult. Theophanu was obviously weaker but the infant appeared to be doing little to help itself, if indeed it was still alive. Emilia sent a girl to alert one of the accompanying clergy, ready for a hasty baptism, and braced herself to manipulate the child out. She was not a trained midwife and the responsibility terrified her but there was no alternative. Seeing her hesitation, the lodge-keeper's wife intervened.

'I've done this before many times, 'she said. 'Let me help the poor lady.'

Emilia dithered only for a moment. Better the expert, provided she washed her hands, than the amateur. The confidence of the burly woman was reassuring and she quickly gave her assent.

After an agonising half-hour, a little girl followed her brother into the world. She never took her first breath and they could not baptise her. By then her mother had mercifully lost consciousness. The delivery had torn her badly and she had lost a lot of blood.

The washed and swaddled baby prince was then taken out to meet his eagerly waiting father. Otto was saddened by the fate of the dead girl but, once he was assured that Theophanu should make a full recovery, his spirits rose again. Nothing could countervail his delight in his son.

As soon as she was well enough, Theophanu was taken to Nijmegen. The original palace had been built by Charlemagne and, although sacked and restored since then, it was comfortable and well-furnished. Here Theophanu could rest in safety and recover her strength. At first she found her spirits very low. She knew that she should be rejoicing at the birth of the heir but she was actually more inclined to brood on the fate of the unbaptised child. She also felt even more guilty about having overlooked Matilda. Was that why this one had been taken from her as a punishment?

Otto was surprisingly patient with her gloomy thoughts when he came to see her.

'It's quite natural to feel like this,' he reassured her. 'You lost an awful lot of blood, Emilia says. I've seen it on the battlefield. Soldiers fall into exhaustion and low spirits when they lose too much blood. As for the little girl, we'll make an offering for her soul when you are well again. She will be safe in God's hands. Now for some good news. Look what I've got here.'

From behind his back he produced a wineskin.

'Is it a special one?' Theophanu asked puzzled.

'Yes. You need red wine to make your blood strong again. This is Burgundy's finest, sent for you by King Conrad at the request of his sister.'

'His sister? Oh, Empress Adelheid! She sent it?'

'She wants to be reconciled,' Otto said beaming. 'She will meet us in Italy. She says she never meant any harm. Now, where's my son?'

When they had finished cooing over the baby, he said to Theophanu

'I think we should build a chapel in the style of your home-country – eight sided – here in the palace, in thanksgiving for young Otto and in memory of his sister. Which saint would you like to dedicate it to?'

Theophanu thought for a moment then smiled. 'Nicholas,' she said with certainty.

'Nicholas?' repeated Otto, surprised.

'Yes, the Bishop of Myra. According to the stories he brought little boys back to life and gave dowries to poor girls. He would be a good patron for our children.'

'Fine,' Otto agreed. 'They'll never have heard of him round here and they'll call him something ridiculous like Sint Klaas, but I imagine his story will make him very popular, particularly with children. We'll start drawing up plans tomorrow.'

CHAPTER SIXTEEN

Theophanu immersed herself in the plans for the new chapel. Although she suspected she was being absurd, she found it comforting to think of kindly Saint Nicholas keeping an eye on her little, lost baby, and as a result, she was able to warm to the survivor. He was a lovely child, gaining weight rapidly now and as full of energy and personality as his eldest sister. The Empress spent more time with Matilda too, which assuaged her guilt. She wanted to see which of the toddler's attendants were closest to her. Once they left Nijmegen, they would head for Essen and there Matilda would be given to the Abbey to raise. She was only just two and if she showed particular affection to any of her nurses, Theophanu was willing to pay the young woman handsomely to stay with the child, at least for the first few years. Fortunately she approved of Matilda's favourite, a young relation of Archbishop Willigis' from Saxony, and the girl was more than happy to accompany her little mistress. Theophanu's mind was much relieved.

After leaving Matilda, they headed along the Hellweg, the great trading route to and from the silver mines at Ramsberg, to Quedlinburg, where Adelheid was to remain; only the baby would come with them to Italy. At three Adelheid was excited to be going to school like Sophia and she had visited Quedlinburg several times. Theophanu had fewer qualms about leaving her there, and again her favourite attendant was willing to stay with her.

They enjoyed some good days hunting and hawking in the Harz Mountains before they turned south towards Gandersheim. This was the real beginning of the long journey to Italy and they would say goodbye to Sophia on the way. She was delighted to see them and entranced by her little brother, to Theophanu's surprise, because Sophia had never shown much enthusiasm for her sisters. The child was obviously happy and busy. She was learning Latin, she told them proudly, and she could sing the psalms properly now. Early progress reports had told her parents that the canonesses had had storms with her at first – accepting discipline had never come easily to Sophia – but Abbess Gerberga said her conduct was much improved recently. All in all they had an idyllic time together exploring and fishing the little streams at the foot of the hill, Sophia having been given a day's leave of absence, but as they were returning to the convent, she realised that they were going to Italy without her. Then the tempest broke and all attempts to pacify her failed. In the end she was simply removed, while her parents pleaded for leniency in the circumstances. In the morning a much-subdued Sophia was brought to bid them farewell. The sight of her woebegone face cut her parents to the quick. Otto quickly produced his leaving-present for her. It was wrapped in rich red velvet and Theophanu was nearly as eager as the child to see what it was.

She gasped aloud when she saw, then had to choke back her laughter. It was the bi-lingual psalter which Otto had 'borrowed' from the library at St. Gall all those years ago and obviously never returned. Theophanu wondered at his nerve. Gerberga only had to mention the gift to her sister Hedwig, who was famed for regularly reading Virgil with Abbot Ekkehard of St. Gall, and the abbot would be demanding his property back. Now Otto was the emperor, of course, he could ignore all protests. Abbess Gerberga, unaware of the book's origins, promised that the child could keep it for herself and a smile transformed Sophia's features. They left rapidly then, while the good mood held.

In the end it was November before they were back over the Alps. They retraced their steps of eight years earlier over the Julier and Septimer passes but the journey was much harder in the cold weather. There was plenty of snow on the summits but the track over the pass was still open, probably the last week it would be. The frost made the stones slippery and they were all relieved to reach the hospice at the top. On the descent the following morning they looked back to see mist sweeping down after them. Soon they were enclosed and isolated in its cold, clammy world and Theophanu took little Otto from his nurse and wrapped her thick waxed wool travelling cloak round them both, trying to give her heat to the baby. By midmorning the sun drove off the mist and the going became easier.

Adelheid and her entourage awaited them outside the walls of Pavia on a fine December morning. The woollen cloaks were all put away and silks and velvets were everywhere. The imperial cavalcade approached in silence, then Otto and his mother dismounted. Still without a word, they exchanged a long, steady look. Then, Adelheid first, they expressed their contrition for having offended each other. In their rich clothes, each lay prostrate on the muddy ground and begged and received forgiveness of the other. Next, rising, they gave each other a kiss of peace and finally a bear-hug.

Then it was Theophanu's turn. The two empresses did not prostrate themselves to each other but each spoke words of sorrow and forgiveness and exchanged kisses. Theophanu said,

'Dear Lady Mother, let me present to you your grandson, Prince Otto.'

Imiza brought the child forward and handed him to his grandmother. For a long moment Adelheid simply looked at him. Standing close to her, Theophanu could see her expression melting into softness and felt a sudden conviction that, at least where the baby was concerned, Adelheid could be trusted. The two women exchanged the most unguarded smiles they had ever given each other.

'Thank you, my daughter,' said Adelheid quietly. 'He is indeed a fine child and worthy of his grandfather.'

The two courts sailed together down the Po via Piacenza and Cremona through the marshes to Ravenna in time for Christmas. Otto had left Willigis in charge north of the Alps but he had brought with him the Chancellor of Germany, the Bishop of Worms, as well as his sister Matilda of Quedlinburg and Archbishop Giselher of Magdeburg. The Italian Arch-Chancellor, Bishop Peter of Pavia, and Chancellor, John Philagathos, had joined them at Pavia, along with a deputation from the Archdiocese of Rheims. Rheims was always politically significant, because its lands straddled the border between the Empire and France and its archbishop, Adalbero, was the most important churchman in France, holding the right to crown its kings.

Adalbero was accompanied by the headmaster of his cathedral school, a famous scholar called Gerbert of Aurillac. He had been Otto II's tutor for a few years and Theophanu dimly remembered meeting him at her coronation. Otto passed some of the time on the boat by telling her stories about Gerbert, most of which were completely unbelievable.

'When he was young,' the Emperor told his wife,' Gerbert was apprenticed to a Moorish sorcerer.'

'I studied at the famous school of Vic in Catalonia,' interrupted the subject of the story.

'He realised that his master's magic powers came from a book of spells which the magician kept locked in a casket,' continued the Emperor, ignoring the interruption, 'so he seduced the sorcerer's beautiful daughter to get the key. Then he abandoned the girl and fled with the book.'

'This is absolute nonsense,' protested Gerbert. Theophanu gave him a sympathetic grin.

'When the magician learned of the theft, he called for his magic horse, which could not be outrun, and his magic hound, which never lost a scent. Gerbert heard them coming' – Gerbert groaned '– and when he came to a bridge, he hid under it, hanging by his hands. Sorcerer, dog, and horse thundered across without seeing him, because he was in neither the earth nor the water, but between the elements.'

'I'm supposed to believe this?' asked Theophanu.

'There's more. He keeps a talking head on his desk at Rheims, you know. The Devil gave it to him and it answers his questions about the future.'

'I keep a skull on my desk as a *memento mori*,' said Gerbert tiredly.

'What is it you actually do that provokes these stories?' Theophanu asked him.

He sighed. 'I've learned many things from the Saracens, some of which would not be news to your people, Lady, but they are new in the West. My new way of counting must seem like magic to those who don't understand it.'

'New way of counting?' Theophanu was baffled.

'Yes. We count one, two, three, but one is not the first number. Nought is – zero. And if you have a symbol for zero and single symbols for the other numbers up to nine, you can calculate huge numbers in very little time. Then there's an invention called an abacus.'

'How does that work?'

'It's a series of rows, with ten beads on each. Each bead on the bottom rung represents one unit. Each bead on the next equals ten units, the next a hundred units, and so on. It speeds the calculation process up enormously, or if you use the Arabic system of numbering, you can do it in your head.'

'He makes his students be a living abacus,' said Otto.

'How?'

'I stand in the pulpit in the cathedral and they stand in rows of ten, each one next to a disc and holding a broom. Each boy represents a bead on the abacus. Then I shout instructions to them to move their discs with their brooms. That way we can calculate enormous numbers.'

'That must be fun.' Theophanu tried to visualise a cathedral full of young men with brooms. 'I can see why people think you're a sorcerer.' she added.

'Tell her about your water-organ,' Otto urged Gerbert.

'That is complicated to explain, but we have managed to use water to ensure that our organ stays at a constant pitch. As you know, that has always been difficult.'

Theophanu nodded wisely, although in fact she did not know. She realised she was looking forward to the debate which Otto had arranged as a Christmas entertainment at Ravenna. He had summoned Gerbert from France and another equally famous scholar, Ochtrich, who had been head of Magdeburg Cathedral School until he quarrelled with his own bishop.

Otto chaired the debate himself. The topic was whether mathematics or physics was more important in the study of philosophy. It seemed to Theophanu, listening with interest and understanding some of it, that Gerbert had the better of the argument. Her own knowledge of mathematics and physics was not extensive, but Philip had trained her thoroughly in logic and much of what Ochtrich said seemed off the point. Otto tactfully refused to declare an outright winner but soon afterwards he appointed Gerbert Abbot of Bobbio, an ancient monastery founded by St. Columbanus. Theophanu wondered what the monks would think of having to push discs around with brooms. Probably not much.

The main reason for going to Ravenna was to meet Pope Benedict VII, who had taken refuge there, and to set about restoring him to his throne. The anti-pope, Boniface VII, had been seen in Rome; to Theophanu's regret this confirmed Byzantine involvement in the ousting of Benedict. As the spring came north, so the court and the large body of troops Otto had brought with him moved towards Rome. Astonishingly the opposition simply melted away and Benedict was back in the Lateran Palace before Easter.

Pope and Empress had talked much on the way from Ravenna and Theophanu grew to like him. He was eager to tell her about a new monastery he had established on the Aventine Hill.

'It's dedicated to Saints Alexis and Boniface, because I want it to be a meeting-place between east and west,' Benedict said. 'Boniface the Englishman, the Apostle to the Saxons, for the west and Alexis for the Greeks.'

'That's wonderful,' said Theophanu warmly. 'What gave you that idea?'

'The Metropolitan Archbishop of Damascus was driven out of his see recently by the Saracens. He needed a home and so I set up this for him.'

'But he would use an eastern-rite liturgy in Greek or Syriac surely,' observed Theophanu.

'Yes, indeed he does. Both western and eastern rites are used there. I want the monastery to be a meeting-place and training-house for missionaries to the pagans and the infidels. Boniface and Alexis.'

Theophanu was caught by the idea of worshipping in her own language again. 'I would like to visit this house, if I may,' she said.

'You would be welcome, Lady. I very much hope that you might be persuaded to support the venture financially.'

'If it lives up to your description, I certainly shall,' the Empress promised. She had not felt homesick for years but she did miss the flexibility of the Greek language.

Theophanu was not short of interesting companions on the ride to Rome. Beside the Pope himself, she spent much time with Gerbert of Aurillac and with the recently appointed Chancellor of Italy, John Philagathos. He was a native Greek speaker from Calabria and Gerbert was also fluent in the language, so that for the first time for some years Theophanu could fully express herself, even to the finest nuances. It brought home to her the strain of always thinking in another tongue, despite her fluency in Latin and Saxon.

She did not quite know what to make of either man. Gerbert was not prepossessing physically; he was too slight and his features too sharp for that, but his intelligence was appealing and he was very good company. All the same Theophanu could not quite trust him. Philagathos was different, a big man with curly, rather greasy dark hair, a high colour and full lips. There was something about him that both attracted and repelled her but nevertheless she revelled in the chance in the chance to use her own language, despite the hostile looks their conversations attracted from men like Bishop Dietrich of Metz and Archbishop Giselher, neither of whom had any liking for Theophanu.

Easter 981 was to see a brilliant gathering of royalty in Rome. Otto and the two empresses were joined by the King and Queen of Burgundy and Hugh Capet, Duke of France. Theophanu was pleased to see such an amicable gathering but when she said as much to Gerbert, he gave her a quizzical look.

'Appearances are not necessarily a guide to reality. According to rumour,' he said with a broad grin,' King Conrad of Burgundy conspired with King Lothar of France to prevent Hugh Capet from meeting the Emperor.'

'You of all men should know that rumour is not necessarily a guide to truth. Proof?'

'Not exactly proof but an amusing story. It seems Hugh disguised himself as a groom to travel through Burgundy, but the groom could not resist giving orders to his supposed masters and so his disguise was revealed and he had to ride for his life.'

Theophanu laughed then added ruefully,

'Well, at least it's pleasant to see my husband at peace with his mother.'

'Yes,' agreed Gerbert slowly, then made up his mind. Better she knew the truth. 'Actually, Lady, the Dowager Empress and her daughter of France were part of the plot.'

'Her daughter,' Theophanu sighed. 'I suppose her loyalties are bound to be divided.' To herself she wondered, if she had to choose between Young Otto's and Sophia's interests, what she would do. Try to find a balance, she supposed, and perhaps that was what Adelheid was looking for.

Theophanu was interested to meet Hugh Capet, although his appearance was rather disappointing, considering the influence he seemed to wield. He was totally unremarkable to look at, with pale hair and thin features. This unprepossessing exterior obviously concealed a quick and cunning mind, but an incident that occurred at a meeting between him and Otto made her realise that the deviousness was not all on one side. When Otto II stood up to go, he left his sword, with its cross-shaped hilt, lying on his chair. Capet automatically moved to pick it up to give it to him but the Bishop of Orleans grabbed his arm and held it back.

He then picked up the sword himself and handed it to the Emperor, who smilingly thanked him. From the smirks and the glances of many of the onlookers, it was clear that there was more going on than met the eye.

'Did you do it on purpose?' Theophanu asked Otto that night.

He laughed. 'Actually, no. I did genuinely forget, but it would have been convenient if Capet had fallen for it. Pity Arnulf of Orleans was so quick.'

'It was the cross, I suppose?'

'Yes, it would have amounted to a tacit oath of homage because of the shape of the hilt. I am surprised Hugh didn't see it coming.'

Theophanu looked at him consideringly. He had denied any intent on his part but she was not sure she believed him. She did not, however, think the idea had been his; it bore the hallmark of the subtlety of Gerbert of Aurillac. She was increasingly realising that, whereas the Saxons were a fairly straightforward, if contentious, people, the Franks were as cunning as the Byzantines. It saddened her a little to see Otto copying them and even more that he did not trust her with the truth.

After the Frankish royal guests went home, life in Rome settled into a routine. Otto and Pope Benedict were much occupied with synods relating to church reform, which was also Adelheid's great enthusiasm. It seemed to Theophanu that, as his mother's influence with the Emperor grew, so she was becoming left out. She and Imiza spent a lot of time with Little Otto and both Gerbert, who knew Imiza through his patron, the Archbishop of Rheims, and John Philagathos often joined them. Even so, for the first time since the early days, Theophanu felt that her finger was not on the pulse of things and she was relieved when plans started to be made for the homeward journey. Then news arrived which would postpone their return to Germany indefinitely.

CHAPTER SEVENTEEN

The devastating news was of the death of Pandulf Ironhead, Prince of Capua, Benevento and Salerno. It was Pandulf whose release from Byzantine captivity had been negotiated as part of Theophanu's marriage agreement, since when he had kept the peace in the south, ruling his buffer principalities under Otto's suzerainty and preventing imperial incursions into the Byzantine south. With his death the peace came to an end.

Events from then on moved with bewildering swiftness. Theophanu sat, almost dazed, at a council meeting where the terms of a muster of imperial troops were decided.

'One hundred knights: Archbishop of Mainz; Archbishop of Cologne; Bishop of Strasburg; Bishop of Augsburg. Augsburg to lead his troops himself; Mainz to stay as regent.

'Seventy knights: Bishop of Trier; Bishop of Regensburg; Bishop of Salzburg.

'Sixty knights: Bishops of Verdun and Liege; Abbot of Fulda; Abbot of the Reichenau,' the Emperor dictated.

'All church and all from the south?' Otto of Swabia questioned.

'I'll get on to the secular lords in a minute. Twenty or twelve knights will do for them. Certainly from the south. I don't want to weaken the northern borders and I don't want to leave any friends of my dear cousin Henry unsupervised for too long.'

By September an army of about twelve thousand mounted men had assembled in Rome and Theophanu was still not certain why. It was obvious that some force was needed to put down the strife that had broken out between Pandulf's sons over who should inherit the various principalities, but that did not need so many men. Rumours abounded. She heard that she wanted to claim Benevento and Capua for herself as part of her dowry. If so, she was the last to know of it and it was nonsense. She had no desire to live there and as imperial vassal states under Pandulf's sons, they were hers anyway. More worrying were persistent reports of increased raiding by the Shiite Fatimids into Calabria and even as far as Apulia, which Constantinople appeared to do nothing to check. Otto's army could be intended to fight this threat, but he could not do so without marching through Byzantine territory and breaking the marriage agreement.

By Christmas the host was in Naples, celebrating the feast peaceably as guests of the Byzantine governor of the independent city-state. While they were there, however, they heard that the Salernitans had driven out Otto's vassal, one of Pandulf's sons, and invited the Byzantine Duke of Amalfi to be their duke. The Empire had its just cause for war and when Otto heard rumours – accurate – of a secret treaty between the Saracens and the Byzantines, he did not stop at Salerno but marched on into Calabria.

Not everyone was happy with his decision. Theophanu opposed it and was convinced that Willigis, had he been there, would have supported her, even if only on the grounds of over-stretched supply lines. Otto of Swabia was also doubtful, because the West did not have even one battleship. Constantinople had the Imperial Navy and the Saracens had a huge fleet.

'We're not going to fight at sea,' Otto II pointed out in exasperation.

'So we shall move like tortoises while they zoom round the coast like hares,' retorted Swabia.

'You know who won in the end,' said the Emperor. 'My mind is made up. We have to defend the Christian people of Calabria and Apulia from infidel attack. If we don't tackle the problem now, then next it will be Benevento, then Rome itself. As their own government won't defend the Calabrians and Apulians, it's up to us. They'll be grateful to us.'

'Your Grace, I am a Calabrian myself,' interposed John Philagathos. 'I know these people. They are Greek-speaking, Greek-thinking, and always have been. They will not welcome a northern invasion.'

'They won't have any say in the matter when they've got five thousand armed knights crashing down on them,' observed Bishop Dietrich of Metz.

A chorus of approval greeted his words, led by the Dowager Empress Adelheid.

Otto and Theophanu had a heated argument that night in the privacy of their bedchamber. He agreed that there was a minor breach of morality in breaking the marriage treaty, but maintained that the greater good of driving the Fatimids out of the Italian peninsula far outweighed the breach. In vain did Theophanu reiterate the practical objections which had been raised at the council. Otto merely laughed until she said,

'Ottone, I think you underestimate the Saracens. They are brave, resourceful, and cunning foes.'

Otto stopped laughing.

'Is that why your father and uncle are so friendly with them?' he inquired nastily.

'You know as well as I do that they're using them to seek revenge. I don't condone their behaviour but the Abbassids are not the Fatimids. That's as silly as saying that the King of France and the King of England have the same interests because they're both Christians.'

'I need to have your support in this matter, because otherwise people will say that you truly support the Greeks and the Saracens.'

Otto's tone was grave and accusatory.

'Otto, you know that's not true. I have even less reason to like the present regime in Constantinople than you have. I admit I am uncertain of the morality of what you are doing, but my main objections are practical.'

'You doubt my military capacity.' Otto was angry now. 'It's fortunate, Madam, that the Empress my mother gives me her full support.'

Theophanu said no more; there was no point. She said nothing as they marched through Calabria to re-take Tarento from the Arabs. When they arrived in March 982 to find the Saracens gone and the city garrisoned by Byzantine troops, she did query the need for military action, but the momentum of the campaign was unstoppable. Otto's men stormed the town and took it. His troops erected a gaily-decorated city of tents around a central parade ground where they would celebrate Easter.

Before that, Otto issued a direct challenge to Constantinople, a decree describing himself as the 'most invincible Augustus and Emperor of the *Romans*'. He was deliberately re-igniting the old quarrel with Nicephorus Phocas about who were the true Romans. The next day scouts brought in the information that the Saracen Emir, Ab'ul Qasim had re-crossed the Straits of Messina from Sicily with his army. Otto's host, thousands of miles from home, was facing two dangerous enemies at once.

Theophanu was kept busy while they were in Tarento acting as an interpreter for the local people, who came flocking to the Saxon Emperor with complaints about the Byzantine Emperor's taxes and other exactions. She was aware from the glares of Bishop Dietrich of Metz and his party, who could not understand a word, that their suspicions of her were increasing and she was certain that they were the origin of the rumours Otto had mentioned. They detested Chancellor John Philagathos, who worked with the Empress on these cases, and she knew that gossip linking her name and his was beginning to circulate. It was an unpleasant situation and she was relieved when the whole army moved off south along the coast at the end of May. As always, she and the baby went too, watched over by a soldier called Nancilinus, whom Otto had appointed to be their special guard.

Ab'ul Qasim set up his main camp near to Sicily but some of his raiders occupied the fortress of Roseto northwards along the coast. Otto's first aim was to recapture the fortress, which he did easily. Ab'ul Qasim was stirred from his nest to try to reinforce Roseto before the imperial forces arrived but he was much too late. Otto had moved on south.

The imperial army was shadowed all through its march along the coast by ships of the Byzantine navy and this gave Otto an idea. He managed to bribe two of the captains to work for him as well by sending him word of the movements of the common enemy, the Saracens. The crucial question, of course, was whether the Saracens really *were* the common enemy, or whether the rumour of a secret alliance between Constantinople and the Fatamids was true. If so, any information would probably be disinformation. To guard against this, Otto stationed one of his knights, a Wendish seafarer from the Baltic coast called Henry Zolunta, on board one of the ships to check the captain's honesty.

The ship was of a type called a *cheladon*, a war-galley with raised decks fore and aft. It had two lateen-rigged triangular sails but also two decks of oarsmen on each side, one hundred and fifty men in all. The captain commanded from the raised rear deck, from where he could see both a wide expanse of sea and his crew down in the middle of the ship. On the forward deck was what made the ship really dangerous, the Greek fire machine. A metal-faced syphon, this could direct blasts of Greek fire, an explosive and combustible substance whose make-up was a closely guarded secret. It burned even in and on water and so it was impossible to extinguish and made the Navy an invincible force.

With these preparations in place, Otto continued his march to the estuary of the River Crati. Once this had been a fertile plain surrounding the city of Sybaris, but centuries ago the inhabitants had fled from the constant pirate attacks and now it was a malarial swamp, impassable at this time of year. Otto's men had no option but to turn up into the mountains and go upstream until they could cross, as their Lombard scouts assured them they could.

Otto now faced a critical decision. They could not take the baggage-train up into the hills. All the wagons and most of the supplies would have to go back to the fortified town of Rossano, along with the camp-followers. Theophanu and the baby would go with them. The army would then have to find Ab'ul Qasim and bring him to battle rapidly, before their food and water ran out.

Theophanu said goodbye to Otto in a clearing in the chestnut forest which covered the hills behind the coast. It blazed with clumps of yellow gorse and poppies and calendulas dotted the ground, an incongruously beautiful setting for their farewell. The rather sickly smell of the chestnut trees seemed more fitting.

They had quarrelled again the previous day when Otto had appointed Bishop Dietrich of Metz to oversee matters in Rossano in his absence. Dietrich was angry at the thought of missing the battle and Theophanu could not understand Otto's choice. From her point of view almost anyone else would have been preferable. Was it that Otto still did not fully trust her? Even so, she realised that it was possible that she might never see her husband again and she took care that their parting should not be marred by argument.

As she lifted Otto to receive his father's kiss, the little boy reached out to touch his father's gleaming helmet, which was fastened to his saddle. Both his parents caught their breath, and Theophanu knew that, like herself, Otto was remembering the famous passage in Homer where Hector bids farewell to his baby son, Astyanax, as he goes off to die in battle, and the baby reaches for the feathers in his father's helmet. For a moment the three of them clung desperately together in defiance of the sudden fear which overshadowed them, then Otto handed the child back to his mother.

'*Absit omen*,' he said to Theophanu with a crooked grin, then they turned to go their separate ways, Theophanu and the baby riding after a grim-faced Bishop Dietrich.

The next few days of waiting in Rossano were terrible. The weather turned unbearably hot. Theophanu divided her time between praying in the coolness of the church and standing on the ramparts gazing southwards over the plain. The town was built on a hill a little way inland but connected to its own little port on the coast. From the citadel she could see a long way and she paced up and down, hugging little Otto to her and trying to imagine what was happening.

On the evening of the fifteenth of July she was watching the sun set gloriously in the west. She started to murmur aloud the old Greek evening hymn 'O Jesus Christ, joyous light, holy glory of the eternal Father of the universe,' but when she reached the line 'We, having come to the setting of the sun,' her voice choked on a sob and she could not go on. She nearly jumped out of her skin when a rich male voice just behind her took up the hymn and finished it. She whirled round to find herself face to face with John Philagathos. As a monk, he would take no part in the battle.

'You startled me, Lord Chancellor,' she said, struggling to regain her composure.

'I have often watched you here and pitied your sadness,' he said in his deep voice. 'I wish you would allow me to comfort you'

'My only comfort will be the safe and victorious return of my lord,' replied Theophanu, 'but all is in the hands of God.'

'I think you need human comfort too,' he answered huskily and to her astonishment he seized her and forced his mouth down on hers. She knew that he had a poor reputation where women were concerned but he had never shown her any disrespect before. She shoved him away as strongly as she could and said icily,

'You forget yourself, Lord Chancellor.'

She turned sharply to leave the ramparts – only to see Bishop Dietrich blocking the top of the flight of steps she must pass.

'Is this how you think fit to behave as soon as your lord is absent?' he barked.

Theophanu managed to answer coldly,

'If you have been watching us, Lord Bishop, you will know that nothing has occurred. The Lord Chancellor forgot himself for a moment. We are all anxious at present'

'So why was he singing a lovesong?'

The scepticism in his voice made Theophanu realise that of course the encounter had been entirely in Greek; the bishop would not have understood a word. Well, there was no help for that. She was not going to justify herself to a man who had reputedly made a thousand pounds profit from a blatant case of simony.

'It was a hymn to Our Lord Jesus Christ, as I think you really know,' she said. 'Please allow me to pass.'

He drew aside, making his contempt plain, and Theophanu walked proudly away without a backward glance at either man.

The next morning any distress she felt was drowned out. The first survivors from the battle reached Rossano and they brought appalling news.

The army had met the Saracens on the coast near a headland called Cape Colonna after the remains of a temple to Juno which once stood on the promontory. By then the soldiers were thirsty and becoming hungry and the five thousand fully-armed knights, the panzers, were baking inside their mail-suits. Reports on the numbers of the enemy from both the Byzantine ships and the Lombard scouts tallied, however, and were much lower than expected. As the armies made camp on the fourteenth of July, hopes were high in the Christian army.

After Mass the next morning the two armies drew up in battle-order. The charge was sounded as the Emperor loosed his heavy brigade first, the panzers, a concentration of sheer force smashing into the Arab centre. The Saracens were much more lightly armed with small, round shields, mail-shirts, and closely-fitting helmets. Their horses were smaller and lighter and when the yellowish-grey cloud of dust raised by the imperial advance swept into them like a tornado, they broke apart, their banners trampled into the dust. Even the Emir's guard could not hold off the heavy arms despite gallant resistance and Ab'ul Qasim himself was killed. At this, his forces seemed to fall into complete disarray. Almost all of them, as if at a signal, wheeled their horses and fled, as the imperial axemen and archers poured in behind the panzers. It looked like an overwhelming victory for the Christians.

Theophanu's heart sank when she heard this. She could guess the sequel only too well. The tale went on as she expected. Otto's men abandoned the chase quickly, having little chance of catching the fleet Arab horses, and returned to the battlefield for the spoils. Most of them dismounted. Some removed their unbearably hot armour. All relaxed their guard and the generals set no watch.

Meanwhile, unseen behind the raised headland of the cape, the fleeing Saracens stopped their pretended flight and regrouped, along with the other half of their army waiting in ambush. They had failed to lure the imperial troops into their trap, but if they made a prompt counterattack, it would be just as effective. Furthermore they now had a personal motive for fighting, to avenge the death of the Emir, and they would give no quarter.

The early arrivals at Rossano were uninjured but as the day wore on, the casualties started to arrive. Although busy, like the other women, with cleaning and bandaging wounds, Theophanu heard enough to realise the full scale of the disaster. When Otto of Swabia rode in, towards the evening, he was able to give her a fairly coherent account, although he had no answer to the main question – what happened to the Emperor?

'We should have set guards,' Swabia said with bitter self-reproach, 'but we thought that if their lord was killed, they would just leave the fight. After all, that's how it was at home when we were pagan. You fought for your lord and safeguarded his corpse, but with that your obligation ended.'

'You couldn't have known,' said Bishop Dietrich.

'Otto could,' Theophanu said angrily. 'He knew about my uncle John's use of the feigned retreat at Adrianopolis and that he borrowed it from the Saracens.'

Bishop Dietrich glared at her and opened his mouth but Swabia shook his head wearily.

'Well', he said hopelessly. 'Some of our men had started to make camp, you see, and then suddenly this huge host came like lightning upon us. Many were killed before they could even reach for their swords or axes. It was utter chaos. Thousands must have died.'

'What of His Grace?' asked the bishop.

'We grouped round him and fought to the end. He did too. They killed Bishop Henry of Augsburg and the sons of Pandulf Ironhead but still we held our ground. Then an arrow shot the Emperor's horse from under him and Richer, the Bearer of the Holy Lance, was shot too. He just had time to toss it to me but we knew we could achieve no more. Six of us fought our way through to the coast, just north of the headland. Six men but only five horses. The Emperor was unhorsed but Calonymus of Mainz took him up on his.

'We had a few moments' grace – the Saracens were too busy taking prisoners. The Byzantine galleys the Emperor had hired were just off the shore. When he saw them, he ordered us all to leave him except Calonymus. With the horses we might still get away overland. So he and Calonymus stayed with one horse, while we escaped. He insisted, Lady. We had to obey him.'

He looked miserably at Theophanu, who stared at him horror-stricken as Bishop Dietrich asked,

'Did you see what happened? Did he hope the galley would put in for him?'

'No, it was too shallow. I looked back as I left and the Emperor was mounted on Calonymus' horse and urging it towards the sea. I think he meant the horse to swim him out to the galley and get away that way.' He knew the answer to his question before he asked. 'He has not arrived.'

'No.' The flat monosyllable was all there was to say.

Theophanu tried to pull herself together. 'Are you wounded, my lord? You must be tended. This Calonymus – a brave and faithful man. He's a Jew, isn't he?'

'Yes, from Mainz. Very brave. If the Emperor lives, he will owe his life to him.'

'He shall be well rewarded, if he survives himself. If not, I will take care of his family.' She turned to Dietrich of Metz. 'My lord, have we closed the gates in case the Saracens besiege us? I have been too busy with the wounded to know.'

'The walls are heavily guarded, Lady. We cannot close the city completely while so many survivors are still coming in, but I think we shall have to overnight.'

Theophanu nodded. 'See to it, please, Lord Bishop. I will go back to the injured. Come with me,' she added to Otto of Swabia. 'That cut on your arm looks as if it needs cleansing straightaway.'

Theophanu worked non-stop through the next twenty-four hours with the physicians and her ladies. She paused only to snatch a bite to eat and to cuddle little Otto when Anastaso brought him to her. It was a relief to know that Nancilinus had a horse ready and waiting to rush the child to safety if the Saracens did come.

Outwardly the Empress was grim-faced, calm, and supremely efficient. Inwardly Theophanu was both frightened and furious. Her thoughts veered between cursing Otto for his stupidity and poor generalship and desperate fears for his safety. She slept fitfully on the night of the sixteenth and when the next day dawned, it still brought no news of the Emperor.

CHAPTER EIGHTEEN

In the half-light before sunrise, a sentry on the ramparts of Rossano grasped his comrade's arm and pointed out to sea. A ship, a galley, heading for the port. Was it the first of the Saracen advance guard? Bishop Dietrich was summoned and, as the ship drew nearer, they could pick out its shape better. It was Byzantine – but that could mean friend or foe.

As the ship docked, there was a sudden flash of flame from its foredeck and the boom of the explosion reached the watchers on the hill a second later. The noise roused the sleepers of both port and town and soon the ramparts were crowded. There was obviously a parley of some kind going on on the dockside, before two little figures landed from the ship. Horses were brought and the two men leapt astride and galloped up towards the town.

As they drew nearer, Otto of Swabia, standing with Theophanu, Dietrich, and Philagathos, cried out,

'That's Zolunta! Henry Zolunta! He was the Emperor's man on the ship.'

The little group of leaders moved down to stand inside the main gate, which was opened just enough to allow the two riders in then slammed shut. Zolunta flung himself off his horse and knelt at Theophanu's feet.

'He's alive, Lady,' he panted. 'The Emperor's alive but in danger.'

Theophanu shut her eyes and for a moment the world seemed to whirl round her. This would not do! She breathed deeply and regained control.

'Where?' she asked.

'On the ship. I will tell you the whole story in a more private place.'

'Don't we need to act quickly?' asked Swabia.

'No, my lord Duke. There is time enough and you have to understand the situation.'

'Very well', said Theophanu. 'Come to my chamber, my lords. What about your companion, Sir? He is from the crew.'

'Yes, sent to watch me to ensure there is no double-dealing. Fortunately for us, he doesn't understand Saxon.'

'Good,' said Theophanu. Then to the sailor, in Greek, 'You will accompany us.'

His face brightened at hearing his own language and obediently he fell into place behind them. When they were all seated in Theophanu's private apartments, Bishop Dietrich said,

'So – what's happened?'

Zolunta sipped his wine gratefully and started his tale.

'When you and the others', - he nodded at Otto of Swabia, - 'left the Emperor on the beach, he intended to get out to the galley on Calonymus' horse, then send it back to give Calonymus a chance of escaping. As the horse swam, the Emperor struggled out of his armour and his cloak and cut his tunic free with his sword, so that he couldn't be identified. Then he let the horse go back and swam the last bit himself. By the time he reached the galley, there was nothing to identify him. The crew did not want the bother of picking up refugees, so they ignored him and sailed on. He could do nothing except swim back to the shore and wait for the Saracens. He thought Calonymus would have taken the horse and gone by then.

'When he got to the beach, he was astonished. Calonymus had seen what was happening and waited for him, even though the Saracens were already appearing in the distance. The Emperor says he had been on the point of giving up, but Calonymus' loyalty steadied him.

'By now my ship was sailing past and he and Calonymus recognised me on board. They knew that I would insist that he was taken up. Calonymus helped him to mount again, saying, "Take my horse and if they slay me, remember my sons." The Emperor promised that he would and plunged back into the sea. I watched it all from the galley. I could see his red head moving painfully slowly through the waves and I could see a troop of Saracens riding fast along the beach. When they reached Calonymus, he fought bravely, but they killed him, of course. At least he died quickly, as his courage deserved. They were armed with scimitars, not bows and arrows, and the Emperor was too far away for them to reach.

'The Emperor got to the ship and we lowered a rope for him. He was nearly naked and utterly exhausted. I wrapped my cloak round him and took him to the captain on the afterdeck. We tried to keep his identity secret but the captain had recognised him. In the end he asked straight out, "Are you the Emperor?" and His Grace wouldn't tell a direct lie. He answered, "I am the Emperor. My sins have brought me to this pass."'

The listeners said nothing. There was too much truth in Otto's comment for them to deny it. Theophanu smothered a sob as Zolunta went on,

'This was dangerous, of course. They were unlikely to hand him over to the Saracens, but their real loyalty is to Basil II, who would be very glad to get his hands on him. That would be almost as bad. In the end we did a deal. "I am only too willing to visit my dear brother, Basil II, in Constantinople," the Emperor said. "I am sure he will be a true friend to me in my need and I have no desire to go home, since I led my army to destruction. Few will wish to welcome me there, but first I need to stop at Rossano, which we must pass near. My beloved wife, who is a princess of your people, awaits me there. She too will want to visit her old home and she has the imperial treasury with her. With that, we can make a fitting gift to your emperor, who will of course reward you for your care of me." He knows, obviously, that the gold is unlikely ever to see Constantinople, but the captain has to keep up pretences too. So here am I, to collect the Empress and twelve chests of gold and silver.'

He stopped and grinned at the horrified outcry.

'We would just be hostages in Constantinople,' Theophanu said, 'that is, if Basil lets us live at all. At the very least, he would demand a huge ransom on top of the treasury.' She was appalled at the thought of being Basil's prisoner, especially after her father's treason.

'Oh, quite,' agreed Zolunta. 'That's where the Emperor's plan comes in. Don't worry, Madam. Nobody's going to Constantinople, certainly not you, but because of our sailor-friend here, we have to make it look as if we're playing along.'

The scheme Otto had devised seemed horribly risky to Theophanu but it was the best they could think of. Bishop Dietrich supervised the filling of twelve chests with treasure and had them loaded onto pack animals, while Theophanu selected appropriate imperial garments for Otto, an important part of the plan. Then she, Zolunta, Bishop Dietrich and two of his knights, both experienced sword-fighters, and the mule-train set off for the harbour. As they went, the two knights assessed the height of the ship, which was also important. High but not impossible, they judged.

When they reached the quayside, the Emperor appeared on the foredeck next to the Greek fire syphon at the highest point of the galley. He shouted that the captain would allow him only on that deck, because it was too high above the water for a rescue attempt to be made, but Bishop Dietrich and the two knights were to be allowed on board to parley. The Empress and Zolunta were to wait on the quayside with the treasure.

They had deliberately left some of the chests partly open, so that the gleam of the gold could be seen. It seemed to addle the crew's wits, because to the Saxons' astonishment, they did not take away their weapons when they went on board. As soon as they reached the captain, Bishop Dietrich insisted that the Emperor had to be given suitable clothing, before they would do any negotiating. Accustomed to the importance of ceremonial in the Eastern Empire, the captain considered this a reasonable request and the three Saxons were allowed up to the foredeck.

Theophanu watched from the quay as they appeared. She heard Bishop Dietrich say,

'Your Grace, I beg you to remove those unworthy garments.'

She saw Otto agree and the bishop move forward with the robes in his hands. Otto threw off Zolunta's cloak and pulled the salt-stained tunic over his head. Then he twisted like an eel, ran to the rails, leapt on them and dived overboard. A sailor grabbed at his ankle as he balanced on the rail, but Livo's sword slashed the man's neck open. The other sailors on the deck stood unable to believe their eyes and in that split second the three Germans pounced on them and hurled them down the companion-way onto the lower deck. This had the effect of knocking the men who were already trying to mount the stairs completely off balance.

Theophanu kept switching her gaze between Otto's head, swimming round the ship, and the three still on the boat. According to the plan, they should all have jumped by now, but Bishop Dietrich seemed to be hesitating. The deck was at least thirty foot above the water and Theophanu wondered how well he could swim, especially in the episcopal robes which he had had to wear to make the trick with clothes convincing. Delay was dangerous, however, and she was glad to see Livo and Richizo seize him and throw him into the sea. The delay allowed more sailors to reach the upper deck and the two knights cut down at least two each before they could reach the rail, where they balanced briefly then jumped themselves.

By now the captain had assembled his archers in the bows of the ship and a hail of arrows shot towards the figures in the water. The Emperor gained the shore and climbed onto the dockside, then, naked as he was, commandeered the nearest available horse and forced the terrified animal back into the water. The Bishop was thrashing around, trying to get rid of his heavy, embroidered cloak, and the sailors had now got the Greek fire machine working. Otto reached him through a storm of both arrows and the deadly clinging explosive. Like everyone else, Theophanu was shouting encouragement as he grasped Dietrich's cloak and pulled him to the shore. The garrison from the town had arrived now there was no more need for concealment and they dragged the Bishop from the water, while the Emperor went back through the Greek fire for the other two.

The archers were now shooting at the people on the quay and Theophanu leapt back just in time as a missile shot in front of her nose.

Once all four men were out of the water, the ship's crew lost heart and stopped their fire. Otto shouted mockingly,

'Here is the reward I promised.' He pointed to the treasure. 'If you want it, come and get it. We won't hurt you.'

Not surprisingly, the crew did not take him at his word. Already the rowers were taking them out of the harbour, as Otto finally turned to embrace his wife.

At first, of course, there was euphoria. The sheer daring of the escape had them all beside themselves with excitement and the story in all its detail was told and re-told endlessly. Eventually, however, the excitement cooled and the mood of all the leaders was subdued when they met to consider what to do next.

Judging from the number of survivors who had made it back to Rossano, the casualty list was dreadful. Nineteen princes, counts and bishops were known to be dead and others had been taken prisoner and would be sold into slavery. Thousands of ordinary knights and men-at-arms had been killed; thousands more enslaved.

'Why can we not ransom at least some of them?' demanded Otto.

John Philagathos explained. 'They will not accept ransoms, Your Grace. In their eyes the killing of the Emir turned the battle into a holy war, jihad. Ransom would not be fitting.'

There was silence until Bishop Dietrich broke it.

'We must not be too cast down,' he said. 'Our cause is just and the Emperor has set us a wonderful example of courage in the face of adversity. We must not be down-hearted now.'

Otto of Swabia grimaced. 'Nobody disputes the Emperor's outstanding courage, or indeed your own, Lord Bishop.'

There was a murmur of agreement, even from Theophanu. Dietrich was no longer young and it had transpired that he could hardly swim at all. He had behaved heroically, as had the Emperor on a personal level.

'But...' Swabia went on, 'the truth is that the defeat was avoidable and we generals were at fault.'

140

Dietrich glared furiously at Swabia, and at Theophanu, who was sitting next to him and had failed to restrain a slight nod of agreement. The Empress was the first to break the awkward silence.

'The fact is, my lords,' she said, 'that despite the enormous courage displayed by you all, we are actually the remnants of a defeated army trapped in the midst of a hostile populace, thousands of miles from home. We have to retreat, at least out of Calabria.'

'Is that so that your father's friends, the Saracens, can walk in unopposed?' asked Bishop Dietrich. 'Or is it your imperial cousins and compatriots you're making it ready for?'

'Enough!' snarled the Emperor but the Bishop ignored him.

'The Empress never wanted us to be here in the first place, but she spent her time enjoying herself in Rossano while brave men were dying for your safety at Cape Colonna.'

'That's outrageous!' burst out Otto of Swabia. 'The Empress exposed herself to danger on the dockside, by all accounts, and I saw myself how hard she worked in the infirmary. You should apologise to her, my lord.'

Theophanu stared Dietrich firmly in the eyes. If you have a valid accusation to make, then make it, her gaze said. After a moment he looked away and mumbled what might have been an apology. Theophanu said,

'There is no need for apologies between us. We have no time for quarrels now. The important thing is to work out how to get the Emperor and the Prince to safety.'

'No!' said Otto II. 'We should stay here and send for reinforcements.'

Now there was an outcry. Philagathos' voice was the loudest in warning that the Calabrians would turn against them now their weakness was revealed. Otto of Swabia said it was not just the Calabrians.

'When the news reaches home, Sir, there could be rebellion, and messengers will need to get to you quickly. I'm worried about the Wends we have with us.'

Everyone looked at him in surprise. 'But without Henry Zolunta the Emperor would have been lost,' protested Theophanu.

'Oh, certainly. I'm not questioning *his* loyalty, but several of the Wendish tribes are forced allies. Their hearts are not really with the Empire and when their comrades get back from here with the message that we are not invincible, I fear the whole northern border could be endangered. All the lands east of the Elbe conquered by your father, Your Grace.'

Otto knew this was true. The north-eastern marches were held down by force and an absent emperor always presented an opportunity to insurgents. In the end, reluctantly, he agreed. He would withdraw as far as Benevento or Capua.

'I'll be back, though,' he concluded the meeting. 'Young Basil needn't think he's seen the last of me.'

CHAPTER NINETEEN

The court stayed the whole autumn in Capua, soon joined by the Empress Adelheid once she heard of the defeat. Otto sent messenger after messenger to Germany demanding reinforcements and Adelheid supported him in this against the wishes of her daughter-in-law. As a result Theophanu became isolated within the family. Otto treated her with cold politeness, describing her in his decrees as his 'housemate', no longer his 'most beloved wife'.

Bitterly hurt by this, she spent most of her time with Imiza and Anastaso, Emilia having returned to Constantinople, saying that she was getting old and wanted to die in her own place. Little Otto's education took up much of their time. He could already chatter in both Saxon and Italian and toddled round the courtyard, enthusiastically slashing the air, endangering anyone foolish enough to venture within range of his wooden sword. His great delight was a diminutive pony, imported from the far north of Britain, on which he would perch proudly. He was an affectionate and demonstrative child, rewarding to teach, but still Theophanu ached for her former closeness to Otto. One thing was sure; at this rate little Otto was never going to have a brother. More than their lovemaking, though, she missed the adult male companionship to which she had become accustomed. Otto, Duke of Swabia, who had been such a friend from the early days of her marriage, had started for home already. She felt that he might have been a bridge between the Emperor and herself, but all such hopes vanished for ever in November with the terrible news that Swabia had fallen ill in Lucca at the end of October and died within two days. The mosquitoes of the Crato Estuary were continuing their devastating work. Nor was Otto of Swabia's the only death amongst those returning home. To Theophanu it seemed as if the whole world of her married life was falling apart. She longed for her daughters; she longed for the north.

'It's strange,' she said to Imiza and Anastaso one day. 'I never thought I would feel homesick for the north, but now even mile on mile of forest seems appealing. Or the gentle heat around Lake Constance, or the green of the meltwater in the rivers in spring. Or boys sliding on frozen ponds in your part of the world, Imiza. Real winter, not this cold drizzle.'

'You don't yearn for Constantinople, then, Lady?' asked Imiza.

'No, I couldn't bear such an enclosed life any more. Anna's letters often seem to me to be about nothing but trifles. No, it's the north I miss. We must take you and show you your home, little fellow,' she added, picking up the child, who was trying to crawl into her lap.

Eventually the disastrous year of 982 drew to an end. Otto's demands for more troops were not answered. Instead his lords insisted on a meeting of the whole Imperial Council, the Diet, to be held at Verona in May. They insisted that no decisions were to be made until after the meeting, which infuriated the Emperor, who could nevertheless do nothing about it. Fortunately, and rather inexplicably, the Saracens had withdrawn to Sicily after the battle and so far had not returned to Calabria.

The imperial party set out for Verona in late spring. They arrived to find the little town bursting at the seams. Verona was unusual in that many of its buildings had survived intact from Roman times, but the whole Imperial Council and each member's retinue could not all be accommodated within the city walls. The imperial family stayed in royal apartments attached to the Abbey of St. Zeno just outside the gate, but most people were in tents.

There were many joyful reunions. Theophanu was delighted to see Otto's sister, Abbess Matilda of Quedlinburg, again. Apart from their long-standing friendship, Matilda had recent news and a message from young Adelheid, now six years old and able to form her letters. Otto of Carinthia had also come to the Council and Theophanu felt that the various strands of her disrupted family life were beginning to come back together. Best of all was to have Archbishop Willigis' reassuring presence with them once more. She trusted his judgement and hoped that Otto might actually listen to him.

Looking round the council-hall Theophanu realised that several leading figures from Saxony were absent. When she asked Willigis, he confirmed it with a sigh.

'Duke Bernhard Billung and Margrave Dietrich of the Nordmark are the main ones missing,' he told her.

Theophanu gasped. To refuse the Emperor's summons to court was tantamount to rebellion.

'No, no,' said Willigis, seeing her expression. 'They're not the rebels. They set out to come but on the way they had word that Swein Forkbeard of Denmark was overrunning the border towards the Elbe. Yes, Swein Forkbeard, your husband's godson,' he added with a bitter grin. 'The latest report is that Prince Mistui and his Abodrites have joined him now they're back from Calabria – if in fact they didn't start the whole thing.'

'The Wends,' said Theophanu slowly. Willigis looked at her, a little surprised.

'Yes. Mistui's lot are. Swein's are Danes, of course.' She must surely know that.

'I know. The point is that this is what Duke Otto foresaw before he died – that the Wends would carry the news of the defeat back and the whole frontier would rise.'

Willigis grunted agreement. 'It didn't need supernatural powers to see that,' he said dryly. 'Still, let's hope they've started their push too soon. They should have made sure Duke Bernhard was on the other side of the Alps before they rose. When the Emperor is back, things may quieten down.'

'I don't think he intends to come north yet. He wants more reinforcements to come south.'

'So he said. Well, he won't get them. If he's not careful, he won't even have a north to get back to.'

'But he's the Emperor.' Much as she disagreed with Otto, Theophanu's mind, formed in Byzantium, simply assumed that in the end the Emperor's will was law.

'And this is the council and electoral assembly of the Empire,' retorted Willigis. 'He will have to negotiate.'

Theophanu realised what he meant as the Council went on. The word 'reinforcements' was never so much as mentioned. In the minds of those assembled, the main purpose of the Diet was to settle the succession, although this matter was actually left till last. If the Emperor wanted his son to succeed him, then he had to listen to the Council.

On the first morning Theophanu sat as Empress at Otto's right-hand side as he declared the Assembly open. She was one of several women present and able to speak: Empress Adelheid, of course; Abbess Matilda; and Duchess Beatrice of Upper Lotharingia, who governed as regent for her young son.

The Council's first business was to appoint members to replace those who had died at Cape Colonna or in the months since, chief amongst them Otto of Swabia and Bavaria. The Emperor was not prepared to entrust such a huge power bloc to any other single person. In the end he had to divide the duchy, giving both halves to members of the local ruling dynasties, rather than to members of his own Liudolfing family. Although his nephew still ruled Carinthia, the appointments represented a definite reduction in Liudolfing power and a reversal of the policy established by Otto the Great. It was undoubtedly a snub to the defeated emperor and he felt it so.

The next item on the agenda was the reception of foreign embassies. First came the Venetians. Venice had been rising in importance for decades, eclipsing Ravenna, but since the days of the Exarchate it had been close to the Eastern Empire. A pro-Byzantine party was in fact in power now, but nevertheless the City Fathers had judged it wise to maintain a treaty of trade and mutual protection with the West. Both Theophanu and Adelheid spoke in favour of this. Theophanu felt a slight resolving of her ambivalent attitudes towards her homeland as a result.

The Venetians were followed by the Bohemians, who had come to request imperial endorsement of a new bishop for Prague. Adalbert, the chosen candidate, was making history, because his given name was Voitech. He was a converted Slav nobleman, the first time a native convert had been appointed to such a post within the Empire. Theophanu saw the appointment as a step towards independent churches on the Byzantine model, even if under the nominal oversight of the Bishop of Rome, and was sure that such an approach was more likely to Christianise Bohemia than the imposition of direct control from the Empire.

With these matters out of the way, the real business started. The Empire needed to know who would succeed Otto in the event of his death. The defeat had made everyone even more than usually aware of the fragility of human life. Used to the hereditary nature of the Byzantine monarchy, Theophanu had not really registered that in Germanic society any man of the royal kin could succeed; the idea of election was not just a formality. Her little Otto was the likely choice but it was by no means inevitable.

The most vociferous opposition to him came from those who argued that the chosen successor should be a man of already proven capability. (The proven man they usually had in mind was Otto's cousin, Henry, onetime Duke of Bavaria, still in prison in Utrecht.) The point was made repeatedly by speakers such as Archbishop Egbert of Trier, Bishop Dietrich of Metz, and other churchmen. If the Emperor should die before the heir reached maturity, the result would be chaos for the Empire. There had to be strong, experienced hands on the reins for the sake of all. Theophanu suspected that an unspoken rider was that the succession of a king still in his minority would give his mother too much power in the eyes of the Church, especially if the said mother happened to be Greek.

Other speakers, among them Willigis, Gerbert of Bobbio, Otto of Carinthia, and Abbess Matilda, pointed out the hypothetical nature of the objection. The Emperor was in his late twenties and in robust health and his son was already three years old. It was reasonable to expect at least two decades in which the prince could be groomed for his eventual role, and so the anticipated difficulties would simply not arise.

This viewpoint finally prevailed. Both Theophanu and Otto were beginning to relax, when the Archchancellor stood up to speak. What he had to say came as a complete bolt out of the blue to them both. After expressing his pleasure at the Diet's decision, Willigis continued,

'Nevertheless we cannot deny that the events of the past year have caused great disquiet north of the Alps. Germania needs you home, Your Grace. At the very least, the little prince must come back. The Council wishes him to be reared as a prince and knight of the Empire amongst his own people. If they never see him, how can they learn to trust him to deliver justice and to defend them? How can he understand our laws and customs if he can barely speak our language?'

There was a unanimous chorus of approval. It seemed the only ones silent were the two empresses and Otto himself. All the blood had drained from the Emperor's face, whether from shock or fury Theophanu could not tell. Finally he rose to his feet, bringing the whole assembly to theirs.

'I intend to continue my campaign against the infidel and their collaborators in Southern Italy,' he announced bitingly. 'I campaign on behalf of the Roman Empire of the West and I wish my son to be brought up in the heartland of that empire.'

'First he will be King of Germany, then Emperor of the Romans, Your Grace,' replied Willigis imperturbably. Again there was a swelling murmur of agreement.

'Is that a condition of his succession?'

'Yes, Sir. Obviously he is Your Grace's son. You may choose to keep him in Italy, but not as your heir.'

John Philagathos stood up. 'My Lord Archchancellor,' he protested, 'surely you are being too high-handed. The Prince will not be King of Germania alone but of Germany and the Italian Kingdom. Why should one half of the Empire be preferred to the other?'

Willigis hesitated. It was so obvious to him that the real seat of the Empire's power was in Germany but an Italian could be expected to see it differently. How could he put it tactfully?

'Italy is more settled, at the heart of the civilised world,' he said. 'You have the Lord Pope and centuries of tradition to keep government running smoothly. In the North the person of the Emperor is paramount.'

The Patriarch of Aquileia intervened.

'I see the truth of what you say, Lord Archchancellor.' His tone implied 'you barbarian', but at least he did not say it. 'I also see that the Italian lords will feel no need of loyalty to a prince who is not their crowned king.'

'That has been considered, My Lord Patriarch,' Willigis answered. 'When the Prince is crowned co-king at Aachen, I propose that Archbishop John of Ravenna conduct the service jointly with me, to symbolise the two crowns.'

'Is he never to become co-emperor?' asked Otto sarcastically.

'In due course in Rome, Your Grace, with the consent of the Lord Pope.'

Theophanu rose to speak. 'Lords, ladies, you must see that this is a weighty decision for His Grace and me. I request an adjournment so that we may discuss the proposal privately.'

Willigis looked at Otto, who nodded. 'We shall re-convene in an hour,' the Archchancellor announced. When they were alone Otto's fury exploded in fluent curses for several minutes. Theophanu waited for the storm to subside, then said,

'Otto, will you not re-think? If we *all* go home, nothing is lost.'

She knew she was risking re-awakening all his old suspicions of her treachery, but the thought of being parted from her son was unbearable. Otto was adamant, however.

'I can't back down, so we will have to let the boy go.'

Theophanu's cry of protest interrupted him. He crossed the room and put his arm round her shoulders.

'Why are you so upset? You left the girls behind without objecting.'

'I thought we would be gone for only a few months, not years, and we had to let the girls go to school anyway. Even so, it wasn't easy, but Otto's case is different.'

'Not that different,' said the Emperor. 'He'll have to start his knightly training in a year or two wherever he is. You can't keep him fastened to your skirts.'

'I don't want to,' snapped Theophanu angrily, 'but I don't want to miss the few years I am allowed to have him.'

'So you go back and I'll stay. Why not? Everyone else seems to be leaving me.'

Theophanu sighed. *'Ubi tu Gaius, ego Gaia,'* she said, quoting the old Roman marriage vow. 'You are the Emperor; I am the Empress. You know I will not leave you.'

Otto's face softened. 'Thank you,' he said more gently. 'The boy will be all right, my love. Willigis will look after him and once he is safely anointed and crowned, maybe I can get him back here.'

Theophanu was silent. Otto's pledged word seemed to mean less and less to him, as she suspected Willigis knew well. It was the way of the world but it marked a change in the man she loved.

Otto stood up. 'We'd better go and draw up an agreement,' he said. 'At least the boy is guaranteed the succession. That's a huge point gained. As far as the future is concerned, who knows?'

The negotiations led to little Otto's being elected unanimously by both churchmen and laymen, but some of the provisions worried his mother. She was reassured that he would travel to Germany under the care of Archbishop Willigis but on arrival he would be transferred to the foster-care of Archbishop Warin of Cologne, a supporter of Henry the Wrangler and no true friend to the imperial family. She objected but the Council insisted. She guessed it was the price for allowing the Archbishop of Mainz to officiate at the coronation, a prerogative Cologne also claimed.

The coronation would take place on Christmas Day in the Palace Chapel in Aachen, where Otto the Great had been crowned and Charlemagne was buried. By then the little boy would be three and a half. First though, now in Verona, his election had to be ratified by the Council and the people, and the nobles would swear homage to him.

Theophanu sent a message to Anastaso and the child was hastily fetched from play, scrubbed, and dressed in his best clothes, a long tunic of fine light-green linen and a red cloak fastened over one shoulder. Her eyes misted with tears as he was brought into the hall, looking about him curiously and confidently. He was so tiny to be sent such a long way.

A chair was placed for him next to his father and there he sat, his legs dangling, looking round questioningly at his mother. One by one all the venerable bishops and grizzled warriors of the Imperial Council knelt before the child. Each put his hardened and calloused hands inside little Otto's soft, chubby ones and swore to be his man. Theophanu's were not the only moist eyes; some of the grimmest and most ambitious lords felt a temporary softening of their hearts.

At the end the boy was led outside the hall to receive the acclamation of the people. In this case the only 'people' present were the knights and retainers of the councillors, but legally they were enough. Otto was by now thoroughly confused, but decided he liked all the attention he was getting and waved happily to acknowledge the shouts of 'Vivat.'

It was a different story a few days later when the time for parting came and the Council broke up. His parents, his attendants, and Archbishop Willigis had carefully explained to him that he was to be king and so could not stay with his parents, and he had seemed to understand and accept it. The reality came hard to him, however, although for a three-year-old he showed unnatural dignity. His white strained face told its own story. As he rode away, perched in front of Nancilinus, who had guarded him since Rossano, he constantly twisted round to look back. For his sake Theophanu and Otto kept their expressions cheerful but it broke their hearts to see the little auburn head bobbing away.

The saddened atmosphere grew even darker when Abbot Maiolus of Cluny came to say his farewells. The elderly man, revered for his holiness and reforming zeal, suddenly leaned across from his saddle and grasped the Emperor's arm.

'I beg of you, Your Grace,' he said urgently, 'do not go to Rome. If you enter the city, you will never see your home again.'

Otto stared at him, transfixed. Then his mind started to work. Was this a warning of a plot or had the abbot had a vision? Or was it a last attempt by Willigis and his supporters to get him to go home? After a moment he laughed uneasily and moved his arm.

'I have no intention of going to Rome, Lord Abbot,' he said. 'My way lies to the far south along the Adriatic shore and I must be upon it. I thank you for your concern, but there is no need to fear for me.'

For all his brave words, the imperial cavalcade, which set off for Ravenna the next morning, rode unusually quietly. At best they had missed the chance to go home. At worst, who knew what might happen? In their bones the Saxons amongst them knew that mighty Fate overrules all things. So, she feared, did the Greek empress.

CHAPTER TWENTY

Looking back, it seemed to Theophanu as if every step of that journey was marked by omens of disaster. It started just outside Ravenna, where they were intercepted by a group of Venetian nobles led by a man called Stefano Coloprini. He was opposed to the pro-Byzantine faction in power in Venice, with which Otto had just signed a treaty. Coloprini claimed to have urgent business to discuss with the Emperor and that evening they had a long, private meeting, from which Otto emerged with a satisfied grin on his face. He immediately summoned a messenger and sent him to Otto of Carinthia, ordering the Duke to blockade Venice. Carinthia extended right down to the sea and included the Venetian hinterland.

As they rode on the next morning, Theophanu observed acidly that he had signed a trade and protection agreement with the Doge only a month ago, and by any standards a treaty was supposed to hold longer than a month.

'Not if there's a fleet involved, my dear,' said Otto cheerfully.

'What fleet?'

'The Venetian fleet. One of the best in the world. The blockade will bring Venice to its knees rapidly, because they have to import almost all their food, and then I shall make Coloprini Doge and he will lend me his fleet to deal with the Saracens – and any other troublesome powers in that region. You were always saying that I was mad to fight the Saracens without ships. Now I've listened to you and you still don't seem to be happy.'

'What about your precious honour?' asked Theophanu rather spitefully.

'Honour is determined by the greater good.'

'You mean, you want your own way at all costs,' retorted Theophanu.

'You've turned into a shrew since the child left. I see little profit in your company, if you can't be pleasant.'

'As Your Grace wishes,' answered Theophanu crisply and dropped back to ride beside John Philagathos. She still did not really like or trust him, but at least they thought alike over Calabria.

While they made their way south, the situation in Germany continued to deteriorate. Prince Mistui had indeed joined with Swein Forkbeard and together they sacked and burned Hamburg, the crucial trading centre between the North Sea and the Baltic. Even worse than that, the Christian Abodrites were joined in rebellion by a still pagan tribe, the Redarii. Encouraged by their success all the Wendish tribes east of the Elbe rose in revolt. The Germanic settlements there were actually quite few and isolated, and through the summer news kept on arriving of yet another loss – Havelburg, Brandenburg, the Abbey of St. Lawrence at Calbe were all fallen by August. Everywhere the idols of the Slavic gods Radigast and Swaroziyc were re-erected and some of the captured clergy were sacrificed to them. In Brandenburg the corpse of the former bishop was dragged from its tomb and desecrated.

'Surely we should go back now,' Theophanu urged. 'Who knows how far the insurrection will spread?'

Otto hesitated. In truth he was well aware that by the time they got back, it could be too late.

'We'll wait a few more days,' he decided. 'Perhaps matters will become a bit clearer by then.'

They did but not in a way anybody expected. The next messages from the north were more encouraging; a force under Duke Bernhard of Saxony had driven the invaders back across the Elbe, so that the original Saxon lands were safe. All Otto the Great's conquests, however, and all the work of the missionaries he had sent out, remained lost.

'This is largely the fault of Margrave Dietrich,' Otto said angrily to Theophanu. 'If he hadn't overtaxed them so much, they would have seen the benefit of staying with us.' Theophanu nodded agreement. 'My great-uncle Nicephorus made the same mistake,' she said. 'That's why he had no support when the crunch came.'

'All the same, I have to find land to reward my vassals with. If it's not the Nordmark, I'll have to find it in Southern Italy.'

'You *do* intend to take the South from the Empire!' Theophanu was startled by his admission into using the wrong term.

'I intend to take it from *Constantinople* and restore it to the *Roman Empire of the West*, where it naturally belongs. I need more land, Theophanu. The Empire can't function without it.'

'But wouldn't it be better to...'

Otto interrupted her. They were standing on the old Roman walls of Fano, a little fishing-port on the Adriatic where the Via Flaminia reached the sea. From there they had a good view of the road coming from the distant Appenines and for some time Otto had been watching a group of men approaching at speed along it. Now they had come near enough for him to see that they were wearing papal colours.

'It's a message from the new pope,' he said. 'There must be more trouble. Just what we need.'

He was correct. Benedict VII, that scholarly, peace-making man, acceptable to most parties, had died, unexpectedly but apparently naturally, in the summer. An unusual achievement for a pope to die naturally, thought Theophanu cynically. Abbot Maiolus of Cluny was proposed in his place, but he declined the honour because of his great age. Otto then suggested and imposed the nomination of his mother's friend, Bishop Peter of Pavia. The appointment had proved controversial.

Only the previous day Otto had shown Theophanu a letter from Gerbert, stuck at his Abbey of Bobbio which he hated. It complained bitterly that Gerbert and his monks were starving to death, because of the excessive taxes and the depredation of land which Peter of Pavia and his patroness Empress Adelheid had inflicted on the abbey. Moreover, added Gerbert, the Lombards were openly referring to the Emperor as a donkey for appointing the tyrants. Gerbert was a great supporter of the royal house. If even he was against Peter's appointment, it was not hard to imagine how much the Roman aristocracy must object to it.

155

That was indeed the envoys' message. Yet again the Pope needed the Emperor's support against the Roman factions and they carried an urgent appeal for the Emperor to come to Rome. Theophanu gasped in horror when she heard that.

'My Lord, remember Abbot Maiolus' warning,' she murmured in a low voice, so that only he could hear.

He smiled reassuringly. 'Maiolus is an old man and becomes fearful,' he whispered back. 'What was the state of affairs in Rome when you left?' he asked the envoy aloud.

'Very uneasy, your Grace. There is much violence in the streets and people are saying that the antipope, Boniface VII, has been seen in the city, as well as a lot of Constantinopolitans.'

'There you are,' said Otto to his wife with a certain air of triumph. 'Basil hasn't given up the fight, any more than I have.'

'It's only a rumour,' protested Theophanu. Honesty obliged her to add, 'but it's probably true.'

Hand of Fate or not, the outcome was inevitable. Against all their intentions and inclinations, they went to Rome, despite Abbot Maiolus' prophecy.

At first all seemed well. They reached the city without incident and the Emperor's presence quieted the restive Romans. Boniface had vanished, if indeed he had ever been there in the first place. They heard from Willigis that young Otto had reached Cologne safely, was settling in well, and all was in hand for the coronation at Christmas. Then Otto II fell ill.

One foggy evening at the very end of November he seemed unusually tired and complained of a headache. By the next morning he was feverish and all his muscles were aching. Most uncharacteristically he agreed to stay in bed all day and seemed to improve slightly over the next two days. On the third day, however, the fever returned and ran much higher. Theophanu and Abbess Matilda, who was still with them, were seriously worried by now. Matilda suggested sending for another doctor to aid the Emperor's own physicians.

'He trained at Salerno,' she said, 'and people say he's the best in the city.'

'It's worth trying,' said the Empress. 'My fear is that it's the same swamp-fever that killed Duke Otto last year.'

'And so many others,' agreed Matilda. 'Well, God knows the local doctors should be experienced at treating it. There's enough of it about in Italy.'

'Yes, but it's strange. Only Germans seem to suffer from it.'

'True,' said Matilda. 'Perhaps it's a sign we should all go home.'

A sudden rush of tears prevented Theophanu from answering. Matilda's words recalled Abbot Maiolus' warning too strongly.

When the doctor came, he examined the patient then shook his head gravely.

'It is indeed a swamp-fever caused by bad air, as you feared, Lady,' he said. 'Whether he brought it from the south, as you think, or from the marshes of the Po Valley, or even from the Campagna, I don't know, but it has established a firm grip on him. We shall need desperate measures to save him. I will prescribe a dosage of four drachms of aloes, but the outcome is in the hands of God.'

'Four drachms?' exclaimed Matilda. 'That's a huge dose.' Like many religious, she had considerable medical knowledge.

'He's very ill, Lady Abbess,' said the doctor simply.

The treatment made the patient worse rather than better, and the next time the fever returned, he became delirious. The doctors admitted failure and it was time for the priests to take over. On December 6th, a bitterly cold but bright day, Otto rallied a little and became lucid. He asked the Pope and everyone else crowded into his chamber to leave him alone with his wife for a moment and suddenly they were surrounded by silence.

Theophanu took his wasted hand in both of hers, leaned over the bed and kissed him. His eyes flickered open again.

'Forgive me,' he whispered.

'Of course, my love. And you me.'

157

His parched lips parted in a painful smile. 'I've always loved you. It was politics drove us apart.'

Theophanu choked. 'Not any more, not ever,' she murmured.

'Pray for my soul and guard little Otto's inheritance,' he entreated her. As she nodded, he went on 'Now call the others back. I haven't got long.'

She did as he asked. Otto, in his hoarse voice, divided his personal property between the Church, his mother, his sister Matilda, and the poor. His wife and children were already well-provided for. Then, divested of all his earthly grandeur, he made his final confession. The Pope gave him absolution, he received the viaticum, and was anointed with holy oil. After that, it was a question of waiting. His exhausted body could no longer fight the fever; the convulsions became more extreme until he finally lost consciousness. On December 7th came a succession of harsh, rattling breaths, followed by silence. Otto II's earthly life was over.

For some time Theophanu and Matilda stayed by his bedside, stunned. Despite the few days' preparation, his actual death was a shock. Otto was still a young man in the prime of his life, only twenty-eight years of age. In her grief Theophanu forgot the ambitious and ruthless politician he was becoming and remembered only the handsome, laughing boy she had married, or the proud, indulgent young father. Where had it all gone wrong? Where had she learnt to be the bitter shrew he had once called her? As the first, numbed shock wore off, she wept for the sheer pity of it all.

Matilda crossed the room and gently put her arms round her sister-in-law.

'Come, child, we must leave now so they can prepare his body. Come to my chamber and weep your fill, then we must take thought for what is to happen.'

Still sobbing, Theophanu allowed herself to be led from the room. Yes, there was the funeral to organise; at least she could do that for him. But more urgently she needed to pray for his soul as it faced judgement.

Matilda was in full agreement there but demurred at Theophanu's wish to go to the monastery of Saints Alexis and Boniface.

'It's too dangerous and it will look bad,' she said flatly. 'We don't actually know where Boniface VII is' – by which she meant that, if he was anywhere, he was probably hidden in Alexis and Boniface – 'and you mustn't seem to give any encouragement to him. Pope John's position is shaky enough as it is.'

'Politics!' Theophanu burst out with passionate disgust. 'Can't I even mourn my own husband as I wish?'

'No, Madam, not while you are the Empress,' Matilda answered quietly.

Her calm reasonableness stirred memories of Philip in Theophanu's mind. She gave one more shuddering sob, then smiled tremulously at Matilda.

'Of course you are right, sister,' she said. 'You should not need to teach me my duty, but it is so hard.'

Matilda nodded. 'Think of the boy,' she advised practically. 'We must be strong for him, you above all, but first we will pray for my brother's soul in St. Peter's.'

There was so much to do so quickly. Messengers went off all over the Empire, especially to Empress Adelheid in Pavia and to Willigis in Aachen preparing for the child's coronation on Christmas Day. The three little girls also had to be told that they were fatherless. Interim decisions had to be made about the Venetian blockade, which was causing famine, and about the security of Rome itself. Pro-Byzantine factions were at work in the city the minute the news of the Emperor's death was made public.

Theophanu's days were frantic but her nights were also troubled. She had a succession of disturbing dreams in which St. Lawrence, the patron saint of the Ottonian dynasty, appeared to her with his right arm mangled and bleeding. He said,

'Why do you not ask who I am?'

'I do not dare, my Lord.'

159

'I am Lawrence,' the saint said. 'What you see in me was done by your lord. He was led astray by the words of a man who has caused great discord amongst the chosen of Christ.'

Then he disappeared. Theophanu remembered the dream in great detail the next morning and puzzled over it. It could mean so many things but it certainly increased her unease about Otto's soul. No king could always rule in accordance with the teachings of Christ and he was bound to have much to answer for at judgement.

Even in winter the funeral could not be too long delayed. Otto had asked to be buried at the entrance to the *paradisum* or courtyard garden of St. Peter's. It was a sign of humility that he did not request burial inside the church, yet he wished to be near the grave of the Prince of the Apostles. Above the tomb Theophanu commissioned a mosaic of Christ himself, standing offering a blessing to all the faithful who entered St. Peter's Church. The body was placed in an antique stone sarcophagus, which was then covered with a lid of the most precious red porphyry marble, the imperial stone. His mortal remains would lack no honour that could be paid to them; his widow prayed fervently that his immortal part would fare equally well.

Even before the notes of the requiem mass had died away, the Crescentii, the leaders of the opposition in Rome, were driving clergy appointed by Otto's popes from their parishes. Pope John seemed powerless to stop them and in the middle of the month Imiza, Theophanu's lady-in-waiting and friend, received a letter from Gerbert warning the Empress that anti-imperial forces were closing the roads to the north of Rome. Unless she wished to be trapped, she needed to move quickly. Theophanu was reluctant to leave her husband's grave so soon and felt responsible for the safety of the Pope, but Matilda and Imiza between them organised the move and presented the Empress with a *fait accompli*.

Their destination was Pavia, where the Dowager- Empress awaited them. Mother- and daughter-in-law clung together in genuine sorrow and sympathy. They spent a quiet, joyless Christmas praying for the soul of one emperor and for the well-being of the other, the three-year-old who was being made King of the Germans and the Italians that very day so far away. So the year ended with even more grief than there had been at its beginning.

CHAPTER TWENTY-ONE

As the bell of the Palace Chapel in Aachen rang out to welcome Christmas morning, a huge crowd gathered in the courtyards outside. At the west door a throne had been erected and a little boy, dressed in his finest clothes, sat in it. To his right and left towered the Archbishops of Mainz and Ravenna, tall men made even more imposing by their mitres and brocaded copes. As in Pavia, Otto's nobles knelt before him one by one to swear allegiance to him, only this time most of them were Germans, not Italians. The child had no difficulty with this part of the ceremony; he had done it once already and he did not have to say anything. Occasionally he glanced across the square at Nancilinus, waiting in the queue to pay homage. As Otto II had promised, the soldier had been rewarded with land for his guardianship of the boy, but to Little Otto Nancilinus was a living link with his parents and with a land where the sun seemed always to be shining. He was reassured by his guard's grave nod of approval.

Once the oath-swearing was finished, Willigis indicated to the child to rise. It was a clear, crisp day and the sun was now high enough to shine into the square. A shaft of sunlight caught Otto's red-gold hair as he moved into position behind the two archbishops and the men carrying the cross and the gospelbook. To either side walked thurifers swinging censers. Fragrant smoke filled the courtyard.

Inside the dark, eight-sided church Otto remembered that he had to take his cloak off. He had a bit of a struggle with the brooch which secured it, but Archbishop Willigis helped him surreptitiously. The chill of the day and the need to have his hands bare for the oath-swearing had left Otto's fingers cold and clumsy. He had wanted to carry the ceremonial sword himself but it was much too heavy for him and at rehearsal Willigis had decided to opt for safety. A young knight therefore followed Otto carrying the sword and now laid it with the King's cloak. Simply clad in a white tunic, the child was led to the carpeted steps of the high altar, where he prostrated himself while the litany was sung. So far, so good; he had remembered everything in the right order.

At the end of the litany he had to stand up again. Archbishop Willigis asked him if he would protect the Church, the clergy, and the people, as his father did, and if he would uphold the catholic faith. Otto had not understood when they explained this bit. It was something about two natures in one body and something else called dual precession. As far as three-year-old Otto was concerned, if his magnificent father was for it, so was he, and he assented eagerly three times. Then the Archbishop of Ravenna asked the assembled nobles if they would be loyal to young king. A roar of 'Fiat, fiat, Amen.' filled the great church.

Next came what he had been told was the most important part of the ceremony. His tunic was removed and he was anointed with holy oil on his bare head, chest, shoulder-blades, and upper arms. It was this anointing which marked him as dedicated to God and to his people. This was what made him really the King. Then he received the symbols of kingship, sword, still too long, cloak, sceptre, and staff. His arms ached with the weight, even before the two archbishops put the crown on his head. This gold circlet had been specially made to fit him, so it was not heavy or difficult to balance, despite its rich jewels.

By now it was well past midday and Otto was beginning to feel both hungry and in need of the lavatory. There was more ceremony still to come, however. Archbishop Willigis led him up the winding stone staircase to the upper gallery of the church. The steps were quite worn and it was difficult to get up them without tripping over his cloak, especially when his hands were full and he could not look down in case his crown fell off. He managed it and came out near the huge throne of Charlemagne, which towered above him, facing out over the body of the church. He had practised climbing up the massive steps to the throne, but not with crowns and sceptres. Suddenly he didn't think he could do it.

Luckily for him, Willigis realised the problem. He signalled with his eyes to the Archbishop of Ravenna and both men closed in behind the child. Concealed by their copes from the people watching from the nave, each put a hand under the boy's elbow and carefully lifted him up the steps. At the top he had plenty of room to recover his balance, turn round, and take his place on the enormous throne. As he sat down the bells pealed in triumph and the choir burst into the hymn *Te Deum laudamus*. A shout of acclamation and rejoicing could be heard from outside and the congregation joined in. Little Otto sat almost stunned as the waves of sound beat round him on the throne of his ancestor Charlemagne. Pride and happiness filled his heart, not least because he had done everything right and his father and mother would be so pleased with him.

The rejoicing carried on all day. The nobles feasted in the Great Hall of the palace and the common people in the square outside enjoyed themselves even more riotously. Evening fell early at that time of year but torches and bonfires outside and candles inside held the darkness at bay. About an hour after dusk, though, there was a sudden silence outside, then cries of horror began at the furthermost edge of the square. Uneasy quiet fell in the hall as well, as messengers were sent to find out what had happened. Otto was rather glad that the noise was getting less. He was tired out and for once really wanted to go to bed.

After what seemed an age to those waiting, the seneschal came back into the hall and spoke to the Archbishop in a low voice. Willigis' face turned ashen and he rose slowly to his feet. There was no need to raise his arm for silence; the hush was absolute.

'His Grace the Emperor,' Willigis said quietly into the silence, 'is dead of a fever in Rome these nineteen days past. God have mercy on his soul.'

Otto looked round uncomprehendingly as all the grown-ups crossed themselves. His father could not be dead. He was young and strong and he would be so proud of how Otto had behaved today. Why were they playing this horrible game? The Archbishop hadn't said anything about this at the rehearsals. Suddenly he desperately wanted his mother, who would explain what was happening to him. Unnoticed among the shouting men and wailing women, the over-wrought three-year-old King of the Italians and Germans began to howl his distress, but he, who had so recently been the centre of attention, was ignored in the mounting confusion.

All of a sudden strong arms grasped and lifted him and enfolded him in their safety. 'Nancilinus!' he gasped with relief and snuggled against the soldier. Then a roar from the Archbishop of Mainz made him almost jump out of his skin.

'Where do you think you're taking that child?'

'To his nurse, Lord Archbishop,' Nancilinus replied. 'He's had enough. He can't take any more today.'

Willigis shook his head to clear it, then nodded and spoke more gently.

'Yes, take him to the women, poor little lad, but don't take him out of the palace.'

Within forty-eight hours Otto and his entourage had been sent back to Cologne. Willigis came to see him before they left, explaining what it meant that his father was dead and Otto would not see him again in this world.

'Where is he then and why can't I go too?' asked the little boy.

Willigis hesitated. Church doctrine was uncertain on this point.

'Wherever he is, he is being cleansed of his sins so that he becomes ready to enter the heavenly kingdom. You cannot go to him because you are still alive, but you can pray for him.'

'What about my mother?'

'She will be praying for both him and you. And I think that, when the snow eases and the mountain-passes open, she will come north.'

With that Otto had to be content. Willigis deliberately gave him no hint of the arguments that had followed the news of the Emperor's death. Some had argued that the little king should be set aside and another member of the royal kin, such as Henry the Wrangler or Otto of Carinthia, chosen. Had the news arrived a day earlier, that would certainly have happened, but most agreed that what was done, was done. Young Otto was the anointed and crowned king, for better or for worse. The fact could not be changed.

Cologne brought more partings for Otto. Willigis, dignified and imposing but with a soft spot for small children, had to leave to attend to the affairs of his archdiocese. Archbishop Warin of Cologne, a tall, thin, humourless man, took his place as Otto's guardian, which did not please the little king at all. Even more distressing was the departure of Nancilinus, sent away to his own estate by Archbishop Warin as soon as Willigis had gone. King or no, Otto was much the youngest boy in the archbishop's household and he spent a miserable few days being teased and mildly bullied by the others, until one of the clergy from the cathedral, a priest named Everger, noticed and befriended him. Everger told him that he was a friend of Otto's mother and allowed the child to look at the beautifully illuminated books in the library with him. This was where they were one afternoon in early January when they received a summons to the Archbishop's private chamber.

Everger escorted him there. They arrived to find three strangers in the room with Warin. One was an elderly bishop, one a fearsome one-eyed individual who looked like a sea-raider, and the last a bald, shortish man with a red face and an angry expression. From Everger's indrawn breath of dismay, Otto realised that he did not like these men.

'So, this is my nephew,' the bald man boomed. 'Do you know who I am, little fellow?'

'No, Sir,' stammered Otto.

'I am – or should be – Duke Henry of Bavaria.'

'But – but I know Duke Henry. He doesn't look like you,' protested Otto.

'Not Henry Liutpolding. He's an imposter. I'm Henry Liudolfing, like you're Otto Liudolfing. I'm your father's first cousin and I've come to be your guardian now he's dead.'

Otto looked at Archbishop Warin.

'I thought *you* were my guardian,' he said.

Warin produced a thin smile.

'That was in Your Grace's father's lifetime. Now other arrangements have to be made.'

'But I have to stay here. My mother won't know where to find me.'

'No, child, you come with me,' said Henry the Wrangler. 'My children, your cousins, are eagerly waiting for you to be their playmate and my wife will take good care of you.'

His words were friendly but his eyes were not and Otto began to feel really afraid. Henry sounded exactly like the Erlking trying to steal away the little boy, in the story his Saxon nurse had told him.

'No, I shall wait for my mother,' he said with all the firmness he could muster.

'His Grace is surely right,' put in Everger. 'The Empress should be consulted over the guardianship of the King.'

'It was his father's wish that he should come to me. The Council gave you his instructions, did it not, Archbishop?'

'Indeed,' snapped Warin. 'You are presumptuous, Everger. This is none of your business. I command you to silence.'

In the end there was nothing Everger could do, other then secretly sending off express couriers to Archbishop Willigis and to the Empress in Italy. He was certain that they knew nothing of these supposed instructions from the dead emperor.

Yet again, Otto's belongings were packed up and that evening he set off towards the sunset in the wake of Henry the Wrangler, his father's most bitter opponent and claimant to his throne. As they went, gently falling snow erased their traces. Everger was not the only man to wonder if the little king would ever be seen alive again.

CHAPTER TWENTY-TWO

Pavia. Candlemas, February 2nd, the feast day of the presentation of the infant Christ by his parents in the Temple in Jerusalem. At Mass that morning Theophanu had begun to feel a faint stirring of happiness for the fist time since her husband's death. It sprang from thinking about how well her own little son had acquitted himself at his coronation in the Palace Chapel in Aachen. Now that first sense that life might still have some promise was quenched by this latest news.

'Where did Duke Henry take my grandson?' Empress Adelheid was the first of the four women, gathered together to hear Everger's messenger, to speak.

'I do not know, Lady. They set out westwards but the snow made it impossible to follow them without being seen.'

'Westwards!' Theophanu and Imiza exclaimed simultaneously. That was the opposite direction from what they would have expected. Bavaria or Saxony would have made more sense.

'Who exactly was with the Duke?' asked Abbess Matilda.

'Bishop Poppo of Utrecht and Ekbert One-Eye.'

'Ekbert one-Eye?' There was a horrified silence. One-Eye's reputation for treachery and brutality was widespread. Eventually the messenger could tell them no more and they dismissed him. He left them staring at each other in mingled perplexity and distress.

'Why on earth did Bishop Poppo set them free?' wondered Theophanu. 'He's always been loyal before.'

The other women looked at her with some surprise.

'Well, your husband is dead,' pointed out Matilda gently.

'What difference does that make?'

'When the lord who imprisons a man dies, the sentence lapses,' explained the Abbess. 'Is it not so in the East?'

'No, I don't think so. I don't really remember.' It was a chastening reminder that she was still an outsider. 'So it could be due process of law, not a plot?' That was important; it would seem to put Otto in less danger.

'Oh yes,' Empress Adelheid replied calmly. 'Duke Henry's release is within the law and he has a good claim to the boy's guardianship.'

'I knew we should have gone north straight after Christmas,' said Theophanu with bitter self-reproach.

'My lady, we could not. The passes were closed, as they still are,' said Imiza.

'The messenger got through.'

'He's had to come a very long way round and he's a young man. We are not.' Imiza glanced significantly at Adelheid.

'There was, and still is, no need to go north,' stated the Dowager-Empress. 'The boy was to be reared by the Archbishop of Cologne. My son's death makes no difference to that.'

'But that's just it. He's no longer in Cologne,' pointed out Theophanu through gritted teeth, trying to hold on to her patience.

'He's in the care of his nearest male kin — nearest geographically, anyway. What is it you fear, Theophanu? The Liudolfings don't murder children.' The remark was barbed, because the same could not be said of the rulers of Byzantium. Seeing her daughter-in-law blench, Adelheid went on more kindly,

'Remember, when your uncle and great-uncle usurped their thrones, they did not kill the little emperors. They simply ruled for them. Henry will not harm Otto. No, our duty is to stay here and keep Italy loyal. If we go, the Lord Pope will surely be killed.'

Yes, well, he's your friend more than mine, thought Theophanu. I'm far more concerned about my son. Her mother-in-law continued unperturbed,

'In any case Lombardy is in such turmoil, now that you've insisted on calling off the blockade of Venice, that we cannot possibly leave.'

This was too much for Theophanu's patience to bear.

'Excuse me, Madam,' she said in an icy tone, 'but you heard what the Lord Abbot of Bobbio said when he was here last week. It was the exactions imposed by you and the Lord Pope, when he was Bishop of Pavia, that have stirred up the Lombard towns.'

Once the news of Otto's death reached Bobbio, both the monks and the local landowners had risen in revolt and driven out their abbot, Gerbert of Aurillac. He had travelled through Pavia on his way back to Rheims, where he intended to stay. He had promised to keep the imperial ladies informed of the situation in France and had established a system of correspondence with Imiza, a kinswoman of his patron, the Archbishop of Rheims.

'Gerbert has a very biased point of view,' observed Adelheid magisterially. Actually she loathed him as much as he loathed her. Matilda decided it was time to intervene.

'We really can't make any decisions until we have more information,' she said to her sister-in-law. 'Imiza, if Duke Henry's gone westwards, perhaps your husband will be able to send us news.'

Both Theophanu and Imiza brightened at this thought. Imiza's husband, Count Heribert, was with his brother and liegelord, Duke Conrad of Swabia, and would be well-positioned to know what was happening. Even so the next few days seemed interminable to Theophanu. One evening Imiza said to her,

'Why are you so worried, Lady? I'm sure Duke Henry won't harm the anointed king, particularly not when he's a child.'

'The French kings do,' said Theophanu.

'Madam, that was the Merovingians, the long-haired kings, and that was centuries ago. The Carolingians never have.'

'Yes, I know that really,' admitted Theophanu. 'It's just – oh, Imiza, I hate to talk about this, because it makes me ashamed of my countrymen, but when I was a child, Basil and Constantine *were* nearly murdered for the crown.'

'I never heard that,' said Imiza. 'Were you there?'

'Sort of. It was when I was about three, the first time I had ever been to Constantinople, just after Romanus II died. My great-uncle Nicephorus had been awarded a triumph for the re-conquest of Crete and I was taken to watch the procession. We were still staying in the townhouse a few weeks later when we heard that he was going to marry the widow, Empress Theophano, and take the throne. The Chief Minister, a man called Joseph Bringas, didn't want to lose power and he sent soldiers to arrest my great-grandfather, Bardas Phocas Senior. They dragged him away from the house; I watched from the nursery window.

'Later that day he escaped and sought sanctuary in Santa Sophia, our great church. The Patriarch wouldn't let Bringas have him, so Bringas went to the palace nurseries and grabbed Basil and Constantine by the arms, although they were the sacred emperors. He frog-marched them to Santa Sophia and told my great-grandfather that he would kill them if he didn't give himself up. So of course, he had to.'

'Then what happened?' asked Imiza, round-eyed.

'The mob was so angry that it rioted and my grandfather was released and came home. But the rioting went on for days and half the city burnt down, before Basil the Eunuch restored order and my great-uncle became Senior Emperor. It was a terrifying time.'

'How old were the boys?' asked Imiza, thinking about it.

'Basil was six and Constantine was three, the same as Otto.'

'And now they're strong young men and your little Otto is in the care of his kinsman, not someone from another family,' said Imiza. 'I can see why you're so frightened but the situations aren't really parallel.'

Despite these reassuring words, when the next news reached them from Gerbert, it was not wholly encouraging. Henry appeared to intend to take the child towards France. He had arranged a meeting in the Rhineland in early February with the Carolingian kings of France, Lothar and his son Louis, who had forced Theophanu and Otto II to flee from Aachen when Theophanu was expecting Matilda. Gerbert thought that he intended to offer the Carolingians Lotharingia, in return for recognition of

Henry's right to either the throne or the guardianship. When Gerbert wrote, the meeting had not yet taken place.

'I think what worries me most,' said Imiza to Theophanu privately, 'is that Ekbert One-Eye is with them. That man would sell his own grandmother.'

'He reminds me of pirate captains in the Aegean,' agreed Theophanu. 'Do you think he would be interested in a ransom for Otto? Perhaps Basil and Constantine would help, in return for our lifting the blockade on Venice?'

Any such hopes were dashed by the steadily increasing unrest in Rome. Spies reported that the Antipope Boniface had been seen in the city again, along with Byzantine agents. Pope John XIV's position looked even more insecure. Nevertheless the next despatch from the north was more encouraging politically, although it did nothing to assuage Theophanu's worry for Otto's safety.

It came in a letter from Count Heribert. He reported gleefully that the Kings of France duly turned up to the meeting but there waiting for them was not Henry the Wrangler but Conrad of Swabia and a force loyal to the little king and the imperial ladies. Henry's whereabouts were unknown but the French had been forced into an ignominious retreat through the hilly, forested country of the Eifel on the Franco-German border. The Swabians dug traps for the French warhorses; as the invaders hurried homeward along the woodland trails, they never knew which tree canopies ahead of them concealed soldiers waiting to drop on their saddles; all the way they rode with the constant anticipation of an arrowhead thudding between their shoulder-blades. Altogether it was an uncomfortable and dangerous journey and with every setback their anger and dissatisfaction with Henry increased. As soon as they got home, they decided to change sides. Count Heribert obviously thought it all a great joke.

Information now began to flow in from all sides. Henry the Wrangler had headed for Saxony, along with Bishop Poppo, One-Eye, the imperial insignia, and, most importantly of all, the child. Otto had been sighted and was not merely alive, but appeared to be in good health. This news came from two counts, who had gone to meet Henry at Corvey, intending to give him their loyalty, although they had opposed him in the past. They approached him with their feet bare, as a sign of conciliation, but he swept straight past and refused to receive them. They were deeply offended by this unregal behaviour and took to encouraging opposition to Henry amongst their friends and families in the north.

In the west, too, resistance was growing. At the urging of Gerbert and his patron, Archbishop Adalbero of Rheims, Bishop Notker of Liege summoned a meeting to consider responses to the abduction of Otto. This was to take place in his cathedral city in late February. The Kings of France would attend, as the little king's cousins, as would Duke Charles of Lower Lotharingia. The leading churchmen of South West Germany would be there, headed by Archbishop Egbert of Trier. Liege was near Dietrich of Metz's diocese, so he would be present but a disappointing absentee was Archbishop Willigis of Mainz. It worried Theophanu that she had heard nothing from him, when she would have expected his support, as she said to her sister-in-law one day. Matilda was reassuring.

'He would have to investigate the Duke's claim that Otto – Otto II – really didn't promise the boy's guardianship to Henry. Archbishop Willigis has to be extra careful about the law. He doesn't have a powerful family to protect him. I'm sure he would have rallied to our side if he felt Otto was in any danger at all.'

When word of the outcome of this conference reached Pavia in early March, it was exhilarating. The assembled lords had swung solidly behind Otto and against Henry, even the French kings and Archbishop Egbert of Trier, who would personally have been happy to see Lotharingia returned to the Carolingians. In front of the high altar of St. John's Church in Liege, all had sworn to protect the rights of the little king and to oppose the abductor. A letter from Gerbert, which followed soon after, however, revived all their anxieties. 'Duke Henry's real aim is the throne,' he warned them. 'Do not believe his protestations that he wishes only to be the King's guardian.' Since this information must have come direct from the Carolingians, who knew what they had tried to negotiate with Henry, it was even more alarming. While Otto lived, Henry could not be king.

Gerbert's letter reached Theophanu in early April and faced her with an unbearable dilemma. Some of the easier passes were now open and she was desperate to set off for the north straight away, but still events in Italy held her trapped. The rumours of Antipope Boniface's presence in Rome had been confirmed in the worst way imaginable; he and his Crescentii allies had seized control of the city and deposed Pope John. Adelheid's friend was now held prisoner in Castel Sant'Angelo, like his predecessor, Benedict VI, who had also opposed Boniface. There was every reason to fear that John too would be found mysteriously dead in his cell. If the empresses went north, his fate would be sealed.

This intolerable situation lasted through early April, while there seemed to be no news coming from the north. Then messages from all corners arrived at once and the ladies were forced into action.

CHAPTER TWENTY-THREE

The first to reach Pavia was a Saxon who had left Magdeburg on March 18th, two days after Palm Sunday. On arrival he was shown straight into the presence of the Empresses, dusty and dishevelled as he was, and sank to his knees in front of them. Theophanu's heart leapt when she recognised, beneath the dirt, the colours of the Archbishop of Mainz.

'You come from the Lord Archbishop of Mainz?' she asked eagerly as soon as the man rose to his feet.

'Yes, my lady. He sent me to you in all haste.' He glanced rather nervously at Adelheid then handed the letter he was carrying to Theophanu. She smiled at him and motioned Adelheid and Matilda to move near enough to read it with her. The messenger continued, 'He said to ask you to read the letter and then I was to add any details you wanted, but above all, I was to say, 'You must come quickly.'

Theophanu looked up and nodded then continued to devour the letter. It contained no good news but somehow the assurance that Willigis was for them outweighed the ill tidings. Henry had found support in Saxony; the imperial palace at Werla had been opened to him. This was important because it gave him control of the silver-mines which had played a large part in Saxony's rise to prosperity and success. According to legend, it had been Theophanu's own father-in-law, Otto the Great, who had discovered them, but Adelheid had merely smiled when asked if this was true. The Empress was more disturbed to learn the names of some of his supporters. They were not negligible men. Prominent amongst them was Archbishop Giselher of Magdeburg, who had allegedly swindled and bought his way into his dignity. His defection was disappointing, although not really surprising. The next name was more of a shock.

'Bishop Dietrich of Metz!' Abbess Matilda said blankly. 'But he was one of my brother's staunchest supporters. How *could* he betray little Otto?'

'It's said he made a thousand talents of silver out of helping Giselher trick the Magdeburg chapter and get the archdiocese,' observed her mother grimly. 'He thinks Henry's going to win. You won't find Dietrich backing a loser.'

'He hates me too,' said Theophanu. 'He always has, since I first met him at Benevento. I don't really know why.'

The messenger cleared his throat nervously and they all looked at him.

'Lady,' he said hesitantly, 'Bishop Dietrich has accused you of supporting the enemies of the Empire and of infidelity to your lord when you were in Italy. Nobody believes him,' he added hastily.

'What?' There was a stunned silence then the imperial women closed ranks.

'Who is supposed to be the recipient of the Empress' favours?' demanded Adelheid with ice in her voice.

'The Chancellor of Italy, John Philagathos.'

'But this is ridiculous!' Theophanu was furious now. 'I like Philagathos as a friend,' she added to her mother-in-law. 'He's clever and competent, he speaks my language and shares my faith, but beyond that....' Then she broke off.

'What is it?' asked Matilda. 'What have you remembered?'

'There *was* one time,' said Theophanu slowly. 'It was at Rossano when we were waiting to hear news of the battle and I was very worried. Philagathos *did* become over-familiar but he backed off as soon as I checked him and he's always behaved since. But Bishop Dietrich *was* there, lurking in the shadows, and of course he couldn't understand what we were saying.'

'Surely your tone would have made your meaning clear?' said Matilda.

'Yes, it must have done.'

'Not to someone who hates Greeks anyway and is now looking for a reason to justify treason,' said the Dowager-Empress.

'Treason?'

'Read to the end of the letter, Theophanu. Henry has claimed the crown for himself, not just the guardianship.'

The two younger women read on horrified. Adelheid was right. With Archbishop Giselher's cooperation, Henry had called a full assembly of the Saxon nobility at Magdeburg on the day after Palm Sunday. There he proclaimed himself king and demanded the nobles' assent. He did not explain whether he intended to rule alone or with Otto as co-ruler. He obviously expected to be acclaimed on the spot.

'How did the Saxon lords react?' Theophanu asked the messenger.

'They did agree to it, but only if the little king gave his consent in person. Obviously, as he wasn't there, he couldn't, so the meeting adjourned until the Eastercourt at Quedlinburg.'

'My son was not there?' Theophanu's heart was racing.

'No, Madam. No-one has seen him for some weeks now. My Lord Archbishop expects the Duke to produce him at Quedlinburg, but we can't be sure.'

'I can't believe the whole assembly voted for this charade,' said Matilda.

'Indeed, my Lady Abbess, many were uneasy but were too uncertain to say so. By the time I left at dawn on Tuesday, a lot of tents had been struck and their occupants gone. . The Duke's anger when he was not immediately proclaimed king made more people fearful for King Otto. My Lord Archbishop thinks they went to seek the opposition.'

'Over in Lotharingia?' asked Theophanu.

'Nearer than that, Madam. The noblemen Duke Henry offended at Corvey have taken up arms against him near Hildesheim, west of Quedlinburg. If His Grace is not present at the Eastercourt at Quedlinburg, then Archbishop Willigis will join them – as will all men of good will, I think. The opposition to the Duke is gathering, Lady, and that is why My Lord Archbishop needs you and the Empress Adelheid' – with a nod to that lady, - 'to come north straightaway.'

Theophanu and Matilda started final arrangements for the trek north, but no matter how much they got packed up, Adelheid still refused to leave Italy while Pope John was a prisoner. The sisters-in-law were discussing the pros and cons of going without her, when the arrival of another messenger, a young knight who held land from Matilda's own abbey of Quedlinburg, began to change the Dowager-Empress's mind.

'Lady Abbess, I have a letter for you from Sister Emnilde.' Looking apologetically at the Empress, he handed the parchment to Matilda, who read it rapidly and groaned.

'Fetch the Empress Adelheid at once,' she directed a servant. Then she turned to Theophanu. 'My dear, this concerns you too, but it is not good news. Perhaps we should sit before you read it.'

Mechanically Theophanu obeyed her and took the letter. On reading it, her first feeling was relief that it was not an announcement of Otto's death, as she had feared. It was almost equally worrying, however; it said that a troop of soldiers under the command of Ekbert One-Eye had arrived at the abbey of Quedlinburg with a writ from the Wrangler, demanding that the Princess Adelheid be given into their keeping. In the absence of the Abbess, nobody had the authority to prevent the removal of the six-year-old princess.

'So, he has two hostages now,' Theophanu said painfully. 'What about Sophia and Matilda?'

No-one could answer that. 'I blame myself so much,' said Matilda. 'I'm so sorry, Theophanu. I should have been there.'

'What could you have done? One-Eye doesn't care whose authority he defies. Only superior physical force could have stopped him, vile as he is.' As Empress Adelheid entered, Theophanu said urgently, 'Madam, read this. You *must* see now that we have to go immediately.'

'My namesake!' exploded Adelheid a moment later. She seemed to take the kidnapping as a personal insult. 'I begin to think you are right, daughter.'

Theophanu let out a huge sigh of relief and turned back to the messenger.

'Does Archbishop Willigis know about this?'

'He didn't when I left on the Wednesday of Holy Week, Lady, but he will by now. Everyone was expecting King Otto and Princess Adelheid to be at the High Mass of Easter and then at the Court on Easter Monday. The court – the retinue – was due to reach Quedlinburg on Maundy Thursday.'

With Adelheid's cooperation, preparations for the journey went better, although it still seemed maddeningly slow to Theophanu. Then messengers from Rome and from Willigis arrived simultaneously. In Rome the inevitable had happened. Pope John XIV, formerly Bishop Peter of Pavia, had been found dead in his cell in Castel Sant'Angelo. The messenger did not know whether the cause was starvation or poisoning and it made little practical difference. Boniface was now firmly in control, although his strings were being pulled by Constantinople and its Crescentii allies, and Rome was lost. Even in his own city of Pavia, only Adelheid really grieved for the dead pope. Philagathos and other great Tuscan nobles loyal to the crown were sure they could hold Northern Italy and Theophanu and Matilda just wanted to be gone.

Because they already knew of little Adelheid's kidnapping, Willigis' message was not as much of a shock as he expected. He confirmed that neither child had been seen at Quedlinburg, which indicated that they were Henry's hostages, not his wards. At Archbishop Giselher's instigation, Henry had been greeted by the singing of the King's *laudes* when he reached the town, a *de facto* recognition of his kingship by the Saxon church. Even worse, many of the Saxon nobles and most of their bishops had sworn homage to him despite the absence of Otto, and so had the West Slavic princes, Miesco of Poland, Boleslav of Bohemia, and even Mistui of the Abodrites.

'Don't they ever go home?' interjected Theophanu bitterly, on reading this.

'No, Mistui's too busy burning Hamburg and everything else he can get his hands on,' retorted Matilda.

The rest of Willigis' letter was more cheering. The loyalist resistance was gathering round the castle of Asselburg, north-west of Quedlinburg. Willigis had sent his own Thuringian military vassals there and he mentioned encouraging names of others who had gone, men like Duke Bernhard Billung of Saxony. The western opposition to Henry, stirred up by Gerbert and the Archbishop of Rheims, had already reached the Asselburg and Willigis was confident that their cause would prevail. The loyalists had discovered that young Adelheid was being held in Ekbert's castle of Ala. An attack on it was being prepared, with the hope that they might find the little king there as well, although Willigis admitted that there was great cause to fear for his future. He concluded by urging Otto's mother and grandmother to come immediately to claim the guardianship and act as a rallying point.

They needed no urging now.

'Right,' said Empress Adelheid, characteristically assuming the right to take charge, 'we're in Pavia already. There's no point in going over the Septimer to Constance, when we're so far west already. We'll go by a western route – the Great St. Bernard. I think Willigis is wrong about timing, you know. It will be worth our while to detour through Burgundy.'

Matilda closed her eyes in exasperation.

'Why, Mama?' she demanded. 'We've wasted enough time already.'

'I think your mother is right,' said Theophanu unexpectedly. 'The rallying is happening without us. So long as we get word through quickly that we are on the move, that is what matters. You intend to visit your brother, King Conrad, don't you, Lady?'

'Exactly,' replied Adelheid appreciatively. 'You understand me well, daughter. Yes, I hope my brother still has influence with his daughter Gisela, who is, of course, wife to the Wrangler. And I hope and believe that she has influence with her husband, which is why I have not been worried about Otto's safety until now. I fear, though, that Ekbert One-Eye is a different kind of threat from Duke Henry and Gisela. I *am* afraid for the children now, but rushing things will not help.'

Later that evening Matilda said to Theophanu,

'Abbess though I am, I don't know how you keep your patience with my mother.'

The Empress smiled ruefully. 'I have to admit that there've been dozens of times in the last few weeks when I'd have cheerfully put my hands round her throat and throttled her, but she *is* clever and we need her support. And after all, it was you who pointed out that while I was empress, I couldn't do just as I liked.'

Matilda nodded. 'Still, this waiting has been terrible for you,' she said.

'Action is certainly much easier, but tomorrow we set out. With St. Alban and Willigis on our side, we should prevail.'

'St. Alban? You're taking the reliquary.'

'Most certainly. That was what Pope John gave it me for. I shall deliver it to the Church of St. Pantaleon that your uncle Bruno founded in Cologne.'

'I never understood why Pope John gave you that particular saint. St. Alban of Britain? Why?'

'Pope John explained,' answered Theophanu. 'It was one day just after my husband died, when I happened to tell him how much I admired Empress Galla Placidia. Of Ravenna?' Matilda nodded and Theophanu continued, 'He said there were relics in the papal treasury given by Placidia all those years ago and that I should have them, because she kept them with her when she had to win back the Western Empire for her young son. He could see even then that I might have to do the same and he thought that St. Alban might look with favour on another empress having to fight the same battle. I don't know much about Alban though.'

'I do. The story's in Bede; it's quite well-known in the north. You can read it in our library if we ever get back to Quedlinburg. Well then, in the name of Alban of England let's go north and rescue the little lad, and restore his birthright to him. A northern saint for a northern king.'

CHAPTER TWENTY-FOUR

The relief of being on the move and doing something was indescribable. They rode fast now up toward the Great Saint Bernard Pass through Vercelli and Ivrea. As they climbed higher, the snow grew deeper, but the trail was passable. They stopped at the two little huddles of grey stone buildings near the top, and were grateful for the hospitality of the kindly monks there. It was always tempting to think that the worst of the journey was over once one reached the top, but Theophanu knew from experience that the reverse was true; it was always more difficult to come down, This time was no exception. They were well below the high peaks heading for Martigny and the relatively easy going of the Rhone Valley when the river they were following suddenly cascaded into a gorge. The path continued straight along a precipice cut into a huge rock face. In summer it would have been no problem, but the valley faced north and snow and ice still covered the track.

With great care they inched their way along the precipice. A quick glance down had shown Theophanu that the rock wall was sheer down to a bank still thick with snow, which sloped gently down to the stream. One look was enough. It was safer to stare straight ahead, where she could see that the path widened and began to descend. She was just thinking that they had made it, when she heard the sound she dreaded, the rasp of a horse's hoof skidding on the ice. She looked round in time to see the packhorse carrying the relic of St. Alban vanishing over the edge of the precipice, dragging with him the man who led him.

Theophanu shouted to everyone else to continue to the safer stretch of path ahead. There they halted. She could sense panic rising amongst the packmen and guards. Accidents in the mountains were commonplace but a disaster befalling the saint was a terrible omen for their cause. Quickly ropes were unpacked and the captain of the guard and three strong, reliable men went back along the trail.

By now everyone could see that both the fallen packhorse and the man were stirring. The man floundered to his feet and waved to his companions. The horse could not get up because of the weight of the chest strapped to him, but he was certainly trying to. Above them the guards were belaying to a fortunately-placed spur of rock and two of them climbed down the cliff. A few strokes of the knife freed the horse from its burden and, to everyone's astonishment, it rose to its feet apparently unharmed. The thick snow, softer in the valley with the imminence of the thaw, had broken the falls, a miracle which was clearly attributable to the intervention of the saint. Morale soared again and more men were sent along the ledge with slings for the horse and the reliquary. Within an hour the cavalcade was back on the road north. The relics too had suffered no damage.

Their new confidence seemed borne out when they reached the Abbey of St Maurice further down the valley and found a messenger from Willigis. The news he brought was mixed, however. The best was that loyalist forces had stormed the Castle of Ala, as intended, and had rescued the little princess, along with much treasure. Young Adelheid seemed unharmed, although she had been badly frightened, and she was now in the Archbishop's care until her mother or aunt came for her. The imperial ladies rejoiced over this but Theophanu and Matilda could not conceal their disappointment that the little boy was not with his sister. The messenger said that there were now widespread fears for his safety, but Empress Adelheid shook her head.

'So long as Henry has him, not that pirate One-Eye, he will come to no harm,' she said confidently. Her daughter and daughter-in-law exchanged despairing glances. The messenger's next words, however, supported Adelheid's determination to travel via Burgundy.

'My master says to take the westernmost routes,' he said. 'A meeting between the rebel Duke and the King's supporters was arranged in Saxony, just to the west of the Harz mountains, but the Duke and his men never showed up. Now he's headed for Bavaria, so it will be safer to stay to the west.'

'He still thinks he's the Duke of Bavaria,' said Matilda. 'Henry the Younger won't like that.'

The messenger nodded. 'Yes, Lady, we think most of the nobility will stay loyal to Duke Henry the Younger, but the other Henry may well find support in the Church.'

'Like in Saxony,' said Theophanu.

'Once the threat to the young king became clear, all Saxony swung behind him,' answered the messenger. 'We can be confident, Madam, so long as all is well with His Grace.'

This was an encouraging message to take with them as they turned westwards to start the chase round the Kingdom of Burgundy to find the royal family, always a problem with a travelling monarchy. Eventually they caught up with King Conrad and were even more heartened by his response. Not merely would he give then his support; he would come with them to Mainz and ride with the loyalist army to meet Henry. Theophanu had a distinct feeling that he was rather used to doing as his elder sister, the Empress Adelheid, told him. It was certainly convenient at the moment that Adelheid had such a forceful personality. Valuable as it was to have Conrad's support, finding him had taken time and May was well-advanced by the time they reached Germany.

Here events were moving fast. There had been sporadic fighting in Bavaria between the two factions, but Archbishop Frederick of Salzburg had declared for the royal cause and his example led such numbers to follow him that the Wrangler had fled into Swabia and the middle Rhineland. On May 10th, on a hill above the river at Bürstadt, his army came face to face loyalist forces, led by Willigis and Duke Conrad of Swabia, who had already chased him away from the failed meeting with the French kings in the winter. This time Henry could not slip away without facing his opponents.

The encounter lasted five days and never got as far as fighting. Argument raged back and forth in secret council. Henry had always been noted for his rhetorical skills but Willigis was his match in that area and had more patience. In the end Henry had to accept what he regarded as a humiliating settlement: he was to give the boy back to his mother on June 29th and meanwhile all the troops assembled at Bürstadt renewed their oaths of allegiance to the little king. It looked as if Henry had lost the main game, although he would be allowed to keep the lands he already had.

This news reached Theophanu quickly, since she was so much nearer now. It cheered the imperial ladies greatly as they travelled north along the Rhine valley. The clear implication that Otto was still alive was heartening, but when they reached Mainz at the end of May, they realised that the Wrangler was not defeated yet.

As soon as Henry and his retainers were safely away from Burstadt, he renounced the agreement. Instead he went to Bohemia, to his old friend and ally, Prince Boleslav, and asked for his help in an invasion of the Empire.

'It's fascinating,' Theophanu said thoughtfully, when they heard this. 'He never brings things to a head. He never has, because what he really likes is the gamble. If the stakes get too high, he withdraws for that round and then has another go.'

'He's still got plenty of scope, then,' said Matilda. 'If Boleslav won't play, there's always Vladimir of Kiev – or how about Ethelred of England?'

Before they heard the outcome of Henry's Bohemian adventure, there was one unambiguous joy. Princess Adelheid was reunited with her grandmother, mother, and aunt. At first the meeting was quite strained. The girl knew who they were, of course, but had little memory of them as people. Theophanu was amused but slightly hurt to realise that to the child her abbess-aunt's approval was more important than her mother's. Always a serious, conscientious child, Adelheid seemed to blame herself for being kidnapped and only Abbess Matilda's assurance that it was not her fault brought a smile to her face. That evening Theophanu had the

185

child brought to her own chamber, so that she could talk to her alone. She deliberately avoided mentioning the abduction at first, but asked her questions about her school-life and the little girl quickly relaxed. Yes, she was happy at school; the other girls were friendly and well-behaved, which was more than could always be said for the choirboys, but the girls didn't have much to do with them, thank goodness. The canonesses were strict but if you kept the rules, you were all right and the lessons were mostly interesting.

'What do you like doing best?' asked Theophanu.

Adelheid considered. 'The offices, I think.'

'All the daily services?' Theophanu was surprised. 'Why?'

'The singing. It's like being in Heaven already sometimes. You know, Mother, there's this new way of singing coming in, where you don't all sing the same tune, or rather you do but not at the same time. One part follows another, but a bit delayed, and the harmonies can be wonderful.'

'You girls join in that kind of singing?'

'I don't yet in church. I'm too young, the choir-mistress says, but we're allowed to at choir practice and maybe next year, she'll let me.'

Looking at the child's face alight with enthusiasm, Theophanu thought, not for the first time, what a pity it was that it was Sophia, not Adelheid, who was dedicated to the religious life.

'You must have been very frightened and unhappy when the soldiers took you away from the Abbey.'

The light in Adelheid's face died. 'Yes,' was all she said.

'Did they hurt you at all?'

'Only if I didn't do what they wanted quickly enough.'

Theophanu's heart lurched. 'What sort of things did they want?'

'Oh, get on or off my pony quickly. Eat my food. I never did things fast enough for them, so they'd hit me. That was a bit stupid,' added the six-year-old judiciously,' because I was being as quick as I could. It wasn't fair.'

Theophanu smiled at the age-old complaint of childhood. So long as that was all it was.

'They didn't hurt you in any other way?' she pressed.

'No, once we got to the castle, they didn't even hit me. It was just boring and I was getting pretty hungry and I missed the Abbey so much. When can I go back?'

'By the end of the summer, I expect. Abbess Matilda will take you with her.' Relieved, she dismissed the child to her bed. It seemed that no lasting harm had been done, although she feared that the experience might make Adelheid reluctant to leave the convent for the world when she was older.

The next week brought news from Bohemia. Boleslav had greeted Henry as an honoured friend and had indeed given him troops. Henry started back for Germany in fine fettle, which changed to fury when they reached the border of Bohemia and Boleslav's troops turned back.

'It seems their remit was only to get him safely off Bohemian territory,' explained Willigis. 'Well, I think all the earths are blocked now. Lotharingia, Saxony, Bavaria, Swabia and Bohemia have all separately rejected him. Of course, he might take up Abbess Matilda's suggestions.'

They all laughed. Ethelred the Ill-advised was in no position to help anybody and Kiev was too far away. Henry's antics were still endangering the Empire, however. Boleslav's troops captured and sacked Meissen on their way home. Henry became even more unpopular as a result and he headed for Weimar south of the Harz, where he thought he might find some support. He arrived to find loyalist troops already besieging the castle and again, instead of fighting, he tried to negotiate. This time the terms were harsher for him. If he produced the King on June 29th, as arranged, he would keep his life and three of his estates, nothing more.

'I don't understand why you don't force the issue,' said Empress Adelheid angrily. 'Why all this endless negotiating when we have such a strong hand?'

Willigis and Theophanu exchanged looks.

'Madam, he still has the key card,' said Willigis simply. 'While he has the person of the King, I will negotiate rather than fight, for as long as it takes. That is your wish too, Lady Theophanu, isn't it.'

'It is,' agreed Theophanu. 'I'm as weary of this cat and mouse game as you are, Mother, but we dare not push the Duke too far.'

She did not voice the fear which dominated all their thoughts, the suspicion that the reason Henry would not hand over the child was that he could not. The boy was already dead.

Willigis was looking at Adelheid speculatively. How much did she know about the news from the west which had only just reached him, he wondered. Their supposedly loyal allies, the Carolingian Kings of France, had taken advantage of the disturbance in the Empire to make yet another grab for Lotharingia. They had succeeded in capturing the strategic fortress of Verdun on imperial territory and had left it garrisoned, commanded by none other than Adelheid's daughter, Queen Emma. Whose side was Adelheid really on, he asked himself for the umpteenth time.

For the time being Lotharingia would have to look after itself. The royal ladies were now ready to ride into Thuringia for what everyone hoped would be the handover. At last the struggle for the crown was moving to its final stages.

CHAPTER TWENTY-FIVE

The ride north-east soon turned into a royal progress. The two empresses rode at the head with King Conrad, followed by Abbess Matilda and Princess Adelheid sitting proudly on her pony. Behind them were Archbishop Willigis, the Arch-Chancellor, and Bishop Hildebald of Worms, Chancellor of Germany. Before long they were joined by Duke Conrad of Swabia and large numbers of Swabian and Franconian troops. Every day more soldiers flocked in and by the time they reached Rohr, the appointed meeting-place, they were a mighty host.

It seemed that everyone was there already. Theophanu had expected the Saxons, both the loyal and those who wanted to make their peace, to be there in large numbers, but she had not been sure that the Slavic princes, especially Boleslav, would attend. Again she found herself muttering to Imiza, 'Don't they ever go home?' and in truth she was not pleased to see them. They could still turn against Otto and they had too many supporters with them for her liking.

The royal party installed itself in a royal manor-house on the hill overlooking the water-meadows where the confrontation would take place. Two rivers flowed together in the wide, flat valley and the scene presented a cheerful sight as the royal ladies looked down from the manor. On both sides of the reed-lined banks brightly-coloured pavilions had been erected, like miniature castles, each proudly flying its owner's colours. Both the pennants and the reeds rippled in the gentle westerly wind. At the centre of the gathering and in a corridor leading to it from the north, a space had been left empty. The Wrangler's tents would occupy that corridor and the central space was for the meeting.

To see the vast number of their supporters put new heart into the imperial ladies and one of King Conrad's men was waiting for them with even better news. All through the journey the King of Burgundy had been firing off messengers to his daughter and to his son-in law, and one of these had just ridden fast from Merseburg, where Duchess Gisela had been living since her husband's imprisonment. Duke Henry had ridden in at speed a few days ago, he reported, and had immediately been closeted with his wife for a long time. When he emerged from her rooms, he had summoned all his personal retainers, effectively a private army, together in the courtyard. Then he lifted his arm for silence and formally renounced his claim to the throne.

The messenger paused for dramatic impact, which was rather spoilt by Theophanu's ironic query 'Again?'

'This was to his own followers, Madam. He seemed to mean it this time, because he then freed them all from their oath of loyalty.'

'He actually sent them away?' asked King Conrad.

'Well, no, Your Grace,' admitted the messenger, 'not exactly. He did ask them to escort him and the King to Rohr as a last service.'

The ladies burst into a babble of excited questions, all interrupting each other.

'The King? Did you see the King? Was the King there?'

'I didn't see him, ladies, but other people have. He has been at the castle for a good time and has been seen in the open air from time to time.'

For a moment the world seemed to Theophanu to shudder, as she tasted the immensity of her relief. King Conrad was frowning, however.

'His Grace was definitely not in the courtyard?' he pressed. 'No oath was sworn to him?'

The messenger shook his head and Theophanu looked questioningly at Conrad.

'All may be well,' he said, 'but if Henry's intentions were honest, he could have made it clear there and then, as I told my daughter.' He looked compassionately at the ladies. 'I would say we're off the mountain, but not yet out of the foothills. We must see what the morning brings.'

The Wrangler's party had still not arrived when Theophanu decided to retire for the night. She was certain she could not sleep at all, but the strain of looking confident in front of so many people was becoming intolerable. Empress Adelheid was made of sterner stuff, or she still had more trust in her niece's husband, and she stayed in the hall until the first sounds of the arrival of a large party of riders were heard. Then, with a satisfied smile, she went to bed.

By this time Theophanu was lost to the world. Imiza had a goblet of warm, spiced wine waiting for her and insisted that she drank it, not mentioning the sleeping draught she had put in it. Consequently the Empress was asleep within minutes. On waking she rushed to the window, to find that the circle round the central space was now completely filled and Duke Henry's banner was waving over his tents. At least he had come.

It was a beautiful day, the sun already shining strongly from a clear blue sky with fluffy white clouds drifting across it. The whole camp was stirring and Theophanu listened to the outdoor sounds of dogs barking and horses whinnying. Somewhere in those tents was her little boy. Happiness and fear filled her to an almost equal degree; she was well aware that in many ways today was the most dangerous day of all for Otto.

She was even more conscious of this an hour later as she took her seat for the negotiations to begin. Chairs of state had been placed at one side of the open space for the two Empresses and King Conrad. The two Chancellors and Duke Conrad of Swabia, their chief advisers, stood on either side of them. Once the fanfare to mark their arrival was finished and the Empresses were seated, all eyes turned to the other side of the circle. After a moment of suspense, there was a ripple in the crowd and again the horns rang out. Through the sudden gap in the crowd stepped Henry the Wrangler, formerly Duke of Bavaria, and at his side, coming up only as far as the top of his legs, walked a small red-haired boy. The King of the Germans and the Italians. Behind them was the dense mass of Henry's retainers.

There was a momentary hush then the babble of conversation broke out again as everyone tried to get a better view of the momentous occasion. Theophanu's first overwhelming impression was that she had forgotten how small Otto was. It made his vulnerability even more poignant and her heart ached anew for him. Nevertheless she reminded herself severely that she could not afford to be sentimental today. The boy's safety depended on quick wits and clear thinking.

Significantly, Henry made the least possible obeisance to his father-in-law and Empress Adelheid. He ignored Theophanu completely but it was she who spoke first.

'Henry Liudolfing, why have you come to this court?'

Her clear voice could be heard all round the field and most of her audience exchanged surprised glances. The Empress' voice was usually soft.

'I have come to return the King's Grace to you, his mother, and to the Empress his grandmother. And to claim my dukedom.'

'You have no dukedom. You forfeited it by your treachery to my husband and your misconduct since.'

A loud murmur of approval ran round the assembly at Theophanu's words. Henry smiled grimly.

'I have the King. I will not give him back for less than Bavaria, which is mine by right.'

'The Duchy of Bavaria is not vacant,' said Theophanu calmly. 'Duke Henry the Younger has no wish for you to be rewarded for your evil deeds at his expense, nor could we treat his loyalty so.'

A bellow from amongst the crowd confirmed Henry the Younger's assent to this position.

'That is your problem,' replied Henry, still smiling.

Angrily King Conrad rose to his feet.

'What exactly are you threatening, you impudent traitor?' he snarled. Willigis put a restraining hand on his arm.

'I would not wish to grieve a mother's heart by being explicit,' answered the Wrangler, 'but you are giving me little choice. My meaning is obvious.'

An angry growl rose from the crowd, but Theophanu noted almost mechanically that the soldier behind Otto had moved closer to him, so that the boy was pressed against him. 'It would only need one dagger-thrust,' she thought, but before she could speak, Willigis had stepped forward to defuse the situation.

So it went on all through the endless morning. Feint and counter-feint, threat and counter-threat. Otto was visibly getting tired and anxious; it was a very long time for a four-year-old to stand still. He kept casting longing looks at his mother, whom he clearly remembered, but equally obviously, he had been warned that he must not run to her. Even so, Theophanu became worried that his self-control would snap and he would make some impetuous move that would bring disaster.

Towards noon there was a brief adjournment for each side to assess its position. Many of the loyalists were now eager to rush the enemy and trust to luck and speed that the King would survive. Both Theophanu and Willigis opposed this desperate plan and their view prevailed, so the negotiating positions were taken up again. Once more they went over the arguments, with seemingly no more progress. By now the heat had become oppressive and humid and the sky was becoming overcast. Tempers were getting worn, when all of a sudden a streak of light flashed across the sky from the east and seemed to hang for a moment, glowing ever brighter, before it moved westwards again and vanished from their sight.

For an instant everyone stood staring upwards. Then someone called out,

'A star! A star at midday!'

A man fell to his knees in awe and the whole assembly followed him. The last man to remain on his feet was Duke Henry. His face wore an expression of chagrin and horror. Then he seemed to realise that he alone still stood and he knew that the game was up, with both God and man. He too sank to his knees and the *Thronstreif* was over.

The Lord God could not have displayed his hand more clearly, although some sceptics still expected thunder to follow the unusual lightning. It never came, and so even they agreed it must have been a star. Men learned later that it was seen as far away as Lotharingia. Willigis led them, both loyalists and rebels, in singing *Te Deum laudamus* on their knees and as they rose to their feet, Henry took his little captive by the hand and led him across to his mother. For a moment Theophanu cast her dignity to the winds and did what she had been longing for all day. She flung her arms round her son and, clutching him to her, smothered him with kisses.

All too soon the world intruded again. Willigis's touch on her arm recalled her attention and she relinquished Otto to greet his grandmother while she turned to the Wrangler, now kneeling at her feet. The instinct to kick him in the face was almost overwhelming but an empress must not behave like an ordinary woman. Somehow she needed to win him to her side.

'Sir, you have done much harm to my son and to me, and the Lord has shown you the error of your ways. I charge you to return the imperial regalia, which you have stolen, and to send your men away. When you have done that, Lord Willigis will debate with you what settlement we can reach.'

Henry inclined his head slowly then looked up at her.

'I will do as you bid, Lady,' he said. 'God has indeed made His will clear and I have no choice. Long live Otto III and his guardians, the Empresses Theophanu and Adelheid. Nevertheless I ask you of your clemency to restore my duchy to me and I will serve you loyally.'

'We shall see. I cannot make that decision alone and we are not prepared to discuss it now. My Lord Arch-Chancellor will arrange another meeting with you at another place.'

'Then I shall return home and wait to hear from him,' answered Henry, rising to his feet. He bowed low and strode off to start the process of dispersing his retainers. Theophanu spoke briefly to Willigis then finally had time to turn her attention to the family reunion. She was determined that, at least for the rest of this day, politics would be forgotten and they would pretend to be a normal family.

By this time Otto was making the acquaintance of his sister, Adelheid, whom he had not seen since he was a few months old and did not remember at all. Very properly Adelheid had knelt in obeisance to her little brother, but neither child seemed sure what should happen next. Laughing, their mother suggested that Adelheid should give her brother the gift his family had prepared for him and his delight knew no bounds. The present was none other than his first dagger, beautifully carved and jewelled round the hilt. It was really to mark his fourth birthday a few days away but when Theophanu had commissioned it from Ulfberts, the most famous firm of weaponsmiths in the north, hardly daring to hope that she would have the child back in time for his birthday, she had thought then that it might break the ice between Otto and his family.

The long northern June evening passed in a glow of happiness. Never, it seemed to Theophanu, had the harpists sung so sweetly, never had the Rhenish wines and the mead tasted so delicious, as she sat at the high table in the hall of the manor-house and looked round at the laughing faces of her children, her family, and her trusted advisers and warriors. Truly it had been worth leaving Constantinople and all its refinement for this. For perhaps the first time since her marriage, she felt completely at home.

CHAPTER TWENTY-SIX

Once the captains and the princes had gone home, the imperial party headed for Quedlinburg, the central shrine of their family. On the way they stopped at Gandersheim and to Theophanu's delight, young Sophia was given leave to join her family for a week or two. She and Otto immediately resumed their close bond from infancy, despite the five years difference in age. Little Adelheid still found it hard to reconcile the reverence she knew she ought to feel for her brother the king, with the awkward fact that he undoubtedly belonged to a category of which she thoroughly disapproved – boys. Theophanu shook her head over Sophia, who at times seemed as much of a hoyden as she had always been, but gradually realised that there was a difference. Sophia now knew how to behave when necessary. More surprisingly, it took only a gently reproving look from Abbess Matilda to bring her to heel.

'Unfortunately,' she said to Willigis at the end of a meeting one day, 'neither her grandmother nor I seem to have the same effect.'

The Archbishop smiled. 'We are both too fond of her to be strict enough,' he replied. 'It is good for her that she will not stay at court, but we need to decide about the King. He has to be at court for obvious reasons, but he also needs to be educated. What do you intend to do?'

Theophanu avoided a direct answer. 'I see a change in him as a result of this last year,' she said slowly. 'He was always a whole-hearted child, enthusiastic about all he did, but there's a kind of intensity of feeling now, whether of joy or sadness. It worries me, Lord Archchancellor, because a monarch must not be driven by his passions. It's bad for him and bad for his subjects.'

'We must choose his tutors with even greater care then,' said Willigis. 'He will need at least two, one for his knightly formation and one for his learning. I think this change you notice is not surprising. It seems he was not ill-treated, but he has been cooped up and his frustration is natural at his age. Weapon practice will burn off the excess energy.'

'From the way he chases that pig's bladder around with the choirboys, he certainly doesn't lack energy. Thank goodness they only have leave for a few minutes a day. They were screaming so loudly yesterday that I could hardly concentrate. One of them had such a high-pitched voice he sounded like a girl.'

Willigis decided not to explain that the Princess Sophia had joined in the football the previous day to show the boys how to do it properly. It was a good thing there were no boys at Gandersheim. Then he saw from Theophanu's grin that she knew exactly who the squawker had been. He smiled ruefully to himself. The problem was that the girl was so like her grandfather, Otto the Great; it would be a shame to break her spirit. He turned his mind back to young Otto.

'So we are agreed?' he asked. 'And Empress Adelheid?' The two empresses and Abbess Matilda formed the regency council.

'Yes,' said Theophanu. 'Somehow we have to educate Otto while he travels. His people need to see him and for his safety I am not willing to let him be brought up at a distance from me, so he cannot go to a lord's household, as he would have done had his father lived. We must find a governor for him who is willing to follow him around.'

'I have my eye on Count Hoiko as his knightly tutor,' said Willigis. 'He was one of the first of the Saxon lords to come out against Henry. He was at the Asselburg and he distinguished himself in the rescue of Princess Adelheid. You could not find anyone more loyal and he is a very steady man, just what His Grace needs.'

So it was decided. Willigis left to send a message to Count Hoiko and Theophanu despatched a novice to bring her eldest daughter to her. Sophia had to learn to show more discretion, much as her mother secretly sympathised with her. The Empress did extract a reluctant promise that Sophia would not play football with the boys again but she refused to renounce the game. Until they were eleven, she explained indignantly, the girls at Gandersheim were allowed to kick a ball around in their recreation time, so long as they did not shout.

'You were undoubtedly shouting.'

'I'm sorry, Madam. I will be quiet in future.'

Theophanu sighed. 'Sit down here and talk to me,' she said more gently. 'What do you think was the meaning of the star that displayed your brother's right at Rohr?'

Sophia looked up eagerly, her face alight with enthusiasm. 'Oh, I can tell you that,' she said. 'We had a lesson on natural phono- no, phenomena once. Did you know, Lady Mother, that an eclipse is caused by the earth's shadow and doesn't necessarily signify anything?'

'Yes,' her mother answered patiently. 'We have always known that in the east, or at least since the time of Aristotle. But that was not what I meant. Perhaps the star was a natural phenomenon, although I have never heard of anything quite like it, but its significance lay in its timing. That was what marked it out as a sign from God.'

Sophia considered this. 'Chance?' she asked, hesitantly.

'A very extraordinary coincidence! Is it not more probable to assume that it was a message?' And why am I arguing with a child, she asked herself.

'Yes, I think it must have been,' said Sophia judiciously.

'Good. Well then, Sophia, the message for you is that royalty is a gift from God, and so, just as you have more privileges than other children, as a princess you also have more duties and responsibilities. And that means that you cannot misbehave in public the way you sometimes do. You are nearly nine years old now.'

Tears sprang into Sophia's eyes. 'I'm truly sorry to have grieved you, Mother,' she said. 'I don't mean to be bad. I just forget.'

The interview ended with hugs, kisses, and promises of amendment. In return Theophanu promised to go and hear Sophia act the role of the eight-year-old virgin martyr Charitas in a play written for the girls of Gandersheim by one of their teachers, the noted poetess Rotswitha. When her daughter asked her to hear her lines and she realised that Sophia's part involved her in saying to the Emperor Hadrian,

'I may be young in years yet I am wise enough to confound you in argument,'

the Empress did wonder whether she had really chosen the right school for her strong-willed daughter.

These domestic concerns provided a welcome relief from the business of government but the break could not be prolonged. All too soon Sophia was sent back, Adelheid re-joined her classmates, and Otto settled down to his exercises in real earnest. The Empresses and the Archchancellor heard without surprise the news that Henry had not gone home as promised, but went straight to Bavaria to try to raise local support for his claim to the dukedom. He had not, however, taken up arms again, and they decided to let matters be until the meeting which had been arranged with him in October at Bürstadt. At the beginning of October the court moved to Mainz and stayed in that part of the Rhineland until the new year. Theophanu and Willigis formed the habit of riding out in the afternoons along the banks of the Rhine. It was pleasant exercise and a good way to talk unheard, because the lack of space obliged their retainers to drop back. Inevitably it also furnished scope for gossipmongers and little rhymes aimed at deflating Willigis' pretensions circulated in the streets of Mainz.

Willigis arranged a private meeting with Henry the Younger, the actual Duke of Bavaria. This proved fruitless. Henry was not prepared to surrender his duchy, nor even a part of it, and saw no reason why a traitor should be rewarded for his treason.

'I'm afraid that's a perfectly reasonable attitude and everyone will agree with him, no matter how inconvenient it is for us,' Theophanu commented, when Willigis relayed the result of the meeting. 'The trouble is that the Bürstadt conference will be a complete waste of time, if we can't persuade Henry the Younger to change his mind.'

It was. Nothing was achieved, other than that the two parties did not actually come to blows. The Wrangler had not broken his agreement, at least not technically, and so the suspended threat of outlawry, which hung over him, could not be activated without winning him sympathy. Nevertheless the situation remained intolerably frustrating and distracting.

'At least there's one bit of news which might please you,' Willigis told the Empress in early November. 'You know Bishop Dietrich of Metz?'

'I'm not likely to forget him, am I?' answered Theophanu. 'I thought he'd gone back to Metz to lick his wounds after Rohr. What's he done now?'

'Nothing. Died of an apoplexy.'

'What?' After a moment Theophanu said, crossing herself, 'God have mercy on his soul, but I could never like him,'

Willigis followed suit, but then said with a hint of amusement, 'I hear he's been dictating notes to his secretary for a memoir. You and I will probably go down to future ages with very bad reputations.'

Theophanu smiled. 'That's the least of our worries at present,' she said. 'What I really want at the moment is your advice about the new Bishop of Verdun. Archbishop Adalbero of Rheims, via Gerbert, of course, wants me to confirm the election of Adalbero's nephew, also called Adalbero, to that see. We owe Rheims a great debt for their support last year, and I am happy with the appointment personally, but it will infuriate King Lothar.'

'As he has this absurd belief that Verdun is part of France,' said Willigis. 'It's so difficult because the archdiocese of Rheims straddles the border. We would *normally* consult with the French kings before confirming an appointment in Verdun.'

'We might well do so, if Lothar had not attacked the castle of Verdun without 'consulting' us last summer,' replied Theophanu, grinning. 'It seems to me a good way to get back at him and reward our allies without starting another fight.'

Through the winter Theophanu and Willigis carried on constant negotiations and discussions with Henry the Younger and Duke Otto of Carinthia and a way out of the impasse with the Wrangler began to appear. Henry the Younger might –just might – give up Bavaria in return for Carinthia. Most of Otto of Carinthia'a own holdings and interests were in the Rhine valley and he might be prepared to hand over Carinthia from a mixture of patriotism and promised grants of large holdings. There was a gleam of light at the end of the tunnel as the court spent a peaceful Christmas at Ingelheim on the Rhine. This was the moment that King Lothar of France chose to retaliate over the appointment of the Bishop of Verdun.

Theophanu and Willigis had underestimated Lothar of France's reaction. The kingdom of France, usually called West Francia, was much smaller than Charlemagne's Francia had been. Normandy, Brittany, Aquitaine, Provence, and Burgundy were all independent kingdoms and dukedoms. What was left was the region round the Ile-de-France, with Laon as its capital, but even there the kings had to share much of the territory and influence with the family of the Dukes of France, whose current representative was Hugh Capet.

To the north of this diminished kingdom lay the Duchies of Upper and Lower Lorraine. The young Duke Dietrich, nephew to Hugh Capet and great-nephew to Archbishop Adalbero of Rheims, held Upper Lotharingia, while Charles, unloved younger brother of Lothar of France, had Lower Lorraine. Both were held in vassalage from the Empire, a source of constant irritation to the kings of France. Lothar was, in any case, disappointed by the outcome of the succession crisis in Germany. He had hoped for the guardianship of the child Otto, to which his claim was as good as the Wrangler's, or at the least to have Henry as a compliant puppet-ruler. Theophanu's provocation over the see of Verdun therefore touched a raw nerve.

His first retaliation took the form of a legal attack on Archbishop Adalbero and his secretary, Gerbert, who was also writing letters for, and tutoring the son of Hugh Capet. He accused them of treachery to French interests and summoned an assembly to meet in March at Compiegne near Paris, to hear the charges and set a date for the trial. Gerbert hastily wrote to Theophanu asking for help.

'Are these accusations based on his support for my son's cause?' Theophanu asked Willigis.

'Gerbert would certainly like us to think so,' answered the Archchancellor, 'and it *is* partly true. The other reason for them is that Lothar is trying to annexe church property, to keep it away from reformist monasteries, and the Archdiocese of Rheims under Adalbero is pro-reform.'

'Hmm. My mother-in-law would say that we are doing exactly the same as Lothar in trying to stop her from alienating the lands in her *wittum* to Cluniac monasteries.'

Willigis did not bother to answer that.

'We're going to have to have a showdown with Empress Adelheid soon too.'

'Yes,' said Theophanu meditatively. 'We've done very well not to quarrel for nearly two years, but all good things come to an end. I'm going to ask Abbess Matilda to join us in Thuringia in the spring. She's expert at making her mother see sense.'

Before that could happen, King Lothar launched the second part of his retaliation. In the new year of 985, he launched another attack on Verdun and, after a siege, captured the fortress and its defenders. These included young Duke Dietrich, Thierry to his French subjects, Count Godfrey, the holder of the castle, as well as many other Lotharingian nobles who had shown loyalty to Theophanu and the child-king during the crisis. Thierry's mother, Duchess Beatrice, who had ruled as regent for him until the previous year, had been a particularly staunch supporter of Theophanu and the Empress was appalled when she learned of the young duke's capture.

'We can't possibly ignore this, not when Beatrice did so much for me last year,' she told Willigis.

Her archchancellor agreed completely but both of them wanted to avoid military action if possible, not least because it could make the position of Gerbert and Adalbero even more dangerous. They looked at each other in perplexity then the same idea occurred to both – Hugh Capet. As Thierry's uncle he had a direct interest and right to intervene and his support for the young duke would not stir up French feeling in the way that an imperial intervention would. After an exchange of letters, they set out for Thuringia in late January feeling confident that at least Adalbero and Gerbert would survive the Compiegne meeting unscathed. Meanwhile they had to deal with Adelheid.

CHAPTER TWENTY-SEVEN

Empress Adelheid was as firmly convinced as ever that the German lands in her *wittum* were hers to give away in perpetuity as she pleased, just as her Italian estates were. Even her daughter, Abbess Matilda, could not convince her otherwise. Adelheid did not have the power to overrule Theophanu and Willigis acting in concert to block her grants to Cluniac monastic houses, but she declared her determination to leave Germany as a result and withdraw to the more congenial atmosphere of Italy. Theophanu greeted this decision with official regret and secret delight; Theophanu's exercise of power north of the Alps would be easier with Adelheid out of the way and yet it would be useful to have Adelheid watching over affairs in Italy in conjunction with the Chancellor Philagathos. Nevertheless the situation in France did lead her to ask her mother-in-law for help in one venture before Adelheid left for Italy

Theophanu felt at fault in that she had not taken Gerbert's alarm over his own and his patron's situation seriously enough at first. The Archbishop of Rheims was the most senior and respected churchman in Lothar's kingdom and she had not imagined that the king would make any serious move against him. If the Empire had responded more strongly to the first warning, they might have pre-empted the attack on Verdun. She needed her mother-in-law to help resolve matters between France and Germany.

One of those most interested in these developments was Henry the Wrangler. He knew, and resented, how much the opposition to him the previous year had been started and directed by Gerbert and Adalbero. If those two had fallen foul of the French kings and were to be removed from the scene, that would deprive Theophanu of two of her most loyal and important supporters. There was bound to be profit for the Wrangler in this somewhere and he immediately despatched envoys to Compiegne to assure the Carolingian kings of his cooperation in anything they wanted, provided there was something in it for him.

The outcome caused the imperial court more amusement than anything that had happened for years. Theophanu could hardly contain her laughter as she told Imiza the news that had reached the council.

'They all met, including Henry's envoys, and they all uttered horrible threats to Archbishop Adalbero. Very blood-curdling, apparently, and everyone was getting completely carried away by their venom against the traitors, but then a messenger came in to say that Hugh Capet and six hundred of his knights were mounting a patrol towards Compiegne. Not even attacking them, just patrolling in the area. So, being prudent men, their Majesties Lothar and Louis, and the flower of French chivalry, decided to go home.'

'Just because of a rumour?' Imiza could hardly believe it.

'It was true. Capet was nearby, but he could have been coming to join them, for all they knew.'

'That wasn't likely, when Gerbert is his secretary. What's happened about the trial?'

'Postponed indefinitely. Hugh Capet is such a wonderfully sinister man, isn't he? He says so little and you never know which way he's going to jump,' answered Theophanu.

'Yes, Lady, but that makes him dangerous,' warned Imiza.

'I do know that,' said Theophanu patiently.

Soon Willigis brought even better news. The incident at Compiegne seemed finally to have opened the Wrangler's eyes to the weakness and unreliability of his Carolingian allies. Through a certain Count Herman, he had continued negotiations with Theophanu and Willigis, even while intriguing with the Carolingians, and suddenly his attitude changed. He had realised that there would be no help for him in West Francia, because the Carolingian kings were such broken reeds. Hugh Capet held the real power and at this time Hugh was a firm supporter of Theophanu. Henry signalled that he was now ready to make a full, formal submission to little Otto. At a Reichstag to be held in Frankfurt in the summer, he would pay homage to Otto and his guardians and ask his pardon for his behaviour.

In return Henry would finally be reinstated as Duke of Bavaria, but Carinthia would remain a separate duchy in the hands of Henry the Younger. The months of patient negotiation were about to bear fruit.

Henry also offered to lend his influence in resolving the difficult state of affairs in France and this pleased Theophanu greatly, although it was not so much Henry whose support she wanted, more that of his wife Gisela. Adalbero and Gerbert now looked safe enough for the moment, but the same could not be said of the loyal defenders of Verdun, still held captive by Lothar through his allies, the Heribertine Counts of Blois and Vermandois. This was also the matter in which Theophanu wanted Empress Adelheid's help.

She was not sure whether the idea had been her own or had come from Duchess Beatrice of Upper Lotharingia, so concerned about her hostage son, Duke Thierry. What had struck both Theophanu and Beatrice was the realisation of how inter-related all the royal ladies in the Verdun dispute were, mostly through Empress Adelheid herself. Emma of France was Adelheid's daughter. Theophanu of the Empire was her daughter-in-law. Beatrice of Upper Lotharingia was her late husband, Otto the Great's niece, as was also Adelaide Capet. Gisela of Bavaria was Adelheid's own niece and Matilda of Burgundy was her sister-in-law. Finally the two imperial abbesses, Matilda of Quedlinburg and Gerberga of Gandersheim, were respectively Adelheid's daughter and her niece by marriage.

'If you would use your influence to prevail on all these ladies to meet together, surely with good will we could broker a solution to the Verdun dispute acceptable to all parties?' Theophanu suggested to Adelheid. 'None of the men involved would be present, so there would not be so much need to save face.'

'It is a good idea,' Adelheid agreed. 'What makes you think that any of the various kings and dukes will take any notice of women's decisions?'

'As far as our side goes, that isn't really a problem, is it? You, Willigis and I all want a reasonable agreement, so that travel between France and

Germany becomes easier again – and trade. We won't insist on the minutiae of honour, just to make a point. Nor will Burgundy. Emma has a lot of influence with her husband. Adelaide Capet doesn't, but her husband wants to keep a balance of power between France and us. It gives him more room to manoeuvre.'

'Indeed and that's why Archbishop Adalbero and Gerbert give us so much backing,' said Adelheid. 'They too want no over-mighty neighbours.'

'I'm well aware of that,' said Theophanu dryly. Why did everyone seem to think she needed warning against ambitious men? That was a lesson she had learned soundly in childhood.

'I'm relieved that you are,' responded her mother-in-law. 'I don't think I've ever met anyone as ambitious as young Gerbert.'

'I should have thought Henry of Bavaria could rival him in that department,' objected Theophanu.

'Yes, but he's royal; Gerbert's a peasant.'

Theophanu sighed; just occasionally she missed Constantinople, usually when she was confronted by the extraordinary blindness produced by the western obsession with noble descent.

'Well anyway, while the royally ambitious Henry is in such a helpful mood, he can help us at the colloquium. He has so many links to both sides in Lotharingia.'

'Colloquium?' asked Adelheid.

'Yes; the *Colloquium Dominarum*. That's what we're going to call it – the summit-meeting of the Ladies.'

'I wish you luck,' said her mother-in-law, 'and I will urge everyone to attend, but I will not be there myself. Once Henry has made his formal submission, I'm going straight to Italy.'

'Very well,' agreed the Empress. 'I will start to set up the arrangements for Frankfurt, if you will write to your kinswomen.'

The arrangements proceeded smoothly and by June the little King, the Empresses, Abbess Matilda, and the Arch-chancellor and Chancellor were all assembled in the great courtyard of the palace at Frankfurt to receive

Duke Henry's submission. Theophanu had chosen the setting for this ritual carefully. Frankfurt had been one of the centres of Carolingian power under Charlemagne and its complex of royal, ecclesiastical, and commercial buildings on the hill above the Main formed an imposing sight. Situated near the confluence of the Main with the Rhine, it was on the chief north-south route through Germany, but access to east and west was also good. The story of what happened there would travel quickly round the entire country.

The royal palace stood at the top of the hill, within the castellated walls of the town. In front of it was a large, gravelled square, where the Reichstag, the imperial parliament, would be held. The upper storey of the palace provided a protective backdrop at one side and a colonnade led from there to St. Saviour's Church. An impressive portico and a flight of steps to the upper courtyard of the palace ensured that all would be able to see the drama.

As at Rohr, the imperial party entered first, once the members of the parliament were assembled. The three royal ladies took their seats, this time with Otto enthroned at the centre. He was nearing his fifth birthday now and looked different from the little hostage of a year ago. He had grown several inches and the constant practice with his wooden weapons and his bow and arrow had made him sturdier, as well as bringing a healthy glow to his sun-burned cheeks. He walked with much more confidence and his mother's heart filled with pride as she surveyed him. He looked so much a king and yet also exactly as a little boy ought to look; if only his father could see him now, she thought with sudden regret.

Otto III swirled his cloak professionally as he took his seat, then everyone else sat down. There was a buzz of anticipation then a sudden silence as Duke Henry entered the square. He was dressed as a penitent in sackcloth and sandals, a point Theophanu and Willigis had insisted upon. They were determined that even the most slow-witted onlooker would not fail to grasp the significance of this meeting. Henry had

208

reluctantly agreed, on condition that he did not have to prostrate himself to the King.

Slowly the former rebel walked across the square and came to a halt before the thrones. He fell to his knees there and lifted his hands in petition.

'You have come before your king in penitence for your rebellion. What is it you seek?' asked Otto, as he had learned off by heart. His clear, child's voice rang out confidently over the square.

'I ask nothing but my king's pardon and seek only my life,' replied Henry. Of course this was not true; the point of the bargain he had made was the Duchy of Bavaria, but it needed to be crystal clear to all watchers that the duchy would be bestowed at the King's pleasure, not at Henry's urging.

'If I grant you my pardon and your life, will you swear to become my liegeman, true of life and limb?' asked Otto. That had been more difficult to remember, but he'd got it right. Unseen, his mother squeezed his hand in encouragement and approval.

'I will, so help me God,' said the penitent.

Otto rose to his feet, as did the imperial ladies. Carefully he descended the steps until he stood directly above the Wrangler. Then he reached out his hands and grasped Henry's in his. Theophanu and Adelheid did the same and together they lifted Henry to his feet. The Duke then exchanged the kiss of peace, first with the little king then with the ladies, followed by bear-hugs all round.

At Theophanu's touch on his elbow, Otto remounted the steps and resumed his throne. Henry again knelt before the child, lifted, and held out his hands to him. Otto placed his round the older man's and Henry repeated the words of the oath of homage. Now at last he was Otto's liegeman and vassal, acknowledged so in the sight of God and man, and the bell of St. Saviour's Church rang out to celebrate.

The grant of Bavaria was confirmed by the parliament later in the day and then all the participants climbed to the upper storey of the palace for a festive banquet to welcome the new Duke of Bavaria. It was also a farewell meal for Empress Adelheid, who would start for Italy almost immediately.

The great hall of the palace was filled with trestle tables, all groaning with food. The main dishes were meat of various kinds, pork, veal, lamb and poultry. Stews of river fish stood on every table. Cabbages of several kinds provided a green accompaniment and to finish off there was cheese, wheat bread, honey and nuts saved from the previous autumn. It was rather early for any fruit from trees but there were plenty of the early berries. Wine, mead and ale flowed freely as the singers, dancers, and acrobats entertained the company, but the finest Rhine wine was kept for the end of the feast, when all stood to hand round the loving cup as a pledge of friendship. At the top table Otto and Theophanu started it on its way.

Solemnly the little boy held the huge cup for his mother to drink from, turning his back on his grandmother on his other side. She turned to face him to protect his back. Then Theophanu stooped for Otto to drink, while the guest of honour, Henry of Bavaria on the Empress' right hand, turned to protect her back. When Otto had finished, he and Theophanu moved back to back, while the Empress held the cup for Henry. So it went on until everyone at the table had drunk. It was an apt symbol, Theophanu thought watching it on its travels, of the mixture of suspicion and trust present in the hall and in the Empire.

CHAPTER TWENTY-EIGHT

True to her word, Empress Adelheid set off for Pavia immediately the Reichstag was over, while Theophanu, the little king, and Abbess Matilda, accompanied by the new Duke and Duchess of Bavaria, set off for Metz for the *colloquium dominarum.*

Once the initial greetings were over, the participants took their seats at a round table, so avoiding difficulties of precedence. Nevertheless someone had to open the proceedings and Theophanu was the only empress present. Feeling more nervous than she usually did when presiding at public meetings, she carefully set out the cause of dispute as objectively as she could, and then asked for comment or suggestions on how to resolve the situation. A long silence followed her remarks, which she was determined not to break, having learnt the value of silence as a tool of diplomacy. It also gave her the opportunity to study those attending whom she did not know so well.

Chief amongst these was Emma of France. In appearance she resembled her mother, Adelheid, but Theophanu sensed her to be a much less strong character. Unlike her mother's piercing stare, her eyes shifted, as if always looking round for approval. She had with her a piece of parchment and Theophanu guessed that it contained her husband's instructions.

Sitting on her left was Adelaide Capet, whose expression was as enigmatic as her husband's. Her choice of seat might indicate a leaning towards the French, but her closest relationship was with her sister-in-law, Duchess Beatrice. It would be difficult for her to show a callous indifference to her nephew's fate.

To Emma's right sat *her* sister-in-law, Queen Matilda of Burgundy. Although she was tied by blood to the French house, Matilda's husband, King Conrad, was such a staunch supporter of the Empire that Theophanu was fairly sure that she could rely on her help. The Empress herself was flanked by the two imperial abbesses, Matilda of Quedlinburg and

Gerberga of Gandersheim, sister to Henry of Bavaria. Beyond Gerberga was Henry's wife, Gisela, sitting next to her own mother, Matilda of Burgundy. All men had been banned from this initial session and no records were to be kept, so that all could talk freely.

Abbess Gerberga was the first to take up Theophanu's invitation.

'Perhaps if we went round the table and each of us said what it is our parties most hope to gain from this meeting,' she suggested, 'we might come to a common mind.'

This idea received enthusiastic acceptance, and Duchess Beatrice volunteered to go first, as her concerns were the most personal.

'Obviously, I most want my young son set free,' she said. 'He has just come to manhood and I do not want his youth wasted in a dungeon.'

Murmurs of sympathy greeted her from all sides, but Abbess Gerberga stopped any comment.

'Speak one at a time,' she said firmly. 'We can discuss later. Lady Adelaide, you are the next round the table.'

'That is to go against the sun,' said Adelaide quietly. 'Isn't that supposed to bring bad luck?'

'It is certainly against convention,' replied Gerberga, 'but our meeting like this is against convention and we hope to find a better way forward than the usual methods. Please speak.' She smiled encouragingly at Adelaide, while the rest held their breath. Were they about to discover what the Capets really wanted?

Adelaide inclined her head. 'Very well,' she said. 'Naturally my husband does not want his nephew Thierry to languish in prison, but we also want the power of the Heribertine counts, vassals of King Lothar, restrained.'

There was a brief silence. No Heribertine ladies were present. After a moment Gerberga nodded to Queen Emma.

'Our position is simple,' she said. 'We want control of the fortress of Verdun but we are prepared to compromise over how that control is exercised. I should warn you that the Heribertine counts will not release Count Godfrey under any circumstances. It is an old enmity.'

'Queen Matilda?' asked Gerberga next.

'Burgundy wants the restoration of free trading between France and the Empire.'

'Duchess Gisela?'

'Recognition by France of the succession of Otto III and of the regency council of the imperial ladies and my husband. I am empowered to say that he will release all his Lotharingian vassals from their obedience to help find a solution.'

There was a sharp intake of breath and heads all round the table swivelled towards Theophanu. She nodded her agreement.

'Myself I desire peace,' said Gerberga. 'Lady Theophanu?'

'I too greatly desire peace, but I cannot buy it at the expense of loyal vassals,' answered Theophanu slowly. She smiled at her sister-in-law. 'You are the last to speak.'

'Like you, I seek reconciliation of the claims of justice and mercy,' replied Matilda of Quedlinburg. 'It will not be easy to find.'

The thought did fleetingly cross Theophanu's mind that it was fortunate that the Abbeys of Gandersheim and Quedlinburg had no holdings in Lotharingia. It made it so much easier for the Abbesses to adopt a high moral tone.

'We have already had one offer of compromise,' said the Empress. 'Perhaps there will be more. Lady Emma, I was interested by your remark about ways of exercising control. The Empire does not necessarily need to hold the fortress, so long as rights of transit and trade are guaranteed and the Bishop of Verdun is given access to his see. And the prisoners are released.'

'If you accept our right to the fortress, all the prisoners except Count Godfrey could go free,' promised Emma.

There was a hastily muffled exclamation of delight from Duchess Beatrice. Theophanu felt a lump in her own throat, remembering how she had felt when Otto was restored to her. Nevertheless, she still had to negotiate.

'The Kings of France would acknowledge my son as King of the Germans and Italians?' she asked.

'Yes,' said Emma firmly.

'Ladies, I think we have the basis for a deal,' said Abbess Gerberga.

Nods all round showed their agreement. Obviously details would still be open to bargaining, particularly the financing of such agreements, but with the help of Willigis and other counsellors, such problems could be overcome. Theophanu was in high spirits when she relayed the news to the Archchancellor.

Willigis too was pleased with the outcome, although he warned that persuading Henry's Lotharingian vassals to transfer their allegiance to the Emperor would doubtless carry a substantial transfer fee. He thought that Archbishop Egbert of Trier would probably prove the most expensive.

'Very likely,' said Theophanu, laughing, 'but he has such good artistic taste and such good workmen. I want to borrow them for several projects I have in mind this winter. I want to see if we can combine the skills of the craftsmen I brought from Constantinople with those of the Trier workshop, to produce work that will astound the age – and resound to the glory of God, of course,' she added hastily, misreading Willigis's expression.

'How much is this going to cost?' asked the Archchancellor.

'It's to the glory of God, My Lord Willigis. And to Art. If we're going to have peace, we should use it constructively.'

'That's a big 'if',' said Willigis. 'Messengers have just come in from Italy.' His tone was gloomy but a smile spread over his face. Theophanu did not know what to make of it.

'Not my mother-in-law?' she asked without much hope.

'She sent the messenger, but she is not the problem this time. It's the Pope.'

'Which pope?'

'Good question. I'd better call in the messenger and you can judge for yourself.'

He rang a small silver bell on a table beside him and immediately the door opened. Theophanu was surprised to see that the messenger was a woman then she looked more closely and gave a cry of delight. Forgetting all dignity, she rushed forward and threw her arms round Anastaso.

'I didn't hope to see you again until I returned to Italy,' she said, when she had calmed herself. Anastaso had married a Lombard nobleman and stayed behind when the Empresses rode north to rescue little Otto. Belatedly Theophanu realised that her friend was dressed in black.

'My husband died of fever and his family had always resented me. We had no children so there was no reason for me to stay. They kept the dowry you gave me, which was all they wanted. When I heard that Lady Adelheid was coming to Pavia, I set off to find her and see if I could serve her.'

'You didn't want to go home?' asked the Empress.

'No, there is nothing for me there. I heard last winter that Emilia was dead.' Theophanu nodded; she had heard the same. 'When I reached Pavia, the Empress received me kindly, but then word came that Pope Boniface was dead and Rome was in turmoil again. A message had to be sent to you immediately, of course, and Lady Adelheid arranged for me to travel with the messenger.'

'Boniface is dead! How? Was he killed?'

'We don't know. The rumours are confused. What is certain is that, as soon as he was dead, the Roman mob looted the Lateran Palace, which they seem to think they have a right to do on the death of a pope, stripped his corpse, dragged it outside and left it under the hooves of the statue of Constantine the Great.'

Theophanu gave a most unladylike whistle. 'Constantine the Great? How appropriate! That will teach him to defy the Emperor', she said. 'I wonder how the Eastern Empire will react to the loss of their protegé? What does Basil the Eunuch think of that?'

'We shall never know,' interposed Willigis. 'There was also an embassy from Constantinople. Your former schoolmate, the Emperor Basil II, has finally wearied of the Eunuch's tutelage and taken power himself. Perhaps the thought of his impending thirtieth birthday made him bestir himself. Anyway he's stripped the Eunuch of his offices and wealth and accused him of plotting with –'

He paused and looked at Theophanu with grim amusement.

'Don't keep me in suspense,' she said. 'Which one of my awful uncles this time?'

'Your Uncle Bardas...Phocas.'

'That's a relief.'

'You prefer Bardas Sclerus to Bardas Phocas?'

'Yes. That's only because I don't really know Bardas Sclerus.'

Then seeing Willigis' look of mock reproach,

'What can I do but laugh? At least my father isn't involved this time. Well, that means the East will be in disarray, so they will be unlikely to worry about the loss of Pope Boniface.'

'Yes. The Italians are urging you to return to Italy, but I think it unnecessary.'

'Indeed. I'm not falling for that one again. We stay here and see who the election comes up with.'

After a moment's thought, she asked,

'Who has the actual power in Rome now?'

'The Roman aristocrats, as always. Particularly Crescentius Nomentanus.'

'Let it be unofficially known that if they produce a pontiff we can live with, we will not contest the election, please, Lord Archchancellor. Meanwhile, Anastaso and I have a great deal to catch up on and my son will wish to see his oldest friend. I will see you tomorrow, Lord Willigis.'

CHAPTER TWENTY-NINE

The next few months were exhausting but rewarding for Theophanu. She, Otto, and Henry of Bavaria rode the length and breadth of the Empire north of the Alps – or so it felt – publicly displaying the newfound unity of the imperial family. From the flat lowlands of Holland to the towering mountains of Bavaria, cheering crowds lined the route whenever they approached a settlement, relieved that the spectre of civil war had been averted. By the time they reached Ingelheim for Christmas, Theophanu felt that they all richly deserved the three months of stability and rest that she planned.

Rather to the Empress's surprise, events did go according to her plan. There were occasional rumblings from France and Lotharingia. Archbishop Adalbero was unhappy that his brother Count Godfrey had been sacrificed for the general good and Gerbert's letters on his behalf and on his own were becoming even more indiscreet. In one of them he even stated openly that Lothar was king in name only; the real ruler of France was Hugh Capet. The fact that this was close to the truth would only increase King Lothar's anger, if a copy should ever fall into his hands. However, Theophanu and Willigis, resuming the habit of their rides along the banks of the Rhine, both agreed that the French could be safely left to get on with their squabbles by themselves, while the two of them worked out their strategy for the coming year.

Here for the first time, they came close to falling out. Theophanu still wanted one more ceremonial gesture to demonstrate Henry's allegiance to her son and she wanted it to take place in Saxony, where she still felt least certain of her support, at Easter. Willigis disagreed.

'You run the risk of pushing him too hard. He's a proud man; there's only so much humiliation he can take, and the other nobles won't like seeing his nose rubbed in the dust again.'

'By a foreign woman, I suppose you mean?' asked Theophanu dangerously.

'It doesn't help. You have to be realistic.'

'I too have my pride.'

'Indeed,' answered the Archbishop, 'and there are some who say that you have too much of it.'

'There are those who say that the Lord Archbishop of Mainz is much too concerned with the wealth and status of his archdiocese,' snapped the Empress.

Willigis bit back an angry retort and they rode on in silence for some minutes. Then the Empress said in a softer tone,

'If I am honest, I know that there is some truth in the accusation. I am too proud, but I only seek to secure my son's position.'

'I admit the same, with the same justification concerning my archdiocese,' responded Willigis eventually. 'To exercise power is to be corrupted by it to some degree, I suspect. Leaving that aside, however, I still think you need to tread lightly with the Saxon nobles for political, not moral, reasons.'

For the time being the dispute was shelved and they turned their attention to pleasanter matters. Theophanu was anxious to mend fences with her archchancellor and a fine afternoon in late January took her to the Archbishop's Palace in Mainz. Anastaso and Imiza both accompanied her. The three ladies were shown into the Archbishop's presence carrying a long carpet-like bundle wrapped in crimson wool and to Willigis' surprise and delight, they unwrapped the wool to reveal a chasuble of white Byzantine silk brocade, embroidered with a pattern of crosses and phoenixes.

'Straight from the imperial workshops in Constantinople,' said Theophanu, smiling at Willigis' expression. 'I asked the Princess Anna to oversee its production last year, and Lady Anastaso brought the material north with her.'

'It's magnificent,' said the Archbishop, for once almost lost for words. 'I...I can't thank you enough. White for Eastertide.'

'Yes. You'll be able to wear it for the Easter ceremonies at Quedlinburg,' said Theophanu innocently.

Their eyes met and they both burst into laughter.

'Madam, I never thought you would stoop to bribery!'

'I learn to adapt to my company,' replied the Empress. 'And now we have learned that the Princes of Poland and Bohemia are both going to be there, we have to maintain imperial prestige and unity.'

'Yes; if we can present your scheme to the Saxons in those terms, it will do no harm,' agreed Willigis. 'I have something to show you as well. You remember the prayerbook you commissioned from the scriptorium of St. Alban of Mainz for His Grace? It is almost completed. Shall we ride out to the monastery and see it?'

The rest of the afternoon passed very happily. Theophanu had asked the scribes to decorate the prayerbook, for young Otto to use at services, in the latest fashion, and they had done even more than she expected in sending to Constantinople for details of what was new. She arranged to bring the King with her the following day to see his treasure.

The little king was enraptured by the idea that something as important as a book had been made just for him. Naturally enough, what pleased and interested him most was a double-page illustration showing him, or a boy who looked very like him, prostrate at the feet of Christ. When he came to the painting of the Crucifixion, he wanted to know why the angels only seemed to have the top of their bodies, rather than hovering in the air as usual. Theophanu looked enquiringly at the scribe.

'That is the way they are depicting them in the East now, Lady,' replied the monk. 'We heard you wanted the book to incorporate the latest designs, so the angels look over the top-bar of the cross at our Lord's sufferings. The other new idea is where we show Him between His mother and St. John.'

He showed then the page. Theophanu stared at it, puzzled. Something was different about it but she could not identify what it was. Otto spotted it first.

'Our Lady is on Our Lord's left, not his right. It should be the other way round.'

The scribe looked at them almost apologetically. The Empress was actually frowning and he suddenly realised that the change could be taken as a political comment.

'Again it is the eastern fashion,' he said hastily. 'We copied it from a book made for the Chief Minister of the eastern Empire.'

'Basil the Eunuch?' asked Theophanu, surprised.

'I think his name was Basil. As you know, Lady, he has fallen from power and I think some of his possessions must have been confiscated and sold.'

'And came west so quickly? Well, *sic transit gloria mundi.* That means 'so passes the glory of this world', Otto; we would all do well to remember it,' said his mother to his inattentive head, then grinned at the Archchancellor over it. 'My Lord, the King and I cannot thank you and the brothers enough for the care you have taken with this book.'

Otto looked up, reminded of his manners.

'Oh yes indeed, Lord Archchancellor,' he said warmly. 'I shall never be bored during prayers again.'

Willigis smiled at his obvious sincerity, however unrealistic it was.

'When you can read the words properly, you will find it even more interesting,' he promised. 'We must find you an academic tutor soon.'

'I have given thought to that,' said the Empress. 'When you are nearer seven, you will begin formal lessons and I think Bernward, from the clergy of the Palace Chapel, will make an excellent tutor.'

Otto noted the name but classed it as a distant threat to his autonomy. He would not even be six until the summer. Meanwhile there was all the excitement of getting ready for a summer on the move. They would go first to Grone, on the borders of Saxony, and then on to Quedlinburg for Easter.

Otto was still too young to appreciate the political significance of the arrangements his mother had made for that Easter but he liked the fact that they all seemed to centre round him. The three sacred days from Maundy Thursday to Easter morning were spent quietly at the convent on the hill, but the long services were enlivened for him by being able to look at the pictures in his new prayerbook and it was fun to watch his sister Adelheid, who was now old enough to sing with the canonesses. Like Adelheid, Otto enjoyed the music, and briefly he envied his old football friends singing in the boys' choir. Such feelings were dispelled, however, on Sunday morning, when he was dressed in his royal robes to 'go under the crown' as it was called, a ceremonial crown-wearing.

The procession assembled at the foot of the hill. All the great nobles of church and state from the north and east of the Empire were there, as well as the Princes of Bohemia and Poland. In splendid array they climbed the steep road that led up to the church on the hill and at their head marched young Otto, next to his mother, with his fleur-de-lys decorated child's crown balanced firmly on his head. it was a bright and breezy early April day and the sunlight gleamed and glittered from the silks of the clothes and banners and the from the polished metal of the jewels and armour. After Mass came the festival banquet, the part of Theophanu's plans which had worried Willigis.

What had disturbed the Archchancellor was the Empress's determination that the little king's table – and, of course, her own – should be served by the four leading dukes of Germany. Henry of Bavaria was to wait at table, Conrad of Swabia to be the chamberlain, Henry the Younger of Carinthia the cellarer, and Bernhard of Saxony the marshall. It was not Theophanu's own idea; Otto the Great had used the same ploy at his coronation in 936, to emphasise the need for internal unity and the subordination of the duchies to the royal dynasty.

Looking round the hall, Willigis judged that she had got away with it. Certainly Boleslav of Bohemia, Henry's former ally, was looking stunned and subdued to see the Duke of Bavaria meekly waiting on the little boy and the Greek woman. The key to her success, Willigis realised, had been the procession. As he followed her up the hill, at the head of the bishops and behind them the nobles, all strictly in order of rank, with incense swirling past their heads, he had understood that she was recreating one of the stational liturgies of Constantinople, when the Sacred Emperor would walk through the streets and show himself to his people. Looking at the faces of the country-people lining the route, Willigis had seen the depth of awe in their eyes and realised that, by elevating the status of the Emperor, Theophanu had removed the humiliation from the table-service of the royal dukes. She was even cleverer than he had given her credit for, he reflected admiringly.

Otto cared nothing as yet for all this but he thought it was good fun to have a great and rather frightening man like Duke Henry waiting on him. It was even better the next day when he received Duke Miesco of Poland in formal audience. After Miesco had sworn an oath of allegiance to the king, he presented his young liegelord with a gift. That was customary, but the gift, a camel, was not. Otto contained his excitement until the audience was over, then rushed off to examine his new treasure. The lack of enthusiasm expressed by the women in his life did not trouble him at all. His mother and Anastaso both said, rather deflatingly, that they had seen plenty of camels in their time.

'Moreover,' said Anastaso, normally Otto's staunchest supporter in the little trials of his life, 'I don't know how Duke Miesco thinks it's going to survive in this climate.'

'Nobody could,' said the Empress, shivering. It had turned cold overnight and she was still in her silken court garments. She could feel a head-cold coming on.

'Your Grace, why don't you go and ask if your sister may come to see the camel?' suggested Imiza, feeling sorry for the little boy. Adelheid would doubtless be a more receptive audience.

In the end it was agreed that all the children of the convent, girls and boys, could have leave to view the wondrous beast, as a part of God's creation. Miesco watched them, smiling in satisfaction. Subtler than

Boleslav, he had guessed correctly that the camel would find a quicker way to a child-king's favour than more conventional gifts.

Otto soon heard the outcome of the negotiations and shouted aloud with joy. In the summer, at the age of six, he would embark on his first campaign, leading his troops to re-conquer the lands which had been lost in the great Slav rebellion before his father's death.

CHAPTER THIRTY

'Why on earth did you agree?' asked Anastaso, when they were alone. 'The boy is not even six years old yet.'

'It was necessary to gain the alliance with Duke Miesco,' explained the Empress.

'But why the *child*? He can't fight, any more than you can.'

'It seems he is needed there in person to represent the Empire's claim to the lost lands,' said Theophanu. 'His presence confirms that the Empire extends right to the Polish border.'

'Why are you making such a fuss, Anastaso?' asked Imiza. 'There are always boys in battle to look after the horses and take messages and so on. Remember, Lady,' she added to the Empress, 'when your late husband campaigned against the Danes and you accompanied him in 974? Young Olaf Tryggvason, who's stirring up trouble in Norway now, was there as a boy of ten.'

'Ten is not six!' snapped Anastaso, close to tears. 'Madam, you *know* it's barbarous.'

Theophanu gave her a tight smile.

'It is the custom here, Anastaso,' she said gently. 'He'll be perfectly safe. He'll always be surrounded by you and me and the clergy of the Chapel Royal, and around us a circle of armoured knights. Of course he will not actually fight, but he will see war for what it actually is.'

The memory of those words rang hollowly in her mind some months later in high summer, as the royal party huddled together in the middle of a clearing in boggy woodland somewhere on the upper reaches of the River Oder. Temporarily, at least, they were lost.

At first all had gone well. Otto was, of course, extremely scornful of his womenfolks' apprehensions and delighted in the pomp and panoply of war. He had a specially-made suit of padded leather, strong enough to protect him but not too heavy to wear, and he was given a long dagger, which fitted into a sheath at his waist. Thus attired, he presided over the muster at Merseburg, where he discovered to his joy that the captain of his bodyguard was to be none other than his old friend, Nancilinus, his protector in Italy in his infancy. Count Hoiko, his tutor, would always be with him too.

The boy, not to mention his mother, coped well with the hardships and privations of being on campaign. Theophanu was sure that she minded the shortage of hot water and the constant dirt far more than Otto did, but the sparsity and simplicity of the food troubled neither of them. Theophanu sometimes felt that she had not eaten a really tasty meal since leaving Italy, so the campaign diet was no great hardship. As for living in a leather tent rather than a permanent building, Otto was enthusiastic. The ladies were less so.

The army marched proud and unresisted along the northern border of Bohemia, until, as arranged, it met up with Miesco's troops. Then the two armies, in reality under the joint command of Marquis Ekkehard of Meissen and Prince Miesco, turned north and headed into lands they wanted to re-conquer. The Lutizi, the particular Wendish tribe they were attacking, could not mobilise an army to oppose them in pitched battle, and so it was a campaign of skirmishes and ambushes. What this led to on the ground, Theophanu realised, was the raiding and firing of villages and outlying farmsteads. The men were all put to the sword, which was savage enough, but what really troubled her conscience were the sad processions of captured women and children. Long lines of them, shackled at the neck, were sent back to the slave markets of Magdeburg, from there to be sold on all over Europe, North Africa and the Middle East.

'Why do they never enslave the men?' she asked Imiza one day, as they watched a group file westwards past the opening to the imperial tent.

'They could become Christians. By law, you can't enslave an adult male Christian. Women and children don't count.'

'It *is* barbarous,' observed the Empress.

'You have no slaves in Constantinople?' enquired Imiza, her tone hard. She was becoming tired of being accused of barbarity by Greeks. 'Strange how some of these will end up in slave markets there then.'

'Yes; I'm sorry,' answered Theophanu. 'As a child you just accept things and don't think about their implications.'

'That's why it's good for His Grace to be on campaign so young. He will grow up knowing the cost.'

'Oh, I think he already knows the cost of many things,' retorted his mother. 'He has not had an easy childhood.'

Today's events seemed likely to make it even harder, she thought anxiously, as she murmured soothing words to her nervous horse. Their campaign had been victorious and they were making their way back westwards. They had all slightly dropped their guard and the royal party was riding with a smaller escort than was customary. On a hunting foray they had just ridden through yet another devastated village when they found their way barred by a surprisingly large band of howling savages.

A fierce fight developed, less unequal in numbers than usual. Every man, including the clergy, had to fight and none could be spared to keep an eye on the little king. He drew his dagger and was waving it, enthusiastically but ineffectively, in the air, when a horsefly stung his pony. It reared then bolted, by chance clean through a gap in the fighting, and shot off into the forest.

Theophanu immediately set spurs to her own mount, a daughter of Windswift, and raced after him, shouting in a high, desperate voice which might carry through the battle to Nancilinus.

Even through the din, he heard, but could not disengage immediately. He sliced down with his sword, biting deep into his enemy's neck, and manoeuvred his horse out of the fray, just in time to see Imiza vanishing through the trees. He spurred after her, following a zigzag course, and within minutes they caught sight of the Empress ahead of them. She had dismounted and was stooping over something on the ground. Cursing,

Nancilinus rushed forward, but Theophanu shouted to him to be wary. The ground was treacherous.

By the time he reached her, she had risen to her feet, with Otto in her arms. He was conscious and his fallen pony lay some yards away. The ground, turning suddenly marshy near a stream, had caused the horse's foot to give way, but luckily, as it fell, it had thrown the boy's light body completely clear and he had landed flat on the soggy earth. He was winded and bruised, but otherwise unhurt.

Once Nancilinus had checked that the King would have nothing worse than bruises as a souvenir of the fall, he turned his attention to the screaming pony. Its leg looked broken and the noise it was making would bring undesirable onlookers. Using his broad body to block Otto's view, Nancilinus quickly put it out of its agony, and rejoined the others, taking the little boy up on his own saddle.

Once the pony's screams died away, there was silence. They were surprised not to be able to hear the noise of the battle, but away from the boggy clearing round the stream, the trees were densely-packed and the thick leaf-cover muffled all sounds. None of them had noticed exactly which way they had entered the clearing and the firmer ground of the forest proper carried no hoof-marks. Away from the clearing the trees marched endlessly, with no sign of a path. They were lost in hostile territory.

Theophanu and Imiza drew their hunting bows and made sure their arrows were within easy reach.

'Now,' the Empress said to her son, who was still showing signs of shock, 'we've got a very important job for you, Otto, because your young eyes are sharper than anyone's, so you need to keep them skinned. You're our tracker, just like on a hunt. You watch for a hoof-mark or crushed grass or a broken twig. Imiza and I will do the same, while Nancilinus keeps watch for enemies. Understand?'

'Yes, Madam,' replied the boy formally, colour returning to his cheeks now that he had an important job to do.

He thought for a moment, then said,

'We never crossed the stream, so we must have come from somewhere this side.'

'Good,' said Theophanu. 'Let's ride along the edge of the clearing on thist side then and see what you can find.'

'Watch above the trees for carrion birds flocking as well, Ladies,' added Nancilinus.

Before too long Otto gave an excited cry. A stand of hazel had several small branches broken back. They aligned their horses with the direction of the damage and set off away from the clearing, with Nancilinus, his sword drawn, peering from side to side, listening for any sound. Soon they found a faint hoof print, then a glade where the blades of grass had been bent and not yet straightened.

Shortly afterwards, Nancilinus gave a whisper of warning, but they could all clearly hear the sound of hoofbeats coming towards them. Theophanu and Imiza fitted their arrows and drew back the strings but cries of welcome and warning came from the new arrivals. As they lowered their bows, Count Hoiko flung himself from his saddle and rushed towards his missing charge.

'All's well, Lord Count,' said the Empress. 'His Grace is unharmed; indeed, it was his tracking skills which brought us home safely. You have trained him well.'

The German force had defeated and largely annihilated the enemy horde. There was a joyful victory celebration that night, at which the young tracker was the hero of the hour. From then on, the campaign concluded as had been planned. The whole of the Meissen area was now back under imperial control, although the pagans still held the land from there north to the Baltic coast. By the autumn Otto and Theophanu were in Saxony again, discovering that while there was internal peace throughout the Empire, on its borders trouble was brewing.

To the north and southeast the upheavals seemed to need watching rather than immediate action. Swein Forkbeard had usurped the Danish throne from his father, Harold Bluetooth, and driven the old man into exile eastwards along the Baltic coast to the island of Rugen, where he died of his wounds in the autumn. Swein would almost certainly be an even more difficult neighbour than his father, but the north was well-fortified and guarded since the Slav Revolt.

The news from the Eastern Empire was more unexpected. Having taken power into his own hands, young Basil II had used the summer to mount a large punitive expedition against the Bulgars. He laid siege to Sofia for three weeks without achieving anything, then decided to withdraw his troops. On the long trail back to Constantinople they were ambushed and soundly defeated. Basil lost two thirds of his army as well as his treasury and baggage. For a new emperor, it was a profoundly humiliating experience and Basil vowed revenge against the whole Bulgar nation. Looking at his record, nobody took his threats seriously, but Theophanu remembered how he had frightened her as a child and shuddered for the Bulgars. As a result of the defeat there were murmurs about Basil's fitness to rule, but no rebel had taken any action as yet.

The real problem, as usual, lay in France. The unexpected death of King Lothar in the spring, at the age of forty-four, had endangered the peace achieved by the *Colloquium Dominarum*, but Louis V, Lothar's nineteen year-old-son and co-king, had succeeded to the throne without trouble. Queen Emma wrote in April that she was confident that she would prevail on her son to continue his father's policy of peace with the Empire, but she underestimated Louis' resentment of her attempts to control him. The situation paralleled the relationship between Otto II and Empress Adelheid in the mid-seventies, thought Theophanu grimly. Funny how her own sympathies were now with the mother rather than the son.

'He's attacking Queen Emma on two fronts,' Willigis told the Empress, when they were re-united in the Rhineland in the autumn, 'and both of them involve us.'

'How so?'

'Duke Charles of Lower Lotharingia has renewed the old accusation that Emma committed adultery with Bishop Ascelin of Laon, an accusation which King Lothar refused to countenance, if you remember, and King Louis is supporting Charles against his own mother. In a queen adultery is a capital charge, because it's treason, so Queen Emma has had to flee the court. She's taken refuge with Archbishop Adalbero at Rheims.'

'In the past I was rather inclined to believe those allegations,' said Theophanu slowly. 'I was weary of hearing so much from my mother-in-law about the ever-perfect Queen Emma, I suppose, but now I know myself how lightly and unjustly such accusations can be made, I'm not so sure. My husband certainly believed them.'

'I doubt whether he cared one way or the other,' said Willigis. 'He *did* want Charles to become a vassal of the Empire.'

'And now Louis pretends to believe them, to get out of leading-strings and to carry on his dispute with Archbishop Adalbero, who just happens to be Ascelin's uncle,' worked out Theophanu.

'Exactly.'

'Can't we leave them to wash their own dirty linen?'

'Not entirely and not easily. I haven't told you the whole of it yet. First, Emma has written a desperate letter to *her* mother, Empress Adelheid, asking her to intercede with you for support – one mother to another and all that.'

Theophanu put her head in her hands and groaned.

'No use groaning,' said the Archchancellor unsympathetically. 'You were the one that wanted to bring the personal into politics. Anyway, the Dowager-Empress is meeting us at Grone to advocate her daughter's cause.'

'What does she have to say about all the complaints about her disastrous administration in Italy that came in last spring?' asked Theophanu.

'Probably that Gerbert was behind them. It will be an interesting meeting,' said Willigis with a grin, 'but the real trouble, Lady, is that Louis and Charles are attacking Rheims and its properties and demanding again that Archbishop Adalbero be tried for treason.'

'And Charles is my son's vassal from the one side and so is Adalbero from the other. Quite apart from Emma's problems.'

'It's a nice little conundrum,' agreed Willigis.

Theophanu gave a short, humourless laugh.

'I can see why men find warfare so appealing. It's so much simpler. So what do you recommend that we do, Lord Archchancellor?'

'We have to meet Lady Adelheid, obviously. I suggest that we give her some rich gifts that she can hand on to her favourite convents and monasteries. That will please her, but more importantly, it will indicate that she is in your favour and, by implication, her daughter will not be abandoned.'

Theophanu nodded. 'Fine. What about Adalbero?'

'That will relieve some of the threat to him. I'm sure Gerbert is in close contact with Hugh Capet anyway. We keep troops armed and ready near the border, but the last thing we want is war with France. That would make all the progress of the last few years pointless.'

'Our real difficulty, in strict confidence, of course,' said the Empress, 'is that the accusation against Adalbero is not unfounded. If I were Louis, I would consider him a traitor.'

'When Gerbert writes letters saying openly that the Carolingians are finished, it isn't hard to see Louis' point of view,' admitted Willigis. 'I think, though, that Louis misunderstands him and we must take care not to make the same mistake. He and Adalbero are actually neither pro-Ottonian nor pro-Carolingian. They are for whatever is best for the Archdiocese of Rheims and preserves the peace.'

'That could turn out to be the most dangerous position of all,' said the Empress sombrely.

CHAPTER THIRTY-ONE

By the early summer of the following year, the Empress's words seemed to be prophetic. Despite the reading aloud of Queen Emma's plea to her mother at a meeting of the court at Andernach on the Rhine in mid-January, the Empire refused to get involved.

'I wish that I might be allowed to love her (Theophanu's) son, since I look on mine as my enemy,' Emma had begged, but it made no difference. Her own son Louis was still determined that Archbishop Adalbero should stand trial and fixed a date, March 27th. To make sure that Adalbero actually turned up this time, he and his army marched on Rheims and to most people's surprise, Hugh Capet went with them.

'What game is Capet playing now?' Theophanu asked Willigis as soon as he entered her audience-chamber one day in March.

'I really don't know, Madam,' answered the Archchancellor. 'Could we leave that for a bit, do you think?'

'Of course. I assumed that was why you wanted to see me.'

'Yes; I do, but this other matter is more personal. Have you had any letters from Princess Anna in the last few days?'

'No. Why?'

Willigis groaned. 'I was hoping she would have broken the news,' he said ruefully, as he seated himself at Theophanu's nod.

'You remember the crushing defeat that Emperor Basil suffered last summer? I'm afraid it's put ideas above his station into your uncle Bardas Sclerus' head. He landed in Anatolia and launched a bid for the throne in the new year. Backed up by troops provided by the Caliph of Baghdad.'

Theophanu was silent, absorbing the full enormity.

'Apostate as well as traitor,' she said tonelessly.

'There's no evidence he's renounced his religion. But all the same, if he becomes emperor, it could only be as a puppet of the Saracens.'

'My father?' Theophanu asked in the same expressionless tone.

Willigis looked at her sympathetically. 'Yes; he's with Bardas.'

'Strange, isn't it,' Theophanu said meditatively, 'how it's always kinsfolk who create the real problems in life? A celibate orphan is obviously the best thing to be.'

'There are gains and losses in every state,' replied Willigis rather stiffly. Theophanu pulled herself together.

'I'm sorry, Lord Willigis. I spoke out of exasperation, without thinking,' she said swiftly. 'I suppose the difficulty for us is that when this news gets out, it will seem to uphold that silly rumour that I supported the Saracens at Cotrone.'

'I don't think it will matter, while your policies remain as popular as they are now.'

'But if I wanted to do something which did not meet with general approval....' Theophanu did not bother to finish the sentence.

'There is also the question of how our relationship with the Eastern Empire will be affected.'

'That will depend on who wins, won't it? How is the great rebellion prospering so far?'

'No news as yet. Perhaps we *should* concentrate on France instead.'

'Well, Hugh Capet would go down well in the East. He's devious enough. Do we have any idea why he's with Louis?'

'It could be that he wants to see fair play.' Willigis broke off as the Empress began to laugh helplessly, then he too joined in. The sheer incongruity of the idea of fair play anywhere was too absurd.

'I think it would be a good idea to remove Gerbert from the scene before he commits any more indiscretions,' said Theophanu, after they had sobered up. 'He's still officially Abbot of Bobbio and therefore my son's vassal. He owes us military service. He can order his knights north to support the campaign in the east this summer and lead them himself.'

'He won't like that,' pointed out Willigis.'

'I know he won't, but it could save his life. Louis will never dare put Adalbero to death, but Gerbert is expendable.'

'I'll send messengers off straight away. Meanwhile, we'll have to delay the court's departure for Saxony as long as possible.'

'Easter is very late this year luckily. The trial should be over by then.'

In the event Easter was long gone by the time the trial started. Adalbero won a little time by agreeing that Louis could dismantle two fortresses belonging to the Archdiocese of Rheims, and the King postponed the trial from March to May 29th. Gerbert and his grumbles were safely out of harm's way by then, just as well, because he had written another letter to a friend saying that King Louis was 'a man most distressing to his friends but not very distressing to his enemies.' It never seemed to occur to him that such comments were unlikely to remain confidential.

Theophanu and Willigis were alarmed by a message Gerbert sent in the spring, warning them that a secret meeting, for unspecified purposes, was being set up by Duchess Beatrice of Upper Lotharingia. It was to be held near Verdun immediately after Adalbero's trial and the list of participants made interesting reading. Predominant among them was Empress Adelheid. The enigmatic Hugh Capet was also to be present. So was King Louis of France. Surprisingly the unswervingly loyal Duke Conrad of Swabia would be there too. Gerbert had sent the warning via the Archbishop of Cologne, Everger, the friendly monk who had tried to comfort little Otto before his kidnap. That Everger considered it worth sending on suggested it was more than Gerbert's usual tendency to see plots everywhere.

'It does look very much as if they've decided to re-negotiate an agreement over Verdun, and perhaps over Archbishop Adalbero too, and leave the foreign woman and the commoner out of it,' Theophanu said to Willigis one day. 'I suppose we were over-optimistic in hoping that a few grants of land would pacify my mother-in-law. If it were Sophia in danger, I should no doubt feel the same.'

'Yes; it's easy to understand, but *we* have to consider the Empire as a whole, not just the Rhineland and Lotharingia, and, frankly, so should the

Dowager-Empress. What worries me is the question of *why* they don't want us there. They must know that we certainly don't want war with France, and I don't believe it's *only* snobbery and xenophobia that keeps us out. There must be something going on that they don't want us to know about.'

'The timing is so odd,' said the Empress. 'Surely they would have done better to meet before the trial?'

'Not if they've decided to sacrifice Adalbero to save Queen Emma, or even Count Godfrey of Verdun,' pointed out Willigis. 'One brother pays for another.'

'I always forget that Adalbero and Godfrey are brothers,' answered Theophanu. 'Possibly they want to ditch them both for Emma. Well, time will no doubt reveal the truth'

What time had in store was, not the true purpose of the meeting, but an irrevocable alteration of the political situation in France. In the fourth week of May Theophanu and Otto held court at Allstedt in Saxony. Here they formally restored to Empress Adelheid the lands in her *wittum,* which had been confiscated from her in 984. This followed a private meeting between Theophanu and Adelheid the previous night. It had not been an easy encounter.

'I cannot understand your unwillingness to help my daughter,' Adelheid had reproached the Empress. 'When your son was in danger, I did all I could to assist you, but you will do nothing in return.'

Theophanu winced. She could feel the justice in the claim all too clearly, but she could not risk war, as she tried to explain.

'I am not asking you to go to war,' said Adelheid with some exasperation. 'I only ask for your influence with Louis.'

'But I have no influence with him. He's your grandson, not mine.'

'And a disobedient ingrate he is too,' said Adelheid grimly. 'Nevertheless, if you would throw the whole weight of the Empire behind my daughter's innocence, he could not ignore you.'

'Honestly, Mother, I think he could,' said Theophanu, temporarily genuinely sorry for the older woman's plight. 'He is a spoilt young man who has little sense of his responsibilities. He was already a spoilt child when I first met him at Margut when he was thirteen. Even his own people are calling him *le roi fainéant*. God knows why. In my opinion he's already done too much.'

'It seems he formed a great admiration for you at that meeting,' replied Adelheid. 'You know how young boys sometimes do form attachments to girls a little older than themselves, and you were always so glamorous and exotic. That is why I think he might listen to you now.'

Theophanu looked at her normally shrewd mother-in-law narrowly.

'King Louis has a strange way of showing his admiration by charging my chief vassal in France with committing treason by supporting my son,' she observed sceptically. 'Come, Lady, what have you really come to say – and is it the same as what you will say at this meeting you have arranged with Louis and Hugh Capet?'

Adelheid bridled angrily, but kept sufficient awareness of her purpose to restrain her tongue. She should have taken a much firmer line with Theophanu when she was still a girl, she thought resignedly.

'I have got an offer for you,' she admitted.

'Let's hear it.'

'If I accepted my *wittum* and retired from all public matters, would that satisfy you?'

Theophanu considered. In reality she had already decided to do what she could for Emma by diplomacy and influence, but had little hope of success. Adelheid's offer was worth accepting, however, because if the dowager were off the political scene, it would make it easier to clear up the mess she had created in Italy.

'I agree,' the Empress said. 'I will do what I can to help your daughter.'

The formal grants were made and the court concluded with the usual banquet, but the next morning astounding news broke. Louis Do-nothing, true to his nickname, had taken time off from Adalbero's trial at

Compiegne to go hunting in the thick forests there. In hot pursuit of a wild boar, his horse had stumbled over a tree root and thrown the King headlong. He hit the ground awkwardly and broke his neck. He was dead within a moment or two.

'I wonder where Hugh Capet was,' was Willigis' first comment, when they could discuss the tragedy. Theophanu looked at him.

'You surely don't imagine...' she started to say, but Willigis shook his head.

'I make no accusations,' he said quickly, 'but you know how many rumours there were that King Lothar was poisoned. Another tragedy so soon afterwards is certainly a coincidence. And so many people stand to benefit, including ourselves,' he added.

'Adalbero, Emma, Adelheid, Hugh Capet, Charles of Lorraine, Godfrey of Verdun,' enumerated the Empress. 'We shall have to go back west straightaway, in case of trouble. The campaign against the Wends will have to wait.'

The cancellation of the summer's campaigning disappointed some and pleased others. Theophanu expected an outburst from Otto but he took the news philosophically. He had just started lessons with his new tutor, Bernward of Hildesheim, and the young man was proving adept at capturing his pupil's attention. Although well-educated and a priest of the Chapel Royal himself, Bernward had acted as estate manager for his family for a time, and had a wide-ranging interest in various crafts, particularly wood-carving and gold-smithing.

Gerbert too was relieved to be going back to France. He wanted to rejoin his master, Archbishop Adalbero, as soon as possible and also to be certain that his collection of organs was receiving proper care. Anastaso was delighted to be spared the brutalities of another campaign in the east, a sentiment which her mistress secretly shared. The sight of the trail of slaves heading west still lay heavy on Theophanu's conscience.

'It's the fact that no attempt is made to bring them to our Lord which appals me,' she admitted to Anastaso. 'They have to suffer as a result of our policies in this life; that can't be helped, but there is no reason to condemn their souls to hell.'

'Is there nothing you can do?' asked Anastaso.

'I shall do what I can to increase missionary effort, perhaps through the monastery at Memleben that my husband founded. When I get to Rome, if I ever do, I shall talk with Pope John about it. The trouble is that the western-rite bishops always seem to think in terms of compulsion rather than persuasion, which is futile, as the Slav revolt showed. Anyway, at least we shan't have to witness any slave processions this year.'

All in all it was a cheerful cavalcade which wound its way towards the Rhine. They heard that all charges against Adalbero and Gerbert had lapsed with the death of their accuser, a relief to all. The next news was that, as Chancellor and Primate of France, Archbishop Adalbero immediately conferred the regency on Hugh Capet.

Hugh decided to convene the electoral assembly to choose a new king quickly, while everyone was still gathered together for the superseded trial. He decreed that the election should be held at Senlis near Paris at the beginning of June.

CHAPTER THIRTY-TWO

Gerbert parted from the court on the way west, so that he could go straight to join his master at Rheims, but kept the Empress well-supplied with information about what was happening, as well as assurances of his loyalty to her personally, not just the dynasty.

'Obviously he wants our support for Hugh Capet,' said Theophanu to her Archchancellor, 'but it seems that Charles of Lower Lorraine has turned up in Rheims seeking to get the Archbishop on his side.'

Willigis nodded. 'In normal circumstances Charles would be the obvious successor. He's Carolingian, he's of full age, he has sons, but he has an unsuitable wife and he's your son's vassal. If they decide to go for an election rather than the hereditary principle, he won't win.'

'His wife's too common for the French nobility?'

'Yes. Believe it or not, they're even more fussed about that than we are. But it's his links to the Empire that are the main problem.'

'As they are for us actually,' said the Empress. 'If he becomes King of France, he'll almost certainly try to take Lower Lotharingia back into the French orbit, which is the last thing we want. As his feudal lord, however, I think there will be pressure on me from many of our nobles for my son to support his claim.'

'I'm sure you are equal to opposing such pressure,' rejoined Willigis smiling. 'Unfortunately for him, Charles has been so devious and made himself so unpopular that his support will be less than one would expect. We shall need a *quid pro quo* from Hugh Capet, though, if we stay out of it.'

'Oh yes. I think we both have notions of what form that might take. I will also do what I've been meaning to for some time, invite Charles's son Otto to come to court as a companion for my little Otto. They are much of an age and it will be good for Otto to have a comrade of high rank, as his father had in the 'Young Ottos'. I have made enquiries and he's reported to be a good lad. It will keep the boy safe too.'

239

'Which boy?' For once Willigis was puzzled.

'Otto of Lotharingia. If Hugh Capet wins, Charles and his family are going to be a threat to him. The deaths of Louis and Lothar probably were accidents, but if we have custody of Charles's heir, we can make sure no accident happens to him. It's perfectly proper for him to be brought up with his liege lord my son.'

'And if word gets out before the election, it will be another good reason for the French not to elect Charles,' added Willigis.

'So, we had better see to it,' finished the Empress.

In the event at Senlis, Adalbero made a rousing speech in favour of retaining the electoral principle, which was enthusiastically embraced by the assembly. When the votes were taken, the result was a unanimous victory for Hugh Capet. The coronation took place at Noyon on July 3rd.

By this time Theophanu was in Lower Lotharingia, Charles's own dukedom, where trouble was obviously most to be expected.

The price the Empire had demanded for not opposing Hugh Capet was the freeing of Count Godfrey and the return of Verdun. Gerbert wrote directly to her, warning her that, although Count Godfrey had indeed been set free on June 17th, the Heribertine counts, who actually held him, had dictated altered terms, which were not to the Empire's advantage, and the Empress needed to intervene again.

This problem was soon overshadowed by Charles of Lotharingia's anger at his rejection. Allies of his seized the fortress of Chevremont on the Meuse and started systematically laying waste the surrounding countryside. The peasants appealed to Notker, Bishop of Liege, their lord, for help. Knowing the Empress to be nearby, he sent to her to meet him with reinforcements to retake the stronghold. With little Otto and a small number of guards, she was preparing to do so, when another urgent letter arrived from Gerbert.

'He says that if I venture near Chevremont with only a small force, he has learnt that I will be attacked, regardless of my rank,' Theophanu told Imiza and Anastaso. 'I am not sure what to do.'

'Surely, Madam, you are not thinking of going back on your word to Bishop Notker?' said Imiza, shocked. Anastaso lifted her carefully-plucked eyebrows to her hairline. Common sense was obviously not going to get a look in.

'No, no. I shall go, of course, but do I take my son with me, or leave him here, when I have such a small force at my disposal? Which is more dangerous for him?'

'The Lord Abbot of Bobbio always exaggerates,' said Imiza, with some truth. 'It's his southern blood.'

Her two interlocutors exchanged amused glances.

'Indeed, that must be it,' murmured the Empress. 'So your advice is to take the King, Lady Imiza. What about you, Lady Anastaso?'

'Are you prepared to chain His Grace up, to stop him following you?' asked Anastaso dryly.

Theophanu laughed. 'True; you know him better than any of us, Anastaso,' she said. 'Very well then; let us take the adventure together. We must be ready to ride in two hours.'

As she had ordered, the small force set out on time but at a steady pace. The commander of the guard refused to go any faster.

'My scouts say we have thirty miles to cover to Bishop Notker's latest position, Lady,' he told Theophanu. 'The greatest danger will arise as we draw near, because we have to pass near Chevremont. The lay of the land in the valley compels us. We can't risk tiring the horses before then, because it could all come down to a sprint.'

'I used to be good at horse-racing in my youth,' Theophanu said. 'Once I even outraced the Emperor, when I was a girl.'

'Good,' said the captain, with a grim smile. 'We will try to stay together, but if you hear me shout 'Go', you and His Grace must ride hell-for-leather, while we hold them off. His pony is strong.'

'Yes; it has Arab blood in it,' answered Theophanu. 'Very well, Captain, we will do as you say.'

241

All went well until they reached a point about a mile from the rendezvous. The valley started to open out and they could see Bishop Notker's tents in the distance, when a warning cry alerted them. Also in the distance, ahead and to their left, there was an ominous cloud of dust. Immediately the captain gave the order for all to gallop and the most exhilarating race of Theophanu's life began. At first they thought they would reach the winning-post before the attackers approached them, but as the trajectory of the attack became clearer, the captain realised that they could not avoid it. By now Bishop Notker's men had seen what was happening and were hastily saddling up to mount a rescue.

'Go!' shouted the captain. Theophanu and Otto dug their spurs into their horses and shot forward away from the protection of the armed guards. Otto was yelling with delight, hurling furious curses at the approaching men.

The attackers, themselves small in number and unwilling to divide, hesitated for an instant before four men detached themselves from the main group and swerved towards the Empress and the King.

Too late. Their heavy beasts could not catch the fleet Arabs and by now, as Otto and Theophanu rushed for the tents, they shot past soldiers coming from the camp. In an instant Theophanu was among the first of the tents and cheering warriors surrounded the mother and child and helped them dismount, before they all turned to watch the result of the skirmish.

That was rather an anti-climax. The attackers realised they had missed their main prey and were more and more outnumbered as soldiers poured out from the camp. Almost immediately, they wheeled their horses and galloped away. Some of Notker's men pursued them, while Theophanu's guard rode on into the camp.

'Disappointing that they didn't put up a proper fight,' said Otto sadly. 'You have to admit, Mother, that that was great fun.'

'Wargames are undoubtedly great fun,' said his mother tartly, 'but, as you should remember from the eastern front, all-out war is a different matter. Now, where's Bishop Notker?'

'The trouble is, the little devil's right,' she admitted to Anastaso later. 'Those came near to being the most exciting and enjoyable ten minutes of my life. Everything became so simple – just winning the race.'

Once the imperial banners joined those of the Bishop of Liege outside the fortress, the defenders lost heart quickly and within a week the castle was surrendered. As a result and to Otto's disappointment, there was no hand-to-hand fighting. He cheered up on learning that they were going on to collect his distant cousin, Otto, son of Charles of Lotharingia, to be educated with him. Theophanu was touched by the gratitude of the boy's 'unsuitable' mother for the favour shown to her son, although she must have guessed that his position was also partly that of a hostage. The two boys made friends quickly; Otto of Lower Lotharingia had the steadiness that the young king lacked. He must have inherited it from his mother, not his father, thought Theophanu, but the boys were good foils for each other and she made much of the child.

Count Godfrey and his newly released men joined the imperial force as soon as they could, then the great fortress of Verdun was handed back to the Empire in the course of the summer. At long last the western border seemed to be at peace and Theophanu and the court headed back to Saxony for the high summer, a short break followed by the autumn hunting. The Empress also had the chance to see her daughters en route. Sophia was now twelve, in theory grown-up, and arrangements would soon have to be made for her veiling ceremony. She pleaded with her mother to delay it for a year or two. She did not yet feel ready for so great a responsibility, she said demurely, which caused her mother to look at her sharply and somewhat incredulously. However, her brother supported her in her plea, as she had, of course, told him to do, and Theophanu agreed to her request. For all her intelligence, Sophia was in some ways young for her age and it was good that she was taking the matter of her dedication seriously enough to hesitate, her mother explained to the Archchancellor.

'Hmph!' was his response.

Ten-year-old Adelheid as usual presented no problems and little Matilda was warmly praised by the sisters at Essen. She did everything that was required of her at school and chapel, but she was extremely good at looking after the smaller girls and her teachers were already finding her helpful in this respect.

'She will make a wonderful wife and mother,' Abbess Matilda told her mother.

The rest of the year passed peacefully within the imperial territories but beyond events occurred to confirm Theophanu's increasingly cynical view of human nature. Some of them, inevitably, concerned her uncles. The Sclerus revolt proceeded slowly and with limited success towards the capital but in August the other Uncle Bardas, Bardas Phocas, also had himself proclaimed Emperor, and he had considerable support from the Anatolian aristocracy.

'I don't know whether to see it as tragedy or farce,' Theophanu complained to Willigis.

'I'm afraid it'll turn to tragedy before too long, whatever it is now,' he replied soberly.

For the Scleri his prophecy was fulfilled before long. Bardas Phocas offered his namesake an alliance, which the other trustingly, and against all advice, accepted. They met at a castle belonging to Phocas to confirm the treaty and Phocas arrested and imprisoned his supposed allies. When he marched on, he left them in the custody of his wife.

'Couldn't my father, just once, have acted on his own initiative and kept out of it, if he suspected a plot?' raged Theophanu.

'I was talking to the messenger,' said Anastaso. 'He claims that General Sclerus is losing his sight. I suppose your father feels he can't abandon him.'

'In one sense none of them has ever been able to see,' answered the Empress. 'We heard officially that Phocas is gaining a lot of support. Was that true, do you think?'

'Yes. The government is said to be really worried.'

'I wonder where they'll look for allies?' mused the Empress, but she was surprised when she learnt the answer. Basil II had sent urgently to Vladimir, Grand Prince of Kiev and son of Sviatoslav, for troops.

The next news Theophanu heard was in the form of a desperate letter from her old playmate, Princess Anna, who still kept up an occasional correspondence. Anna dispensed with all formality.

'Dearest Theophano,' her letter began. 'You must come to my help for the sake of our old friendship and because it is your uncles who have brought me to this pass. The Prince of Kiev is only willing to help defend Constantinople if I am given to him in marriage. Theophano, he is truly a monster and I cannot possibly marry him. People say he has four wives and eight hundred concubines already.

One of his wives refused him, so he attacked her father's kingdom, raped her in front of her parents, then killed her father. That's the kind of pagan brute he is.

My brothers, who should be my protectors at this time, have abandoned me. Is there nothing you and your little son, who sounds an absolute darling, can do to help me? Do please, please try. Your loving sister, Anna.'

Theophanu and Anastaso shuddered when they read the letter. They could both remember stories of Rus brutality from when Thrace was under attack and knew Anna was not exaggerating much. How could a girl who had spent all her life in the silken confines of the Great Palace possibly cope with such a fate?

'I'm sure they'll insist that at least he converts to Christianity,' said Anastaso, her tone more doubtful than her words.

'It probably depends on how desperate they are,' replied Theophanu heavily. 'In any case, what does a political conversion or a promise mean in reality? Look at Hugh Capet.'

She was referring to recently-arrived news from France, where the new king, who had made so much of the elective principle to gain the throne, had just associated his son Robert in his rule, thus ensuring that the next king of France would succeed on a hereditary, not an elective basis. The defeated candidate in the election, Charles of Lower Lotharingia, was naturally furious. Theophanu was more annoyed by the fact that Capet had sent envoys to Constantinople to ask for one of Constantine's daughters in marriage, when Theophanu had intended to do the same for little Otto, thus uniting the two empires. She devoutly hoped the daughters had not inherited their father's sluggish idleness.

'Do you think we can do anything for Princess Anna?' asked Anastaso, bringing the Empress back to the present.

'Very little that Basil and Constantine would accept,' answered Theophanu regretfully. 'We could send troops overland from Italy, but they would be nervous that such an army would never go home. I am so compromised as the daughter and niece of the rebels anyway,' she added bitterly.

She was obliged to write to Anna, saying that she could do nothing to help beyond urging her to bear her trials with fortitude. In the circumstances it was rather a relief when the Christmas court broke up early in 988 and she and the child set off for an area of Germany that they had never visited before, the far north-west.

CHAPTER THIRTY-THREE

Their destination was the monastery of Wildeshausen near Bremen, where Theophanu issued a series of decrees designed to ensure the future of Christianity in Scandinavia. Ever since the campaign against the Wends to recover the lost lands in the east, the Empress had been troubled by the fact that no effort was made to persuade the conquered peoples to conversion. At present there was little she could do about that, and anyway she knew that most westerners would understand persuasion as another word for coercion, but Denmark, Sweden and Norway were outside the Empire and so there only persuasion could be used. She strengthened the position of the existing Danish dioceses and founded a new one at Odense on the island of Funen.

The young usurping king, Swein Forkbeard, had had an adventurous and, for his people, expensive career since he had seized the throne from his father. He had attacked the Wendish tribe which had sheltered his father in exile, and had been defeated and captured. The Danes had to pay a large ransom to get him back. On his return he showed his opinion of Theophanu's arrangements for the Danish church by interring his father's body, which he had reclaimed, in a church at Roskilde, not one of the cathedrals designated by the Empress. Nevertheless the presence of Theophanu and Otto in the north-west, and the fortifications which she had had repaired throughout the north since the Slav revolt, made it clear to Swein that there was no point in looking at raids into Germany to recoup his ransom. England would offer much easier pickings under its ineffective and ill-advised young king, Ethelred.

Otto loved the far north. For a short time he wanted to be a Viking instead of a knight. He was entranced by the sleek lines of the great dragon-prowed long-ships as they danced on the water, just as much as by the roistering sailors on the quayside. In vain did his mother point out that going a-viking was another name for piracy; in vain did his tutor Bernward try to direct his attention to the less romantic North Sea trading-cogs and get him to learn lists of imports and exports. Otto wanted to be a sailor. He would listen for hours to the mariners' tales, whether they came from Kiev or Dublin, Sweden or Iceland, but the sailors who really fired his imagination were those who reported the discovery and settlement of a whole new country far the west, which they called the Green Land. There were even rumours of more lands further west still. Theophanu and Bernward had to drag him away, when they set out south again to Essen, where he held his youngest sister, Matilda, and her classmates, as enthralled by the stories he repeated to them as he had been himself.

Theophanu was relieved to get away from the north. Saxony was always cold in spring, but it was a dryer cold. In any case the spring had not even begun to reach the North Sea coast in early March and she had shivered through many sessions of the court. Although she wore a thick bearskin cloak over her ceremonial garb, nothing seemed to keep out the freezing damp and she had developed a persistent cough, which aggravated the pain in her aching joints and muscles. She was more than usually pleased to see the castle of Ingelheim rising above the Rhine, as they drew near to spend Eastertide there.

Inevitably the peace and seclusion from Maundy Thursday to Easter morning led into another court on Easter Monday and this one presented her with an intractable problem. Again Duke Charles of Lower Lotharingia presented himself at court, both to see his son and to petition for the Empress' support to regain the throne of France from the treacherous Hugh Capet. Yet again Theophanu was bound to refuse him, but she knew that public opinion was uneasy about what many saw as a dereliction of Otto's duty as liege-lord.

'What do you think, my Lord?' she asked Willigis, as they met in a brief break from business.

'I think Gerbert is right,' answered the Archchancellor. 'He urges us strongly not to listen to Charles. Hugh is the anointed king and you would weaken the position of your son, and all rightful kings, if you give aid to a rebel.'

'Yes, but Gerbert would say that, wouldn't he?' snapped Theophanu, her patience not helped by the constant headache she had brought back from Wildeshausen. 'He's always been Capet's creature. I am nevertheless breaking my feudal oath to Charles.'

Willigis looked at her with a mixture of surprise, concern, and irritation. 'Your *son's* feudal oath,' he said coldly.

'You forget, Lord Archchancellor. I am a *partner* in my husband's rule.'

'Your husband is dead, Lady. You rule as regent *for* your son.' Then he broke off. 'Madam, why are we arguing like this? You have always seen as clearly as I have the need to be flexible. You know Capet is a better king for France.'

'Charles's young son Otto might suit us better than Hugh's son Robert in the long run. We have to think for his Grace's future, Lord Willigis. But let us not quarrel; I will take your advice this time – and Gerbert's.'

Charles was, of course, furious at this lack of the support which he regarded as his due and promptly withdrew from the court, to Theophanu's relief. Her mind was full of her intention to return to Italy for a time. There were good and necessary reasons for this. Otto was now nearly eight years old and the ground needed to be prepared for his coronation as emperor, which would happen when he came of age at fourteen. The ceremony could only be performed by the Pope and therefore presumably would have to be in Rome. Theophanu needed to mend fences with Pope John XV and felt that this would be more easily accomplished if most of the German nobles were left behind. Then there were the incessant complaints about Adelheid's financial mismanagement of the Italian Kingdom, which the Empress could ignore no longer. She also wanted to visit her husband's grave, to pray for his soul and oversee the creation of a fitting monument to him. Having borne the burden of empire herself, she was not so critical of Otto's mistakes as she had been and was looking for a way of making amends. Lastly, she found herself longing for heat, real heat. She had shaken off her racking cough but was still plagued by aching muscles and joints and constant headaches. Worst of all for someone in her position was her lack of energy. She could hardly bring herself to concentrate on all the trivial details of state business which her councillors kept bringing her, the endless making of judgements and hearing of petitions, and the thought of getting into the saddle was excruciating.

She was resting one afternoon in a darkened room with a particularly severe headache when a commotion at the door drew her attention. The two little Ottos burst into the room, followed by a protesting Anastaso, for once really angry with her favourite. Otto of Lotharingia looked doubtfully at the two women, but the young king had no such qualms.

'I'm very sorry to disturb you, Mama, when you're not well, but Otto has news that is too important to wait,' he said urgently, as he approached the bed.

'Otto?' said his mother, confused. 'Why would such important news come to you boys, rather than to me or the Archchancellor?'

'He's had a message from his father, of course,' King Otto answered impatiently.

'My Lady Mother!' Theophanu corrected sharply.

'My Lady Mother. This is too important for manners. Please try to listen,' begged her son.

'Nothing is too important for good manners. Now, Otto of Lotharingia, tell me what's happened, but keep your voices down.'

In almost a whisper, the boy began his tale and Theophanu did indeed forgive them their interruption. It seemed that, immediately after leaving Ingelheim, Charles had collected troops and gone to the French capital at Lâon. Rather like Quedlinburg, the town and castle were built on a huge bluff of rock that towered steeply above the plain and were virtually impregnable to attack. Charles therefore used guile to win his way in.

'My father has many friends in the city,' little Otto murmured, 'including my uncle, Father Arnulf.' Theophanu nodded. She knew the priest was a by-blow of either Charles himself or his brother, King Lothar, she could not remember which. 'He opened the gate to my father and some friends just before dark. Nobody much noticed them. Then once it was really dark, my father and his friends overpowered the gate-guards and opened the town to all the soldiers they had hidden in the hills around, amongst the vineyards. They took control of the city. A lot of people escaped over the walls into the hills, but they had left soldiers there to round them up and bring them back.'

Theophanu looked at the boy thoughtfully. There was something he was not telling her.

'Were King Hugh and Queen Adelaide there?' she asked.

'No, Madam.'

'You'll have to tell her,' said King Otto. 'It wasn't Queen Adelaide, Mother. It was my aunt, Queen Emma.'

'What exactly do you mean?' asked his mother. 'And let Otto tell me; he had the message.'

'Queen Emma was there, with Bishop Ascelin,' said Lotharingia miserably, 'and my father has put them in prison. He always says very bad things about them.'

Theophanu did not want him to specify these things in the hearing of her slightly younger and possibly still innocent son, so she merely nodded.

'Bishop Ascelin was one of the ones who ran away and left Queen Emma to take the punishment,' said Theophanu's own son indignantly, 'only they caught him and brought him back.'

'I could never see what she saw in him,' commented Theophanu, then looked sharply at the boys to see if they had caught the implication of her remark. Fortunately, they merely looked puzzled.

'You do see why I had to disturb you, Mama?' asked Otto.

'Yes; you were right to do so,' answered his mother. 'Would you go now and send Archbishop Willigis to me? Anastaso, do you have any more of that remedy for headaches you made yesterday? I can hardly clear my head to think.'

It was obvious that the Empire could not ignore this *coup d'état*. Emma was Empress Adelheid's daughter, Ascelin was Archbishop

Adalbero of Rheims' cousin and Charles was King Otto's vassal. The situation worsened when Ascelin climbed out of his prison after a few days, again abandoning his supposed lady. He rode straight to King Hugh Capet, who was, of course, delighted to welcome him.

All that summer Theophanu struggled to overcome her lethargy and negotiate a solution. The court had to travel to Lotharingia again, which meant she had to ride, since the Rhine did not flow to the right places. Letters went back and forth between Hugh Capet and herself, his becoming increasingly irritable in tone as he pointed out that he was prepared to accede to her proposals but Charles was not, so she was in the wrong to give Charles any help at all. By August the attempt at mediation gave way to warfare, as Hugh and his son Robert laid siege to Lâon, and Theophanu, completely exhausted and unable to achieve anything more, withdrew to Lake Constance, still intending to carry out her Italian journey.

Meersburg, where the court made its first stay on the shores of the lake, came under the influence of the Italian Chancellery, not the German. At first Theophanu was well enough to conduct some business, including appointing Otto's Greek tutor, John Philagathos, as Archbishop of Piacenza. He had served as chancellor for Italy before, in 979, but he needed increased status if he was to sort out the muddle Adelheid had created. Since his advances at Rossano, he had always behaved with extreme propriety towards Theophanu, and she had come to value his amusing company, although she knew that many of the more staid Saxons disapproved of their friendship. Even Willigis had advised her to see less of Philagathos, because the old slander would not die until she did.

Sitting holding court one day, Theophanu glanced from one man to another. In his late forties the Archchancellor was still an impressive figure. His tonsured hair was greying round the temples but neither his face nor his powerful body showed an inch of spare fat. His life of constant mobility had seen to that. In Philagathos, in contrast, his excesses had begun to show in unhealthy fat and a slackness of face and body. His abundant hair was greying and greasy and his lips had become fleshy rather than full. Only his large dark eyes retained their attractiveness. Theophanu could not imagine how anyone could suppose her sexually drawn to such a man and she repressed a slight shudder. Since his appointment his manner had become more familiar and his transfer to Italy was probably a good thing, although she would miss the chance to use her own language. At least Willigis would be pleased and perhaps stop scolding her so much for not responding to Hugh Capet's letters.

The King of France was demanding that the Empress return to Lotharingia, where he would give his queen, Adelaide, plenipotentiary powers to negotiate with Theophanu, an attempt to repeat the peace-making success of the Summit of Ladies. Theophanu could see no point in this. Nobody would negotiate with Charles's unfortunate and unsuitable wife, and there was no evidence that he would listen if they did. The stalemate in France dragged on.

As August wore on, the Empress grew less and less capable of conducting any business at all. The physicians could find no cause for her malady. Perhaps she had a low fever, but that should not cause such extreme lethargy. The warm days slipped away; the Italian expedition was abandoned for the time being, and the Empress' lassitude deepened.

'She's just exhausted, my lord,' Anastaso said angrily to Willigis, 'and if you gentlemen would leave her be for a time, she'll recover.'

For once Imiza, who had been recalled to see if her presence would enliven her mistress, agreed with her colleague.

'These last fifteen years, Lord Archchancellor,' she said, 'my Lady has done everything you have done but she has given birth to five children as well. Her body can take no more jogging through endless forests and marshes. It certainly can't cross the Alps. You must give her time and complete rest, and then perhaps she will regain her strength.'

There was no real alternative. The court stayed at Meersburg until October, the first time since leaving Constantinople that Theophanu had spent two whole months under the same roof, then moved only a few miles to Constance itself. By late November the Empress was well enough to make the boat-trip down the Rhine to Cologne, where she would spend Christmas in her favourite city.

CHAPTER THIRTY-FOUR

The long rest served its purpose sufficiently to allow Theophanu to enjoy the Christmas season. The royal palace next to Cologne Cathedral was one of the most comfortable and up-to-date buildings in Germany and while icy winds wailed outside, she revelled in the roaring fires and underfloor heating. The glazed windows kept out the sleet beating against the panes and rich tapestries held the draughts at bay. It was almost possible to be comfortable, she observed privately to Anastaso, who laughed.

'I think, Madam, that you're forgetting how cold Constantinople is in the winter. At least they take steps to combat the cold here.'

'True,' her mistress agreed, 'but they can't really do anything about the damp – although this heating under the floors does help.'

'I always imagined you felt more at ease here than anywhere else?' said Anastaso, surprised.

'Indeed, I love this city, partly because it *is* a city. I sense that the old Roman Empire never really went away here. People come and go from all over Europe and it's the only town I can think of that has extended beyond its Roman walls. Here you don't feel as if you're living in the ruins of a greater civilisation, like in Rome, or in a town that's just starting to grow.'

'Like most other places,' said Anastaso laughing.

'Yes. This is a city and this afternoon I'm going to go outside the walls to see how the building is getting on at St. Pantaleon's monastery, then I shall join Otto and Father Bernward in the Street of the Goldsmiths; a real street with shops, Anastaso, just imagine! They're going to be working on the shrine for the relics of St. Alban, which I gave to St. Pantaleon's Church, and Bernward wants Otto to see how the gold is worked.'

'I thought we agreed with the Lord Archbishop of Mainz that Alban was to be called Albin in the Empire.'

'True, I'd forgotten. You know, I'm sure that it was Albin's intercession which won me back my son. I've asked to be buried next to his shrine when I die.'

Glancing sharply at her mistress, Anastaso frowned. She had been delighted by Theophanu's renewed interest in life, but talk of death seemed a step backwards.

'That will not be for a long time yet,' she said firmly. 'May I come with you this afternoon?'

Theophanu laughed, sounding genuinely amused. 'Of course. I knew no true daughter of Constantinople could resist shops. We could probably do with your advice too. The German smiths are working with those craftsmen from the east I imported a few years ago and they want our opinions on various designs.'

All too soon the peaceful atmosphere was disrupted by news from east and west. From France messengers came to announce the death of one of Theophanu's most loyal and effective supporters at the end of January. Adalbero, Archbishop of Rheims, had gone to meet his maker, no doubt hurried on his way by the tribulations of his last years. The obvious assumption, made by Theophanu and Willigis and nearly everybody else, was that the headmaster of his cathedral school, Gerbert, would succeed him. After all, the appointment lay effectively in Hugh Capet's hands as King of France, and Gerbert, an undoubtedly able man, had acted both as Capet's secretary and tutor to his son. His tireless letter-writing had played a large part in securing Capet's succession to the throne, at least in Gerbert's own estimation. His succession was a foregone conclusion and deeply satisfying to the Empire.

Perhaps that was the problem. At any rate, when the Empress and the Archchancellor learned the name of the next Archbishop of Rheims, they stared at each other aghast.

'Arnulf!' exclaimed Theophanu, 'King Lothar's bastard – or Charles of Lotharingia's own. Nobody seems to know for sure.'

'Possibly the brothers shared a mistress,' said Willigis delicately. 'Yes, it is unsavoury.'

Theophanu grimaced. 'He's the man who betrayed Hugh by opening the gates of Laon to Charles last summer,' she pointed out. 'Above all, he's a Carolingian. What on earth is Hugh playing at? There must be some deal involved.'

'I think we can be sure of that,' agreed Willigis. 'The question is what? It's not good news for us, and even worse for our poor friend, Gerbert. There's a promising career thwarted.'

'You sound almost amused,' said Theophanu suspiciously.

'Not exactly, but when a man is so obviously ambitious, somehow it makes one cautious.'

'He should have learned to cloak his ambition more effectively?' suggested the Empress. 'Like the rest of us?'

'Just so.' admitted Willigis without irony.

'Nevertheless, he has served us faithfully,' said Theophanu.

'That's why I'm worried. What recompense will he want from us now, which it will be impolitic to grant?'

Initially, at least, Gerbert seemed to accept the situation. It was obvious that King Hugh had his own doubts about Arnulf's loyalty, because when he was made archbishop, against all western custom, Hugh made him state his loyalty in writing, including an acceptance of damnation as the penalty for oath-breaking. Hugh's doubts proved valid later in the year, when Arnulf appeared to suffer a grave misfortune. Appearances, as so often, were misleading.

What seemed to happen was that Archbishop Arnulf invited two important local noblemen to dine with him. The episcopal table groaned with food and drink and by the time the feast finished, it was late. Suddenly there was a knock at the door and Duke Charles of Lower Lotharingia and a group of his retainers were admitted. Archbishop Arnulf appeared to be terrified; after all his acceptance of the archbishopric had been a betrayal of Duke Charles's claim to the throne. At his urging, his

257

guests joined him in a flight to the upper storeys of the palace, where they barricaded the stairs, but eventually they had to surrender. Meanwhile Charles's men had occupied the town of Rheims.

The three prisoners were taken under guard to Laon, where Charles himself confronted them again. Bitter accusations of treachery and counter-treachery flashed between duke and archbishop, but in the end there was no help for it. If Arnulf and the two counts wanted their freedom, they had to swear allegiance to Charles and give him access to their holdings. So Rheims and Soissons joined Laon in Charles's hands, a much more substantial threat to Hugh Capet's authority.

What set Europe laughing at Hugh was the leaked revelation that the whole affair was a set-up. Charles and Arnulf had been in league all along and the trading of insults was just a charade, designed to secure Soissons as well as Rheims. So much for Hugh's hopes of pacifying the Carolingians by Arnulf's appointment. He would have done better to stick with Gerbert.

That was certainly Gerbert's own view. He sent letters to Theophanu asking for employment and was even prepared to swallow his pride enough to seek service with Hugh Capet again. He was genuinely sickened by Arnulf's duplicity.

Theophanu, meanwhile, was having a relatively uneventful year herself, enlivened by letters and despatches recounting the latest situation in the Eastern Empire. Princess Anna had recovered from her first distress over her proposed marriage to Vladimir of Kiev and managed to persuade herself that it would never happen. This only increased her anguish when the first dragon-prows were spotted approaching the Black Sea entrance to the Bosphorus the previous Christmas. The ships carried six thousand fully-armed Kievan Rus warriors. The winter was hard throughout Europe that year, so much so that the Bosphorus froze over and the hardy Rus simply walked across the straits one night late in February and massacred the half of Bardas Phocas' army which slept in its tents by the eastern shore, half frozen into unwariness.

Bardas Phocas himself was with the other half of the army, encamped southwards opposite the Gallipoli Peninsula. Hastily he tried to move his troops across to the peninsula, to start the march on Constantinople, but a heroic resistance by the inhabitants of the little port of Abydos enabled the imperial army, including the Rus, to catch up with him. On April 13th the armies faced each other.

'Would you believe it?' Theophanu said to Anastaso, as they read Anna's letter. 'Constantine led the advance guard and he fought quite well. I find that incredible.'

'Well, he has sired three daughters as well,' Anastaso pointed out. 'He's not been completely idle. So what happened in the battle?'

Theophanu scanned the letter. 'Anna says....Oh, I must read it to you. It's extraordinary. 'The first imperial charge scattered the rebel army, but your uncle managed to stem his fleeing troops and draw them up again facing my brothers. Then a battle-madness seemed to come upon him. Yelling horribly, he charged towards my brother Basil, who stood in the centre of our line with his sword in his right hand and an icon of the Mother of God, Bringer of Victory, in his left. Everyone stared transfixed, unable to move, but even as Phocas thundered towards him, Our Lady moved to protect the Emperor. Phocas swayed in the saddle and crashed from his horse just in front of my brother. He was taken up dead and his rebellion was over.'

Both women were silent for a moment, overwhelmed.

'So perish all traitors,' said Theophanu, crossing herself. 'I wonder what will happen to my other rebel uncle and my father now?'

Before the summer was far advanced, she found herself preoccupied by the activity of yet another rebellious relative. This rebellion had as much to do with adolescence as politics, and the perpetrator was her beloved daughter, Sophia, aided and abetted by her godfather, Lord Archchancellor Willigis. Imiza was shocked by Sophia's attitude, whilst Anastaso was openly amused. Theophanu kept her real feelings to herself.

The subject of the dispute was Sophia's veiling, the taking of her vows as a canoness. Theophanu had wondered whether her daughter might baulk at the life laid out for her, but to her relief that was not the problem. Sophia was well aware that it would be extraordinary if she did not end up as abbess and the prospect of the automatic seat on the Diet, the mint, her own troops and all the other benefits of being an abbess were not lost on her. If someone could tolerate the lack of husband or children, to be an abbess was the pleasantest and most interesting life a woman could have. The issue for Sophia was the question of who should conduct the ceremony.

'Why can't it be Lord Willigis?' she demanded indignantly of her mother. 'He's the foremost churchman in the north and I am an emperor's daughter. And he's my oldest friend.'

'That's the only good reason you've produced so far,' said her mother repressively, 'and just because you *are* the Emperor's daughter, you cannot consider only your personal feelings.'

Sophia glared at her defiantly.

'I had not noticed that you yourself are indifferent to rank, Lady Mother.'

'I am not embarking on the religious life, for which humility is a necessary qualification.'

Sophia gave her mother a look which said all too plainly 'You must be joking,' but had the good sense not to put her thought into words. She was regularly accused by the other girls and her teachers of being 'too like a queen'. She decided to make the argument less personal.

'Bishop Osdag of Hildesheim really shouldn't have jurisdiction over us,' she said. 'When the convent moved here, we moved out of his diocese.'

'That is a matter of dispute, and by tradition and canon law, Sophia, the Bishops of Hildesheim have always professed the canonesses of Gandersheim. You cannot change the law just to suit your convenience.'

'My brother's on my side,' said Sophia, realising she had lost and reverting to childishness.

'Your brother is still child enough to support your every whim.'

'He is the King.'

'Yes. One day he will be a man grown and the Emperor. Beware he does not grow to resent your domineering, my daughter. Your arrogance will be your undoing yet.'

'Will you not at least discuss it with Lord Willigis,' was Sophia's last, despairing shot.

'I shall certainly speak to Lord Willigis,' replied her mother grimly.

'Well done, Madam,' exclaimed Anastaso mockingly, when Sophia had gone. 'You sounded exactly like Empress Theophano – the first one.'

'I know,' said Theophanu ruefully. 'There was a time when she said almost exactly the same things to Anna and me. I could hear myself repeating her. But whatever Sophia may think, I'm not really such a hypocrite as my godmother was. I genuinely do often yearn to put aside the distinctions of rank and be an ordinary woman. Imiza, would you ask Lord Willigis to come to me. I'll have to try to find a compromise – as usual.'

This proved surprisingly difficult. Willigis, supported by Abbess Gerberga and several other bishops, was not minded to be very accommodating and Bishop Osdag and his supporters not at all. As a result, when the imperial family entered the half-finished church for the ceremony the next day, it was to find that two episcopal thrones had been set up, one on each side of the altar. Both bishops were still determined to conduct the profession.

By this time Theophanu's patience had run out. There was to be no more negotiation. Taking Otto with her, she strode down into the body of the church and summoned the antagonists. When they arrived, she informed them curtly that they would jointly bestow the veil on Sophia, but that only Osdag would officiate at the celebratory Mass. Willigis directed a look of astonishment and reproach at her, but received such an angry stare in return that he recollected himself, bowed, and walked stiffly back to the vestry. Osdag, of course, was triumphant, but another withering look from the Empress moderated his rapture.

The ceremony proceeded without further incident. Canoness Sophia was content that, at least in her own mind, she had received her veil from the Archbishop of Mainz, and her farewell interview with her mother and brother early the next day was happy. This reconciliation pleased Theophanu. Exasperating as Sophia could be, her mother had not wanted to go off to Italy without making up the quarrel with her, and she was still a long way north. Time was pressing if she was to cross the Alps before the snows came.

CHAPTER THIRTY-FIVE

They had to travel fast but they did manage to reach Rome at the beginning of December. It felt strange to be making a major journey without Willigis's company and even odder to have left young Otto in his care, but Theophanu and the Archchancellor both felt it was safer so. Rome was always unpredictable territory for the Ottonians and it would be foolish to risk having the King seized as a hostage. After Adelheid's exactions, even Lombardy might well prove hostile, as John Philagathos had warned when he had come north at Easter to ask for the Empress' presence to put matters right. In the end Theophanu was travelling with a small escort, in the hope that, by presenting no obvious threat, she would not provoke retaliation.

She had to admit she was pleased when they reached the royal palace at Pavia and found that Adelheid had tactfully removed herself to Burgundy. Theophanu wanted to reach Rome in time for the anniversary of Otto II's death on December 7th and had been worried that a confrontation could hold her up. It would have to come, of course, but she was glad to be spared it now.

Tears filled her eyes as she stood beside Otto's marble sarcophagus at the entrance to St Peter's. Above it on the wall was the mosaic she had commissioned of the Redeemer, his hand raised in blessing, gazing compassionately out over the remains of the dead emperor. As she looked up at it, Theophanu felt, almost for the first time since Otto's death, at peace about her husband.

'I have guarded your heritage as best I could,' she whispered, before turning away into the church for the Mass in his memory. She had been right to come back.

After the anniversary, Theophanu enjoyed her time in Italy. Against all expectation Pope John gave her a magnificent welcome, even inviting her to stay with him in the Lateran palace, although she sensibly opted for the greater security of the royal palace near the Vatican, no distance from the

Borgo, the quarter where Saxons, both English and German, tended to cluster.

She found she quite liked the Pope, although she had no doubt that he was as venal as Willigis had said he was. Nevertheless he raised no objections to the prospect of Otto's imperial coronation and was willing to discuss the details. They both agreed that his *Schwertleite*, the coming-of-age ceremony at fourteen when he would be dubbed knight, should take place in Germany, and then his coronation should follow when he was about sixteen, nearer the age, as the Pope pointed out, when a Roman boy would have received his *toga virilis*. Given the fourteen-year-old Sophia's recent behaviour, Theophanu was perfectly willing to accept the later date.

John XV was a scholarly man, fascinating to talk with, but his religious interests seemed largely focused on maintaining the power and status of the papacy. There was, however, one area which roused him to genuine enthusiasm and fortunately this was a concern which Theophanu shared. John was eager for the conversion of the still pagan areas of Eastern Europe. He supported the monastery of Saints Alexis and Boniface on the Aventine Hill and urged the Empress to visit it. He also maintained many envoys in the east and it was in a despatch from his man in the Crimea that Theophanu heard the outcome of her friend Princess Anna's protracted wedding negotiations.

Poor Anna had finally had to go to marry Vladimir. The Rus had grown impatient after the defeat of Bardas Phocas and had shown it by attacking and taking the Byzantine colony in the Crimea.

'Basil II cannot afford to lose control of the Black Sea and anyway there were still six thousand Rus warriors threatening him in Constantinople itself,' explained Pope John. 'It seems the princess protested bitterly. She accused her brothers in public of selling her into slavery, and she wept and screamed and struggled, but it could make no difference, of course. She was forced onto a ship and when she reaches Cherson, Vladimir will put aside his wives and concubines and receive

Holy Baptism. Then they will be married. Princess Anna will do much good for Our Lord's sake,' he added encouragingly, seeing Theophanu's face.

'True,' replied the Empress, 'but it will be a long martyrdom for her.'

'Oh come,' said the Pope. 'You must have felt much the same when you came west.'

'It was not the same. I was coming to a Christian kingdom and I was a child, young enough to welcome new things. And my husband was young, handsome and loving, not a raddled old barbarian. Is it eight hundred concubines he's supposed to be setting aside? What will he do with them, if he does? Kill them off or sell them into slavery?'

'Anna could build convents for them,' said the Pope, beaming. 'You must see, Lady, that this marks a whole new chapter in the northeast. I thought you would be pleased.'

'Indeed I am,' replied Theophanu, 'but I must spare a thought for the sacrificial lambs. I shall consider what wedding presents it will be best to send her. Tell me, Lord Pope,' changing the subject, 'do your envoys have any word of my father and uncle?'

'Bardas and Constantine Sclerus? Yes, they have been fortunate beyond their deserts. After Phocas' death, his wife, who had them in prison, released them but the Emperor Basil soon captured them. They were brought before him and it seems it was an interesting encounter. Bardas Sclerus has gone blind from cataracts during his imprisonment, you know, and had to be led in. When Basil saw him, he exclaimed, "Is this old dotard the man we have feared for so long?"'

'He always had a cruel tongue,' observed Theophanu with feeling. 'What happened then?'

'Then Basil noticed that Sclerus was still wearing the imperial red buskins. He refused to look at him until he was taken away and dressed properly.'

Theophanu laughed. 'It was the Byzantine obsession with proper dress that saved my husband's life at Rossano,' she said.

'When the prisoner was brought back, the Emperor forgave him his rebellion and gave him the title of *curopalates* provided Sclerus renounced his claim to the throne – which he did, of course. Now he and his brother are on their way back to their estates in Thrace, where they'll stay for the rest of their lives, if they have any sense.'

'Amen to that,' said the Empress fervently.

The one big disappointment of her time in Rome was that a meeting she had planned with Gerbert of Aurillac could not take place. Gerbert should have been in Rome with his master, Arnulf of Rheims, who was to receive his *pallium*, the garment which marked his office as archbishop, from the Pope. It seemed that Hugh Capet had learned of the projected meeting with Theophanu and had forbidden either Arnulf or Gerbert to leave France. Capet was displeased by Theophanu's refusal to negotiate with his wife the previous year and did not believe that the Empress had been too ill to respond. He possibly feared that Arnulf would win her round to the Carolingian cause. Theophanu had been looking forward to hearing Gerbert's assessment of the situation in France face to face. Hugh Capet's hostility to his erstwhile imperial allies seemed to be growing, which was worrying. It was probably also a warning that she should not stay away from the north too long.

She moved on to Ravenna rather reluctantly at the end of March, as the beginning of the trek home. She had so much enjoyed being in a climate where spring started in February rather than late April. Her bones stopped their endless aching and she felt filled with a new energy. It was refreshing too to have more scope to make decisions for herself without the endless consultations with her advisers. Partly to celebrate this, she abandoned the legal fiction that all her decrees were made by her son at her intervention and issued them simply from *Theophania divina gratia imperatrix augusta*. On one occasion she even went so far as to use the masculine form, *Theophanius etc*, grinning to herself at the thought of how shocked Willigis would have been, but it was standard practice for a Byzantine empress regnant and the Italians, closer to the east, did not turn a hair. The grants she made gave her great pleasure anyway. One, her favourite, was to establish a monastery on the Tiber Island for refugee priests from lands conquered by the Muslims or from the threatened south of Italy. Here she was able to help her own eastern-rite church in a way that she never could in the north. Then a few days in Ravenna contemplating the indomitable features of the Empress Theodora in the mosaics stiffened her resolve to challenge her mother-in-law – again.

Easter in Pavia beckoned all too soon. Fortunately the Dowager Empress stayed put in Burgundy, so avoiding a personal confrontation, which made it easier to grasp the nettle of her financial mismanagement. Theophanu gave John Philagathos, as Archbishop of Piacenza, sweeping powers of reform and took oversight of the Italian Exchequer away from Adelheid and transferred it to him. The problem was that Adelheid was by no means the only one with her fingers in the pot and most of them wanted the money for far less altruistic reasons than she had. For the first time, Theophanu wondered if she should have brought more troops to Italy. It was asking a lot to expect John to impose her reforms by force of personality alone. Well, what was done was done and she wanted to see her son. Leaving John with instructions to send immediately for help if trouble arose, at the beginning of May she set off again, retracing the journey of her early marriage over the Graubunden passes to Reichenau, her heart filled with bitter-sweet memories, but also with a strange feeling that she had said a final goodbye to the south.

CHAPTER THIRTY-SIX

Theophanu enjoyed the journey down the river to Mainz. Best of all was the anticipation of her reunion with her son, which would happen in Mainz, but the voyage was enlivened by the company of Henry of Bavaria's sister, Hedwig. The sharp-tongued duchess, who had intimidated the inexperienced girl that Theophanu had been when they first met, merely amused the Empress and her comments on the nobility of Southern Germany were often illuminating.

Otto had grown in the six months she had been away and his mother felt she detected a new confidence in him. It had been right to leave him, a view confirmed by Willigis. The King had listened with more attention to court cases and on occasion been asked for his opinion. In general his decisions had been wise and he listened to reason when they needed to be modified. He had also spent more time with the other noble boys around the court, and was building a group of loyal supporters. Theophanu could not keep the pride out of her eyes as she looked at her son across the loving cup at the welcoming banquet.

The next morning, however, it was time to move on again. There would be a court at Frankfurt, where those who had guarded the realm in the Empress' absence would be rewarded, then the court would travel east immediately.

There was a new crisis to deal with on the eastern border. 'Boleslav of Bohemia's fallen out with Miesco of Poland,' Otto explained to his mother. 'It's all so complicated I don't really understand it but Lord Willigis says I have to attend the council meetings now, and then, of course, I have to go to war.'

'Hm,' said his mother. 'Did Lord Willigis make both those statements, or just the first?'

'Well....just the first really, but I could be useful on the battlefield now. I can shoot brilliantly and I'm getting better with a sword.'

'I'm sure you are,' said Theophanu tactfully, 'but this won't be a battle. Just a lot of skirmishing with nobody sure who's on whose side and a very easy way for a boy to get accidentally killed. Not this year, Otto. Maybe next, when your shoulders have broadened to match your long legs'

Despite Otto's protests and sulks, Theophanu remained resolute.

'I'm sure he wishes I'd stayed in Italy out of his way,' she said half-laughing, half-rueful, to her ladies, as they waited at Magdeburg for news, but the outcome of the campaign justified her caution. She had no great liking or trust for the imperial leader, Giselher, Archbishop of Magdeburg. He was widely considered an ambitious and avaricious man and in the past he had often sided with Boleslav and Henry the Wrangler against Theophanu. Now he was supposed to be leading imperial forces in support of Miesco against Boleslav, but when most of his men re-appeared in Magdeburg without him some days into the campaign, Theophanu's suspicions were awakened. The men said that they had been sent home after a meeting with Boleslav in the forest, but the Archbishop and three of his men had stayed behind to negotiate peace.

'So you see,' Anastaso said to Otto,' you wouldn't have got any fighting anyway.'

'No, but Boleslav might well have got him,' muttered Theophanu.

'He would surely not harm his liege-lord, Madam,' protested Imiza.

'He murdered his own brother Wenceslas inside a church,' answered Theophanu. 'You can't trust him an inch.'

Nor Giselher, she thought to herself, but events took an unexpected turn when an envoy came in haste from Miesco, saying that Boleslav had the four Saxons prisoner and had threatened to kill them unless Miesco removed his troops from the area. The messenger added that Miesco was totally indifferent to the fate of Giselher and his men and had no intention of withdrawing his army.

'Now we'll have to go their rescue,' urged Otto eagerly, his eyes shining with excitement.

Not so fast, my dear,' answered his mother.

'But he's my vassal, and he said you hadn't given him enough troops,' argued Otto mutinously.

There was a sharp intake of breath from the three women.

'He did, did he?' said Theophanu. 'But remember, Otto, he has already sent back the troops he did have. I think you will find that his Grace the Archbishop will be perfectly safe with his old friend Prince Boleslav.'

She was of course correct, but it was a closer run thing than she had expected. Boleslav had allied himself with the pagan Lutizi at the start of the campaign and found his allies more difficult to control than he had thought. When his attempt to bluff Miesco into surrender failed, he found himself in an embarrassing position. The Lutizi wanted blood and the hostages' lives were forfeit. Boleslav tried to mollify them by allowing them to capture a town and sacrifice its Polish governor to their gods outside the walls. This was not enough; the Archbishop of Magdeburg would make a much better sacrifice.

One July morning the court was awakened by shouts from the guards on the ramparts. Archbishop Giselher and his three companions were racing towards the town, pursued by a horde of screaming Lutizi. Just in time the great gates swung to behind the Saxons and the enemy retreated, still howling.

As soon as he was washed and rested, the Archbishop was summoned to explain himself to the Empress.

'Prince Boleslav released us secretly before dawn,' he said. 'Then he kept the pagans arguing about the rights and wrongs of it all. They like a good debate almost as much as human sacrifices, but unfortunately someone saw us on the edge of the forest and they gave chase.'

'I am pleased for your good fortune, Lord Archbishop,' said the Empress formally. 'Did you actually achieve anything?'

'To some extent, Lady. Prince Boleslav will renew his fealty to the King's Grace.'

'Good. What about the quarrel with the Poles?'

'Unresolved. Perhaps we should have a properly resourced campaign next year.'

They regarded each other steadily until finally Giselher looked away.

'Nevertheless,' Theophanu explained to her son later, 'the main danger has been averted. We have not been forced into an open breach with either Poland or Bohemia. On the whole Archbishop Giselher has done well.'

Otto obviously disagreed but was easily distracted by the court's departure for Gandersheim, where he would see his favourite sister. They spent happy days there before he left for the autumn hunting.

By October they were in the Rhineland ready for Christmas. A solar eclipse on the 21st caused much speculation and foreboding, particularly as there had been a comet the previous year. People muttered darkly of the death of princes, but Bernward constructed models to show Otto how the moon was passing between the sun and the earth. It was a purely natural phenomenon, he said, and no doubt the comet was too, although he could not explain it.

Autumn, winter and spring rolled by peaceably within the Empire, contradicting the bad auguries. Throughout Saxony, Thuringia, Swabia and Bavaria there was a feeling of content. The harvest had been good and the peasants had been able to reap it without fear, as they had for several years now. Despite the harsh winters there was no famine. Theophanu prepared for the 991 Easter court at Quedlinburg with a feeling of great satisfaction. If her subjects' lives could not be said to be civilised by Constantinopolitan standards, at least they were peaceful and her son's inheritance seemed assured. An impressive array of foreign potentates was coming to the court, including Miesco and Boleslav. She should be able to bring about some settlement between them, which would clear the way for an all out attack on the Lutizi in the summer. Things seemed almost as settled as at Otto the Great's last Easter-court in 973, she thought, then shivered at the memory of how soon that triumphant court had been followed by his death.

All went as she planned. The campaign was set up and this time Otto would go with the troops. Constant practice with his weapons over the last year had indeed broadened his shoulders and his presence on the campaign would not be entirely as a mascot. He certainly looked every inch the young king. Theophanu tried to insist that he should not be exposed to any front-line fighting but in this she was overruled by the nobles, ardently supported by the King himself. He would face the same degree of risk as all the other boys there. Knowing that her husband's lack of battle experience as a youth had contributed to his problems as a general, the Empress reluctantly yielded.

The one unpleasant surprise which the Easter-court delivered was the unexpected presence of John Philagathos and Margrave Hugh of Tuscany. Although Theophanu was pleased to see both of them personally, they brought bad news.

'The Dowager Empress entrusted the execution of her financial affairs to particular noble families,' the Archbishop of Piacenza told the court. 'They have been taking handsome commissions from their exactions, which they will not give up.'

'The whole economy of the Italian Kingdom is endangered,' added Margrave Hugh. 'The harsh weather of recent years has affected the more tender Italian crops badly and the peasants are hungry anyway. Lady Adelheid's taxes push them into starvation.'

'Unless we have more men, we can do nothing to stop this,' concluded Philagathos, looking at Theophanu.

Her reaction astounded everyone there; it was so uncharacteristic. She exploded with rage.

'If I am still alive in six month's time, that woman will rule over no more than the span of one hand,' she shouted furiously.

Stunned silence greeted this announcement. Anastaso and Imiza, atanding in attendance behind the throne, glanced round uneasily. Someone would undoubtedly relay these words to Adelheid.

Willigis, looking troubled himself, intervened to suggest the authorisation of a commission to conscript more troops in Italy and the court agreed. Philagathos was to be sent back with the authorisation, but Theophanu kept Margrave Hugh with her. She had come to respect his wisdom and judgement when she was in Italy the previous year and felt she needed him now.

'Are you not feeling quite yourself again, Madam?' Willigis asked her that evening.

'Because I spoke unguardedly, you mean? What a lapse!'

Willigis smiled with sympathy. 'Believe me, I understand. Nevertheless, it was not like you.'

'I made no threat against her life,' Theophanu pointed out.

'No, but you threatened her power, which she loves more than life.'

'As both you and I have done many times before. This will blow over, but I confess I am feeling weary again.'

The Archbishop looked at her with concern. He had suspected as much when he noticed her struggling for breath, as she and the King led the Easter procession up the hill of Quedlinburg. He hoped the illness of two years ago was not coming back and resolved to take as much of the burden from her shoulders as he could in the coming campaign. However, he could not stop her from worrying about Otto's safety, which was probably half the trouble.

The court moved as planned to Merseburg, where the muster would be, but then the messengers from France finally caught up with them – and every plan was changed.

CHAPTER THIRTY-SEVEN

The news the messengers brought concerned a spectacular act of treachery. Theophanu and Willigis listened with grim faces and then sent for the two boys, both the King and Otto of Lower Lotharingia.

'Otto, have you had news from home recently?' the Empress asked the latter.

'Not since well before Easter, Lady,' he replied with surprise. 'My father has been reconciled with Bishop Ascelin of Laon and there was going to be a big celebration banquet for my father on Palm Sunday in Laon itself, given by Bishop Ascelin. Archbishop Arnulf of Rheims was going to be there as well. I haven't heard how it went but my mother was very pleased about it.'

Theophanu almost groaned. 'I'm afraid it didn't go well at all,' she said gently. 'The banquet itself was fine, but your father and Archbishop Arnulf drank rather too deeply. When they went to bed, they just threw themselves down and left their weapons lying by their beds.'

She paused and Otto looked at her, puzzled. He knew such behaviour was nothing unusual for Duke Charles but he could not say 'So what?' Even the young king did not like to interrupt and after a moment the Empress went on, her voice almost toneless.

'When they were asleep, the traitor Ascelin entered their chambers and took their swords, without waking them. Then he brought his own guards and arrested your father and the Archbishop, although he had sworn fealty to them. He summoned King Hugh Capet from Senlis and handed them over to him on the Tuesday of Holy Week.'

'Judas!' exclaimed King Otto but young Lotharingia was silent. The Empress continued

'King Hugh put them both on trial for high treason and they have been imprisoned at Orleans, although most of the French asked him just to take oaths from them. Hugh wants to depose Archbishop Arnulf. We do not know what he will do with your father.'

Otto of Lotharingia's face had gone white with shock.

'My mother will be so distressed. I must go to her,' he murmured.

Theophanu swallowed. This was the worst bit to tell him, unprecedented in recent years in the west, although common enough in Byzantium.

'Your mother and brothers and sisters are also in prison.' There were no words that could soften the blow.

Otto gave a great cry and doubled up as if in pain. King Otto knelt down and put his arm round his friend's shoulders.

'We'll take an army to France and free them. Just you wait and see,' he urged.

But Otto of Lotharingia, a year or two older than his friend, knew that it could not be that simple, an opinion which Willigis and Theophanu were obliged to confirm. Basically they would do all they could for Charles and his family short of going to war, but all of them knew that war was probably the only means of saving them.

It was decided that the King and the Empress would go to Lower Lotharingia immediately, where they could monitor the situation and their presence might have a restraining influence. Only a small group would accompany them at first, so that they could travel with maximum speed. The army would stay in Saxony in readiness for the campaign against the Lutizi and the rest of the court would catch them up at Nijmegen, where King Otto had been born.

The ride was a hard nightmare for Theophanu. She was feeling unwell even before they started and they kept up a relentless pace. To make matters worse, the weather broke and it rained for four solid days. Even their thick, waxed-leather cloaks could not keep out such rain and she was permanently drenched and frozen. By the time they reached Nijmegen, she had a high fever.

Ignoring her throbbing head and agonising throat, Theophanu insisted on holding court on May 28th. There she confirmed young Otto of Lower Lotharingia in his father's dukedom, even though Charles was still alive.

This action would make it impossible for Hugh Capet to pressurise his captive into transferring the duchy to France. It was to be hoped that it did not also sign Charles's death-warrant.

After the court was over, Theophanu gratefully collapsed into her bed. At first the rest seemed to help, but then the fever came back more strongly and her entire body ached unbearably. Many people offered remedies but her attendants, alert to the ever-present danger of poison, especially from the French direction, allowed no potions other than those prescribed by her Greek physician. Again she seemed to rally a little and when a flagon of the best Burgundy wine arrived from the Empress Adelheid, Theophanu was eager to try it.

'She sent me some when I was so weak after the birth of the twins,' she said to Anastaso. 'Do you remember? It was delicious and it did me a lot of good.'

Anastaso did remember. She also remembered what Theophanu had said about her mother-in-law at Quedlinburg at Easter. Adelheid was now in Quedlinburg attending a family funeral and Theophanu's words would no doubt have been repeated to her many times. When she mentioned her worry to Theophanu, the Empress smiled faintly and reached out to take her oldest friend's hand.

'Anastaso, I think I'm dying anyway.'

'That's not true,' insisted the Greek through her tears. 'You'll come through this like you did through the last lot.'

The Empress shook her head.

'I can feel my death in my body already,' she said. 'Lady Adelheid's wine can do no harm and at least it may ease my going. She would be glad to know that,' she added ironically, with a flash of her old humour.

Whether it was coincidence or not, that evening Theophanu sank into a state of semi-consciousness, which lasted for several days. In a lucid interval she called her son to her and urged him as his greatest charge to care for his sisters as well as his empire. Then she made her final confession and received the last rites from Archbishop Willigis.

276

Before the others came back into the room, she roused herself to speak again.

'Willigis,' she whispered, and he turned, startled. Never, in all their long partnership, had she called him just by his name.

'There is one fault I have not confessed. Not a sin. I have always resisted it. But in another world, if we had been different people, you and I...' she broke off, unable to say any more.

'Yes, oh yes,' he answered her. 'If everything had been different. But in Heaven, where there is no marrying nor giving in marriage, it will be different.'

'Till then,' she murmured, already lapsing back into apparent unconsciousness. When Anastaso and Imiza removed her jewels and dressed her in a nun's habit, as she had requested so that she might enter the heavenly kingdom as a simple servant of God, not an empress, they thought Theophano smiled, but they could not be sure.

She never spoke again and as the June dusk closed in round the palace, the laboured breathing grew still until it finally stopped.

EPILOGUE

The Empress-Regent was dead; long live the Empress-Regent. Adelheid, Empress-Regent of the West, ensured that her daughter-in-law's funeral instructions were followed to the letter. Theophanu had asked to be buried next to the newly-constructed shrine of St. Alban in St. Pantaleon's Church in Cologne. Rather an obscure choice, reflected Adelheid, but that's what she wanted. The service itself, conducted by Everger, Archbishop of Cologne, lacked nothing in splendour or an illustrious congregation and when young Otto, his eyes still tear-stained, came to bid his grandmother goodnight, he thanked her warmly for her care for the day's ceremonies.

'What arrangements have we made for her *memoria*, Grandmother?' he asked, as he turned to go.

Adelheid smiled. 'Memorial Masses said for her to shorten her time in Purgatory? We haven't, my dear. She should have used some of her revenues to make such arrangements, but she never did. Indeed, she objected when *I* used my wealth for that purpose.'

Her grandson stared at her in dawning horror.

'But you can't take revenge on her after death like this,' he protested. 'She'll be trapped in Purgatory for ever.'

'She will be released when she has paid for her sins,' Adelheid said calmly.

Otto kept his eyes fixed on hers.

'My mother grew much more ill after she drank that wine you sent her,' he said accusingly.

The Empress-Regent returned his gaze impassively.

'You are becoming hysterical, child,' she said. 'It's not surprising; it's been a hard day for you. You need to go to bed now and in the morning you will see matters more sensibly.'

Otto II's gaze did not waver.

'In the morning, perhaps I shall have to, Grandmother,' he allowed. 'But in three years time I shall be King and Emperor, in reality as well as in name. Then, I warn you, my mother will be properly remembered.'

AUTHOR'S NOTE

About 90% of the incidents in this book are 'true' in the sense that they are recorded by contemporary chroniclers, however improbable some of them may seem. Similarly all the characters, except Philip the tutor, Emilia and Anastaso, were real people. As far as I am aware, this novel is the first book to tell the story of Theophanu's life in English but German-speaking readers wishing to know more about her can find a scholarly study in Ekkehard Eickhoff's magisterial work, *Theophanu und der Konig* (Klett-Cotta). There is also a book of essays about Theophanu's times entitled *The Empress Theophanu: Byzantium and the West at the Turn of the First Millennium* (Cambridge University Press).

I am grateful to many people for help, advice and encouragement, including Paul and Joan Crossley, Peter von Steinitz, Roland Mainstone, Paul Winner, and Wendy and Peter Duffy. Particular thanks go to Lynn Bridger, Mary Handford and Andy Crooks for their patient assistance in getting the book into print. Above all I thank my husband, Chris Herbert, for constant support and brilliant ideas.